MURDER IN ARGELÈS

A THIRD-CULTURE KID MYSTERY

MURDER IN ARGELÈS

D-L NELSON

FIVE STAR
A part of Gale, Cengage Learning

GALE
CENGAGE Learning

Detroit • New York • San Francisco • New Haven, Conn • Waterville, Maine • London

GALE
CENGAGE Learning

LIBRARY OF CONGRESS CATALOGING-IN-PUBLICATION DATA

Nelson, D. L., 1942–
   Murder in Argelès : a third-culture kid mystery / D.L. Nelson.
  — 1st ed.
    p. cm.
   ISBN-13: 978-1-4328-2551-5(hardcover)
   ISBN-10: 1-4328-2551-8(hardcover)
   1. Women authors—Fiction. 2. North Shore (Mass. : Coast)—
Fiction. I. Title.
PS3614.E4455M83 2011
813'.6—dc23
                                                  2011033159

First Edition. First Printing: December 2011.
Published in 2011 in conjunction with Tekno Books and Ed Gorman.

Printed in the United States of America
1 2 3 4 5 6 7 15 14 13 12 11

To Robin: may both our hearts heal

ACKNOWLEDGMENTS

To Julia of the twenty pages a deep appreciation for having an eagle eye. The Rennes-le-Château Musée was always a source of information. Over the years I have read many books that became part of my general knowledge but these were the base: *Montaillou* by Emmanuel Le Roy Ladurie; *Holy Blood, Holy Grail*, by Michael Baigent, Richard Leigh, and Henry Lincoln; *Ecritures cathares* by René Nelli; *L'héritage du diable T1: Rennes-le-Château* by Félix (text) et Gastine (drawings). I used the website www.renneslechateau.com to check when I forgot a date. The television station France 2 produced a documentary that I saw so long ago, I have forgotten the title. During the past twenty years I have been up and down all around Languedoc and Roussillon and have encountered many history buffs and treasure hunters anxious to share their knowledge and theories whose names were shared over a cup of espresso then forgotten. If they remember me, it would be only because of my terrible French accent. The *Maires* of Argelès, current and past, are not murderers or proven crooks. There is a website for Third-Culture Kids, www.tckworld.com. And for those who know and love Argelès, I've rearranged the position of the angels slightly with the church, but over the years they have been moved. Although I've tried to make the French understandable, there is a French/English dictionary at the back. And yes again, thanks to the Geneva Writers Group, Sylvia Petter, Susan Tiberghien and my editor, Gordon Aalborg. Also thanks to Jennifer Mc-

Dermott, my favorite Third-Culture Kid. For those that want to find out more about Third-Culture Kids, you can visit http://tckid.com for additional information. And finally, Llara, I'm still working on your inheritance.

CHAPTER 1
RENNES-LE-CHÂTEAU

" 'I saw the bitch burning the money,' isn't that what your grandmother told you? Well, isn't it?" Michel's eyes, the eyes I once loved, were so dark I couldn't see the pupils. Now they merely annoyed me.

How I wished someone would enter my shop, but it was late enough in the tourist season as well as late enough in the day that it was unlikely anyone would wander in to look at my oils and charms. None of the latter was strong enough to make Michel disappear. I didn't want him to disappear entirely—just for now—and to take with him the man waiting for him outside who was shifting from one foot to the other while pretending to be interested in my window display of books on the healing power of plants. In reality I knew that he really wanted to hear what was happening inside.

"Just have a drink with him. Talk to him, *Chérie*."

Here come the endearments, I thought. Michel and I were divorced, a happy divorce, if such a thing were possible. Michel still shared my bed many nights, and I still shiver when I wake to feel him holding my hand in his sleep. However, I no longer have to shiver when the bills come in wondering what irresponsible thing he had done with our money, what crazy scheme he was working on that would throw our lives into yet more disarray.

Granted, I didn't make a fortune in the shops here and in Carcassonne, but with my website, I run out of bills before I run out of money each month. Well, almost each month. By nature I'm frugal, not wanting much. The two rooms over this little shop in Rennes-le-Château, a village perched on a mountain top with views of the valley below, suit me just fine. The walls are gaily painted. I'd even painted my *frigo* with blue sky and sand and then cactuses, a balance to its cold insides preserving my food. I love dichotomies—which may explain my relationship with Michel. I love him but can't tie my life to his.

"Just talk to him, *s'il te plaît Chérie.*"

His prematurely white curls contrasted with those big brown eyes that were part of the reason I married him in the first place despite every omen being against it, but I already mentioned his eyes. Maybe that's a sign I'm getting old, but I refuse to think of fifty-nine as old.

"*S'il te plaît?*"

"There's no one to watch the shop."

"I'll do it."

I gave one of those sighs that I knew he knew meant I'd given in. I handed him the money bag I hang around my neck. It took only one time for two robbers, one who engaged my attention while the other emptied the cash drawer, for me to never leave money so easily available again.

Michel grabbed me by the shoulders and kissed my forehead, then shoved me into the autumn air. Down in the valley it would still feel like summer, but up here I needed a sweater. With one it was still possible to sit in the café for hours and read or talk to neighbors; at least it was on those warm autumn days when the *Tramantane* stayed calm rather than blowing so strongly that if I stood on the edge of the wall I could lift my arms and fly all the way to Carcassonne.

"Miriam Fournier," I said to the man. He was dressed in gray slacks and a blue shirt with ridge marks where it had been folded by a professional laundry, open at the neck revealing a gold chain entangled in slightly graying chest hair. He held a blue suit jacket over his shoulder with his finger. His dark hair, also with a few streaks of gray, curled over his collar. He handed me his card. Sebastian Nicholas, Producer, France 2. "Pleased to meet you. Where should we go?"

I led him around the corner to the café. Red metal tables with red wire-backed chairs were placed outside, but only two of the twenty were occupied and those by locals, who could be found in those same chairs every afternoon with their beer and cigarettes. We nodded as I chose my favorite place, under the chestnut tree and next to the fountain that burbled companionably. A few chestnuts were on the table. I half hoped that a chestnut would bonk this Sebastian person on the head. As for myself, I sat just out of reach of the falling nuts.

He ordered a beer, and I debated a kir royale, because he would obviously pay, but I didn't want anything alcoholic. I still had the month's end books to do, and with my hatred of paperwork, the last thing I needed was a fuzzy head. It was too late in the day for an espresso and the café's hot chocolate was merely a store brand served in a packet and a cup of hot milk. *"Diabolo frais."*

While we waited for our drinks, he leaned back and smiled. He was a good-looking man, the kind that plays the lover besting a husband in so many movies. "Michel said your grandmother knew Père Bérenger Saunière."

"Know is the wrong word. She was a little girl when he died."

"January 22, 1917," he said.

The waitress brought our drinks. She knew not to put any ice in mine. The fizzy strawberry flavor burst in my mouth. The drink was too sugary to be healthy, but at the same time I was always stick-thin—more from nervous energy than diet—so I never worried about my weight. My chubbier *copines*, especially those who gained weight merely by walking by the *pâtisserie* might have cursed me, had they not half-suspected that I really knew how to cast spells with my charms and love potions rather than make others believe that they worked.

Rather than tell Sebastian I knew the date was correct, I shrugged. I once heard an English tourist say that the French can hold an entire conversation with shrugs and facial movements. She didn't know I understood English, and I had never thought of it, but after that I observed conversations from afar. She was right.

"And your grandmother?"

"Was very old when I was born. And I'm old."

"Not old and still lovely."

He was right. I've often been told I look like I'm in my mid-forties, whatever the mid-forties look like. Thanks to good genes and my oils, my face is unlined and my hair is a rich chestnut (Number 45 of the hair coloring product that I prefer). Despite growing up in this village with less than five hundred people and leaving for university and work for a few years (one of the few people who did), I've come back, but my years away in Toulouse and Carcassonne taught me how to dress. Now I favor the flowing skirts, peasant blouses, shawl-like scarves and huge earrings that make me look like I should operate a store that sells oils, potions and charms. I'm vain enough to want to look young, especially if I don't have to sacrifice the experience that is written in my soul but not on my face.

"And you knew Marie Denarnaud," he said.

"It's hard in a village this size, to not know everyone. She died in 1953. I was a child. My grandmother had died in, when was it . . . 1975, but her mind had died long before her body." I took another drink of my strawberry-flavored fizzy water and picked up a potato chip from the dish that the waitress had left closer to me than him. "Why don't you tell me what you want?"

"I don't have to tell you about the village," he said. Of course he didn't, and people who say, "I don't have to tell you" annoy me. I could tell him a lot more than he knew, if I were so inclined. I'd seen it go from unknown to the center of a mystery thanks to books and documentaries that started in the U.K. and had spread out through the world. And just when the furor was dying down along came a best-selling novel followed by a movie and a whole new batch of tourists arrived to peek into the church and whisper of buried treasure and strange ancestries.

I had been happier about the influx than many of my neighbors. The onslaught of attention allowed me to return and open my little shop. I was a mountain girl, happier to wake where I could see the sun come up through the slats of my shutters, then throw them open to see the hills and sky rather than the red bricks, which was the view from my Toulouse flat or my neighbor's kitchen window in the small development where we lived below La Cité wall in Carcassonne. I don't care if she always kept a flowering plant in her window. Thus the publicity was a gift: I could finally come home and still earn a living.

In the beginning, I loved being in a city. I knew other students. After graduation I landed a job in marketing at Blagnac, the Toulouse airport where I met Michel through a colleague. Lord knows, Michel would never have had a practical job. But each time I visited my parents and sister and brother, who stayed here at least back then, it was harder to leave. Michel dreamed his dreams, sometimes worked as a painter, sometimes as an *ébéniste,* whose way with wood would have made the tree proud to give up its life for the furniture he created, so in a last attempt to save our marriage he came with me.

Sebastian turned his beer around and around on a coaster. "This place has a very strange feel, not a bad one, mind you, and spooky is too strong a word."

While growing up here, I hadn't noticed it, but he was right.

13

I chalked it up to the fresh air, the winds that rocked the trees, but *there was* a strange feeling in the village. Michel had commented on it when I first brought him here and he'd never heard of the mystery at that point. Many of the tourists mentioned it, too. I brought Sebastian back to the subject.

"We want to make a documentary to air in the spring."

"There've been lots of documentaries."

"This one will be different."

I cocked my head and waited. I learned long ago that sometimes silence brings forth more information than questions do. He must have learned the same thing. He remained silent, a tug of silence against silence. I wondered if I'd break it for the first time in my life, but he was the one who surrendered.

"It'll have a different slant. We'll be looking at it from the villagers' point of view. What happens when a little place high in the Pyrénées becomes the focus of international attention?"

I still kept silent.

"We'll touch on the mystery, of course."

Still I was silent.

"What your grandmother knew will be important, of course. And naturally, your memories will be invaluable."

I said nothing.

"And of course, we will reward you, because you have both the point of view of a villager and someone who has a broader background, the experience of the modern day-to-day life down in the valley."

"Of course." I finished my drink and stood up. "Let me think about it."

I wanted to slap Michel for bringing this man into my life.

Chapter 2
Argelès-sur-mer

The cock crowed at the fifth and final bong of the steeple bell. The priest sat straight up in bed. Today was the day. Annie was coming back. He had so much to show her, and he knew, just *knew* that she would be as excited as he.

Cold morning air pierced his rough sheet and single blanket. Within an hour the September sun would prove that summer hadn't quite slipped away yet. He threw the covers back.

The cold bricks of his bedroom floor, laid at least two hundred years before, were faded to soft terra cotta. A path worn between the bed and door from other priests' feet left the floor uneven. He always felt a kinship with those who had slept in this same rectory as they cared for the souls of Argelès just as he did. He wondered if he were the only one to lose belief in the Church's teachings.

He threw on a pair of jeans and a cotton sweater over the underwear that he'd slept in. He put on battered felt slippers that had taken him a good two months to mold to his feet.

Her train was due at 5:20. He had time to make coffee. The kitchen window looked out onto a square courtyard flanked by eight buildings on each side with a peek-a-boo walkway to the street. One of the buildings was the back of his church, another, the back of his rectory. A tree and small fountain stood in the center. Madame Dumas, his neighbor to the left, had planted pink and purple begonias in cement boxes surrounding the fountain.

At one time it had been the sole source of water for each home on the square, but in the last sixty years the village fathers had added the necessary piping for both indoor toilets and running water, hot water even, when the residents could afford water heaters. Some were electric, but the rectory's was old-fashioned gas in a device that looked like a small metal garbage can suspended from the wall. To ignite it he had to have the force of at least two different taps flowing through it. First he turned on the water in the kitchen and then the bath. As water ran through the contraption, he held a lit taper to the pilot light until it ignited with a woof, more than a bang. Only this morning it didn't work. Not for the first time, he vowed to buy a new water heater. His superior had turned his request down, but he would go into his own funds if necessary.

This morning, however, the priest lacked the patience to fiddle with the apparatus. He ran cold water into the coffeepot, added three spoonfuls of ground beans, screwed the top of the pot on and placed it over the burner. He splashed cold water from the tap on his face and shuddered. Not as bad as during his training in the monastery, but certainly nothing like his Paris childhood where the maid would run his hot bath and hold a warmed robe for him before he got out of bed.

Still, despite his lack of faith, he couldn't bring himself to change his life. It was the Bible with its human interpretations that he rejected, not God or a god or a powerful being. He wished it weren't so, that he could return to his childhood certainty that had carried him through the first five decades of his life. He had made vows; he would stick to them. He would help others. If faith brought them the comfort that he couldn't find for himself, then he had accomplished something in the world. Maybe that made him a fake, but at least he was a fake for a good cause: the well-being of his parishioners.

While he waited for the coffee to perk, he put the photos that he wanted to show Annie in a large manila envelope. She would be so excited when she saw the aerial photos. He had circled the indentations, a large square in the ground, with a red magic marker. He laughed at himself. That something was there was so evident, no highlighting was necessary. What he couldn't understand was why no one had noticed it before. Surely, his aerial photos weren't the first. There was always the possibility that any other photographers weren't searching for proof of an earlier civilization.

A noise on the street caught his attention. Probably garbage men picking up the trash. Until two years ago, *la poubelle,* the trash, was hung in bags from hooks on the side of the house. But as the village attracted more retirees from northern France, Denmark, Holland, Germany, the U.K. and Ireland, the old mayor had decreed that all garbage must be left in bins purchased from his office. How much of the profit of the trash bins went into the man's pocket, the priest could only guess.

He shook his head as he poured himself a demitasse of black liquid. The old mayor was an idiot, and if that was an ungodly thought, so be it. More than once during the old mayor's confession, he had pronounced a penance of doing something nice for those whom the National Front party demonized. The priest was all for inclusion, not the exclusion practiced by the mayor's party. Thus the mayor found himself, under threat to his mortal soul, having to grant a permit for the Algerian family to operate a grocery store while in his heart-of-hearts he would have preferred to run them out of the village.

The priest smiled at the memory. The mayor had lost the last election to a socialist, not even one from the few families that had ruled the village for centuries. Small village politics: the faces and issues might change, but the mentality was always the same.

That was why the priest so liked the influx of new blood and especially Annie. She was the only woman to tempt him from his vow of celibacy. There was the age difference. Had he been younger or she older, her thirty something against his forty-three . . . no that wasn't it. His vows again, got in the way, and that was something with which he would have to live.

It didn't matter how feminine she was with a smile that was never far from her lips. He thought of her mass of red curls that would put Medusa's to shame and her brown eyes that sparkled. All the outward appearances were wonderful, but it was her intellect that appealed to him. She not only shared his love of fairness, she was as passionate about history as he was. She had been an incredible help in his research of the Cathars and other medieval heresies in between her jobs that stole her from the village to cities all over Europe.

Holding the coffee cup in one hand he grabbed the ancient church door key in the other. The key was six inches long and its unknown metal weighed far too much to put on any key chain or wear around his neck.

Outside, a dog sniffed around a garbage can, pushed his nose against the cover, and when it wouldn't budge, lifted his leg and moved on. The garbage men left the bins on the ground and open after emptying them, so the noise he'd heard must have been street cleaners or someone sneaking home at dawn.

The priest strode the twenty-second walk over the cobblestone courtyard to the church. Had he left the door unlocked? The wood was original, creviced and cracked. Part of him felt that churches should always be open, but too often kids came in at night to smoke grass or shoot up. More than once the priest had gone out to talk to them, win their confidence and get them to stop, although his successes were rare. Last night, in any event, he had remembered to lock up. The door creaked open.

The church smelled stuffy. Seven hundred years of burning

candles and incense had infused their smoky odor into the walls. The altar itself was new, by comparison—only two hundred years old, and even that had just been refurbished with fresh gold leaf on the cherubs. The walls had been white-washed and the dark pews replaced with light wood chairs, a far less depressing place for prayer than when he had first been assigned here.

He let himself into the tower and climbed the stairs. The early morning sun filtered through the slit windows, lighting the rough wooden steps leading up to the bell tower.

At the top of the stairs, he gazed at the three bells that rang out the hours, half and quarter hours. He certainly wouldn't want to be up there when the bells struck twelve o'clock, but he loved being down on the street when they rang for Mass or a wedding. He picked up a pair of binoculars that he always kept hanging right inside the door leading to a walkway that encircled the top of the tower.

He often came up here to survey the area. Depending on which direction he faced he could see Canigou with its snowy peaks, the smaller Pyrénées, all of the village or the Mediterranean.

Today he looked toward the tracks. The night train was coming over the bridge and heading into the small station. Even with the binoculars he had a hard time making out if Annie was at the station, but he knew she would be on the train. She had called him last night from Zurich to tell him that she'd make the connection for the 21:55 out of Geneva. Had her plans changed, she would have let him know. Together they would look at his discoveries. He could hardly wait to see her reaction.

He didn't hear the footsteps behind him but felt a shove against his back a second before he was catapulted over the edge. He landed on the green bronze angel below.

CHAPTER 3
ARGELÈS-SUR-MER

Three rapid knocks or maybe more penetrated Annie's dream. She wasn't eight years old. She hadn't been plunked down in a place where people talked funny, but where was she? She heard another knock bringing her back from her dream to the present.

"Perpignan." The voice was deep, male and insistent. A lock clicked and a door slid open.

Annie forced her eyes open. She was on a train in a *couchette*. From her bottom bunk she saw three bunks on the opposite wall of the narrow sleeping car. A woman slept opposite her. The other beds were empty. Had it been July or August every one would have been filled and the car stuffy with hot bodies anxious to escape Geneva for the Côte de Vermeille, the poor person's Riviera.

The conductor bent down so his mouth was next to her ear. *"Les prochains arrêts après Perpignan seront Elne et, Argelès. Vous avez twenty minutes."*

"Merci," Annie whispered to not disturb the sleeping woman whom she knew was going on to Barcelona. They had chatted from Geneva to Lyon, not unlike new college roommates, sharing the easy confidences that sometimes happen when Annie met strangers as she rode this train to the village she now thought of as home. What home was had been the crux of their conversation last night.

The door slid shut. Annie shook herself, tasted her morning breath and rummaged in her backpack for a mint. All she had was the small backpack. Everything else was already in her studio—her nest, she called it.

"*Bonne chance,*" the woman mumbled. "You, Third-Culture Kid, you."

"*Vous aussi.*" And Annie did wish her good luck.

She left the compartment, closing the door behind her. Out the window she saw the Perpignan station. Although it was still dark, the platforms were well lit. Another high-speed TGV train, dark and locked with its sleek white nose pointed toward Spain, sat at the farthest point from the station. Three people disembarked from Annie's train with their suitcases either slung over their shoulders or dragged along on little wheels. No one got on.

Annie, as always, peeked at the bright multicolored whirls of the station's ceiling. The centre of the universe, she thought, or at least that's what Salvatore Dali had declared it when he finished painting it. She had never been a big fan of the painter from the Spanish side of Catalonia. Perpignan was on the French side of the border, so when Annie first moved there, she had made the mistake of calling the natives French. With icy voices they informed her they were Catalans, not French no matter what their passports said. She had not made the same mistake twice.

Fully awake and outside her compartment, she knew that once the train started up, it was only twenty minutes until she was home. The female computer voice boomed out the destinations: Elne, Argelès, Collioure, Cerebère, Port Bou. The conductor who had awakened her blew his whistle and swung himself up onto the train.

Third-Culture Kid, Annie thought. She'd never heard that term before, but it was one of those clicks in her life: a lock falling into place. That was the missing piece. Certainly it described her.

Sometimes she felt that her life was a series of good accidents. When she needed something, it appeared. Not that she always had the sense to recognize it. Nothing screamed "Hey! Listen, Dummy!" But last night she had recognized that her sleeping-car mate had been there to give her information she needed, but hadn't known she needed. That is, she didn't know it until they had started talking as they shook their sheets out of the plastic wrappings to make up their bunks. She didn't know the woman's name, nor did it matter.

Annie watched the countryside flash by. Only an occasional house light or car headlight broke the early dawn until they came to Elne, the village before Argelès with its lit-up abbey. She and Père Yves had gone through the abbey for the first time three months ago.

She could hardly wait to see him. He had sounded so excited when she talked to him last night. What had he found? She knew how much he liked teasing her, making her wait until she got to Argelès, before telling her. More than one weekend she'd gone down based on his teasing, but she'd never been disappointed.

She glanced at the closed compartment. Third-Culture Kid— that was what she was. No wonder she dreamed about her childhood after her pre-sleep conversation.

For her first eight years she'd been raised in Sudbury, Massachusetts. Her father worked for Digital. Her mother was a commercial artist who tried to do her own work between clients. Annie was an only child, not like most of her friends who complained about brothers and sisters. Annie would have loved to have had brothers and sisters to complain about, but her parents had said that since they had been given the most wonderful child possible, why in God's name would they want another? Annie suspected it was more that her mother didn't have the patience for a second.

Everything was normal until one night, over the first corn of the season bought from Aunt Sadie's stand down the street and obviously picked fresh hours before, when her father announced they were moving to Njimegan.

"Njimegan?" her mother had asked.

"Holland," her father said.

It seemed like the next day that Annie was on the plane, her dog stored with the luggage, and then in a school where people spoke in strange grunts. None of them wore the wooden shoes, long dresses or starched caps of the illustrations of her story about the little boy who stuck his finger in the dike. They dressed normally, although she did see windmills as she biked to school. Even grownups biked places.

Never had she felt so alone. Children came up to her but soon lost interest when she couldn't respond. When she cried at night, her mother and father talked about switching her to the International School, but decided the chance to learn another language was invaluable. Her mother signed them both up for Dutch lessons.

The television showed many American programs with Dutch written underneath. Annie had her first click when her teacher said something to her and she understood. Another Anne, one girl who still tried to talk to her often, realizing that the new girl had begun to understand, came over and from then on Annie didn't feel as alone. There were still things that were strange, like restaurants with tiny carpets in place of cloth on the tables, but soon these things became normal.

Then her father came home and said, "Stuttgart."

Another language she must learn. Annie looked at the German and thought that if you took out a vowel it was almost the same thing as Dutch. Learning this time wasn't as long.

Then her father said, "Geneva."

She and her mother had groaned.

As a teenager Annie found French the easiest of the languages, once she learned to wrap her tongue around the sounds. In Geneva almost half of her classmates were from somewhere else. Their parents worked for the UN or at various diplomatic missions. They came and went with their parents' assignments. As soon as Annie developed a good friend, that friend would be off to a home country or another assignment in some distant place. Promises were always made about letters and visits. Two or three would be sent within a few weeks reporting new adventures, but then they would taper off.

Although she didn't dwell on it, Annie never felt like she really belonged. When it came time for university she asked to be sent to the States.

"But it costs almost nothing here, and less in Germany," her father said. "It's not like we can't afford it, but with your languages . . ."

"I want to spend more than a few weeks in my own country," Annie had insisted, thinking back to her visits to her grandparents, when her parents rushed from friend to friend, relative to relative, then out to buy whatever at a small percentage of the cost in Geneva for themselves and other ex-pats who handed them shopping lists adding the words, "If you get a chance, could you . . . ?" Getting back to Njimegan, Stuttgart or Geneva was the vacation.

When she enrolled at UMass in Amherst, Annie felt as much of a stranger there as she had when she first moved to Holland. Granted, all the other freshmen were new too, but they had many shared experiences. Annie knew Elton John, Depeche Mode and most American and English singers, but none of them had heard of Johnny Hallyday, Jane Birkin, Serge Gainsbourg or Claude François. Some of her classmates had never left the state. Some even confused Switzerland with Sweden and Swaziland, although those who had read *Heidi* immediately pictured her milking goats and having a friend named Peter. After a year, she decided to finish her studies at the University of Geneva.

Her train car mate had voiced similar experiences. Her father had been a diplomat and they had lived in Africa, Asia and the Middle East. "You Americans are wonderful. You even have an organization for people like us," she'd said as the train rocked its way through the French countryside. "We don't belong in our birthplace, we don't belong where we live, but we have our own culture, *voilà*, a third culture, a mixture of it all."

Click!

The train slowed and Annie could see the large plumed reeds that hid the cemetery from the view of arriving tourists. She was home. From the first time she had set her foot in the village, she had known that this was where she could put down a root, a place to come back to between assignments. She had deliberately chosen to be a freelance tech writer, working enough to make her expenses, but not so much that she didn't have time to indulge her passion for historical research.

That was how she had found Argelès. She'd been roaming the area investigating the Knights Templar as an offshoot of her research on the medieval heretical sect, the Cathars. When she'd come through to look at a wall, supposedly built by the Knights, she'd seen one street, narrow as befitting a place constructed in the twelfth century when the width of cars wasn't an issue. Every window had flowers flowing down the wall and pots of plants lined the street. All the houses were connected.

Two older women were sitting on kitchen chairs, one snapping beans and the other peeling apples. They exchanged the ritual *Bonjour Madame* as required by politeness. Annie patted the dog, which had come out from under the bean snapper's chair, his tail wagging. He was an unclipped poodle who seemed to say, "I know I am cute and adorable."

Glancing up to the top floor of the building across from where the women sat, Annie spied the sign in the top window, *A VENDRE,* and twenty minutes later she was climbing the three stories to the *grenier,* the attic, with the real estate agent. Up until this century, the space would have been used to store seed or hay for animals that would have lived on the ground floor. Family quarters would have been on the second and third floors.

Someone had renovated the entire building, assigning a single flat to each floor. As she walked up the stairs, she guessed each apartment would be dark with only two windows opening onto the street. The back of the building was against another building facing out onto the parallel street.

When the agent opened the door, light filtered down in a welcoming ray from an overhead skylight. She climbed the additional staircase flanked by a wall that still had the original stones in tones of beige and rust but mostly gray. They reminded her of the stone walls throughout the New England of her childhood, the kind Robert Frost wrote about in his poem. There was a fireplace, a wooden cathedral ceiling held up by thick beams. The kitchen area was perfect with a flat stovetop and an *au four,* the miniature ovens that resembled an American toaster oven, but which most of Annie's French friends used to turn out incredible meals. A waist-high refrigerator was under a counter that jutted out.

The French talk about *coup de foudre,* love at first sight. Annie had a *coup de foudre.*

Each time she got off the train, she fell in love all over again as she walked to her nest, for that was what she'd named the apartment—*mon nid,* my nest. Each time she arrived she mentally said hello to the smells of pines, of sea air and of the bougainvillea in the summer or wood smoke in the winter, baking bread from the *boulangerie,* the wine from the caves and if it were after nine in the morning, the chickens roasting on spits in front of the three *charcuteries.*

Gabriel Martinez, who owned the best bakery and tea room in the village, would have been up baking since three o'clock, for no resident of Argelès would want anything but fresh bread, croissants, brioches or *pain au chocolat* to start their morning. Fresh, still warm to the touch. And they might come back again at noon and again at dinner for the next batches of bread.

Usually Annie stopped at the tea room for breakfast, having a *tartine,* a long, thin baguette slathered with butter and whatever berry jam Gabriel's mother had made. Because it was still early, the tea room was shut. Although Annie knew she could knock on the door and after the ritual cheek kisses and "you're-back-for-how-long-this-times," Gabriel would start the coffee and sit with her to catch her up on village news, but just now she was anxious to get home and even more anxious to see Père Yves.

Annie passed the only traffic light in town, walked past the *charcuterie,* the green grocer and turned the corner to the church.

After a shower and breakfast she would go see Père Yves. How lucky she'd felt to discover his passion for history matched hers. Her friends humored her interest, but Père Yves thought passion for original research as normal as eating. She respected that most of his free time for the last seven years had been spent roaming the area around Rennes-le-Château with all its mysteries. He'd written her that she would have to see his latest find. Maybe he'd proved that the ancient buildings he suspected were underground really existed.

The clock on the church tower struck twice: 5:30. Père Yves won't want to see me at this hour, she thought, no matter how excited he is. She glanced at the church. There were normally two bronzed angels flanking the ten-foot wooden doors leading to the sanctuary. The wood had the deep crevices of centuries-old wood. Slumped across a toppled angel was a big pile of cloth. Vandalism was Annie's first thought. She almost walked by, but instead she reached into her pocket for the glasses that she needed to see anything more than a few feet in front of her.

When she realized it was a person, she assumed it was a drunk. Père Yves would be really pissed off when he saw that his angel was broken. Its head had rolled a few feet away. Her imagination brought up the idea of an angel walking to a guillotine and having its head chopped off. She hoped that it could be reattached. She knew the village had worked hard to raise the funds for the angels in the 1800s. At least the head was undamaged. Another few inches and it would have rolled down the six stairs to the sidewalk, probably denting its serene face.

Then she saw the white, white hair. Although Père Yves was only forty-three, he had pure white curls. He was so handsome that more than one young woman, including Annie, had shaken their heads that this perfect specimen of manhood was removed from any potential relationships other than spiritual or friendship. At the same time his priesthood removed any tension that normally lay under the surface with a male friend, the way the husband of a good friend would be off limits—appreciation without follow-up.

None of these thoughts were in her head as she took the stairs three steps at a time. Her thoughts were a prayer to his God asking that he would be okay. In the mysteries she loved to read or watch on television, people put two fingers on the jugular vein or reached for the pulse, but Père Yves's wide, staring eyes made that unnecessary.

"I wish I knew the last rites," she whispered to him. Looking around she wanted to holler, but instead she dug into her backpack and pulled out her *natel,* her mobile phone. She knew the *gendarmerie* number by heart. Let someone be in already, she prayed. The battery was dead.

"Shit." She didn't want to leave the priest alone. Although

she wanted to close his eyes, she knew she shouldn't. She raced around the corner to her house, unlocked the door and bounded up the stairs. As always the key stuck. She niggled and jiggled until it gave. She then raced up the last flight to her studio.

The phone sat on the desk between the two windows next to her computer. She dialed, gasping for breath.

The phone clicked. *"Gendarme Boulet, j'écoute."*

Double shit! Gendarme Boulet, the stupidest policeman she'd ever seen, was the former mayor's son. No matter where else he was assigned, he was always sent back to Argelès after having messed up something, somewhere, somehow. Or so the gossips said. Annie loved listening to the gossip, although she prided herself on being a collector of information, not a repeater. Still she cursed that the ex-mayor's influence reached far enough into the national force to have this idiot back in the village. "Annie Young here. Père Yves is in front of the church and he's dead. Come quick."

"Where are you?"

"Home. My *natel* didn't work. I'll meet you there. And call your *patron*."

She hung up before he could argue. Of course she could have called the chief herself, but the last time she had seen Roger, they'd parted with a fight. He'd wanted her to give up her assignment and stay with him. She'd said that being a tech writer was her livelihood. She went where the work was and if he didn't understand, tough shit. Only she'd used the phrase, *"C'est la vie, connard,"* which translated a little stronger than she had meant it.

He'd turned red and walked away.

They hadn't spoken since, no matter how much she had stared at the phone wishing he would call to admit he was wrong. She had no intention of admitting that possibly *she* might be wrong, although if she thought she were—which she wasn't in this case—she would have. Maybe.

Annie's bathroom was so small she could touch all four walls. She peed, splashed water on her face and brushed her teeth. No way did she want to go back to the church and see the body of her good friend. Instead, she wanted to vomit, take a long, hot shower and crawl into bed. She wanted to check out each thing in her nest, the special mirror designed by a Spanish craftsman, the African baskets bought on a trip to Burkina Faso. She wanted to look at her skylight and see the underside of a little bird walking across the glass, letting her know there were gentle creatures alive and healthy. She wanted to do anything but face the fact that her good friend was dead.

Instead, she grabbed her house keys and ran back to the church.

The police cruiser, a small Renault, was parked up in front of the church. Gendarme Boulet stood with Gendarme Gault. Boulet strode up, hulking over her small frame, blocking her view of the church and Père Yves. "I don't like jokes, Annie." His words were almost a growl.

"What are you talking about?" she asked.

He moved away so his body no longer blocked her view of the church. She looked. The angels and the base it had rested on still lay on the ground. The head had rolled down the six stairs and was staring heavenwards. The nose had been chipped. Père Yves was nowhere in sight. The spot where he had been was swept clean.

The butcher arrived at his shop across the street from the church in his Citroen and barely scraped by the cruiser. At best the street, one of the widest in the village, was two tiny cars wide if the drivers pulled in their rearview mirrors.

"*Qu'est ce que c'est, Boulet?*" he asked through his rolled-down window.

A third car pulled up behind the butcher's. It was a Renault like the cruiser only with no markings. Chief Roger Perrin stepped out. He was not in uniform, but in jeans and a cotton knit beige sweater that showed his well-shaped body. Annie, at any other time, would have sighed, remembering how his hands felt as she had nestled in his arms after long hours of making love. "What's up?" he asked. He did not look at Annie.

"She," Boulet said, pointing to Annie, "calls us to tell us Père Yves is dead. We get here and look. *Voilà. Rien.* Nothing except for the angel. Broken." He smirked. "I know you've got lousy eyesight Annie, but there's a lot of difference between a knocked-over statue and a dead priest."

Roger looked at Annie's forehead as he said, "Can you tell me what's going on?" He spoke in English, their language when they didn't want others to understand. Neither Boulet nor Gault spoke English, although they both spoke Spanish and Catalan as well as French.

Annie told him. As she talked, he nodded.

At least he doesn't think I'm blind or stupid, she thought. But Roger's respect for her intelligence had never been a problem. It was her love of freedom and sense of independence that had come between them.

"Dead men don't walk away," Boulet muttered.

"No they don't." Roger turned and went up the stairs. He reached down and touched his fingers to the angel's right wing. He smelled it. "Blood."

Boulet shrugged.

"And statues of angels don't bleed," Roger said.

Gault, who had said nothing until now, spoke softly, "But it could be anything." He looked between the chief and Boulet.

"Gault, go over to the rectory and see if the priest is there," Roger said. "Boulet, get a sample of the blood. We might want it for DNA."

Within minutes Gault was back. "Doesn't answer his door,

Patron. Knocked loud enough to wake the dead." Realizing what he had said, he looked down at the ground.

"You sure he was dead, Annie?" Roger asked. This time he looked into her eyes. "Were you wearing your glasses or lenses?"

"Glasses. His eyes were wide open, staring like a fish."

"Look in the church," Roger said. "Wait. Use gloves in case there are prints."

"Always prints in a church," Gault said.

In a few minutes both policemen were back and shaking their heads.

"Come on Annie, I'll buy you coffee. Gault, Boulet, go back to the station."

A few minutes later they were the first customers in Martinez's just-opened tearoom.

Gabriel kissed Annie on both cheeks. "Nice to have you back," he said. Without asking, he opened a bottle of apricot juice. Then he brought her a *tartine*. For the chief he put down a *café, double crème*.

"You believe me?" she asked when Gabriel had gone back behind the counter and was placing a strawberry pastry next to the chocolate tarts.

Roger nodded. "However, without a body, there's not much I can do. You're looking good. Not much of a tan."

"Hard to tan when you spend most of your summer in front of a computer describing in terms so simple even a moron can understand how a software package works," Annie said. When she reach for her apricot juice her hands shook so much that had the glass been a little more full it would have spilled on the small round tabletop. "Père Yves—I saw him dead. Not a half hour ago!"

Roger started to reach for her hand then stopped. "I can launch a search. But we both know that he disappears days at a time whenever he can."

The street in front of the tearoom was filling with early morning shoppers. Men and women came into the tearoom to line up for their morning bread. Some had a basket to hold several baguettes. Gabriel chatted with each of them by name, asked about their spouses, children and dogs.

"He wouldn't disappear before saying Mass," she said. "And I know what I saw!" She'd also seen Roger's hand motion and had to fight her own impulse not to stroke his face. They were so good together and not so good together. But maybe, just maybe, they could work toward being friends. At thirty-three she had gathered many friends from her exes.

Gabriel brought a large cup of hot chocolate to the table. He made it differently from the woman who worked for him. His had black, dark chocolate, serious chocolate, reserved for his special clients. "Better than the Swiss?" he asked regularly. She always said, *"Bien sûr."*

She ate her *tartine* and drank her chocolate. Roger played with his spoon.

"If he doesn't turn up for Mass, I'll start a search. Want to wait with me?"

She shook her head as she finished the drink. "I'm going home to sleep."

"May I call you later?"

"If you learn anything." She leaned over and gave him two kisses, one on each cheek the way friends do, resisting the desire to kiss his lips.

"A bientôt." She decided to go the long way so she wouldn't have to pass the church. What she felt was sadness so deep that even tears couldn't find it.

CHAPTER 4
ARGELÈS-SUR-MER

The striking of the church clock shocked Annie awake. Where was she? A skylight shed a stream of light down on her. She was in her nest. She looked at her clock: noon. Then she realized her nightmare was real. Père Yves was dead, but she couldn't prove it because his body had mysteriously disappeared. And why should I have to prove it anyway, she thought? I know what I saw. Now it's up to Roger to deal with this madness.

Roger. Seeing him again under the worst possible conditions was a lousy way to start a holiday. A wave of guilt swamped her. Thinking of a vacation, ruined or otherwise, when a good friend was dead was just plain horrible.

Her stomach growled. Annie had a metabolism that if she didn't eat regularly her blood sugar did whatever blood sugar does to make her feel sick and weak. The shops would be closing for their three-hour noonday break, and frankly she didn't have the energy to either run around to buy anything nor to cook anything. One nice thing about making good money: she could choose a restaurant whenever she wanted. She grabbed her backpack, double-checked to make sure she had Euros and not just Swiss francs and ran down the three flights of stairs to the street.

Two of the three *mamies,* who always put their chairs out in the street to sit and talk together, were just putting their knitting into their baskets. Annie had picked up the term *les mamies,* the grandmothers, from the neighbors. At first she had thought of them as three mother superiors with their black dresses and hair slicked back into buns. But instead of fingering rosaries they snapped bean, shelled peas or peeled potatoes into big ceramic bowls. Sometimes they knitted or crocheted. Once she got to know them, and realized their earthy humor, the image of mother superiors evaporated into the blue sky. Usually they would have been in their houses fixing lunch long before noon. The street would be flooded with the odors of frying onions and meat roasting.

"*Bienvenue*, Annie," Mamie Couges said. Her white roots contrasted with the rest of her black hair tucked into a no-nonsense chignon. "When did you get home?"

"You know when she got home," Mamie Boudin said. She had not bothered to dye her hair. Its whiteness contrasted with her lined sun-beaten skin. For years she had worked the harvest picking grapes to supplement her husband's income. He had worked in the cork factory that supplied wineries throughout the country. Pushing the small cylinder measures through the bark had provided enough to support the family, but Mamie Boudin liked a few luxuries. She still boasted that she had been the first woman in Argelès to own a washing machine, although from time to time she still lugged her washing down to the river where a shed filled with soapstone sinks had allowed women for centuries to provide clean clothes for their families. Old women still went there to see friends.

Both Monsieur Couges and Monsieur Boudin were long dead, but the *mamies* fixed lunch for their sons each day because their daughters-in-law worked in Perpignan and couldn't get home to do it. One son worked in the local *Crédit Agricole* bank and the other for Gan insurance. Likewise when school was in session, they made their grandchildren's lunches and then sent them back for the afternoon session.

"Is it true? Did you really see Père Yves's body?" Mamie

Couges asked. She leaned into Annie as if to protect the information from the others.

Annie told them what had happened. This wasn't gossip but facts. And she knew if she wanted to keep abreast of what was happening on her narrow street, she did need to give some information to the *mamies*. Thus she knew how much the Danish journalist, who spent summers here, had paid for his new roof and why the Dutch woman was selling and going back to The Hague. And how many times Michel beat Chantal, although what interested her more was her desire to save Chantal, mousy though she was. What she did reveal was as little as possible and only things that the subject would not mind being shared. The mixture of people whose families had been there since the time of Charlemagne and people from other parts of France and Europe who used Argelès as a summer or retirement home somehow worked, against all logic, to form a community.

She was told at one time the Catalans both resented the newcomers while chortling at what fools they were to pay such high prices for the properties and for the crazy way they renovated them. There were three price structures—one for Argelèsians, one for French and one for foreigners—with the amount going up with each category of buyer. But then one of the Danish journalists and his wife, who had the house across from her own, had thrown a street party including champagne. He'd hired a grandson of one of the *mamies* to bring his band, and everyone, the natives and the interlopers of Danish, Dutch, Swedish and Swiss nationality danced, ate and drank. The tenor changed and now the *mamies* would ask when this or that person might be coming back with an eagerness to see them.

They peppered her with questions until Annie almost gave in to the desire to make up facts.

"Idiot," Mamie Couges said, referring to Gendarme Boulet.

"But his father wasn't as bad as the new mayor."

Mamie Boudin wagged her finger. "*Sais-tu ce-que cet idiot a fait?*" It wasn't clear which idiot mayor she was referring to. The old woman added, "It's about equal who's more stupid, but this time it is the new one."

Annie shook her head. She had no idea what the new mayor might have done, but she was sure that Mamie Boudin would tell her in detail. No way was she going to admit she preferred the new mayor to the old. Idiot was often defined by the point of view of the person assigning the term.

"He brought all these ruffians from Paris for the summer. Poor kids." Mamie Boudin used the word *poor* as if she was talking about leprosy or cancer. "We were all scared to be on the street."

Annie couldn't imagine the cane-swinging Mamie Boudin being afraid of anything including King Kong on a rampage. "Are they still here?"

"*Merci Dieu*, thank God, most of them have gone back, but crimes were way, way up. Robberies galore. Cars broken into almost nightly. Mostly tourists'. They left ours alone. Maybe next time the old mayor will be reelected."

Annie swallowed her words. The new mayor was the first mayor in decades that hadn't come from the powerful Boulet family and he was also the first mayor who hadn't been a lover of the far-right beliefs of Jean Le Pen, whom Annie described as being slightly less liberal than Genghis Khan.

The *mamies* considered anyone whose families hadn't lived in Argelès at least since the sixteen hundreds to be newcomers and upstarts, although they'd showed an amazing fondness for Annie from the beginning even before the ambience-changing street party. She'd guessed that because they had invited her in to eat. She figured she'd won them over by knocking at their doors on rainy days and asking if they wanted her to pick up some bread when she went to buy her own. Also she was the only American they knew, although they grouped other Americans with *Les Pied Noir*, the Black Feet, those French who had left Algeria when independence had been declared, Arabs, blacks, Parisians and anyone else who wasn't them.

"Did you know that he was back with another woman?" Mamie Couges whispered pointing with her thumb back over her shoulder to the Danish journalist's house after they had drained Annie of all the information they felt she could give.

"*C'est vrai?*" Really? Annie wasn't about to say that she knew the woman they thought had been Christian's wife for years was in fact his mistress, and that it was his wife who had been with him this last trip. She and Christian would chat by e-mail, and he'd told her of his deteriorating relationship with his mistress and his improving marriage. She had asked him if he thought there might be a connection, and he'd said no. She smiled at the old ladies.

The church bells rang the half-hour. "*Excusez-moi*, but I really need to get something to eat."

"Shops are closed by now," Mamie Couges said. "Come eat with me. My son's not coming today. Some meeting somewhere."

Annie weighed the idea of the food against the activity of Mamie Couges' tongue. Even things Mamie Couges threw together were heaven. One time she'd whipped up eggs and spinach in some kind of sauce. Not normal eggs, but little eggs, which she'd found in the woods. Annie had tried not to think how upset the bird would be to discover an empty nest.

"That's so nice, but I'm meeting someone," she lied.

"*Un gendarme par chance?*" Mamie Boudin asked. She tilted her head.

What a flirt she must have been when young, Annie thought. "The Chief has his hand's full right now, *je pense*, I think." Let them guess if Roger were still in her life. Lord knows, whenever they'd walked hand-in-hand down the street, one by one the old women suddenly felt a need to shake rugs out their windows or to hang out washing. Roger had pointed out that the washing was often dry. Annie had guessed they'd telephoned one another as soon as they'd been spotted.

Les mamies, with hearing that seemed to work through thick stone walls, were the reason that English had become Annie and Roger's language. He had spent a year in the States at some special training program and spoke English so well that Annie often forgot it wasn't his mother tongue. His facility had let them speak freely knowing their talk wouldn't be reported throughout the village. Although some of the younger residents spoke excellent English, most of the older people didn't.

She bent down and kissed both women on the cheeks. As she walked to the restaurant, she wasn't sure if her headache was hunger or just the result of the emotion of the morning. Hunger she could take care of. She knew she'd miss Père Yves, her research buddy, forever. And she needed to do something to find out what happened.

CHAPTER 5
RENNES-LE-CHÂTEAU

After I locked up the shop, pulling the metal gate over the store window and door, I walked upstairs. The living room had a tiny kitchen area at one end. There was a small bedroom that barely held my double bed, nightstand and bureau. My armoire was in the living room and that was for my clothes, not that I had all that many, but I loved every piece I had. Clothes should be like old friends, treasured more each year.

Ptah, my big black cat, woke up long enough to consider whether to greet me or not. He was getting old. Few people realized that the original Ptah was the Egyptian god who called the world into being. He and the goddess Isis probably had a wonderful time hanging out together.

I had considered naming him Satan, but one can carry the witch thingie too far. As my neighbors have known me since I was born, they consider the whole witch thing a marketing ploy, although none have the sophistication to use that term. More likely, they just would say I'm pulling the wool over the tourists' eyes, poor bastards, although it serves them right. They will send tourists to my shop. If they have a shop, like Jean-Pierre has the blown glass store, I return the favor.

I wasn't all that hungry to start with and the *diabolo frais* with the producer had taken away the rest of my appetite. I sliced an apple into paper-thin slices, one of the early ones in the season picked from Robert's tree near the entrance of the village. I sprinkled the pieces with cinnamon and arranged them in a circle on a plate.

I didn't feel like putting on the news. It would probably be the same-old, same-old: corruption, one politician contradicting another, etc., etc., etc. I sat in my rocking chair and ate the apple, taking my time to let the sweetness and the bite of the cinnamon tickle my tastebuds.

The producer had triggered memories. I hadn't thought of my grandmother for a long time. She was one of those *mamies* that created the stereotype. Unlike my mother, who was often sick, Mamie Josephine (my father's mother was Mamie Rosa) always had time for me. She was a wonderful storyteller. When I was at the University of Toulouse, we had an oral history project and I had taped the story of Mamie Josephine's life using an old transcribing machine. I wondered if I still had it.

I've an attic crawlspace with a pull-down ladder outside my bathroom. My tendency is to throw stuff up there when I'm not sure if I will want it in the future, although most things I know I won't. Those go out immediately. But things like Christmas decorations, old records (accounts—not musical), photos I don't want hanging around and things like that get sentenced to the crawlspace.

I found a flashlight, pulled the string and mounted the stairs, something I disliked doing alone. Now I am more aware of falling then I was even five years ago, and if I fell at night no one would notice until the next day when I didn't open my shop. Just because I looked younger, my body, although in good shape, could humble me every now and then with some new limitation or ache.

The light beam played around the different boxes. Most I could immediately eliminate because I'd labeled them: *Papers 1984*, for example. Three boxes were called *Misc.*

When I say crawlspace, the roof is slanted and I can almost stand in the middle, but I immediately have to hunch over when

I take a few steps in any direction. The ladder opens in the middle. I sat with my legs crossed on the floor, aware that my skirt would gather so much dust it would need washing, and pulled the *Misc.* boxes to me.

The first was full of books: I shoved it to the opening. I wondered why I had kept them in the first place, although at the time they probably were not so yellowed nor had had brittle pages that broke when I touched them—as they did now. It could go straight into the *poubelle.* I always thought the word for garbage was much too pretty the way it rolled off my tongue.

The second box had some yarn for sweaters and patterns I hadn't had time to knit, along with a few pieces of cloth for dresses I hadn't sewn and a few baby clothes that Chloë never lived long enough to wear. I no longer mourned her actively. She'd lived less than an hour. I'd never seen her alive, never held her. It's not that I'm callous. For years, each baby I looked at caused a pain unlike any other, but now enough scar tissue has formed to keep the wound from reopening, but it is there nevertheless. Thinking about Chloë, who would be in her late thirties, was not something I wanted to do.

The third box was sealed with tape that was old enough that it pulled off easily and crumbled. Inside was an old fashioned reel-to-reel tape recorder only slightly smaller than a mini microwave. Those were the pre-cassette days. What a novelty it had been. Neighbors came in to try it out. Most people had radios, but only one or two had televisions in those pre-1968 Revolution times when France began to gain financially thanks to people not accepting the status quo. One thing I love about my country is that people strike at the possibility that maybe somewhere someone might be remotely considering thinking about maybe considering making things more difficult such as a wage freeze, a factory closing or god or goddess forbid reducing our vacation time or raising the cost of a doctor's visit. It may e inconvenient but it is better than degrading our quality of ife.

But even after 1968 this village was too far from anywhere to ave a factory that provided jobs and most locals either went to he valley to work, or scraped out some small existence by hemselves.

My prof had given me the recorder for the project when he bought a new one. Well I have to admit, I'd been sleeping with iim. Now there's a wrong word. We never slept. He was young nd handsome, unfortunately married (at the time I believed he line, "My wife doesn't understand me," although I've earned that probably the wife understands the man all too vell) and I was imagining myself young and sophisticated nstead of being a tiny mountain village girl. He was from Paris nd I had hoped his sophistication would enter my body along vith his sperm, although in truth it was trapped by the con-lom.

The tape recorder was heavy and I had to struggle to get it lown the ladder, but I am still strong. Lifting it out of the dust-covered box, I was surprised that it wasn't dirtier.

I remember the day I recorded the tape. Mamie Josephine vas scrawny, wearing a black dress as she had since her husband iad passed away twenty years before. She didn't mourn him. By ill accounts my *papi* had been a mean son-of-a-bitch and berhaps my grandmother's sunny disposition had more to do vith her freedom. However, widows wore black and she fol-owed tradition. How surprised I was when I helped clean out ier things after her death to find she had made herself red silk oras and panties.

Her hair never turned entirely gray, but half and half, and she orced it into a little bun on top of her head. She always pinned up the stray hairs in the back with a little gold barrette that ooked like a butterfly. I never knew where she got it, but she promised it to me when she died. I was still in Toulouse at the university but away in England with my lover-prof when she passed, and when I asked my mother about it upon my return three days after the funeral, she told me they had buried her with it. I always felt badly.

At the time I was doubly sad. The prof had told me at the end of the trip that he was going to stay with his wife and I had better forget him, but not to forget all I had learned because I was going to make a wonderful sociologist. I never worked in my degree field, first working in marketing, which I hated, but then in a shop much like mine in Toulouse near the airport, met and married Michel and as they say the rest is history, and not all that interesting.

A marriage is made up of cooking meals, cleaning the house, arguing about money, making love, not always in passion. I've made love in anger and in submission. I've had every eon of my body involved and more than once I've planned my next day's menus while my lover thinks I'm admiring what he is doing to me.

As I plugged in the machine, I wondered if the tape would be too brittle to play, but what could I lose? The transcription was underneath, a faded script in old-fashioned courier type tapped out on my old Olivetti typewriter with my name Miriam Fournier; the title *Poverty and Wealth in a Small Mountain Village, An Oral History*. Then came *his* name: Dr. Hughes Andres, Professor Sociology and the date May 1, 1962. If I destroyed the transcript and the tape broke then the information would exist only in my memory, clouded by a lifetime as a busy adult.

I prayed that I could hear my grandmother talk about the village before the mystery or the information went international. I pushed the button and Mamie Josephine's reedy voice brought me back to a time when I would burst into her house and be greeted by a smile that erased any doubts I had that I might not be loved.

I placed the tape recorder on the kitchen table and plugged it in. The clock showed it was almost time for bed, but if I went now, my mind would keep wandering back to what was on the tape and to the France 2 producer. Instead, I made a *tisane* with my freshly dried mint, even if it meant I would have to get up a couple of extra times in the night to pee. I flipped on my electric hot water kettle, one of the few trendy things I have, trendy by shape and trendy by its sky blue clear plastic.

I suppose it is almost old-maidish how much I like the blue mug with the triangular insert placed against the rim, which steeps the leaves in the hot water. I bought it from the potter around the corner, but the ritual in things that make my eyes happy is comforting. Besides whom does it harm? Finally, with the *tisane* brewing, I turned on the machine. Several feet of tape rolled before my grandmother's voice began quivering, giving me time to settle in my comfortable chair. I shut my eyes to listen and be taken back to the day I had made the recording. Hearing her voice makes me all warm inside, the same way my feet are warm in my cozy heavy socks that I now put on at night after the sun goes down. I followed her words on the transcript.

MF: What is your name?

JA: Don't be silly, you know.

MF: Don't think of me as your granddaughter, think of me as a stranger.

JA: (laughter) "Silly girl, I'm to forget I diapered you, dried your nose when you had a cold and sewed your first communion dress? I'm Josephine Azéma. I was born an Azéma and married an Azéma, although we were no relation.

MF: And how old are you?

JA: I was born in 1880. I'll be 82 this summer, and I don't feel it, let me tell you. I can still walk up and down the mountain if I have to.

MF: Tell me about your early life.

JA: I was one of six children, the baby and the second girl. My brothers were Pierre, Bernard, Raphaël and André. He died, André, when he was four, bitten by a snake while he played in the grass going down the hill. Raphaël died during the flu epidemic in 1918. Pierre was killed in World War II and Bernard was shot by the Germans. He was a Maquis, a real resistance fighter, who risked his life every day from the second the first German boot touched French soil. Your Aunt Marie-Claude and me, we are the only two still alive, tough old birds that we are. (She laughs).

MF: (laughs)

JA: My mother was often sick and spent time in bed. Only when I was grown up did I learn that was because of pregnancies mostly ending before the baby was born. I suppose I knew at some level, but by the time I came along, it was mainly Marie-Claude, the oldest, who looked after us all.

The village was poor: not poor like today, but poor like you've never seen . . . even when you were little during the war. We all lived off the land more or less. Because my father was a baker, we were slightly better off. People traded a chicken, lamb, fish, vegetables in place of money for their baguettes, but my father had to insist on coins sometimes. The people down below would not trade the flour he needed to bake the bread for anything but hard cash.

Of course, we didn't know we were poor. We thought the whole world lived like us. And I'm not sure we were all that unhappy either. All that changed when the priest came. When he enriched the village we discovered what we didn't have and some of us longed for more instead of thinking that what we had was all there was. I will say this for him, he shared his wealth with the village in many ways.

MF: How many people lived here then?
JA: I never counted, but I guess about 300— not many more.
MF: When did the priest arrive?
JA: It was early summer or late spring, I'm not sure which, but it was one of the first really hot days of the year. I was barefoot and sitting by the stream that runs all the way down the mountain. The road wasn't paved then, that's one of the things the priest did with his money. It was more a dirt path but if you sit just right you can see to

where it bends. He appeared, pulling a small cart with some things in it. I couldn't see what, but I was curious. My whole family used to say I was too curious for my own good.

I would pepper my mother with whys as she lay in bed until she would call Marie-Claude to take me somewhere, anywhere.

MF: How did you know he was a priest?
JA: We'd been expecting him for a long, long time. Our little church certainly wasn't one of the desirable posts. In fact, some priests considered serving in our village God's punishment.

Anyway, this priest was young, or so they told me. When you are five or thereabouts all grown-ups look old. He stopped more than once to dip his hand in the stream and wash his hands, splash water on his neck and drink.

I forgot to mention, most of the villagers were inside, not because of the heat, but it was lunch time and like now people took naps and didn't come out until three or four depending on the seasons and the work in the gardens.

When he rounded the last bend before entering the village he found me sitting on the rock, right by the ruin of the tower that has been a ruin since long before I was born and will probably be a ruin forever and forever, unless people decide to use the bricks and stones for something else. Why they haven't done it yet, I'll never know. Some say it is haunted, but I think parents say that to keep their children from playing there and having it collapse on top of them.

MF: That's what *maman* told me.
JA: And I told her. Do you want me to tell my story or not?
MF: Yes, sorry.
JA: When he saw me he stood straight. He had been bent over slightly as he pulled the cart. I almost imagined him as a donkey.

"What do we have here?" he asked.

I thought he couldn't be too bright because I was obviously a little girl.

"What's your name?"

"Josephine Azéma."

"Can you show me where the church and rectory are?"

He had that tone people use with little children that implies that they're really stupid. The same way they are always saying, "My you've grown" as if they are surprised you didn't shrink.

I nodded and started to run.

"Slow down," he called. "This cart is heavy."

I walked back and showed him the church.

The front step was broken, the graveyard was more like a meadow, the front door only had one hinge. You didn't swing it open, you lifted it open, which he did. Inside the church was light. There was a hole in the roof that let in the sun, also the rain so not many people prayed on stormy days.

"Jesus, Mary and Joseph," he said. Those were things Marie-Claude told me never to say, but Marie-Claude spent her life telling me what to say, what not to say, what to do and what not to do. Even now she tries it. You'd think, after all these years, she'd realize I ignore her. (cackling laughter)

I was too scared to say, If you think that is bad, wait till you see the rectory. He would hate the rats that had taken over, the holes in the floor, the shutters that were stacked in the kitchen doing nothing to protect the windows. I didn't mention that the rectory still had windows, about the only thing that wasn't broken.

I stood at the door and watched him sink onto one of the benches inside the church. He put his head in his hands. I thought he was praying, but as we got to know him better, we learned prayer was something he did the least of, unless someone was looking, of course.

Chapter 6
Argelès-sur-mer

Les Arbres is a typical Catalan restaurant in a small hotel serving dishes prepared with tomatoes, garlic and pepper. From the outside it looked like any other restaurant, but inside Jacques and Marie-France had created a paradise in a courtyard complete with fountain and plants. In winter and on rainy days it was covered with a glass roof, but when Annie walked in, the weather was perfect. The sky was so blue that had it been in a painting people would have said that it was impossible for any sky to be that color and that clear. Last month every table would have been taken and a line of people waiting, but now only a local couple, whom Annie recognized without knowing their names was sitting at a table.

Marie-France kissed Annie on both cheeks. "*Bienvenue. Jacques, regardes!* Look who's here. How long this time?"

"At least a month," Annie said. "Maybe longer. It's so good to be back."

Jacques came from the kitchen, wiping his hands on his apron before enveloping her in a big hug. This was so un-French, but Jacques believed hugs were necessary to get through any day. "Have you heard?"

"Père Yves?" Annie no longer was amazed at the speed information traveled in a small village: more efficient than the Internet any day. "I found him, but he disappeared again."

"*C'était toi?* It was you? I'd heard Gendarme Boulet found and lost him." Jacques looked at her closely. "Have you seen

51

Roger yet?" He ignored Marie-France's speed-of-light hand signals. "I'll ask her anything I want. She can always tell me to not be so nosy."

No way did she want to go into a Roger-saga with them. She knew, since they had fixed her up with Roger, that they'd felt responsible when the two of them had broken up. Marie-France had been making plans to have the wedding reception at the restaurant even though Roger hadn't proposed. If the restaurant owners had had their way, the couple would have married and had at least one child by now. Annie wanted to say she didn't want to talk about it, although she knew that wouldn't work. "*Oui. Ça va.* It was fine. I'm starving."

"I'll bring some fish soup," Jacques said. "Just made it to today with fresh *aioli*. Croutons baked with olive oil." He kissed his fingertips.

"Champagne? Kir royale?" Marie-France asked.

Annie may have loved both of them and although the greetings from her friends made life seem normal, it wasn't. Just the idea of alcohol made her shudder. Under normal circumstances turning down champagne or a kir royale was against her religion, but it was this oft-repeated joke that seemed so inappropriate now. How many times had Père Yves teased her that if he used champagne for communion wine she might convert? She didn't want to think about him because when she did, her first thought was of his eyes staring lifelessly at her.

Within minutes Marie-France had Annie installed at a table with a bowl of steaming brown fish soup before her. Annie threw in croutons, the *aoili* and a bit of the shredded cheese. When she tasted it, her stomach told her she had done the right thing.

Marie-France sat down opposite her. Annie saw her stiffen as she glanced at the entrance. Annie turned around to see Roger walk in the door. She patted Marie-France's hand. In turn the woman slipped into the kitchen. She'd once told Annie that years of running a restaurant had taught her the best time to be invisible.

Roger had changed into his uniform. He was still drop-dead handsome with the gray forelock in his otherwise thick black hair. He kissed Annie on both cheeks. *"Pourrais-je m'asseoir?"*

"Bien sûr," she said, pointing toward the free chair opposite her. There ought to be some international law that old boyfriends develop wrinkles and lose all their teeth plus gain 100 pounds all in the gut. However, if there were such a rule, Roger certainly was in danger of being arrested for its violation.

"I've been thinking," he said in French.

Annie knew when he spoke in French around his country-men that there was nothing personal in it. Too bad. Not too bad. Okay, she could admit to being ambivalent. *"Et . . ."*

"Père Yves still hasn't turned up. My staff, especially Boulet, thinks you've an overactive imagination." He looked around. "But they're . . ."

"Male chauvinist pigs," they said together and both smiled.

"Not only that, they think you made it up to get my attention." As she bristled, he held up both hands, "I don't. There's blood on the statue, and Père Yves missed morning Mass. He had told several people he wasn't going to go back to Rennes-le-Chateau until you got here. Something has happened to him, but I haven't got a body and . . ."

". . . without a body, no crime."

Roger smiled. "And you're still finishing my sentences." Annie blushed, which he politely ignored. "Despite our differences, one of the things I always appreciated about you was your intelligence. You were closer to Père Yves than any one of his parishioners. Any ideas?"

Marie-France came back to the table. "Do you want to order, or should I leave you alone?"

"Just give me what she's having," he said, "and a glass of wine."

In minutes Marie-France was back with his soup and wine and disappeared so quickly that she could have been a spirit. Annie knew that her friend was watching. When another couple entered she came out from the kitchen and herded them to a table as far away from Annie and Roger as it was possible to be without seating them in the kitchen.

"He'd written me that he had definite proof of a find. I suspect it is something about a building that he thought had once been there—nothing more. We were going there tomorrow."

"Would you be willing to help me search his place? You would know more than me what's important."

Annie wanted to say no because then she could pretend everything was all right, but even more she needed to know what had happened to Père Yves. She also wanted to know what he had intended sharing with her. She nodded.

"Have you sealed his rectory? Dusted for prints? I mean if it's connected to his disappearance, someone might want to search it."

"I'll ask Boulet to do it." Looking at Annie's face he added, "I'll have Gault do it."

Marie-France cleared their plates and then put down two salads with hot melted goat cheese, walnuts, avocados and small toasts. *"Bon appétit."*

"I've missed you, Annie." He switched to English.

She picked up her fork and moved a piece of avocado to the goat cheese and back again. She wanted to say she missed him too, but that was more than she cared to admit. "It hasn't been easy, I guess." That could mean not easy for him or her. And there was no way she was going to say what she really wanted to do was to take him by the hand and lead him back to her nest

54

and strip him of clothes and make love to him. She pictured the three *mamies* shaking their rugs and wishing they could see inside Annie's apartment. Without being able to stop it, a smile played over her lips.

"What are you smiling at?"

She put the avocado in her mouth. "The salad. When do you want to look at the rectory?"

"After lunch?"

"Fine. If we wait too long the murderer could find something himself."

"We only know he's missing." Roger drank about a quarter of his wine. A wistful look crossed his face. "When I worked in Paris I handled a lot of murders. I'm out of practice. In fact, I came down here for a quiet life. And we can't even prove it is a murder."

Annie knew that it was also to get over the fact that a criminal had hired someone to shoot and kill his wife in revenge for Roger having gathered enough evidence to send the crook to prison. Not that he'd told her: the *mamies* had filled her in. Roger, they'd said, wanted to raise their daughter Gaëlle outside of the messiness of Paris.

"How's Gaëlle?"

"She misses you too."

"Not fair. Gaëlle knows she can always reach me by phone or e-mail."

He held up his hands. "Okay, cheap shot on my part. Another thing: the body, how far could it have gone? There's always the possibility he was hurt and got up and went to see a doctor."

Annie's first reaction was to pour her glass of water over his head. "He was dead, Roger. Dead. And I told you I was gone only a short time, to call the police and to calm down. At that time of the morning there's almost no one around. Whoever moved the body was taking a risk that someone would be up early, walking a dog, catching the early train to Perpignan, something."

"So either the alleged killer of the alleged dead man had a car nearby or he hid the body."

"There's no alleged body." Annie spoke through clenched teeth. "If Père Yves only fell, no one would have moved him." She could not say the word *suicide*. Père Yves was not the suicidal type, but what was the suicidal type?

Marie-France replaced their empty plates with two *crèmes brûlées*. "This is regular, not the Catalan one?" Annie asked.

Marie-France, who'd started back toward the kitchen, turned and said, "For Roger, yes. For you normal. Not a whiff of anything *réglisse*. Licorice."

Annie reached for her wallet, but Roger grabbed the check. "Consider it pay for helping me. Now let's go and see what's in the rectory."

Chapter 7
Argelès-sur-mer

The rectory was over 500 years old and flanked by houses of the same age. Annie and Roger walked through the stone archway that led onto the square of connected houses around a tiled courtyard with its fountain in the middle.

Fountain was what Père Yves had called it, but Annie had often told him "fountain" might be the wrong word. "It's a metal post with a face in the center," she'd say to him. The face could have been that of a God or a normal Roman man carved into the metal with its laurel wreath buried among curly tendrils of metallic green hair and bushy eyebrows. The mouth was open: water ran down the tongue into a small basin for recycling, except today. Someone had left a red plastic pail under the stream that was overflowing into the catch drain. Whoever had put the pail there would have to step over the pink, white and purple begonias clogging the ceramic boxes surrounding the fountain to retrieve their water.

How she wished Père Yves was the one who had left the pail, but she knew he wasn't. His pail was blue. She wished the face could tell her what had happened to her friend. She wished Roger wasn't half treating the case as a possible missing person. She wanted him to commit to the case as a missing corpse.

When Annie started a work project she knew there was a way to crack it. This situation had to be the same, if only she could think hard enough. Maybe the rectory would help and by her delaying with the examination of fountains or other tactics only postponed the inevitable.

The square was empty as they approached the rectory. At this time of day, all the residents were inside either washing up from lunch or napping. After buying her nest, Annie had quickly adjusted to the three-hour noon shutdown, missing it whenever she accepted a new assignment in a more modern place where people rushed through the entire workweek with only short breaks for lunch. Part of her love of the village was its slow-paced days. Today wasn't one of the times she appreciated the siesta break. "Do you have the key?"

Roger reached into his case for a key that a small boat might have used as an anchor. The key seemed to match the age of the house. "I found this not far from the angel. Since it didn't work in the church door, I guessed it might be for the rectory."

"How did Boulet get in then? I can't imagine Père Yves giving him one of the extra keys."

"There were extra keys?"

"He kept one in his office at the church, and vice versa."

"We *flics* have lots of skeleton keys." Although he said it lightly, his face was serious. "Let's check his office in the church to see if there's a missing key to the rectory."

They walked into the icy cold church. Roger dipped his fingers in the font of holy water and crossed himself. Annie, as a non-Catholic, did not. Their footsteps echoed on the ancient stone floor as they walked down the aisle and behind the altar to the small room where Père Yves had his office.

When Annie's hand reached to touch the latch, Roger grabbed it by the wrist.

"What?"

He reached into his pocket and pulled out two pairs of white rubber gloves like surgeons use. "Just in case we can get usable prints," he said. "Which I doubt, since anyone in the village could have a perfectly good reason to be here."

The office had a small table, three folding chairs and a two-drawer file cabinet.

"Someone has looked through here already," Annie said.

"How do you know?"

Père Yves had joked he was almost obsessive–compulsive when it came to his paperwork, and she knew from the way that every folder would have the papers inside perfectly lined up in correct order, that it was only half a joke. Although he was nowhere as near as Monk on TV to having OCD, because his need for order was mainly centered around his work, he still was a bit fanatic.

Several files were stacked on his desk, the file drawer from which they came still open. In the pile to the left, all the files were in pristine order, the one to the right had papers sticking out willy-nilly.

"He would never leave his office like this. Whenever I waited for him, even if we were going to be late for whatever, he never left without putting everything back just so."

"I doubt if you can tell if anything is missing."

"Everything here should be confidential," Annie said as she read the names of parishioners from the labels. She opened the bottom drawer. Here were the financial and other business records of the church. They did not look like they had been touched. "Whoever looked through those files did not get a chance to finish."

Roger took out his phone. "Gault, I need someone with something over here to seal Père Yves's office. Not with yellow tape. With a solid lock."

"As police we can look through the records, but I don't think it is right you do, since these files must contain confidential counseling notes and things."

Annie felt relief. She knew enough gossip without having to carry the secret of whatever had missed the village grapevine.

"Let's go on to the rectory."

The rectory's door had a bronze knocker shaped like a hand with well-tapered fingers. Roger lifted it and let it fall against the metal plate. The noise echoed in the silent square. He gave her a look that echoed her hope against hope that they would hear footsteps, and Père Yves would open the door, and they would all have a good laugh over the gossip he'd caused. There was no answer. Roger inserted the key and twisted; the lock gave immediately.

Behind the entryway, hidden by a door, was the kitchen. Annie had eaten there enough times to know every crack in the tiled floor. She could picture Père Yves lighting the gas hot water heater to wash the dishes or putting in a load of laundry, although the chugging would drive them to the next floor where he had his private study. It suddenly struck her that he had never worried about the propriety of his being alone with a young woman.

Annie opened the top door of the washing machine. It was the typical French kind with a metal drum inside that had a door. She turned the clasp. A soggy load, with black socks on top, was waiting to be hung. She knew from talking to the priest that often he put a load in before going to bed because the wash cycle alone lasted well over an hour and a half followed by an equally long rinse cycle.

"He didn't have time to hang up the washing before he was killed," she said.

"We don't know he was killed. How does the kitchen look?" Roger asked.

"Like a kitchen." Père Yves's coffee cup was still on the drain board. She opened the refrigerator, which was only half the size of an American one. There was a ceramic bowl painted with huge purple and blue flowers filled with couscous next to a plain beige bowl of different meats and vegetables. A half-drunk bottle of wine sat on the rough black wooden table. Next to the wine was a bowl of fruit that included grapes, apples, pears and figs.

"This too would rule out suicide. People don't buy this much fruit if they are going to kill themselves," Roger said.

"Which means you think he's dead too and all the blather about *if* is just that—blather?"

He shrugged. "Nor do people who want to kill themselves start their laundry. Why bother? And Père Yves would never die before finishing his couscous. I remember eating with him at *Poivre et Sel* down at the beach. I thought he might consume the bowl as well as its contents."

"I know he was planning to have some people in for couscous earlier this week. Those are definitely leftovers. When Père Yves makes it, the amount is four times what's left in the *frigo* now." Annie was so swamped with memories that she needed to sit. How that man loved his food. Even when they were walking on the rough terrain around Rennes-le-Château, he would find a rock and pull out a feast from his backpack. One time they'd had chicken orange salad. Another, a tomato and cheese pie, and he'd confessed to making the pastry from scratch.

He would be more apt to commit suicide if he *couldn't* finish a meal, she thought, only half jokingly for she knew the priest's deep morality would keep him from that sin. Although he disagreed with much that was happening in Rome, the more they talked about the different heresies and political movements during the Middle Ages, it was evident to her that Père Yves still believed in the moral principles to which most religions conformed even as he separated those from his Church.

Roger opened a cabinet. "No housekeeper. Amazing how neat."

"He liked puttering around by himself," Annie said. She opened the door under the kitchen sink and pulled out the garbage. There were the normal coffee grounds, carrot peelings and an envelope, the kind that was used for the mail development of photos. Père Yves often sent his digital photos for development rather than look at them on screen or print them himself. He'd bought a photo printer, but had never gotten it to work as well as he wanted. His patience with mechanical and technical things was about a nanosecond, although he could spend days or weeks researching some historical detail.

The envelope was empty. Not even the CD in the pouch for that purpose was there. A plain white envelope, without even a return address to tell them anything, was torn.

"Nonclues," she said.

Roger took the envelope. "If we don't find any photos, their absence might be a clue. Look, it's dated last Tuesday."

"The day he e-mailed me saying he found something to show me." She fought tears. "And he teased me about it last night before I left Zurich."

Roger rubbed her back. "I wish I'd known him better. Everyone loved him."

"Well one person didn't. Let's go upstairs."

As narrow and shallow as the house was, Père Yves's study was the biggest room, occupying the entire floor. Unlike the kitchen, which was monastery minimalist, the walls were covered with books, a CD player and CDs, mostly jazz, gospel and blues in alphabetical order. He had files in multicolored folders. Annie remembered him bragging on how he color-coded everything: green for crusades, red for Rennes-le-Château, black for Black Madonna and Isis material, yellow for Cathars and other heresies, purple for Septamanie, the Visigoth community that was supposed to have flourished in the region around the 400s. She, in turn, had tried to follow his example, but was not as successful in maintaining order. Too many papers ended up in the wrong place.

Looking at the black folder reminded Annie of all the discussions they had had on various theories. Some, including Annie and Père Yves, believed in the possibility that Mary Magdalene had fled to the South of France when different early followers of Christ saw her as a threat to where they wanted to take the foundling Church. This was one of the things the two of them had been researching. Père Yves wanted to prove Mary Magdalene was the black Madonna and was related somehow to the goddess Isis. For a second she wondered if he had told his Bishop and if so, there had to be repercussions.

"Do you think the church killed him because of his questioning some things about the Virgin Mary?"

Roger gave her his "don't-be-ridiculous" look.

"Okay, I've been reading too many stupid conspiracy books."

"Where do we start?" Roger asked. When Annie shook her head, he asked, "Do you feel funny going through his things?"

"I kind of wish I did more because that would mean I believed he was still alive." She shivered. "But I saw his eyes."

"We'll do this methodically: drawer by drawer, folder by folder," he said. He started with the top left drawer. This included the records of the church and personal bills. "Nothing out of the ordinary, although I'm no accountant," he said.

"Don't tell me you think he was fiddling with the books?"

"As a policeman I shouldn't overlook the possibility, as a person who is fairly confident in my instincts of human nature . . ." He shrugged.

Annie pulled out the first yellow folder labeled Cathars. Père Yves's handwriting was instantly recognizable. Not because he always used brown ink or a real pen, but because it looked like calligraphy. He said if any sin would send him to hell, the sin of pride toward his penmanship was a guaranteed one-way ticket to eternal damnation.

Annie knew how much she would miss going to her mailbox,

thumbing through her bills and finding an envelope with his handwriting. They had become few and far between the last year because Père Yves had fallen in love with the computer, e-mail and the Web, saying to her that so much of their recent research would have been impossible without the Internet. For the Internet he had unlimited patience, and pooh-poohed the inconsistency with his attitude towards other technical stuff, saying that consistency was the product of small minds and lack of flexibility. "The Internet, my digital camera and mobile phone are useful, but why should I waste my time programming something when I am not going to use it? I'll learn and do what's necessary and no more."

She thumbed through the pages and Post-it notes. Most said things like, "Duality/The fight between two equals. Good and Evil. Check out spring 762 A.D. Merovingian Jewelry, Sion in Switzerland." These made sense with their research. Others, like "dissonance in social structure, semantics of delinquency, 15th October," meant nothing. She went back to the notes under the title "Good and Evil."

The priest had written, "As set down in St. John's Gospel: good being the kingdom of the good lord, evil being the material and time passing reality of the visible physical world." The Post-it said to file it in the folder "Cathar." She picked up that folder and started reading the first page. "The entire contents are the basic beliefs of the Cathar faith, that some had said was wiped out when French soldiers had killed 200 Good Men and Good Women, as the Cathars called themselves in 1244." However, the faith, as she and Père Yves had discovered, was still being practiced in hundreds of small villages in the Pyrénées. She had no idea what contents the paper referred to, but there was nothing in that file or any of the others that they hadn't discussed to death. A bad choice of words, she thought.

Roger finished with all the drawers about the same time Annie finished with the folders. "He was certainly organized," he said. "Anything out of place would stand out like a sore thumb. What's upstairs?"

"Never been up there. I would assume his bedroom."

They walked up the stairs. "Now it really feels like an invasion of his privacy," she said.

"I got used to it in Paris, except most times I didn't know the victims."

He was silent and Annie wondered if he were thinking of his wife, but that was a subject they had never gone near. As curious as she was, she felt people should tell her what they wanted her to know when they wanted her to know it. As much as she'd hoped that someday he would want to, there was part of her that never wanted to hear about someone else whom he'd loved. No one arrived at her age, much less his, without having a past love, but that didn't mean it should be a topic of conversation. Instead of saying anything, she followed him up the narrow staircase.

The single bed was made with such military precision that if they had wanted to drop a Euro onto the blanket, it would bounce. Père Yves and Annie had talked about how Annie never made her bed when she lived in an apartment where she could close the door but always turned her bed back into a couch in her Argelès nest because she couldn't hide the mess.

Annie slipped her hand under the pillow and pulled out neatly folded pajama bottoms.

"It could mean that he didn't sleep here last night." Roger ran his hand along the cotton blanket.

"He claimed he always made the bed first thing when he got up. Even before brushing his teeth."

"Do you notice anything strange?" Roger asked.

Annie looked around. The small casement window was open, nothing unusual there. The curtains were of blue striped Catalan fabric, as was the dresser scarf. The priest's shoes, sneakers and loafers were lined up.

"No slippers?"

"Hadn't noticed that, but something else." She wandered around and around. There was a cross-shaped part of cleaner wall. "No cross over the bed."

Before Annie could comment they heard the front door slam.

"Hello, anyone there?" A voice came up from down below. Roger and Annie scrambled downstairs. They were narrow and slippery under Annie's sandals, although Roger's police shoes had thick gripping soles. When they reached the entryway, they saw Mayor Pierre Galy. He stood there in his khaki pants and open-necked blue shirt, his sandy brown hair tousled; he needed a trim as always. The mayor was young, Annie's age. Most village officials, at least until the last election, had been in their sixties when not only had two young men come in, but people from other than the ruling Boulet family and the Boulet cronies. The silent revolutionaries, some of the locals called this new bunch. Unfortunately, enough of the old group remained on the council to hamper many new ideas from being implemented.

"I saw the door open, and I thought I'd see who was here," the mayor said. He shook Roger's hand and kissed Annie on both cheeks. "Welcome back. Any word on the priest?"

Roger briefed the mayor within seconds.

"I know you'll do everything you can. The best thing I can do is to not get in your way," Mayor Galy said. He did not have to add, "not like my predecessor," who would have followed Roger around peppering him with questions and demanding results if not at that moment then yesterday. The glance that Roger and Annie exchanged said wordlessly they both thought that this new mayor was a breath of fresh air in the village. The Boulet family had strangled it too long.

Still Argelès was not totally released from the Boulets, who owned the biggest hotel and much of the rental property, commercial and residential, at the beach. They had been instrumental in developing the port and no one could rent at the marina without adding to the Boulet fortunes. When Galy had won the election, Boulet had told him to find another place for his boat. The Mayor of Collioure, one village down the coast, no friend of the Boulets, made sure that Galy's boat had a place. He'd offered it free, but Galy had insisted on paying. Their negotiations had been in the opposite direction of most buyers and sellers.

"Two hundred," the Collioure Mayor had offered when he realized he'd have to accept something.

"Thousand Euros," Galy had countered.

"Three hundred," the mayor had said.

They'd settled that the Argelès mayor would pay five hundred for the slip.

The story had kept the town buzzing for over a week. A few people even spoke about honest politicians with a shake of their heads.

"Anything I can do to help, let me know," Galy said. He shook Roger's hand again, patting him on the back, and kissed Annie's cheeks for a second time.

"He's an improvement," Annie said after the mayor had departed.

"Still, he's stirred up a lot of controversy by bringing in those kids. Kept us hopping this summer. The idea was fine, but the kids needed more supervision. Unfortunately, he'll never get a chance to iron out the kinks." When Annie frowned, he added, "too much political liability to do it next summer. Let's go back upstairs."

Roger started going through Père Yves's armoire. There was two of everything, hung on hangers—except there was only one sweater and pair of pants. He mentioned it to Annie, who was going through the drawer on the nightstand.

"He was wearing his beige cotton knit," she said. There was a large envelope under Père Yves's well-thumbed Bible. Inside was an aerial photo. She could tell immediately that it was of Rennes-le-Château and the surrounding countryside. An indentation in the ground had been marked with a magic marker. "Hello, I think I've found what he wanted to show me."

Roger came over and sat next to her on the bed. Priest's beds, Annie thought, are not arousing. This was a good thing. "He wrote me that he found something that we believed. This looks like it's a missing building. God, we talked so often about how it would be if we could only do a dig." She pointed to the outline, a minor indentation, rectangular and large. There were some smaller indentations, which could be walls. "There is definitely something underground here."

"Why is that important?" Roger asked. "This entire region must be layers and layers of civilizations. People have lived here from the days of cavemen." He looked at her. "And cave-women."

"He thought it was a Roman temple, a temple to Isis or to Mary Magdalene if they aren't one and the same," she said. "Lots of people look for the Cathar treasure that was supposedly smuggled out of Montségur prior to the final battle, but there's also the treasure of Rennes-le-Château that's both more recent and certainly more plausible or at least easier to prove."

"Do you want to go there tomorrow?"

"Sure," Annie said.

Chapter 8
Argelès-sur-mer

The priest spoke Dutch and kissed Annie on both cheeks and told her to eat Boston baked beans on Saturday night because that's what her grandmother had done. When he turned into a skeleton with dead fish eyes in his orbital sockets, Annie jolted herself awake. She sat straight up in her bed. Shit—another dream that mixed different parts of her life. I am a Third-Culture Kid, she reminded herself. It's okay to feel like a stranger everywhere.

She resisted curling into the fetal position and threw herself back on the bed and put her hands under her head. A small bird patted across the skylight glass. "I don't normally get to see the underside of a bird in such detail," she said to it as it danced in a circle above her head, "except here." As if he heard, he stopped to peer at her. Except for robins, blue jays and crows, she couldn't tell one wild bird from another. Oh yes, and pigeons, although one boyfriend she dated told her what she had called a pigeon was really a dove. As for crows, until she heard them caw, she was never a hundred percent sure.

"No use feeling sorry for myself," she said to the bird. "I bet if I grew up in a small town anywhere in the States I'd be jealous of the life I'm living here. However, how do you tell someone that no matter where you live, you still have to take out the garbage and vacuum the rugs?" Talking to myself again, she thought. Or maybe Hoover the rugs, as her Brit friends called vacuuming—or maybe neither. In her nest there was only one small rug in the bathroom that could either be shaken or thrown in the washer. The rest of the floor was a light beige tile that had looked very pretty when she'd chosen it, but showed every crumb. Sometimes she thought the crumbs hid until after she swept, reappearing to mock her. Still, this flat, as tiny as it was and with its less than pristine floor, felt more like home than anywhere she'd ever lived since her early Massachusetts childhood. The other places were strange, then familiar but always had a feel about them that any moment her father would be called to a new location or she would. Annie never considered it a problem, just a fact of life, like her red curly hair.

Mornings Annie liked to gentle herself awake, setting her clock radio a good hour before she had to get up so she could listen to music, plan out her day. Think time.

Nightmares were not the way she wanted to wake up.

The second she thought that, her radio went off. The Québécois singer Garou rasped that someone couldn't love if they'd never experienced being alone. It wasn't a message Annie wanted to hear first thing. She'd been alone. She'd loved it. Especially when she compared being alone to having her wings clipped. "Excuse the expression," she said to the bird, which was turning circles like a small child trying to make its self dizzy.

Her bladder was so full she could almost feel the pressure of the bird on it. One nice thing about a studio, the toilet was only a few steps away. She staggered into the bathroom. Annie slept in T-shirts. This T-shirt was from a Johnny Hallyday concert.

A pile of ancient *Gourmet* magazines, a gift from her mother found at the Geneva Plainpalais Saturday flea market, was in the magazine rack next to the toilet. She picked up one with a cherry pie on the cover. She'd promised Père Yves she'd make him one. She had no intention of reading recipes for cherry pie or anything else, but she thumbed through the pages, trying to ignore the image of her grandmother telling her never to put off kind deeds. Sitting in France thinking of New England wisdom made her smile. Maybe it wasn't New England wisdom, but grandmother wisdom. She wondered why she had never visited them in Europe. She and her parents had always gone to them.

Her thoughts drifted back to Père Yves. Where could the priest's body be? Maybe someone had moved it, but to go any distance they would have had to have a car. She didn't remember seeing a car. If they'd stashed it some place it would have to be close, in one of the houses. Whose? Why? There were a couple of houses, shells really, holding up the walls of the neighboring houses. She'd mention that to Roger. Then there were the secondary residences, summer homes. But by this time the body would start to smell, and would be discovered.

The destruction of the angel statue with the angle of the priest's body made her think he fell from the tower. There was no way someone could fall from the tower accidentally, unless they were leaning over. But if Père Yves were leaning over the edge, and she could think of no reason why he might, his weight would make it almost impossible for him to fall. She'd been up with him in the tower enough times to admire the view, yet he always stayed back from the edge. He'd confessed he was afraid of heights unless there was a wall at least waist-high between him and the edge, although he hadn't had to tell her. They had been on top of too many mountains where he always stood back far behind her. That would mean someone would have had to do more than just push him. They would have had to flip him over the half wall at the top of the tower.

But that would be dangerous with too much chance for someone to be seen. Granted, Argelès didn't begin to wake up until eight A.M. No, that wasn't true. The baker and the butcher were always up early, preparing their products for the day. But the baker would have already been in his shop by four and the butcher came between six and seven, usually on the later side if he had had too much wine with dinner the night before, which was the case most of the time. Still, there were people like herself who got off the morning train or people who would catch the early train to Spain or Perpignan.

"Annie? You up?" A male voice drifted through her open window.

Annie pulled up her panties and peeked out her window. Her doorbell substitute was to have guests call up from the street below. She had at one point installed a small bell with a long string reaching to three stories, but every breeze made the bell ring, driving her neighbors and herself crazy.

Roger stood on the street gazing up. It made his head look like it was put on his neck the wrong way. "Ready?"

"No. Come on up." She tossed her keys out the window.

He picked them out of the air. By the time he'd climbed the three flights of stairs, she'd pulled on jeans. When he entered, there was the awkward foot shifting of former lovers who were used to hugging and kissing but weren't comfortable with the casual double-cheek kiss of casual friends.

At one time they would have tumbled into the unmade bed. They looked at it and each other for a minute before she said, "Want coffee?" She let him mull it over. "Let me try an easy question. What's your name?"

He laughed, breaking the tension. "Let's grab something at the tea room. Anyway, I know that if you get hungry, you'll be a real bitch. And then you'll hit me up for lunch."

"I can't help it. My blood sugar drops. And I'm hitting you up for lunch anyway. That's my fee for helping you with the murder."

He ruffled her hair, which was still messed from bed. "At the moment all we have is . . ."

". . . a missing person's case."

"Stop finishing my sentences."

"Speak faster." She went into the bathroom and started to brush her teeth then wandered out with the toothbrush in hand. "You don't really believe that he is just . . . missing?" She mumbled through the foam.

"Officially?"

"Unofficially."

"Murder," he said. "I don't think he'd have jumped. Besides, I trust you." When Annie cocked her head, he held up his hands and said, "No, I'm not jumping on your idea and claiming it as my own. I confirmed the idea when I walked by the church this morning. Unfortunately, I think I should have posted someone near the church last night to watch the street. They could have moved the body in the middle of the night. Not sure where, but out."

Annie went back into the bathroom and spit.

All eight tables at the tea room were occupied, but Annie and Roger only had to wait a few minutes before a table for two, next to the standing case filled with handmade chocolates, was freed.

The owner, Gabriel Martinez, his apron dusted with flour, waved the normal waitress aside and put a demitasse under the hissing espresso machine. He filled a tray with *tartines,* croissants, two freshly squeezed orange juices and a hot chocolate and brought it to them. The couple at the next table left, and Gabriel took one of the chairs and sat down. "*Alors,* what happened to the priest?"

"*Sais pas.* I sure as hell don't know," Roger said. "We're working on it."

Annie felt a wave of warmth for him. One of the things she loved, or had loved about him (she reminded herself to put it into past tense), was his ability to admit he didn't know something. If only he could apologize for giving her such a hard time about her last assignment. Of course, she could have stayed and changed her life, moved in with him, but giving up her independence would have destroyed their couplehood even faster.

At least now they seemed to be building some kind of friendship. She brought herself back to the conversation between Gabriel and Roger.

"Madeleine Boulet was in here a few minutes ago. Raging on about who will marry her on Saturday."

"She's about as smart as her brother," Annie said. She knew Roger would have liked to have said that, but couldn't disparage one of his own men.

"Except her brother doesn't think he's a prince. She's worse now even than when her father was mayor, if possible." Martinez leaned toward Annie. "Her wedding makes Princess Diana's almost impromptu."

"How so?"

Gabriel leaned back in his seat and shook his head. "When I was frosting the cake, she stood over me and made me redo some of the roses. Now I ask you, don't I make a beautiful rose?"

Annie had to agree. Martinez was a master. The window decorations were works of art at which she loved to look. She'd never been able to decide which one was her favorite, although she had narrowed it down to the chocolate copy of the church and a frosting painting of the port, which could have been mistaken for a photo at a quick glance. And as proof of the taste of his creations, she held him responsible for at least two of the five pounds added to her body since moving here.

"Look," he said, dragging them behind the counter and through the door to the baking room. Three six-foot racks with torpedo-shaped white dough waited to be rolled into the floor-to-ceiling ovens. The heat was stifling. They followed him to a second room that was twenty degrees cooler. He pointed to a glass-door refrigerator. Two wedding cakes were inside. One had an almost photograph finish of a bride and groom on top, but was painted in frosting. "Does that look like the work of someone who needs to be told what to do?"

Roger and Annie both agreed that it didn't.

"Is that hers?" Annie pointed to the other, which had white frosting roses cascading down six tiers of cake. A plastic bride and groom stood on the top.

Martinez rolled his eyes. "Look at the cheap plastic orna- ment. *Ooh, la la!*"

Annie and Roger made the necessary sympathetic noises before they went back to their table to finish their croissants and tartines silently. At the next table they could hear Renaud, one of the village *notaires,* talk about the new mayor to his wife.

"I like the idea of having a car parts manufacturer in town," he said. "It will bring in jobs."

"The mayor will have a hard time getting it through," she said.

"Don't tell me. Boulet still controls the council, and all they want is tourist business. If it isn't a restaurant or a boutique, they don't know what to do with it."

Madame Renaud tapped the tabletop with her spoon. She let out a huge sigh, the kind that could almost cause a curtain to move in the current. "If there had been some good jobs here our children would never have moved to Toulouse."

"*Ma Chérie,* we've been over that so many times," Renaud said as Roger stood to pay the bill.

Annie followed him to the car. "You drive. I'll tell you what we're going to look at," she said.

Chapter 9
Argelès-sur-mer and
Rennes-le-Château

To get from Argelès on the sea to Rennes-le-Château in the mountains, it took Annie and Roger almost two hours. They ignored the *Autoroute* for the beauty of the national road, which wandered its way through the Pyrénées. These were old mountains, worn down by millions of years of windstorms blowing from Spain. Today's wind was mild, rustling the vegetation along the side of the road.

Vineyards dotted the lower slopes, but scrub pine dominated the upper regions. Infrequently, they passed through hamlets that were little more than a few houses. The larger villages, larger being a relative term, might have a bakery, grocery store, restaurant, butcher, or perhaps even a gas station.

It had been ten minutes between towns when Annie felt the well-known pressure in her bladder. "Can you stop at the next station, *s'il te plaît?*" The window was rolled down and she had fastened her hair back to keep it from blowing in her face and, more importantly, from snarling to the point where a pick, never mind a brush, would mean heavy-duty pain.

Roger's window was down too. His left arm, tanned darker than his right, rested on the door frame. The car was an old Renault that he'd had for ten years. He never replaced anything that worked, a quality that matched Annie's. "Gotta go, Bitty Bladder?"

Annie stuck out her tongue, but didn't say that the size of her bladder was no longer a topic for discussion. It was fine when they were lovers, but bladders, periods and other bodily functions should be out of bounds now.

"I'll be happy to stop, but there's a price," he said.

Her head snapped around to look at him. "What?"

"Tell me ten ways I'm wonderful."

"What!" Her voice was considerably louder.

"You heard me. Better get going, gas stations are far and few between and we might pass one before you finish."

Seeing his grin, Annie thought she would be a good sport. "Okay, one you're a *bon flic,* a good cop. Two, you're a good father. Three, you make a good omelet. Four . . ."

Roger reached over and patted her knee. "It would help your case if you could make my qualities more personal and less professional, or how do you say . . . functional."

The pressure in her bladder was increasing. She should have known better than to drink anything before hitting the road, but she never did remember, so there was no point in beating herself up about it. They saw the white sign with the red border and black letters announcing the next town was St. Paul. "Four, you've got wonderful curls."

"Better."

There was no gas station in St. Paul, but there was a small café. "We can stop for coffee and I can use the loo," she said.

"Six more." He drove by the café slowly.

Annie watched as they passed a middle-aged couple sitting at a white plastic table in front of the café. "You've a lovely smile, a flat stomach, a good sense of humor except when your ex-girlfriend has to pee."

"Careful, the man who controls the wheel, controls the passenger's bladder," he said. "It's a long way to the next gas station."

Annie wanted to hit him. "I can use a bush."

"And if someone drives by?"

"Who cares? I'll probably never see them again, anyway."

He was cruising at about five kilometers an hour as they came to the sign with the village's name and a line drawn through it. Only mountain road showed ahead.

"When you wear a suit jacket, you have the sexiest shoulders; you're intelligent and have a strong sense of ethics. When you smile, your eyes laugh too, you like to read and you tie your shoelaces great." The list came out as fast as she could speak.

He slammed the brakes and turned the car around then parked it in front of the café.

Annie hopped out and ran inside. As in most cafés, the toilet was downstairs, and she just made it, placing her feet on the porcelain squares for the purpose and angling her body over the hole. There were fewer and fewer of these old-fashioned toilets in France, and when they were all gone, she wouldn't miss them one bit.

When she came upstairs, he was sitting at the table sipping an espresso. His wallet and keys were next to the bill that had been torn in half, indicating that he'd paid. He pointed at his cup. "Want one? Or are you afraid it will act as a diuretic?"

Without saying a word she reached for the keys. "I'm driving. She who controls the wheels, controls the bladders."

"Tie my shoelaces great?"

"Desperation."

When he laughed, she had to join him.

Back on the road with Annie at the wheel, he said, "We've fooled around enough." He gripped the arm rest.

"Too much."

"Tell me what it is about Rennes-le-Château that makes it so important. Careful, there's a curve coming up."

"Want the long or short version? The long one could take years."

He braked a second before she did, going around the corner.

"Short and what is relevant to Père Yves."

Annie took a long breath and let up on the accelerator. "Okay. Researchers have considered the village everything from the place Jesus Christ and Mary Magdalene were buried to the center of some kind of magnetic field with pentacles between mountaintops."

"Pentacles?"

"Pentacles. If you draw lines between the mountaintops in the region they form a perfect pentacle."

"An accident of nature," he said. "More nonsense from the crazies."

She had to fight to ignore the remark. "They have some symbolic meaning, especially when you consider the construction of certain churches on these points. And if that's not enough the Romans and Merovingians were all over the area. There's also talk of secret societies that had Isaac Newton, DaVinci and Jean Cocteau as the leaders, which may be guarding the secret of either Christ's relatives who are living today or it could be Dagobert's."

"Who the hell is Dagobert?"

"A Merovingian king from the Dark Ages. Died 679 and allegedly his son was secreted away to this town. Some think Christ was his direct ancestor. Some think there was a treasure that came with him through Mary Magdalene, while others just think his gold is buried here. Pick a time, you'll find someone saying there is the possibility of treasure."

"Sounds like it could be named The Center of Crackpots Anonymous. Slow down."

Annie let up on the gas. "Crackpots Un-anonymous is more like it. Any of the theories can be backed up and some of those have been studied by university professors. Not to mention novels and movies, which you never wanted to read or see. However, lots of the theories have been debunked."

"I rest my case," Roger said as Annie careened around a corner. "Watch out."

"Let me tell you what we know for sure. Béranger Saunière became the priest there in the late 1800s. The church had been dedicated to Mary Magdala since 1050. Now, the priest was dirt poor and so was the church, holes in the roof and all that. All of a sudden he was rich. He repaired the church and wait until you see it. He built a road up the mountain and a beautiful house: a tower for his library. And he put in a water system for the entire town. We're almost there."

She turned the car onto a smaller road that would not allow two small French cars to pass. "This is the road he paved." After a few minutes steep climb, she pulled into a parking lot. They got out and walked through the deserted streets. All the shutters were closed, although many of the windows had window boxes with geraniums and begonias. "What do you notice?"

"No people."

"In all my trips, I've seldom seen any residents, only tourists, unless residents walk around with cameras all the time. That may be because of the number of tourists that come through. Books about this place are almost an industry in themselves."

They turned a corner and passed two closed shops, one that had blown glass animals in the window and one that recommended plant remedies along with healing oils.

"More bunk," Roger said, pointing at it.

Annie started to say something but decided against it. From the time she first dated Roger, she was aware that fantasy was not his strong point. His imagination as far as his work was concerned was great, but not necessarily on arty, arcane or out-of-the ordinary things. He couldn't visualize a recipe, but he would savor it when it was in front of him. The only fiction he read was detective and crime stories, preferring newspapers and science stuff. The former they shared, the latter she didn't like.

They came to an old stone church. From the outside it was like hundreds of other old churches throughout France.

"I'm not going to say any more. You tell me what you see." She pushed the brown wooden doors open.

Roger walked ahead of her. Inside she saw him shudder. He turned around and around. "Bizarre. Especially that." He pointed to a monster holding a fountain. On it stood a statue of the Blessed Virgin.

"That's Rex Mundi," Annie said. "A satanic figure."

"With the Virgin standing on him. Does it mean she's vanquished him or is he controlling her from underneath?"

Annie sat on one of the chairs. "Now you're getting it." When he looked more confused she patted his arm. "Everything in this church can be interpreted hundreds of ways."

"It's all nuts." He pointed to a station of the cross. "I've never seen a kilt on a biblical figure."

"There are some who say that ties the whole mystery into the Scottish kings. Others consider Rosslyn Castle outside Edinburgh is connected in some way with the Knights Templar."

"That doesn't prove anything. They had outposts all over. Even in Argelès."

She took him by the hand and led him outside. She could feel him relax as soon as sunlight hit their faces. "Gives you the creeps doesn't it." It was not a question. "Let me show you some more stuff." She stopped at another statue. "It was in here."

"What?"

"Parchments with codes about treasures and Dagobert. The priest allegedly found them when he moved an altar stone under this statue, which he later moved out here. We think this is Lady Blanchfort, who was the last descendent of the Knights Templar. One theory is that she had the documents hidden, but we don't know for sure. King Philippe, The Fair, destroyed the order in 1307, supposedly for their treasure, which was never found. Unless, of course, that was what Saunière found and used for his building projects."

"Treasure here, treasure there. Good God, Annie, it sounds like everyone has been bitten by a virus that makes them think treasure is under every stone." Roger shook his head.

"Remember Juan Perez?"

"The one who worked for the *Mairie* taking care of all the planters along the main streets until he moved back to Barcelona or the drunk who died two months ago?"

"The gardener. He spent every spare minute here looking for treasure."

"Before my time, but I remember hearing how his treasure hunting took so much time that they fired him and his wife left him."

They walked out of town to the edge of the mountain. A slope was strewn with boulders and looked into a valley, wild with vegetation. "See that path between all the plants?"

He nodded.

"It was part of the main Roman road from the Atlantic to the Mediterranean. It has never been totally overgrown. Now look at this." She dragged him into a ruin. "What do you think this was?"

He looked around and pointed to a grinding wheel. "Mill?"

"Yup. And the grinding stone based on the placement and size had to be part of the original building. Probably from the construction it had to be built before 1400. Now what else is strange?" She watched him pace around inside, touch the rock-layered walls.

"My God! There's a fireplace. Mills don't have fireplaces. They could cause an explosion from all the grain dust."

She went outside, and he followed. "Be careful. There are

vipers around. I forgot to wear my boots." She pulled up her pants to show him.

"Great. What if we get bitten?"

She reached into her backpack and pulled out the white, green and yellow snakebite kit.

"You're kidding."

"Nope, city boy." When he looked embarrassed, she said, "I didn't think of it either until Père Yves taught me."

"So have you seen any?"

"Maybe every third or fourth trip when we wander down the rocks. There's one with diamonds, not too big, but gives a nasty bite."

"I've never liked snakes," he said.

"Me neither. Gotta admit I sometimes consider it a successful trip here when we haven't seen any as much as if we've learned something. Now look there." She pointed to a water tap poking out from a stone heap.

"So?"

"As long as both Père Yves and I've been coming here, there's been a fountain. However, remember the flooding we had about five years back?"

He nodded.

"The fountain was washed away. Someone rebuilt it."

"That's not so strange."

"There's water in the village. There's a stream. There's no need for a fountain. And no one we talked to ever admitted knowing who did it. And don't ask me what it means. The only thing I ever get here are more questions."

"And Père Yves?"

"He wasn't looking for treasure. He was tracking down the goddess Isis, who some think was believed in by Christ."

Roger threw up his hands. "Do you expect me to believe any of this crap? It isn't even coherent."

"No, but some people do believe all or parts of it. And Père Yves had a lot of questions about the historical Jesus. He also thought that there might have been a temple to Isis or to the Black Madonna, who could have been Mary. There are lots of Black Madonnas around Southern France."

"They could have been statues that got old and dirty," he said.

Annie pulled the aerial photo out of her backpack. The two of them looked at the lines and indentations in the ground that could be the remains of a building covered with dirt. However, from their view, they couldn't make out anything.

"This is stupid," he said.

"You wanted to know what Père Yves was doing here. I've told you. If you don't like it, tough shit." She stomped off. He looked into the valley again, turned and followed her. She had the car keys.

CHAPTER 10
THE NATIONAL ROAD TO
ARGELÈS-SUR-MER

Annie's hands clinched the wheel. As often as she'd spent time in Rennes-le-Château with Père Yves discussing the different possibilities, the word *crackpot* had never appeared in their conversations. She didn't want to count how many times Roger had used it in the last hour.

She could just picture Père Yves, who had earned a degree in history from the Sorbonne before taking his vows, sitting back in the chair in his kitchen, a cup of coffee in his hand saying, "The victors are the ones who write history. Imagine how your Revolution would have been written had the English won?"

"Or if Louis XVI had defeated the rebels?" she'd replied.

"We'd have missed out on Napoleon and Robespierre. So think of how much history has been lost when all knowledge was limited to a few monks in monasteries who had their own point of view. History was propaganda. No Internet then."

She smiled as a picture of medieval monks surfing with quill mice flashed through her mind. Now there was a crackpot idea, but the idea of dismissing the unknown as crackpot bothered her. Even crackpots were right sometimes.

"Feeling better. No longer mad at me?" Roger reached over and put his hand on her neck. When they'd been a couple that was his opening move on making up.

She definitely did not want those memories. What also surfaced was the memory of not being able to explain to him in the detail that he considered necessary how she felt about things when they differed from his experience. Nor could she explain to him that half of why she was angry was not just his use of the word *crackpot*.

Seeing Rennes-le-Château again made her miss Père Yves even more. Knowing they'd never share another trip and bounce ideas and theories off each other made her want to cry or hit something or someone. Poor Roger was the closest someone. It wasn't his fault that he didn't share her passion for history.

And to be fair, although she wasn't sure she really wanted to be fair, there were things she did with Roger that she could never have done with Père Yves. Making love was one, but she wouldn't do that with Roger again either. However, he'd taken her to football games and played tennis with her, which the priest would never have done. There were just things that you could do with some people that you couldn't do with others, and it was nobody's fault. However, despite all her reasoning, she was still mad at Roger.

"Pull over." Roger pointed to a parking lot. Ahead was a cliff of sheer rock with a road cut through. Cars were wending their way up, slowly twisting and turning. "I'm going to feed you."

Annie bit back the words, "Like an animal at the zoo." Her blood sugar was probably low, adding to her bad mood.

According to the sign written in swirling calligraphy, the restaurant had once been an abbey and mill built during the thirteenth century. Inside it was totally deserted, but they walked through the old refectory to the outside where the own-ers had arranged eight tables. All had pink linen tablecloths with pink or green linen napkins, folded like small Napoleonic hats. The sides of the linen moved in the slight breeze. Above the wind was blowing harder, but the rocks protected them.

Only one table was occupied by two German tourists. Annie knew because she could hear German floating across the lawn.

"Next to the river?" Roger asked and when she nodded, he

used her elbow to guide her to a table next to the water that really was more of a brook. When she looked into the water gurgling over stones covered with green tendrils she could see small fish.

Roger scanned the area for a waitress. Finally, a woman in black slacks, which could have been painted on, came out. Her white peasant blouse showed ample cleavage. Her black hair was cut in a child's Dutch boy, the only childish thing about her.

She handed them the menus and waited. After staring at the water, the sky, the fish and Roger she asked with a thick Catalan accent, "What will you have today?"

"Gazpacho," they said together and laughed. *"Salade verte,"* spoken, also in unison.

"Entrecôte for you?" Annie asked.

"Bien sûr, bleu. Poulet Catalan for you?"

"Apéro?" Roger asked.

Annie looked at the rock cliff and the winding road. "Not if I'm driving that."

"If you really want a drink or wine with lunch, I'll drive."

She stuck her tongue out at him. "Water will be fine." The waitress left.

Annie stared at the brook.

"It's hard to believe that little brook cut through all that rock," he said, "but this is the end of summer. In spring it's a torrent. The abbey's been flooded many times."

She knew. She and Père Yves had stopped here often. "Okay, any ideas on how Rennes-le-Château fits into the murder?" She noticed his raised eyebrow. "Disappearance then."

Roger played with his fork, turning it prongs, handle tip, prongs, handle tip, prongs. "If people thought he had found a treasure, someone might have been trying to make him tell where it was."

"Or if he found some secret that would dispute Christianity's basic tenants, the Church might be trying to shut him up," she said.

"Both are far fetched. The Church isn't in the habit of killing off its priests. And, if someone wanted to know about the treasure they wouldn't have pushed him off the church tower."

She looked at him sharply. "How do you know anyone did?"

"Based on what you told me about the position of the body, I went up to the church tower at about where he would have had to have fallen from to land on the angels as you described. I found a piece of cloth, actually a bit of yarn from what was probably a sweater, that I guess could have been ripped as he went over the edge. He wouldn't have fallen on his own. It's too high. Someone would have had to shove him over."

Annie shuddered. She pictured the scene in her mind, like a movie, only in slow motion. She also imagined a face hanging over the edge watching the priest fall. The waitress arrived at the same moment. Maybe hot tea would have been psychologically better than cold soup. Instead of ordering tea, she dipped her spoon in the soup. "If someone wanted information about a treasure, killing him would not be the way to get the information."

"Unless the killer already had the information."

"He could have forced Père Yves to jump." Roger watched her closely. "Okay, I can tell by your face you don't like that one."

"He'd have fought with the man first, even if he had a gun. It's too much like suicide. He was too opposed to that. Thought it was the most horrible death possible. Not just because the Church teaches that the soul goes to Hell, but because of what it does to the family."

Roger rubbed his chin. "Do you know another reason I think it was murder?"

"So now you are definitely thinking of murder."

"I can't officially think of someone being murdered without a body, but I do trust your powers of observation, which is why I keep going back and forth between murder, suicide and disappearing on his own. I don't mean to drive you crazy. It's *flic* talk."

He reached for her hand, which she withdrew to pick up her spoon, then he picked up his. "Besides suicides don't dispose of themselves."

"It's a puzzlement," Annie said. When he looked confused she said, "It's a line from *The King and I*." She cocked her head. "Because you speak English so well, I sometimes forget it isn't your first language and that we had different cultural childhoods. Yul Brynner used the phrase."

"You've lived in many places, in many countries. I've lived in two places, Paris and Argelès. To be sure I spent some time in the States for special training, but they worked us so hard that we barely got off campus." He took a mouthful of soup. "When we get back to Argelès, want to stop by and see Gaëlle?"

"Not a good idea; she might think we were getting back together."

Roger reached out and put his hand over hers. "Might not be such a bad idea."

For a minute she covered his hand with hers, and then put his back on his own side. "Not really a good idea. The stuff that drove us apart is still there."

He reached across the table and stroked her cheek. "We could talk about it."

Before she could answer the waitress arrived with a tray. She scooped the soup dishes and put down their main meal. *"Entrecôte bleu. Poulet Catalan."*

When they dated, he always attacked his rare steak, inhaling it, very un-French, she used to say. Frenchmen savor their food, but he always said he could savor anything but steak. This time he pushed it out of the way so he could take one of her hands in both of his. "Gaëlle's missed you."

She thought of his teenage daughter, her body developed ahead of her years, struggling between her father's expectations of her to go to the *lycée* in Perpignan and on to a university, against many of her friends' plans to get out of school as fast as they could. She had teased Gaëlle about being so smart to be in college at her age, but Gaëlle would roll her eyes and remind Annie that college in France was the same as an American junior high. Gaëlle often told Annie things that began with "Don't tell Papa, but . . ."

"I'm not so sure she'd be glad to see me."

"Try it," he said.

CHAPTER 11
RENNES-LE-CHÂTEAU

I shut off the tape recorder and sat there, my hands in my lap. Mamie had been dead a long time but after listening to her, I felt her in the room with me. I could see her eyes glisten, I could watch her do a little dance step after she made a poignant remark, I could smell Sunday dinner cooking: onions, always lots of onions to stretch whatever meat, the one time a week that meat was on the menu. And I imagined her saying, "Miriam, Miriam, Miriam," whenever I did something she didn't like. Her saying, "I'm disappointed in you," was a worse punishment than being sent to my room, hit on the back of my legs with the fly swatter she used to brandish or being deprived of something I wanted.

What would she have made of all the hoopla over this village?

Thunder rolled outside. My mother had been terrified of thunder and after we had added electricity in the early 1950s, she would unplug every lamp and the radio. She made us all sit in the middle of the living room and we could see the flashes of light through the slits in the shutters and we'd count 1-1,000; 2-1,000; 3-1,000 to see how close the storm was. Here in the mountains it often was so close we felt like we could touch a lightning bolt if only we could stretch enough.

As an adult I love bad weather; it is so much more interesting than good. Instead of huddling and being afraid, I picked up my raincoat from where it had fallen off its hanger and went out. The rain drenched me almost as soon as I left my doorstep.

I didn't care as I walked up the hill to the edge of the wall overlooking the valley near the Magdala tower where the priest had built his home and library. It's now a museum, a must-see for tourists coming through. Certainly not that luxurious compared to the huge mansions of the rich, but for this village, it was Versailles and Buckingham Palace rolled into one.

By the time I reach the edge, I wished I'd remembered boots, because my feet were sopping, but the storm made me feel alive. I only feel like this during electrical storms, but that was maybe because I grew up here. For me Toulouse, Carcassonne felt strange, dead, where here life crackles like the lightning, fireworks from the gods.

As much as I hated to leave the power of the storm I went home to finish the transcript from so long ago it must be done before the producer from France 2 comes back. He said he would be here later in the week. I've decided I would probably, notice I've said probably, help him. It might bring another round of tourists and more business.

CHAPTER 12
ARGELÈS-SUR-MER

Annie stared at the clear field on the left side as she and Roger pulled through his gate and started up the long driveway. "What happened to the pines?" She'd loved how his house had been hidden from anyone who stopped to peer over the high wall surrounding his land. There had been seventy-five pines on each side. Although she wasn't a numbers person, one day she'd counted them. Their smell, the pinecones that she'd collected to make Christmas wreaths as gifts, telling friends it had nothing to do with decorating gurus on television: she just liked giving homemade gifts. The trees were part of her good memory bank. Now every single tree on the left-hand side had disappeared. She felt as if someone had compromised her database.

"I'm going to put in a pool. And a tennis court. Maybe." He pointed to the right as he parked in front of the house. "There're still lots of trees over there." He pushed the buttons on the remote, closing the gate behind him.

As she parked the car next to the one-story, white stucco house, a German shepherd burst through the beaded curtain that was supposed to keep mosquitoes away, but didn't. The dog put his front feet on the window ledge of the driver's side where Annie sat. Within seconds he was through the window turning and twisting in her lap, giving her face big, slobbering licks. His rear hit the horn, and it beeped. The dog jumped, rearranged his body and resumed kissing her.

The animal continued his outpouring of love for Annie

without greeting his master. "*Alors,* you unfaithful creature, Hannibal, remember me?" Roger asked. He protected his face from being lashed by the dog's tail and tried to grab hold of his collar.

"Guess he remembers me," she said as she tried to push the dog away long enough to get a good breath. She wasn't sure how she would be able to extricate herself from the car with eighty pounds of writhing dog flesh all over her. "Calm, Hannibal, calm." Thrusting her hand under the dog's stomach she failed to force the door open.

Roger went around and grabbed the handle to open the door. Hannibal, at the same instant, lunged again at Annie with kisses, and fell through the car door, knocking Roger down. The dog got up, shook himself and ran to get a pinecone.

Annie scrambled to help Roger up. She was dusting him off when the dog dropped the pinecone at her feet. "Still remember our old games, Hannibal?" She tossed it as far as she could. Within seconds the dog and cone were back.

"He obviously missed you," Roger said. "But before you get conceited, he'll do this with anyone who is willing to throw the stupid pinecones."

She heaved it once more, turning away so Roger could not see her face. Her expression showed how much she'd missed this place. How many hot afternoons had she, Roger and Gaëlle cooked out on the brick barbecue built into the wall on one side of the patio? She could almost see herself walking through the pines, over the footpath spanning the creek to the orchard to pick fresh plums. She remembered how she and Gaëlle had spent an afternoon making preserves and baking plum tarts. Weary and hot, one of them had annoyed the other, and a flour flight had started. Neither ever admitted who started it, if indeed they were even sure.

"Think your daughter's home?" Annie asked as she brushed

the bead curtains aside and entered the kitchen. It was the kind of kitchen that had to have been designed by a woman, with enough electrical sockets and comfortable working spaces making it easy to go from counter to sink, counter to dishwasher, counter to stove. Annie had often marveled at how many homes had the sink against a blank wall. Bad enough to wash dishes, but so much better when there was something to look at.

Both Roger and Gaëlle cooked. She'd helped teach them, although they complained that her cooking was too American. Another argument, which ended with both of them apologizing for looking a gift cook in the mouth, especially when Annie pointed out that the meals she'd showed them were from Holland, Germany and Switzerland as well as America.

The fact that Roger owned this house was a fluke. Had not the couple who sold it been splitting up, he would never have been able to afford it. He'd even admitted feeling a bit guilty, but his desire to find a suitable home for his daughter after both her mother's death and tearing her away from her friends in Paris assuaged his guilt. "Probably in her room. She hibernates there."

"She's thirteen; of course she hibernates. I'll check it out."

Annie tiptoed down the hall, past the room that she and Roger had shared so happily. It had been Gaëlle who'd suggested Annie sleep over the first time. "I know you're doing it, so why not save Papa from having to creep out of bed in the middle of the night to drive you home."

The teenager's door was closed but Annie could hear Patrick Fiori singing *"Que Tu Reviennes."* She knocked once and then knocked harder. Her knuckles stung.

"Go way Papa. I'm doing my homework."

"It's not Papa."

The door opened and Gaëlle flung herself on Annie with the same force as Hannibal had only without the face licks. Annie staggered for Gaëlle was large for her age, standing almost five eight and with a figure that would have given Marilyn Monroe a run for her money.

Every square inch of Gaëlle's wall was covered with pictures of Patrick Fiori cut from magazines or posters she must have stolen from the way they had torn patches. Annie stepped in and lowered the volume on the CD player to a level where they could talk. "I gather you like him."

"Let me show you something." Gaëlle grabbed a video and took it into the living room. Patrick Fiori was riding in a car with several others. When they came to a small village, he got out. The crew hooked him up to a microphone, and he began walking toward a house where he entered without knocking. The camera forwarded him in. A teenager, about thirteen, was playing violin with a group of her friends, when she saw and heard Patrick singing *"Que Tu Reviennes."* The girl screamed.

"Her mother arranged it," Gaëlle said. "Isn't it a great idea? It's called *Stars à Domicile.* Do you think you could arrange with TF1 to have him come here and surprise me?"

"I'm sure they'd want to use a different star." It was like nothing had changed. Annie would show up at the house, and Gaëlle would launch into whatever was interesting her at the moment. She told Annie things that she never would tell her father, often more than Annie wanted to know.

"He's playing in concert in Perpignan, but the show is sold out. Already for November. Can you believe it?"

If there were as many infatuated teenage girls as Gaëlle, she could believe it, no problem. "Where?" Annie asked.

"Palais des Rois Majorque."

"Tant pis, too bad."

Gaëlle kept one eye on the television as she talked to Annie. "So near and yet so far. If I were older, I could go and hope there were scalpers. Watch this part where he imitates Quasimodo." The teenager flopped on the couch. "Papa would never let me go alone anyway." A smile crossed her face. "Does this mean that you and Papa will be an item again?"

"This means that your Papa and I are friends, nothing more."

The smile disappeared from Gaëlle's face.

Annie took her hand. "But what happens between your Papa and me doesn't mean diddly damn for things between you and me. We've a relationship that has nothing to do with him anyway." Annie ruffled the teenager's hair. The last time she'd seen her it had been long and straight. Now it was short and spiked.

"Even if he finds another girlfriend?"

Annie was really unhappy with the gut stab that she felt at that thought. "Even then. Now tell me all the news, including about the haircut."

When Annie finally got back to her nest she flopped on her couch before doing anything else. She'd turned down a dinner offer, but she had accepted some fresh tomatoes, basil and onions from their garden to make herself a light meal, all she had the energy for. She plugged in her refrigerator for the first time since her arrival. Good God, this was nothing like she'd planned. During the last three weeks of her assignment with the UBS in Zurich, she'd come home at night too tired to eat. In bed she'd count the days until she could get to Argelès. And what had happened now she was here: the same feeling that her arms and legs were too heavy to function or falling asleep only to wake in the morning fully clothed.

Well, she certainly hadn't fallen into those long, lazy days where the big decision of her day was if yesterday's bread was good enough for breakfast. Had she a chance to read all night and sleep all day if she wanted to? No. This was too much like work with no time to herself and too many things to do that she didn't want to do. *Merde!*

She turned on the radio. Someday she would get a television, but for now she liked the isolation. She watched too much television when she was working, letting it lull her to sleep or act as background noise as she got ready to leave the house in the morning. The radio announcer said Patrick Fiori would sing *"Que Tu Reviennes"* next. Annie suspected she could learn to hate that song as she realized that she had not so much returned to what she expected but had fallen into a world she didn't like and hoped would go away.

Mustering what little energy she had left, she turned on her computer to find Charles' address. He was the head of the board that managed the *Palais des Rois Majorque*. And she had done a project with him when he worked for HP. The phone rang several times before he answered.

"*C'est moi*, Annie."

"Annie, *Bon, tu es ici encore, ça va?*" Charles was always glad when she came back.

"*Ca va bien. Très bien.*" She wasn't *très bien*. She felt awful. A hole was in her life with the loss of her friend. She allowed herself self-pity. So few people shared her love of history, and who would share her delight? God, I'm being selfish, she thought. Père Yves had lost his life, and she was worried about herself. Charles wasn't a good enough friend to share this.

"Annie, will we get a chance to see you this visit?" There was pleasure in his voice.

"Probably, I'm here for at least a month. However, this isn't a social call. I need a favor." Because she was a person who regularly kept in contact with her friends and acquaintances when she didn't need a favor, she felt no guilt in asking when she did. She never called people only when she wanted something. Favor insurance, she called it.

"Anything."

"I need six tickets for Patrick Fiori." She heard him suck in his breath.

"I hate to say no to you, but it's impossible. Sold out. Too many teenagers in love with him," Charles said.

"And it was impossible when your IT person got drunk and wrapped himself around a tree and you needed someone to figure out the code of everything in your system. Didn't I find a genius for you?" Her find had been able to solve the problem of the specialized program that held the secret to everything at the *Palais*, which had been his client before he joined their staff. "And I got him there in forty-eight hours."

"It's sold out," Charles said.

"I had to search in Japan for you. You said you owed me your life. What's a few tickets?" She didn't tell him that the person she had contacted was desperate to get back to Europe and with that single deal she'd chalked up two grateful friends.

"Aren't you a little old to be a groupie?"

"They're not for me. I've a good friend, a teenager who lost her mother and has been uprooted from Paris, and it would mean a lot to her. We could get by with two."

There was a long sigh. "What's that phrase you Americans use? Guilt trip?"

Annie bit her tongue. People thought of her as American when it suited them. Yet the little time she spent in the States, there she was accused of being too European. "Not so much a guilt trip as a reminder."

There was another long sigh. "I suppose I could put in an additional two chairs."

"At the front?" She'd asked for six tickets hoping she could get the two.

"Tell you what, I'll send you a note that will get you in to see me, and we'll arrange something."

"Think we could meet him?"

He laughed. "You do exact your pound of flesh."

"I save your life; you save mine. Besides, it'll mean so much to this kid."

"*Bien sûr,* you could never resist a stray animal. I should have said no when you first worked for me years ago. I thought I'd escaped you when I left HP to take this job."

"You'll never get rid of me," Annie said. She didn't want to point out how he usually called her for work. "The next time you need a super-tech writer you know where to find me."

"Not a bad idea. When are you free? We've new software that is messing up our purchasing system. Part of the problem is that no one understands it because the manual is *merde.*"

"Not until the end of the month. This is a holiday." Holiday, hah, she thought. This is anything but. She noticed she had messages. One was from her agent, and two others told her of two jobs in Switzerland and one in Belgium. She needed working papers for Belgium. It would be so much easier for her to have a European Union passport. Charles could bill her in Switzerland if they went ahead with the project, even if it was stretching the law. Working papers were just one more example of being out of place—not having the right just to take a job. She sighed. Of course she could go back to the States, but that felt even less like home than Europe. Too bad! There was none of her type of work in Argelès. Then again, she could always waitress in a restaurant during tourist season or pick grapes during the harvest, except again, she didn't have working papers even for that type of work.

She had considered applying for her Swiss nationality, which would give her the right to work anywhere in the European Union. What had stopped her? Nothing—except procrastination.

What the hell, eating was better than moaning. Not that she was starved, but she was just hungry enough so that if she didn't eat, she'd get that sick, low-blood-sugar feeling, just as she would be crawling into bed.

Her pans were suspended from the wooden beam over the counter marking off her kitchen area. She took down a pot and fry pan. The area under the counter produced a half-used bottle of olive oil, shell macaroni and a half head of garlic: a meal for a goddess or at least a Catalan goddess. She fried the onions and garlic and added the tomatoes. As they bubbled she cut the basil into the smallest possible bits with the kitchen scissors. The macaroni was cooking. Her six-bottle wine rack held two bottles, both local wines. She wondered if she opened a bottle would it go bad before she finished it. To hell with it, she could afford to throw it out if it did go bad. She'd only paid four Euros for it. Or she could use it for vinegar.

She still missed the old money, especially the 50-franc note with the Little Prince and his plane. She loved the color. She missed her money jar where she threw coins from other countries. Now she only had Swiss Francs and Euros, much simpler.

No reading till all hours tonight. Her new book about the Cathars would have to wait. Probably there wasn't that much new. If emptiness could cause pain, then a pain hit her. She and Père Yves had been hoping to go to a memorial service held at Montségur next month for the second time. Only a few people knew about the pilgrims that climbed the mountain once a year to honor those who had perished during a siege in the thirteen hundreds. There they had met people from the Cathar Institute in Narbonne, who had opened up their research files. They felt like dancing for joy, despite its being a cliché, because it meant that even without university credentials, they were accepted as serious scholars. Asking anyone else to go to the event was out of the question. It would be too disrespectful.

She puttered around, washing dishes, dusting, reclaiming her space. She opened her clic-clac and threw a sheet across the exposed mattress hidden in the couch. Within minutes she was asleep.

At two she sat straight up in bed. She was sure she knew where Père Yves's body was. She wanted to call Roger, but decided to wait until early morning. Sleep didn't come again and she heard the church clock ring each hour, quarter hour and half hour.

Chapter 13
Rennes-le-Château

I dipped my baguette into my bowl of hot chocolate, my favorite breakfast since I was a child. Being grown-up can be overrated. When we can recapture the joys of childhood, we should at every chance.

The rooster, who lives behind my house and is owned by old Madame Perez, is at least sleeping later now that the days are shorter. In June he goes off before four in the morning. Once he crows, I can't get back to sleep. In winter, I can sleep in to almost eight. In June with the early-early dawn, I have fantasies of chicken stew: the rooster is too old to make a roast and would need long hours of simmering.

I was the first one at the bakery this morning, as I usually am. I love the yeasty smell of bread baking. Henri now makes a special bread he calls *pavé d'Henri* that has an extra hard crust and big holes where the yeast has been activated. This morning, like most, my loaf was still warm when he put it in my hands. This is the bakery of my great grandfather, grandfather, and father, although it has not been in the family since my father died.

Enough about bread. I'll listen to the tape until it's time to open my shop. I can look out my window and see if the village has many visitors then decide if I want to stay upstairs a little longer. I've also posted a note on my door for customers to ring the bell, but they don't often. I don't know why. Enough procrastination. I click on the machine, pick up the old transcript and follow the words. It is as if she is back in the room with me.

MF: You said everything changed after the priest came.

JA: Not at first. The priest said Mass. He fixed a few things, like making sure the hinges on the door of the church were attached, and he climbed up onto the roof and hammered wood over the hole. I'm not sure how he did that because of the tiles. Everyone said, he obviously didn't know what he was doing, but at least people didn't get as wet if it rained during Sunday Mass.

MF: So what changed?

JA: You have to remember, I was just a little girl. I know my mother's friends were scandalized when he brought Marie Denarneau to be his housekeeper somewhere around 1890 or 91.

Housekeeper—hah!

Of course as a child, I didn't understand what the objections were. The rumors flew and more than one good woman of the village walked by the house on a summer evening before the rectory shutters were closed to see them sitting together after dinner. I was with my mother, during one of the times she wasn't sick.

I didn't see anything wrong with the housekeeper sitting there sewing. His nose was in a book, which wasn't that different from what my mother and father did, sit together, not read, although my father often went to bed early to get up well before dawn to begin making bread. My mother would use the time to mend clothes or knit.

My mother said housekeepers didn't sit with their employers. Marie was the only housekeeper in the village, and I asked her how she knew because it seemed strange that she thought that without having anything to compare it with, but she just said, she knew what she knew.

MF: What else did people know about the housekeeper?

JA: She had been trained as a hatter but that wasn't unusual in Espéraza where she was from. Hat-making was a big thing back then and lots of people worked as hat makers. She had three brothers and maybe a sister, I can't remember. The priest had lived with her family and according to gossip they were none too happy about her new job with him. Still it lasted longer than the hat-making would have. She spent the rest of her life here.

MF: You didn't like her?

JA: No one did. She protected him from his parishioners and although I can't prove they were lovers, because I never saw them in bed together, it seemed reasonable. Why else would she inherit everything he had? Of course, she couldn't keep the property up. That's why she sold it all to Noel Corbu when the war ended.

MF: Let's go back to the change. What changed?

JA: The priest wanted to fix up the church, not that that is so strange, but, as I said, we were poor, and the Church would be much more interested in putting money into the Cathedrals elsewhere. Again, I was a girl, more interested in my friends than the priest, but the rumors had him going to Narbonne to meet with powerful people. I heard the Countess of Chambord gave him money. Rumor had it that he met her through the mayor of Narbonne, but who knows. How would a small-town priest get to know people like a Countess, for God's sake? We knew he got into trouble over his political beliefs. He was even suspended for a while but I have no timeline for that. Really Miriam, how do you expect me to remember all these things from so long ago? Everything from my childhood melts together these days.

MF: (I reached out to cover her hand with mine. The veins were like mountains on the skin and dotted with freckles that she had never had when younger.) I don't expect you to remember everything, but your life really interests me.

JA: (laughs) I don't see why. The past is the past. However, it was quite an event when there were workmen all over the place. Some came from as far away as Toulouse, although the priest used as many locals as he could. It was a prosperous time for us. My father sold more bread than ever before, because the workmen needed lunch. He bought meat from the valley and sold that too. Some people resented my father for earning more than they did. When everyone is in the same house, there is a certain equality, but if one moves out and has a bigger house, then jealousy spreads just like *la grippe*.

Others hated the confusion. Carts arriving with wood and metal and bricks, hammering and sawing all day long. Oh la la. (She rolled her eyes just like a young girl. My grandmother never lost her ability to flirt.)

The church was rebuilt, and he built Bethany for his home and the Tour Magdala for his books. Books? Who has time to read all that blah-blah, I ask you?

And the road, we can't forget the road. He had the road paved from the village up here. It all had to cost a fortune.

MF: So where did the money come from?

The tape ends there. I shut off the machine. Mamie didn't know. She suspected the priest of selling indulgences, citing how every week he or his housekeeper descended to the village below and came back with a sack that some people said were full of envelopes. She never saw them herself, so she couldn't prove it one way or the other, and she told me she didn't care. After the tape stopped, I made her a *tisane,* and we listened to the tape play back.

"That's not me," she said. The more she listened to her voice, the more she shook her head. "Well, you sound like you, but I cackle."

She died long before books and television programs caused hundreds and hundreds of tourists and treasure hunters to traipse through the village. As for me, that was good for business. Although I had done well in university despite dropping my ex-lover's class, it took me a while to figure out how to earn my living. There were no jobs in sociology and I didn't want to study more to teach in university.

After getting a degree, the idea of continuing working in a shop like I had to help me meet my expenses made all my friends cluck. "You need a real job, a professional job," they said.

Through a friend who worked for Airbus, I found a job in their marketing department. Some of it was really fun, developing all the materials, etc. Almost all my co-workers were excited about bringing the airline from concept to reality.

I loved when we were making the films to show prospective buyers. I would go with the film crews and watch them as they filmed the planes flying next to us. We would go over the Alps. There is nothing like a snowy mountain to set off a plane.

But being cooped up in an office for long hours got to me and my four-week vacations only brought the taste of freedom so I quit.

Everyone thought I was crazy, except my husband Michel. He, too, was a free spirit, which is the one good *and* bad thing I can say about him. I then went to work in that shop near the airport that sold oils. I had gotten to know the owner when I was a customer, and when I told her how unhappy I was living the corporate life, she offered me a job. That was one of my best decisions.

All of a sudden I felt so free. Poorer, because my salary was much smaller, even with commissions. When the owner moved everything to Carcassonne, we went with her. Oh, I know I had to be there to deal with the clients, but the owner and I switched off on slow times so I really had more free time and she taught me so much. When she died, I inherited the shop and then opened this branch up here and put someone in charge of the shop in Carcassonne. And business has expanded thanks to Web sales. I would have made more money had I stayed at Airbus, but I wouldn't have been as happy. I couldn't have come home to Rennes.

And I am grateful to the mystery of where the priest got the money from—without all the hoopla business wouldn't be so good.

Mamie wasn't educated, and I did check out some of the stories for the report. Of course, the Visigoths were all over the area but the idea that this was the main center is stupid. That was Narbonne.

And there is all that stuff about Jesus's wife coming here with his child and that the child and all its descendents have been guarding the secret two thousand years give or take. No, not possible. People aren't that well organized and certainly aren't well organized over centuries and centuries.

Chapter 14
Argelès-sur-mer

Annie's eyelids opened, closed and then stayed shut. A slamming door, two dogs barking, a woman calling to her daughter: each woke her in turn and each time she rolled over and fell back asleep. When her neighbor with the bad disposition once again berated his wife so that everyone on the street could hear, she forced herself to look at the clock. It told her that she'd slept at least three hours. 9:15. She reached for the telephone to dial Roger's number.

"Nous ne sommes pas ici maintenant. Après le beep sonore laissez un message." Beep.

"C'est moi, Annie. Call me if I haven't reached you before you pick up this message. *Salut Gaëlle. Je te parlerai plus tard."* She didn't want to leave a message about the Patrick Fiori concert. There were some actions that demand the giver get the pleasure of seeing the recipient's face.

Her next call was to the station. Gendarme Boulet told her Roger was at the church.

Annie's preference for starting a day was to shower until she puckered, letting the water warm every muscle. However, this morning, she turned around quickly under the spout, ran her fingers through her curls, threw on yesterday's jeans and bolted out the door and down the stairs.

The church was less than a two-minute walk. No sooner had she turned the corner than she heard a woman's screams coming from the church. She took the stone stairs two at a time, but just as she pushed open the heavy wooden door there was silence.

As she stepped inside the familiar dank smell hit her. It was the smell of age, from stone that hadn't seen bright daylight since the roof went on in the thirteen hundreds. Lord knows the small stained glass windows did little to bring in any warmth. Perhaps in the summer when temperatures soared, the cold might be refreshing, but not today. She had never understood Père Yves's statement that he found the atmosphere comforting.

For her it was depressing, but she hadn't been raised in any religion other than her parents' set of ethics that said that everyone was responsible for themselves and everyone and everything in some way was interconnected. Therefore, do no harm. Help where you can. Be honest not just with others, but with yourself. Their code was simple: one that Annie had no problem adapting to her own generation, although from time to time being honest with herself was difficult. As her father often said, "All we can do is our best." That last statement was why Annie was totally comfortable with the lifestyle she'd chosen over the more traditional get-ahead careers of her contemporaries.

No matter what philosophy guided her life, she still didn't like the inside of this church and it took a nanosecond to assess the situation. Shivering she saw both Roger and Madeleine Boulet, back to back, punching numbers into their cell phones. In normal tones that echoed off the stone walls they talked into their phones in such a manner that it was as if they were talking to each other.

"Papa, he wants to ruin my wedding." *Madeleine.*

"Pierre, I have a little incident here." *Roger.*

"He's talking about sealing off the chapel." *Madeleine.*

"It might help if you came down here." *Roger.*

The church door let out its ominous creak as a man came

through the door. In his arms he held two urns of white roses and stood there, waiting for someone to get there.

"*Et puis,* to make matters worse the florist just arrived." *Madeleine.*

"I know we talked about it and I talked to the area Bishop. He says we have no choice." *Roger.*

"Where do you want to start?" the florist asked.

"I'll show you." *Madeleine.*

"Put them down, and come back this afternoon." Roger advanced toward the florist.

"Don't you dare leave." Madeleine beckoned to Roger. "Papa, come quick." She clicked off her phone and walked over to Roger. "You know how close I came to *not* finding a priest for my wedding? And now you are so busy playing policeman . . ."

The florist was backing toward the doors. She stopped yelling at Roger long enough to grab the florist who had deposited the urns of flowers at the entrance. Madeleine moved as fast as she could behind him, blocking the door.

Annie had taken a seat in one of the caned chairs in the back. Like many old churches in this part of the world, pews were rare. Chairs were not. Both were uncomfortable, but in watching this drama, comfort wasn't in her awareness level. No one had seen her.

Roger dialed another number. "I need the full crime team here. Now." He looked around and in the dim light that filtered through the small stained glass windows and the flicker of long white tapers at the small altars spied Annie. "What are you doing here?"

"I think I know where Père Yves is."

"Me too."

"*Parlez en Français,* stop speaking English. It's very rude," Madeleine screamed.

"Screaming isn't polite, either," Annie said in a French that was colder than the church.

"You're just jealous." Madeleine had lowered her voice, but even in a normal tone she had a tone that grated.

Annie racked her brains of one thing that she could be jealous of as far as Madeleine was concerned. "Of what?"

"I can find a husband; you can't."

Annie turned her back and looked at Roger. She had always thought of brides in terms of yet another girl gone bad. Too many of her friends had been divorced. She was expert at making tea as she listened to the woes of the hurt spouse. No way would she dignify Madeleine's comments with a response. Instead, she rolled her eyes as Roger held his mouth rigid to keep a smile from breaking out. "I think Père Yves is in one of the tombs."

"So do I. And I think I know which one as well." Roger led her to one of the side chapels where many candles burned. Madeleine trailed along behind, spewing reasons why Annie wasn't lucky enough to be a bride. Both ignored her.

"Look," Roger said.

Annie looked. There was a stone gray coffin that belonged to a priest who had died in 1708, Bernard Fournier. Unlike earlier tombs, there was no stone effigy on the cover, just flat rock. However, Argelès had been so poor at the time that the price of the carving was beyond what the parishioners could have afforded for even the most beloved of priests. The other stone tombs were dusty. This was not. The cover was slightly ajar.

"I'm convinced he's in here," Roger said.

Before Annie could tell him she agreed, the church doors slammed open and ex-mayor Jean-Pierre Boulet burst in. As usual he was dressed in crisp slacks and a short-sleeved shirt. He never wore a tie, but almost no man in Argelès wore a tie, not even the bank manager or the head of the insurance company. "What the hell is going on here, Roger? Why are you ruining my little girl's wedding?"

"I'm not. I think I know where the priest's body might be."

"He's not dead, just off on one of his wild goose chases," the ex-mayor said.

"What the hell is going on here?" Pierre Galy, the current mayor, came in and shook hands with the ex-mayor. Both men acted as if touching the other might cause some kind of skin disease. "I know you must have a good reason, but why are you trying to stop a police investigation?"

Boulet, who had been roundly defeated by Galy, not just by a few votes but by well over two-thirds, advanced on the current mayor just close enough to make Galy step back. Boulet was fifteen years his senior and between the family's successful businesses and his years of being mayor he still was not used to being challenged on anything. "This is my daughter's wedding. She needs to decorate the church."

"And the police need to conduct an investigation," Galy glared at Boulet. "You've no authority."

"You don't either." Boulet was right. The police were part of the Ministry of the Interior and were responsible to Paris authorities, not local ones. However, politics made it wise to keep the mayor on the police's side. In Boulet's time as mayor, he tried to keep the police as his private employees, which necessitated more than one call to Paris and a great deal of tact on Roger's part. His predecessor had told him that he could handle the crime, the kids, the drunks, but the mayor had driven him *fou*, nuts.

Just as the two mayors advanced toward each other as if about to exchange blows, five gendarmes from the larger police station in Perpignan walked in. They all carried bags; one had a camera.

Roger pointed to the tomb and told them to photograph it before lifting the cover. When the photographer finished one *flic* came forward and using the sidewall as traction he pushed as hard as he could, but it didn't budge. The veins in his neck stood out. The slab gave with a great skreak. He staggered back, gagging.

"Strong smell for someone buried almost three hundred years," one of the Perpignan crew said.

Roger, holding a handkerchief over his mouth and nose, went to the edge and looked in. "It's Père Yves."

Chapter 15
Argelès-sur-mer

Annie almost fainted from the stench. In the mystery novels that she loved to read and on television, shows from *Columbo* to *Julie Lescaut,* the odors were never described strongly enough if at all. She staggered out of the church and vomited on the remaining angel. The one Père Yves had landed on had been taken away. She had no idea where. God, what a thing to worry about: the disposition of a broken angel when her friend lay broken for good in the crypt behind her.

People walking by stared at her. She wondered for a second if they thought she were pregnant, and she bet that a rumor that she was would be around the village by tomorrow at the latest. The price of having neighbors who watched out for your property was that they also wanted to know what kind of toilet paper you used.

She headed back to her nest where there were no bodies and where she could cry without witnesses. It wasn't that she hadn't known that Père Yves was dead, but until the body had been found, she had been able to play mind games with herself, even if she knew it was stupid. Stupid was okay. Lying to oneself was not.

When she had first moved to Holland she used to pretend each class day was only a field trip and the next day she would be back in New England where everyone spoke English. Don't beat yourself up, she chided herself. Using one's imagination to cope is different from being dishonest to yourself and about yourself.

That she'd been right about where Père Yves's body was, as much as she loved being right and hated being wrong, gave her no pleasure. Roger and she had both figured out where the body was. Maybe they shared more than she thought they did. If he wanted a conventional relationship, she shouldn't blame him. Not his fault. That didn't make her right for him. Nowhere was it written that whomever she fell in love with had to love history as she did. Her mom and dad had different interests and their marriage was one of the few successful ones she knew.

Getting back to thinking about being right and wrong, she usually was able to admit she was wrong, often out of laziness. It got things into the open. After all, how much could someone argue after you said, "You're right, I'm wrong." How she wished she could say she was wrong about this whole thing. She wanted to tell Père Yves's God he was wrong in letting the priest die, but although she wasn't a believer, there were challenges she just wasn't willing to take on.

She decided to take a long shower, steaming until the hot water ran out then wrapped herself in her terry-cloth bathrobe and her hair in a towel. Flopping down on her unmade bed she lay there doing nothing. The empty kettle took too much work to fill. Getting dressed brought about the need to open drawers and that involved turning the bed back into a couch to make room.

Her hair was drying into something wilder than normal—she just knew it. That led her to limited action. She got up and grabbed her pick, pulling at the tangles until she cried. I'm crying because it hurts, it has nothing to do with Père Yves, she told herself. She went to the table and put her head down and bawled at the universe.

By the time the church clock struck noon, she had dressed,

made a cup of tea, turned the bed back into a couch and settled with her laptop on her lap. The screen saver read, "The success of a rain dance has much to do with timing." When the clock struck one she was still staring at the screen.

She shut down the computer. Stupid again. What was she going to do? Play Free Cell? She had no work projects: She wasn't going to do historical research. That brought Père Yves too close, along with the awareness that she could never talk to him about history again. There would never be another e-mail from him telling her of what he'd found: a book that she must read, a document in some archive or a new website. She needed to delete his name from her address book, but she wasn't about to turn her laptop back on. As long as his address was there, he was still there in a way.

Bereft—that was the word she was looking for to describe how she felt. She'd never felt it before. When she had lost lovers, she'd been sad, but she knew that they would still be around. Okay, so she was lucky to get to thirty-three without ever having lost a close friend. She still had three grandparents, and her dead grandfather had died long before she was born.

She wanted her mommy and daddy—so stupid for a grown woman.

It's okay to be stupid sometimes. David and Susan Young had been good parents to her. In fact and perhaps because of their bouncing from country to country, they had grown closer because with each new assignment, they only had themselves as they built new networks of friends. Or maybe it was because she was an only child. Somehow they had always known just when she was ready for a new freedom, which at the time had made her angry. She had planned rebellions only to find that they weren't necessary.

They never asked her like other parents did, "When will you settle down and raise a family?" Her mother's biological grandmother time clock might be going off, but she muffled the alarm if Annie were near. Only once had Annie caught her looking longingly as the grandson of her best friend had toddled across the living room floor. If she asked them, Annie could imagine their admission that they would like grandchildren, but would add that she had to do what was right for her.

And it was her father's love of history that had been transmitted to her. He had resurrected his Landmark book collection and would read them to her nights when she was in bed. Although David Young was an executive, he refused to put in eighty-hour weeks and insisted on being home at least to eat with his family, although it might be eight-thirty or nine before they sat down at the table. That might have been one reason Digital had transferred him to Europe, which he considered a prize while others who had been sent felt exiled. And he had never aspired to being president of a large company. He'd found his level in upper-middle/lower-upper management and was content.

The Landmark books had been the brainchild of Bennett Cerf, and as a child Dave Young was bought one every time he was good at the dentist. Annie always pictured her father rushing directly from the dental chair to the bookstore. Thus she had read about the Tudors, the Battle of Britain and the Romans before any of her friends had even heard of them. Together father and daughter had scoured the town library for good histories. Before they moved to Europe, they had walked over every step of the Concord battlefield, and had laid flowers on the grave of the British soldier. Her father had insisted that they look at the American Revolution from the British side.

He was part of the April 19 reenactment of the shot heard around the world and insisted on being a redcoat. Annie suspected that had he lived in the 1700s he would have gone to Canada with the rest of the Tories who sided with King George.

Once in Holland, he took her to Leiden where many of the Puritans had sought refuge before making their way to the New World. In each place they lived, the two of them would set out on weekend expeditions to find what local history there was.

It was the same relationship that Annie had cultivated with Père Yves. Had her father been dead, a shrink might have told her that she was looking for a new father figure, but her relationship with the priest had grown out of casual conversations first over vegetables at the *marché* then over coffee at Martinez's.

Almost like a robot Annie dialed her parents' Geneva home, willing them to be there. With each ring she imagined them walking through the duplex where they'd settled permanently, saying they had lived outside the U.S. too long to go back except for visits. It had become a foreign country to them. Annie wondered if there was any such thing as Third-Culture Parents or were they more trapped then she was between nations?

Her father picked up the phone. "Hi Kitten, where are you?" This was his standard question whenever she called. Although she'd told them she was going to her nest, she had also said she'd be exploring Rennes with Père Yves.

Instead of answering she started to cry.

"Wait a second, sweetie. I want your Mom on the extension."

Annie heard him bellow, "Suze, our daughter has a problem, get on the phone."

"What's the matter, Annie?" Her mother's voice was tense.

As she poured out her story her parents took turns with the *how awfuls* and *poor yous,* and all the words that Annie needed to hear at that moment. Although the comments were only verbal, Annie felt as if they were hugging her.

"Why don't we come down?" her dad said.

"That's not necessary. I'm a big girl," Annie said. Why had she said that? She wanted them there. Now!

Her Mom did the "tut" sound she'd perfected years ago. The

"tut" was never overdone and interjected when the offending statement was just not in the realm of believability.

"Get a room in that nice hotel around the corner from your nest. You know—the one with the great restaurant," Dave said. "And if they've no room, the one by the post office."

"It's a little late to leave today, but we'll be up and about early in the morning, and should be there by noon. Is that okay, Dave?"

"It certainly is. And Annie, although we want to be there for you, I'd like to go to the funeral. You know Père Yves was my friend too."

Annie felt ashamed that she needed reminding. Although both men had not spent much time together, as soon as they'd met about five years ago, they were off on tangent after tangent, often talking long into the night. One time Annie and her mother had left them in Annie's nest and gone back to the hotel to sleep. When they came back for breakfast both men were still at it, deeply engaged in tracing the crusades.

"Thank you. You're right. I do need you here."

The planned arrival of her parents made her feel better. However, her eyes were still heavy from crying and her muscles felt as if she'd run a marathon using her legs, arms and shoulders. She threw herself on her couch and shut her eyes, just for a moment she told herself. The next thing she knew it was morning and she was stiffer than before.

CHAPTER 16
ARGELELÈS-SUR-MER

La Tramontane blew over the Pyrénées from Spain. Annie stood at the end of her street and wondered what Madeleine had done about her wedding. Not that she really cared, but after two good nights of sleep and a good day with her folks yesterday, she was beginning to feel human again. And part of feeling human was curiosity. She headed into the *épicerie* before going to meet her parents for breakfast. She wanted to pick up some flowers for her mother. The shop had assorted bouquets in buckets next to the peppers and pumpkins.

Most Sundays, people bustled about buying meat and vegetables for dinner before shops closed at noon for the rest of the day. This day her neighbors made none of the usual comments—accompanied by sighs—about how long the wind would last. They only talked of the dead priest and what possibly could have happened to him. But unlike ordinary gossip that seemed to hiss, the tones were heavy, as if beaten down by the wind.

No Mass was scheduled, another difference from an ordinary Sunday. An announcement pinned to the door listed the times of Masses in Collioure, Elne and Port Vendre. A yellow tape sealed off the church, letting the villagers know that the forensic people hadn't finished their examination. The only thing that was normal was the bells. They rang automatically, oblivious to the absence of Annie's friend and not caring what happened in the village.

As Annie walked to *Les Arbres* where her parents were staying, a piece of paper accompanied her, twisting and turning in the breeze. The sky, when she looked up over the buildings that crowded both sides of the street, was almost royal blue, typical of when *La Tramontane* swooped down on the region. This was the first day. When she'd heard it come up during the night, she'd pulled the covers around her neck and remembered the Nor'easters of her childhood that had blanketed New England in snow and resulted in school being cancelled. However, *La Tramontane* carried no snow, no rain. Today the color of everything was like someone had added diamond dust to all the surfaces, the flowers, the walls of the buildings, the leaves that swirled around her, making the world iridescent.

Annie loved bad weather almost more than good. A pelting rain could mean a day at home reading, a fire in the fireplace and soup bubbling on her stove. As for wind, whether it was the *La Tramontane* in Argelès or its sister wind, *La Bise* in Geneva, the fury appealed to her for the first two or three days. After that it got on her nerves. For some reason that no meteorologist had ever been able to explain, the winds seemed to last three, six or nine days.

The paper continued its spiral dance as Annie turned the corner. She entered the restaurant where she and Roger had eaten the other day. The waitress, who was folding napkins, looked up and smiled and pointed to the staircase.

The three rooms that Marie-France and Jacques rented to select tourists were up a staircase, as was the guest breakfast room. Annie took the stone stairs two at a time. The room was cheerful, painted yellow with bright patterned blue and yellow curtains and matching tablecloths. There was a strange man, probably in his early fifties, sitting at the table that overlooked the small courtyard. Her parents, Dave and Susan Young, were at the other one. The third was empty.

Her father stood up as Annie approached. "Join us, Kitten."

She did.

"I hope the flowers are for me," her mother said.

"They are. As always, I don't know what they are, but I liked the yellows and oranges."

"Cheerful," her mother said. "We need it."

Her father took a final swallow of his espresso. "Strong enough to chew. What's on the docket for today?"

Annie wasn't sure. This wasn't the normal type of visit where they would explore the region. She shrugged and took a croissant from the basket on the table and broke off the burnt end, her favorite part. She usually left her favorite part to the last, but since the death of Père Yves, she found herself choosing the thing she most wanted first.

Annie's mother said, "Frankly, I'd be happy to go to Annie's and do nothing in particular. Maybe read, play a little backgammon, if you're up to it, Annie."

"Like the old days." How many weekends had she and her family spent in their individual corners reading, and then coming together for a snack and maybe a game of cards or backgammon as they talked about what they had been reading? "I forgot to tell you about a woman I met on the train."

" 'Third-Culture Kid,' that's a good term," Dave said when Annie had finished.

"Maybe that's a reason we're closer than some other families," Susan said. "We only had each other for so long. Annie, do you think . . . ?"

Before she finished her sentence, the other guest came over. He spoke with a thick French accent. "Excuse me, but are you the Annie that was friendly with Yves Bressands?" When she didn't respond immediately, he said, "The priest?"

"Yes."

"I'm his brother, Paul."

Dave Young stood to shake the man's hand. "I'm sorry we

meet under these circumstances. I knew your brother and liked him, although I certainly wasn't as close as my daughter. We were all fascinated by the history of the region." He indicated that Paul Bressands should sit, which he did. "Please accept our condolences."

"*Merci, c'est difficile.* It was only my brother and I who were left. Our parents are gone. My wife died last year, although I have two children in America."

Susan Young reached out and touched Paul's arm. "Have they learned anything?"

"I've talked to the police chief. He appears competent enough."

"He is," Annie said. "Got most of his training in Paris, which has a lot more murders than Argelès."

Marie-France came into the room. "You won't believe this, but the ex-mayor has called a meeting in the *Salle des Fêtes* this afternoon at four." When she saw the confusion in their eyes, she said, "To take action in searching for the murderer."

Dave Young said in the right degree of sarcasm exactly what Annie was thinking. "Roger will love that."

CHAPTER 17
ARGELÈS-SUR-MER

The *Salles-des-Fêtes* had been remodeled from a series of attached reddish brick buildings that were relatively new by Argelèsian standards, going back only to the eighteenth century. It was used for any number of things from exhibitions to meetings. The local library was housed in the same building, as were rooms where craftsmen gave lessons in pottery, painting and other handicrafts.

One side opened onto a narrow street, but the back faced a series of terraces decorated with huge plants, trees and benches, where the old folks came to sit and talk. Beyond the terraces a parking lot had been created when two streets full of houses were demolished, a project of ex-mayor Boulet. No matter who was for or against him, this project had added a bit of spirit to the town. In summer there were plenty of activities for the tourists, but after the tourists departed, the *Salle* became the center of most of what happened during the rest of the year.

Today, people of all ages—from the older people, dressed in mourning perpetually for this or that relative, to jean-clad young professionals—came in groups, quickly occupying all the seats until there was standing room only.

Ex-major Boulet paced up and down on the small stage where local plays were produced. He was dressed well by local standards. Most locals wore work clothes. Most retired people wore jeans or sweats. As usual Boulet wore well-pressed trousers and a shirt that had a triple crease in the back. Annie suspected he would have loved to wear expensive suits, but that would have separated himself too much from the common voter, his power base. She had no way of proving her theory.

He lighted on the edge of a table, the only piece of furniture on the otherwise empty platform. One leg rested on the floor while the other tapped the air. Several times he looked at his watch. At ten past the hour he called the meeting to order.

Annie and her parents were in the fourth row, close enough to observe the ex-mayor's expressions as he began his harangue against the current mayor and his putting the town in danger by inviting all the Parisian socially rejected youth to the town for the summer.

"He is like an actor in a bad French movie," Dave Young whispered to his wife and daughter.

"Shh," Susan and Annie said together.

A figure slipped into a seat behind them. When she turned she saw Paul Bressands. He was dressed in pressed jeans and an Irish knit sweater. They exchanged half smiles, the type that says, I-recognize-you-but-this-isn't-a-smiling-time.

"It was those ruffians that did it. Killed the priest then ran back to Paris," Boulet said.

Several of the villagers nodded their heads. Others folded their arms and frowned.

"We must make sure the police follow up on the kids who were here," someone called out.

"Who else could it be? Everyone loved Père Yves," another voice.

"Does Roger have any suspects?" Dave whispered to his daughter.

"It's like the last person said. Everyone loved Père Yves, which makes motive hard to establish."

"What if someone lost their temper?" Susan whispered, then shook her head. All three of them knew that if Père Yves had been a diplomat, the country he represented would never be at war and all people would sign treaties—smiling.

"Mayor Galy should be here." This came from one of the *mamies'* sons.

Mumbles ran like waves through the room. Talk of acting, although no one was sure what the action should be. Then a voice was heard among the rest. "May I have the floor?"

"Who are you?" Boulet asked.

"Paul Bressands, Père Yves's brother."

The room was so still only an occasional wheeze from Michel Moly who had emphysema could be heard. Boulet nodded and Bressands made his way to the stage.

"*Merci.* My brother spoke to me often about the program; he felt that it was a good program. He tried to get close to a number of those kids. He was frustrated that he didn't succeed with many, but he would be extremely upset if he thought his death would be the cause of the end of the program. He was hoping to see it continue next year."

"And if one of those kids he didn't succeed with was the one who killed him?" Boulet asked.

Bressands stepped back as if hit. For a moment he didn't say anything. When he did his voice was softer, and people in the back leaned forward to try and hear. "It is my understanding that the kids were gone."

"Most," said the ex-mayor.

"All, according to the police," Bressands said.

The ex-mayor looked at Bressands and looked at his audience. The audience was watching Bressands, not him. Because Boulet's most admiring supporters had loved the priest, the ex-mayor had never criticized him in public, although there were rumors that he'd said the priest was too liberal in private. "We in Argelès share your loss, albeit in a different way," he said to Bressands. When Bressands had sat, the ex-mayor said, "There's a murderer loose. We must all take steps to protect ourselves. We need to help the police."

"Roger will love that," Dave Young whispered to his daughter. Annie's mouth twitched, but she didn't say anything.

"If our current mayor were more of an activist . . ." and then Boulet ranted for another ten minutes about the failings of the person who now sat at his desk in the village town hall, for he had said more than once that the *mairie* was his home away from home, or perhaps the reverse.

At the end of the meeting Susan asked, "What did that accomplish?"

"Made our ex-mayor look like he cared more about the village than the present mayor. He has another five years before the next election, and he's going to be campaigning every minute."

The ex-mayor came up to Annie. "Our American resident and history buff. Are these your parents?"

Annie introduced them.

"Madame Young, I see where your daughter gets her beauty."

Annie wanted to tell him that compliments would not lead to votes even if she could have voted. A glance at her mother and she knew that her mother hadn't been fooled either.

The ex-mayor turned to her. "Annie, I've been meaning to talk to you about our priest's trips to Rennes-le-Château, although he should have spent as much time tending his flock as he did in hunting treasure."

"It wasn't treasure, but knowledge," Annie said.

"That's what he wanted us to believe. I think whichever kid killed him knew he'd found something."

"From what I hear, the kids didn't spend much time in church," Annie said. "Père Yves used to see them at the beach and try and get them involved in handball. That's how he engaged them."

"And our good mayor should have made church attendance a requirement," Boulet said.

Annie looked at her watch. "Mom, Dad, we're late. We should get going."

Outside her father asked, "Was that late bit just to get away?"

Annie smiled, then frowned. "Shit. I let that slimy little man distract me. I left my bag back in the *Salle*." She headed back in, feeling much like a salmon going upstream at mating season as she bucked everyone else coming out. When she got to where she'd been seated, there was no bag. She asked the janitor who was putting the chairs away, but he shrugged and said he hadn't seen it, but promised to call her if someone handed it in.

"Did you have much money in it?" her father asked when she rejoined her parents outside.

"Passport?" her mother asked.

"Neither. I left my wallet at home, but there was my journal and address book." There were duplicate addresses on her PC, but her journal—that was something else.

Chapter 18
Argelès-sur-mer

Annie left her parents at the hotel the night after the ex-mayor's meeting. Her legs hurt from the long hike in the mountains they had taken together, but it was a good pain, the type that said she'd exercised well. Tomorrow, it might tell her that she should exercise more regularly.

Her father had been right. They needed to do something normal, something that celebrated life rather than dwell on what they could not change. The wind, instead of being a detriment, had added to the walk, making the mountains appear even more savage as the trees howled above them. The wind had also blown away some of the heaviness she had been feeling, although she knew it would take a lot longer for her to totally forget Père Yves. Oh, that was wrong. She'd never forget him, but as her father had told her, "He has left a hole, and someday there will be a cover over it. When you look at the cover, you'll remember the good things instead of the pain."

The church bells rang five times. Street activity was picking up as parents walked toward the school to pick up their small children. Older children rushed along, their book bags on their backs. Boys pushed each other. Girls huddled, talking together. Annie wondered, not for the first time, what it was that made boys shove each other so often. She'd even see it among the Swiss soldiers, grown men greeting each other in the train station, as they met to go on their regular reserve training with one another. Were men always little boys with their own signals?

131

Were women just overgrown little girls?

Her parents had declined a dinner invitation *chez elle*, opting for a quiet night in their room.

Annie was just as glad because she did not feel like cooking or cleaning up. Sitting down with a cup of tea and piece of fruit was more her speed.

The smell of wood fires hung in the air as residents fired up to take the chill off the early afternoon autumn air. It wasn't usually this cold, but the wind was responsible.

Life felt almost normal. Then she saw Paul Bressands.

He crossed the street and shook her hand. "*Bonsoir*, Annie." His voice was melodic like Père Yves's had been. If Annie closed her eyes she wasn't sure she would be able to guess which brother was speaking, except Paul still had the Parisian accent, while Père Yves's speech had taken on the slowness of the south without ever gaining the Catalan twang.

"*Comment-allez vous?*" she asked. Even though he was dressed casually, it was not the village casual of jeans or sweat pants, but of quality pants and open-necked shirt with a well-knit cardigan. His shoes were shined and she was sure his socks would match the rest of his outfit. Annie didn't feel right using the more casual *ça va* to either tell him how she was or to enquire about how he was. Funny how she had been able to *tutoyer* Père Yves the day after they'd first met, not for lack of respect but in response to the warmth of his personality. Even after all these years she never knew when to drop the formal *vous* for the informal *tu*. The fact that the Swiss were more formal than the local Catalans did little to make her more comfortable with any switch. Maybe had she been Catholic, she would have stayed with the more formal *vous* with Père Yves. However, Paul Bressands looked like a *vous* case. And definitely not a *ça va*.

"*Ça va*," he said. "I left a message on your cell phone. Have you time for coffee or a glass of wine?"

She nodded and patted her pocket where she kept her phone. "I keep it off most of the time." Then she asked, "How did you get the number? Almost no one has it." Annie was the first to admit that unlike most techies, she wasn't a cell phone fan, finding it intrusive to be interrupted. As for all the bells and whistles, she found no need for instant information every minute of her life. Maybe her love of the past made her look beyond the latest moment, or maybe she just liked the control of determining by whom she would be disturbed.

"It was in my brother's address book. I hope you don't mind my using it."

She shook her head. Politeness. She didn't imagine that he would call her often.

As he led her to the café on the main street, he asked, "Do you think it's warm enough to sit outside?" The area was sheltered from the breeze and caught the end of the day's sun, but she was glad she had on a heavy sweatshirt. When she nodded, he chose a table.

"*Banyuls,* two," he said to the waitress who had woven her way between the tightly placed white plastic chairs and tables. About half had at least one person reading a newspaper. The tree acting as an umbrella over the tables was making all kinds of twittering noises, probably, Annie thought, migrating birds settling in until morning. That could lead to some interesting additions to the tables, except just as she thought it, the waitress and the bartender rolled out an awning protecting the tables.

She found it half annoying, half amusing that Paul had chosen her drink for her. Had she not been satisfied, she would have said something, but felt no need to make an issue of it. At one time in her life she made instant impressions of people and refused to change them. Time had proved her wrong often enough so that she now let impressions build.

Her reactions to Paul Bressands were mixed. She found him

handsome, with a Parisian sophistication that spoke of good schools and high positions. It wasn't his clothing alone, for Père Yves had spoken of his brother's success without a trace of jealousy but pride. "My mother was from this region and talked about personal happiness, but my father expected us to do our best at whatever we tackled," the priest had told her. "In fact, we were expected to do more than our best."

"Were they pleased you were a priest?" Annie had asked.

"Yes and no. Part of them was glad to give a son to the church, but they had thought of me as the son who would be the scholar." He'd smiled. "They got both. As for my brother, he was to be, and is, the businessman."

She brought herself back to the present. "What was the message?" When he looked confused she added, "That you left for me. On my phone."

"*Alors,*" he said as he settled back in the chair. "I wanted your advice. You were closer to my brother these last couple of years than I've been. Not that we had words, but I was too caught up in my business. In fact, this is the first time I've taken time off since I don't know when."

Annie fiddled with the empty ashtray on the tabletop. "You certainly aren't a typical Frenchman who must have his four weeks."

"When you own your own small company, it's different. Besides, after my wife left me, it wasn't much fun to go away alone."

The waitress appeared leaving two glasses of ruby red wine on the table. She put a small rectangular piece of paper under the ashtray with the cost of the drinks printed on it.

"*Santé.*" Paul lifted his glass toward Annie, who returned the salute.

The local wine was rich and fruity.

"Yves always brought me some *Banyuls* when he came to

Paris." He sat forward in his chair and fiddled with the base of his glass. "The police will release the body tomorrow. Originally I was going to take him back to Paris for the funeral, but I'm beginning to think it would be better to do it here. Have you any feelings one way or the other?"

Annie pulled the bill out from under the ashtray and rolled it into a cigarette shape between her fingers. "That depends."

"On?"

"If he has a lot more friends in Paris than here."

He took a small sip of his *Banyuls* almost as if he were a woman trying to appear extra ladylike. "Here. At this point, he's been away from home too long to know many people."

Annie straightened the paper out and put it back under the ashtray. "I'm sure Père André from Collioure would do the Mass." She instinctively reached into her backpack for her address book but stopped with her hand in midair. "Damn." She explained that her pocketbook had disappeared after the ex-mayor's meeting. "No one has returned it."

Paul shrugged and reached for the paper and took out his wallet. He looked around for the waitress who was chatting with a man about her age with curly hair and a movie star smile. "I'll take a drive down tomorrow. I'd like to meet him before I invite him."

Annie stood and gave her hand to him. "If I've helped, I'm glad. Please let me know when the service will be."

The waitress still hadn't come. He counted out eight Euros and put them in the ashtray, tore the bill halfway through and slipped it under the money. He stood. "I'd like you to do a eulogy."

Annie sighed. Words, she could always find. Good ones, but she hated speaking before a group. However, she nodded. It would be the last thing to do for him, Père Yves.

Her street was only about three minutes away from the café.

One thing she enjoyed about the village, everything was in walking distance. Although she had her license, she lived her life in a way that made owning a car unnecessary.

As she walked by Mamie Couges's house she could see her stirring something on the stove. Good smells came from each doorway. Although Annie hadn't been that hungry, the smells stimulated her appetite. Maybe she'd cook up some eggs along with the tea.

She took her key and opened her mailbox. Another reason she'd miss Père Yves. He'd gathered her mail and divided into *keep until later, throw away* and *forward to wherever Annie was working.* Now she'd have to bother with having the post forward everything. Although she was sure one of the *mamies* would be more than willing, she knew that each envelope would be discussed up and down the street.

Her insurance was due as was her *taxe d'habitation,* which wasn't that much, less than three hundred Euros for everything. Not only was her nest cozy, it was economical. By foregoing space and possessions, she was free, free, free to work less.

Long ago, she knew that she would have to be a wage slave, but that didn't mean slaving nine-to-five ten to eleven months a year. She couldn't imagine working in the States with just two weeks of vacation. Even the stingiest European country offered four. And by not working for any corporation, she was able to only work six or seven months a year with her contract work. Maybe some day she'd need a full-time job, but she intended to postpone that time for as long as possible.

"Make sure you have savings and a plan for retirement." She imagined her father saying that, although he wouldn't have. What he said was, "I always had savings and put some away for when I was old." She smiled. Her parents did deliver their messages without making her feel forced.

A Carrefour flyer told her about all the great food buys and there was another envelope from the *Palais des Rois Majorque* in Perpignan. When she tore open the envelope there was a note and two press passes.

Chére Annie,

I couldn't get you seats, but I've got you press passes. But I could only get two.

Forgive me? Charles

Forgive him? She loved him. She dashed upstairs to call Gaëlle.

CHAPTER 19
ARGELÈS-SUR-MER

Annie waited in Martinez's tearoom for Gaëlle. It was Wednesday afternoon when the schools were closed for teachers' meetings. Instead, kids attended classes Saturday mornings. More than one working mother had bitched about the schedule as did any parent who wanted to go away for the weekend. The girl was late.

Gabriel sat with Annie. He was talking about his new nut-olive bread, which he had given her to sample slathered with sweet butter, when her mobile phone rang. At least that hadn't been stolen because she'd shoved it in her pocket at the last minute rather than put it in her purse. She held up her hand, and Gabriel stopped listing ingredients. *"Allo."*

"I've your pocketbook." The voice was a muffled Catalan accent but loud at the same time.

"Formidable." Wonderful.

"You're a beautiful woman. I've seen you around the village, and from your journal, I know I'd like to know you better."

Annie shuddered. Someone had read her personal thoughts. Strangely enough, when she was writing personal things she resorted to French. Practical things were in English. Just like when she and Roger made love they spoke French. Now she regretted it because the person on the other end of the line probably didn't read English. Stay calm. "Thank you. Can you drop it in my mailbox, please?"

Gabriel mouthed, "Is anything wrong?"

She pulled a pencil out of his pocket and wrote on a napkin *"Un con."* An asshole. Gabriel looked confused.

"I may keep the journal for a while," the voice said.

Annie heard a click and she looked at the phone. *"Merde."* She explained the problem to Gabriel. By the time she'd finished Gaëlle had arrived, breathless, her hair well spiked with the ends dyed blue. They kissed on both cheeks then Gaëlle did the same to Gabriel.

"I'd love to have seen your father's face when he saw your hair," he said.

Annie, too, would have loved to have seen Roger trying to control his temper.

"There were threats about not letting me leave the house until it grew out," the teenager said, "but he always threatens that whenever I do anything different to my hair, or put on too much makeup, or, or, or . . ."

"Well, I see he wasn't too sincere on that," Annie said as she unzipped her jacket pocket and handed Gaëlle the press passes. The girl scanned them then looked closer and her mouth dropped open. "You mean . . ."

"Absolutement."

Before Annie could add anything, Gaëlle had grabbed her, knocking the napkin holder off the table, and hugged her into pain. "Take it easy."

"I can't believe it. I mean, I can't believe it. I'll see Patrick. Do you think we can interview him, these being press passes and all? Or does it just mean we'll get closer, or maybe we'll just have regular seats? Can we get in early?"

Annie held her hands up. "I really don't know. I just know we can get in, that is if you don't mind going with an old lady." For a moment she wondered if it were better to let Gaëlle go with a girlfriend.

Gaëlle's smile as well as her words put Annie's mind to rest.

"Of course I don't mind. I'll be the *only* one in my class going. All my friends will be oh so jealous."

Gabriel brought over two hot chocolates. "Not sure what you guys are celebrating, but the hot chocolate is on the house."

"By the way, Papa said he wanted you to come back with me. For dinner. He also wants you to bring the dinner. Pizza is my vote."

Annie frowned. This was too much like the old days. Gaëlle didn't notice.

The new Gendarmerie was halfway between the beach and the village. When anyone walking left the old village, they saw several oversized one-family houses built in the 1800s or early 1900s by the village's few wealthy families who owned the vineyards beyond.

That was until about ten years ago. One by one the families sold their land, taking the quick money over the long term and regular, but much smaller income from grapes. Up went ticky-tacky vacation houses. Their builders squeezed as many in as possible, selling the proximity to the village, the beach and the view of the Pyrénées. A few were occupied all year round by retirees. Each house had a fence around it, not the white picket fences of Annie's early New England childhood, but cement and brick. Some were decorated with concrete latticework. Others were topped with colored stones. Most were between waist and neck height and it was possible to peek over to see the small front gardens. Although many were planted with flowers, most were flagstones. Grass was uncommon.

Gaëlle and Annie critiqued the gardens as they walked by. "I'd put a huge pot, maybe salmon colored, and add plants," Gaëlle said.

"Weeding around the tiles would help that one." Annie shifted the pizza box a little. It was hot.

The Gendarmerie was new, built on the last vineyard next to the village swimming pool and sports field that had been named for the politician who had married the daughter of the man who invented cigarette papers. Their Art Deco château was perched on the mountain that could be seen from where Gaëlle and Annie stood at the metal gate outside the police station. They pushed the button. The gate opened silently.

Inside the station Gendarme Boulet sat behind the counter.

"Watch him suck up to me," Gaëlle said in English. The girl didn't like to speak English despite having studied it for three years in school and hearing her father and Annie speak it. The latter had been the best motivation for her to learn, so they couldn't have a language that kept her in the dark about this or that.

Annie did a double-take. "Suck up?"

"I'll explain what it means later," Gaëlle said.

Annie swallowed her laugh as she watched Boulet jump to his feet to offer Gaëlle a seat, a chocolate and a Coke that he paid for himself.

Gaëlle offered her a sip. *"Et?"*

"Big-time suck-up."

They laughed, and Boulet looked at them. Maybe he's only half as stupid as we thought, she said to herself. But then again anyone that obvious could not be called bright, only political. Even the most stupid animal could find food if it were hungry enough.

Roger came out of his office and opened the gate between the public reception area and the police offices and cells, ushering Annie and Gaëlle into his office.

"What do you think of my daughter's hair?" he asked as soon as they were seated in the room that was almost completely dominated by his desk.

Gaëlle's eyes pleaded with Annie, who said, "Matches her

jeans." The young girl flashed a grateful smile. "I used to wear ten different-colored nail polishes all at the same time when I was her age."

"I should have known you women would stick together." He took a folder. "Look at this, but don't tell anyone I showed you."

Annie took the folder. It was the kind that had flaps and elastics so that the papers inside were loose but wouldn't fall out. The label read–*Autopsy BRESSANDS, Père Yves*. She flipped through the pages and handed it back.

"You couldn't have read it that fast," Roger said.

"She speed reads, Papa. Have you forgotten?" Gaëlle's voice was almost a whine.

"I read that he had died of injuries to the heart that were consistent with a fall: crushed ribs that penetrated the heart. Death was almost instantaneous. Internal bleeding. And also, there's the DNA results showing the blood on the angel matches Père Yves's DNA."

She gave her head an I-told-you-so nod and caught Gaëlle's smile out of the corner of her eye.

Roger's living room was double the size of Annie's entire apartment. A small fire crackled in the fireplace. Hannibal curled up in front of the brown leather couch where Roger and Annie sat, their feet on the heavy oak coffee table covered with books and magazines. Gaëlle was in her room supposedly doing her homework, but definitely listening to Patrick Fiori on her CD player.

The empty pizza box was on the floor and if anyone had smelled Hannibal's breath there would be anchovies and onions from the one piece he'd been allowed at Annie's and Gaëlle's insistence. The final argument was that since Annie had bought the pizza she could decide those that would eat. Four-footed lovers of pizza rated as high with her as the two-footed variety.

"What do you think of Paul Bressands?" Roger asked.

"Police question or just curious?" Annie turned and curled her legs underneath her and propped her chin in her hand using the back of the couch as a rest.

"Both."

"Cultured, intelligent, cool, not in the hip sense but emotionally cool. I suppose I thought he would be as warm as his brother."

"Siblings aren't always alike; in fact, it's rare when they are."

"So you think he could be a suspect?"

"I've looked at him a bit. I wish when I told him over the phone, I could have seen his face, but the shock seemed real enough."

Annie reached out and patted Roger. She knew how much he hated that part of his job, telling families bad news. He'd been on both sides, and neither was a good side, he'd said time and again.

Annie thought back to some of the things that she knew about her late friend. "Père Yves had money, or at least his family did. But it was left in such a way that he couldn't give it to the Catholic Church. I mean, he could call on it for things, like hiring a plane to photograph Rennes-le-Château. A poor priest couldn't have done that."

"How do you know he couldn't get at it?"

She shifted position and rubbed her leg where it prickled. "He told me."

Roger took her hand. "You were really close to him."

"We were good friends. My mother said that he was the older brother that I always wanted."

"He approved of me," Roger said as he pulled Annie to him so her head rested on his shoulder and kissed the top of her head.

She froze, half wanting to nestle, half wanting to pull away.

"He told me to give you plenty of space and maybe you would see what a great guy I was."

Annie shot up. "That's not fair."

Roger smiled. "True. I love you, Annie Young. I miss you. Can you honestly tell me that you no longer love me?"

She shook her head. "But that doesn't change that I have a certain way I want to live. You don't like it." She got up off the couch. *"Tisane?"*

He nodded and followed her to the kitchen.

On the way she asked Gaëlle if she wanted one, and the girl replied, *"Menthe, s'il te plaît,"* through the closed door. By busying herself getting out the dried mint leaves and turning on the electric kettle Annie allowed her emotions to calm down. "Let's get back to Bressands."

He nodded and got out three spoons from the drawer next to the sink. "I know his business is in trouble. I had one of my old colleagues run a check on him. He's just about pulled it out of debt. Perhaps the money from Père Yves's estate would be what he needs to secure it totally."

"Doesn't feel right," Annie said. "Besides, he was in Paris, wasn't he?" She reached for the teapot from the cabinet over the stove. It was round and dark green with yellow and brown streaks, typical Catalan pottery. All Roger's dishes were like that. She and Gaëlle had picked them out together about three months after father and daughter had moved in. The youngster had announced she was tired of eating from paper plates and wanted the house to be a real home. It had been the break-through between Annie and Gaëlle, who had been Annie's friend before she had met Roger and wasn't sure how she felt about her friend and father as a couple. They'd meet in Martinez's tearoom where they both went for a chocolate crepe in the late afternoon. When they'd started to chat they discovered they liked the same music, melting the first of many barriers that would fade into nothing.

When Gaëlle said she still felt strange in this area after living all her life in Paris, Annie shared her experiences of shifting around from country to country. The girl had begun to laugh and had said, "At least I'm not the only one, and they do speak French here despite the horrible Catalan accent." She'd rolled her eyes. At that time her father had walked in and Gaëlle had introduced them. There had been no immediate spark, no *coupe de foudre*, but Marie-France and Jacques had kept pushing the two of them together whenever they showed up at lunch alone at the same time at *Les Arbres*.

Time and attention to Gaëlle by both Annie and Roger together and separately had helped the youngster decide that having them as a couple didn't diminish her relationship with either adult. Annie let the memories drop at that moment and went back to listening to Roger.

"He could have hired someone," he said.

As Annie took the kettle and poured water into the pot, Gaëlle came into the kitchen. "Fingerprints?" the teenager asked.

"You really are a *flic's* kid," Annie said and looked at Roger.

"Fingerprints on the tower were numerous. Remember there are tours of the tower at least once a week all during the summer. We must have found at least seventy-five readable different sets and uncountable unreadable. In the rectory they were mainly his. Those that we ran through the national database only turned up a few locals. Some others were from tourists, and we contacted them by phone but none of them seem even remotely plausible. And by the way, I need to get yours."

"They'll match some in the house. I haven't been up in the tower for years." When she poured the water into the kettle, the smell of mint permeated the kitchen.

"Funnily enough, there were no prints at all on the tomb where we found him."

"On the other tombs?" Gaëlle asked. She held her nose near the pot and sniffed. "Hmmm."

"Not many," Roger said.

"People don't touch tombs a lot, I guess," Annie said. "Have we any biscuits?" Shit, she thought, I said *we,* not you. This isn't my house.

Gaëlle brought out a package of LU chocolate/orange biscuits. She cut open the rectangle package, pulled out the brown plastic tray and put several on a dish.

"When Annie isn't here, we eat them out of the box," Roger said. "And who will wash?"

Annie's cell phone rang. She pulled it from her pocket. *"Allo."*

"How nice you are spending some time with the chief of police." It was the same voice from earlier in the day.

"Who are you?" Annie demanded.

Roger looked startled. Annie knew the tone of her voice was out of character.

"Someone who thinks you are a real sexy . . ."

"Leave me alone," Annie said and hung up.

"What was that all about?" When Annie told him he said, "Change your phone number."

They sat at the table, letting their tisanes cool. What a pain that would be. She would have to send out new CVs to all the agents she did business with. "I will," she said finally. "Get my number changed."

"You agreed awfully quickly," he said.

"I always do when you make sense. Besides it makes me really uncomfortable that he knows where I am and can call me and tell me whenever he wants."

"Do you recognize the voice?"

Annie scowled. "If I did, I would have told you."

Roger held up his hands. "Sorry, stupid question."

"I think you should stay here tonight, Annie." Gaëlle sipped her *tisane*.

"I do too," Roger said.

Annie thought about it. The apartments beneath hers were empty. All the owners had returned to Paris, Toulouse and London after their holidays. No one was renting. She knew Roger would check everything out. What if her parents called early in the morning? They'd think she was out getting bread and had been waylaid by some neighbor, that's all.

"Okay," she said.

It felt okay.

CHAPTER 20
ARGELÈS-SUR-MER

"How did I get on the Star Ship Enterprise?" Annie stretched on the couch in Roger Perrin's living room, where she'd slept kitty corner during the night. He had opened it up, turning the couch into a queen-sized bed for her before giving her an unmatched sheet and pillow, which always bothered her. Hers matched. She even ironed them, chiding herself for being fanatic, but she maintained that they felt better against her skin. Although she'd thought she wouldn't sleep because of all the things that had gone on since she'd come back from Switzerland, her eyes had closed almost as soon as he had turned the light out. She hadn't even heard him close the door and go to his own bed—one that she'd once shared.

The next thing she knew, Roger was padding across the floor and opening the shutters on the windows and door leading to the patio. Light flooded the room.

"What?" he asked, coming back to the couch and sitting on the corner.

"Your pajamas. They look like Captain Kirk's uniform." Only Roger was a lot cuter than Kirk. His gray-streaked curls were messed and his thick eyelashes gave new meaning to the term "bedroom eyes" even if he needed a shave and smelled of sleep, the musty odor that she'd woken to so often.

"Oh." He'd never been a morning talker. He rubbed his eyes with the back of his hand. For a moment she thought she'd peeked at the little boy inside the man and imagined him standing there, a teddy bear in one hand and a blankie in another.

She lifted the covers. "Come on in for a cuddle. Just a cuddle." The words were out of her mouth before she could call them back. However, it felt right. "What time is it?"

He lay down next to her, propping his head up with his hands and looked at her. "Eight-thirty. Gaëlle's left for school already."

"What about work?"

He took a strand of one of her curls and pulled it. After it spiraled back, he wound it around his thumb. "Annie, I've been on duty now for nine straight days, most of them, except for yesterday, twelve hours or more. And I'm the chief."

"I guess you can go in a little late, Chief."

"I guess."

"I need to call my parents. If they tried me last night and this morning they'll be worried."

He reached over to the table next to the couch and handed her the phone. For the first time she noticed a glass of water. She hadn't put it there. She stared at it. His eyes followed hers.

"I know you like water by your bed, so I brought it to you. I thought you'd still be awake, but you were out like a light." He continued playing with her hair. "I like watching you sleep. You look almost like a little girl."

She felt a wave of warmth for him. At no time did she resent his coming in and watching her, for she knew she was physically safe. Her heart? Well, he hadn't left her; she'd left him. Still it hurt to be the leaver. Although anger could help her feel justified in her *pique*, it didn't make any difference when she wanted to share some story with him.

"You're a million miles away," he said, putting his fingertip on her nose and withdrawing it so fast she could have imagined it.

"Sorry." She took the phone and dialed the hotel. Her mother was summoned from the breakfast room.

"We were just about to call you," Susan Young said.

Annie explained she'd spent the night at Roger's and didn't want them to worry if they couldn't locate her.

"Aha," her mother said.

"Not an 'aha' at all. It was just too late to come back," Annie said. "I slept on the couch." The last thing she wanted to talk about was the scary phone calls.

"As an adult, you don't have to tell me about your sexual habits," her mother said. "I think it would have been nicer had you shared his bed. He's a good man. Good men are . . ."

". . . hard to find."

"But it's your life and we'll back you in whatever you do."

This phrase was like a Catholic saying "Hail Mary" followed by "full of Grace." She'd heard it over and over. Her parents had let her make her own decisions early. At eight she began setting her own bedtime. At ten she was given a clothes allowance and allowed to decide what she wanted. However, her mother made it clear that if she made bad choices, she'd have to live with them. One winter she had chosen a beautiful pair of boots. Her mother had issued warnings that they wouldn't last. In mid-December they sprang a leak, but her mother refused to replace them, sending her to school with dry socks and a pair of shoes in her book bag. However, she never said, "I told you so." From then on her choice of boots had been wiser. Annie knew that her actions with men would be handled the same as boot-buying.

"Let's meet up for lunch," her mother said. *Les Arbres?*"

"Of course. Love ya." She gave the phone back to Roger.

"Did she tell you I was wonderful and you really should come back to me?"

She raised an eyebrow and said nothing.

He rolled over on his back and pillowed his head with his

hands. "I really don't want to go to work at all today, but I do have to."

She still didn't say anything, waiting for him to go on.

"I'm frustrated. I haven't one good clue as to who killed him. I haven't even any bad clues. Not one. Not a fingerprint that could mean anything, not a motive. I mean, how do you find a motive when everyone loved him? You tell me the treasure wasn't gold, but proof of his theories. Maybe proof. Definitely not treasure as most people think of it."

She turned to face him. "Something doesn't have to be real for people to think it's real."

As the sun streamed into the room it stole the chill from the night. Annie pushed off the covers. She had borrowed a pair of Gaëlle's pajamas that were too big for her. "Can I take a shower?"

"You never used to ask." He stroked her face. "Annie, I was wrong. You have a right to work where you want. What else can I say, but how sorry I am."

She was halfway out of bed and she turned and looked at him. "What are you saying?"

"I miss you. I want us to be a couple again. I'm a big boy and can learn to amuse myself when you're away. Or we can commute weekends."

His eyes didn't leave hers. "Even if it's Japan?"

He shot to a sitting position. "Japan? Is that where you're going next?" Because he was usually soft-spoken, Hannibal, who had been sleeping under the couch, scrambled out to see if everything was all right. He jumped up and lay down between them.

"Off the couch," Roger said. The dog rested his head on his paws and stared into his master's eyes, as if begging him not to ruin the moment. Instead of ordering him off a second time, Roger began scratching the dog's head. "Annie, let's try again.

What we had was good."

It was, she thought. She had missed him. Although she had always enjoyed the company of men, they weren't a necessity in her life. In fact, before she'd dated Roger, everyone she'd gone with had reduced the quality of her life, usually by trying to change her. So many of her girlfriends, who after saying "I do," spent the rest of their life saying, "I can't because my husband won't let me" or "I can't because my husband wouldn't like it." Roger hadn't been like that, except for their fights over her going away. It had been their last fight over her going to Zurich for four months that had made her say she was through, she had had enough.

"Get off the bed, Hannibal," Annie said. He obeyed with a sigh that made them both laugh. She took the dog's place. "I love you."

He kissed her and reached for the top button of her pajamas.

"Maybe we should be a platonic couple," she said.

"Bloody hell, I don't think so." He kissed her again, this time her tongue met his: she didn't worry about her breath. He still tasted of sleep, but she liked the flavor. It seemed real to her, not some advertising man's concept of what a human should taste like.

She rubbed her hand against his stubbly cheek.

"I can shave and come back," he said between nibbles on her neck.

"Nah," she said. She thrilled at the rediscovery of his body, the mole to the left of his right nipple, the scar where his appendix had been removed. It was not like having a new lover where she needed to find out what worked and what didn't. There were no embarrassments for either of them about hitting a ticklish spot. Nor was there the take-it-for-granted feelings that come when people have made love for a long time and it has become routine. This was tender lovemaking, with an air of thankfulness that it indeed was happening again.

They came, not together, but first her and then he followed, his back arched, his head toward the ceiling as if he were about to challenge Hannibal to a howling contest. He collapsed beside her, gathering her into his chest. "Yes," they said together—and laughed.

"Now about Japan . . ."

"I'm not going to Japan. But if I were, you'd have to deal with it."

He sighed. "I'd deal with it, but I wouldn't like it."

"Liking it isn't required," she said.

They stayed side by side playing catch-up, sharing the frustrations they'd had while apart, recounting the temptations to call the other and then resisting. Annie told of one date she'd had and left the man halfway through dinner. Roger said he hadn't been tempted to date at all, although had someone interested him, he might have thought about thinking about it.

"Breakfast?" he asked. "I'll make it. You shower."

They took their toast and bowls of Earl Grey tea onto the patio. Hannibal followed and settled under the white iron table. Roger had plucked several kaki fruits from his tree on the other side of the creek. They sat soft, light-pumpkin-colored fruit in the middle of the table. Had there been a breeze, it would have been a bit too cool, but the September sun felt good on her skin.

"After we eat we'll go into the village to change the cell on your telephone and get you a new number."

"I feel as if I should argue in principle, but I really don't want to," she said.

He reached across the table and patted her hand. "Good girl."

She held up a finger. "Don't patronize me."

"After what we've been through I wouldn't dare."

Annie and Roger pulled out of his drive. She turned and aimed the remote. The metal gate closed, leaving a disappointed Hannibal sitting there. Instead of heading to the village, he turned toward the highway. "We're going to Darty," he said. "Get you a new mobile."

"The only problem with changing my phone number is that the entire world has the old one. It's on my CV and everything. All the agencies I work with, all my old jobs. Shit."

"What if I keep the old one. Take your messages. That way you won't miss out on work. I can give the good guys your new number." He pulled into the shopping center's half-filled parking lot and parked next to a large cactus with thick slate green-gray leaves.

"Including the ones from Japan?" she asked as she opened her car door. Slithering out, she was only just able to avoid getting stuck.

"Excluding those from Japan. But all others."

"I'll take you to the hotel to meet your folks," he said once they were on the road again. "I'd like you to stay with me tonight."

"I think I'd like to stay at my place." She thought of all the notes on the black Madonna and Isis that she'd stashed away waiting to go through.

"Annie, who else is in your building these days?"

"No one. The people downstairs are away. The other two units aren't rented this month at all."

"I don't like you being alone."

She felt him closing in on her again in the way she had hated before they broke up. Instead of answering back, she picked up her old cell phone. "I'll check messages before I hand it over."

As soon as she pushed the button, the voice she didn't want

to hear came on the line. "Listen you American *putain*, if you're not careful you'll get what the priest got. Of course, if you could tell me more about what the priest was working on, then you won't have to worry."

Roger stopped the car and pulled over. He took the phone from her and pushed the button that showed the number of the caller. "It's a Swiss number."

Why hadn't she thought to do that before letting Roger take the phone? Well, she was a historian and tech writer, not a *flic*. "A Swiss with a Catalan accent?" She was shaking but didn't want him to see it.

"It could be a stolen phone. No *abonnement* means the caller just has to use up the message units when he took the phone. You're shaking."

"I just realized that the person who took my bag was in the hall during Mayor Boulet's tirade. We could have been in the room with the killer."

He put his arm around her. "And if it has anything to do with the alleged treasure, he may just come after you next."

"But there's no treasure."

"Whoever is calling you thinks there is. That makes it real, at least to his mind."

"Or it could be someone just playing a terrible joke." Annie couldn't even convince herself of that. She imagined herself at three in the morning hearing creaks on the stairs. There was only one exit from her nest unless she jumped out the window, and that, at best, would cause a broken body if not instant death. In the movies, the heroine would hear a noise and go toward it. Annie had always thought that stupid. She had often joked that when you heard scary music that was the time to go in the other direction. Still she wanted to spend time in her own home. And she didn't want Roger to think he controlled her.

He put his hands on her shoulders. "Listen, I know you think you don't want me to boss you around . . ."

"Get out of my thoughts," she said much more roughly then she felt.

"Look at it from my point of view."

"Which is? I'm being stalked, not you."

"I lost one wife . . . one love to a killer."

Annie chose not to think of his use of the word *wife*. He had corrected it, quickly enough.

"I don't want to lose another woman. I just found you again."

"Just don't tell my parents," she said. "I don't want them to worry." Unlike in the movies when the music is scary it's better to not go to the danger, she decided. Then she grabbed the cell. "If we have the number, we can call him."

Roger grabbed it back. "But we need to think this out," he said.

Shit, she thought. He was right.

"Annie?"

"Hmmm." She hoped it was cool-sounding.

"I was so worried about you that I didn't think of it. See what you do to me."

Okay, he was a man who could admit being wrong and not having all the answers: nothing to make her regret her choice to start over with him.

They redialed the number of the caller. No one picked up.

"He probably used a cell phone, maybe a different cell phone for each call, and has thrown them away afterwards," Roger said. He went back through the past calls. They were from three different numbers. "This man must be a specialist in stolen phones," he said.

"Which is one reason I always try to keep my phone in my pocket: it makes it harder to steal."

"So how did he get your number?"

"Probably from my business cards, which I do keep in my

pocketbook." Roger had once asked her why she had the number on the business cards but would not give it to her friends. She told him her friends got her personal visiting cards without the number. She didn't want to miss a chance at a contract. He had shaken his head because he did not totally understand her logic or lack thereof. Annie's hatred of cell phones was only increased by these annoyance calls. She knew that had the phone been in her pocketbook, the voice would never have been able to call her. But what else might he have done?

The realization that she would need new business cards with a new number and to send them to all her contacts did nothing to improve her mood.

CHAPTER 21
RENNES-LE-CHÂTEAU

When I first met Père Yves, I didn't know he was a priest. A man in jeans and a turtleneck is just a man in a turtleneck and jeans. He was good-looking, I'll grant you that, although good-looking and priests have no correlation one way or the other. Sometimes I think unmarked priests and nuns should wear warning signs.

He came into my shop as any tourist would. It was probably late September or early October when many of the tourists had gone back to wherever they came from: Paris, London or Shanghai. I was packaging some rose oil for a woman from Barcelona, I thought. She had done business with me over the Internet and wanted to see my shop in person, one of the few that didn't come for the history of the village. He nosed around the shop, sniffing the tester bottles of the different oils until she left.

The day was ending and he started to ask me questions. Finally, he said, "Can I buy you a drink?" Usually I say no, but he was a bit different. Of course it wasn't a pick-up. I'm obviously much older, although I think for a woman in my fifties, I'm still attractive, thanks to good skin genes and staying skinny, but not of interest to men in their late thirties or early forties, which was what I guessed he was despite the white hair.

Later when we were seated in my favorite café sipping kir royales, he was playing with the base of his glass as bubbles from the champagne worked through the pink kir. "You don't recognize me, do you?"

Whenever someone says that, I rack my brains, although that is a silly expression. Anyone who can imagine brains spread out on that medieval torture device certainly wouldn't connect it with memory. I ran through customers, people from when I worked in Toulouse, in Carcassonne, although given the age difference that was unlikely. Then I wondered if he were a customer whom I hadn't seen for a while. All the time I was thinking, he wore that cat-with-canary-feathers-in-his-mouth look.

"Give up?" He reached for one of the chips that they always put down with any alcohol, although chips and a champagne drink really don't belong together. I nodded.

"I'm your nephew, Yves."

Flabbergasted, I didn't say anything immediately. I had not seen him since his voice had just begun to break. My older sister and her two sons had come to Rennes without her husband when our mother was dying. I'd thought perhaps she was alone because she didn't want the husband to be reminded of how humble her roots were. Although I'd been tempted to ask, her coldness stopped me. My sister never returned, nor did she allow her nephews to come, after that visit.

My parents used to joke that either my sister or I was a foundling because we certainly couldn't be from the same family. We were only eighteen months apart. That we both went to university was amazing. People from Rennes did not usually do that, but the same teacher in our seventh years of school decided we were too smart just to get married and pushed us, then followed us through the *lycée* making sure we never gave up on our studies. She had subsequent teachers talk to our parents. My father didn't see why girls needed an education, but when my mother saw that it was what we wanted, she wore him down.

Advanced schooling to my sister was like a snob tablet elevating her to some kind of superior status. I am not sure that she ever loved her studies but saw them as a path out of Rennes and to Paris. I never knew how she managed to snag her husband, a graduate of a *Grand École*. Probably it was her beauty along with her ability to be a chameleon in any social milieu.

To be fair, she didn't totally hide her background from her husband. However, the only time she brought him here was after her Parisian wedding: a wedding to which none of our family was invited. He seemed like a nice enough *mec*, although even the word *mec* might be too common for him. I found him a bit pretentious, but correct.

As for her sons, she sent birth announcements and photos from time to time. The only reason I had met either boy was that when my mother was dying she brought them with her. Yves was the type of kid that was fascinated by everything while his older brother, Paul, was more sedate and seemed to adopt his mother's distaste for Rennes.

My sister and I had a real falling-out immediately after my mother died. She was always a bit over the top when it came to religion and she felt that my work had Satan's hand. Within an hour of my mother being buried we battled over my evilness. She had packed up her sons and left so fast that it could be doubted she had ever been there.

When she died, her husband sent an engraved announcement for the funeral. I thought about going, but to me it would have been hypocritical.

I looked at my nephew. "Welcome."

He smiled. He had one of those smiles that if someone was having a bad day, that smile would make a rethink necessary. I could understand how his flock would appreciate him. Although I have few regrets in my life, not knowing him for the first part of his life will always be one.

That man knew his history. I swear he could almost tell me what different French kings and queens ate for breakfast along with the important things of their reigns. But he was also interested in people history, what the peasants ate for breakfast, too.

That first day he said that he thought that at some point there had been a temple here to a Roman deity. Like many he said the village had a feeling, a feeling of something . . . if not holy then different.

The fountain under the chestnut trees where we risked being bonked on the head by the nuts in their thick green casings gurgled. I would get even with those nuts by picking them up and roasting them.

I wore a light jacket and he pulled a sweater from his backpack. We had finished our kir royales and then he suggested we order hot chocolate. The old owner of the bar/tearoom had his own special chocolate, not a powder but a syrup, thick and almost black, that was not sweet, not bitter, but that warmed your body and your soul. The new owner did away with it.

"Are you a witch?" he asked.

"Why?" I prefer to ask questions when asked that question so I only answer what is necessary.

"Because of your shop, your oils, the book on charms. And also because my mother told me you were."

"No, I'm a pagan though."

"You realize that pagan originally meant rural."

I stirred my hot chocolate. The syrup was at the bottom of the glass cup and I liked to watch it snake up through the frothed milk. "Maybe it would be better to say that I'm more of an animist—someone who believes spirits or souls—as Christianity would say—exist in everything."

"You weren't raised that way?" He stared into my eyes.

"Good grief, no. I was christened in the church here. Just like your mother. And I walked by Rex Mundi being trod upon by the virgin to make my First Communion." I didn't go into how much the ugly statue at the entrance of the church scared me and how I had thought that maybe after my First Communion, I would no longer be afraid. I was wrong.

He held my gaze. "And when did you lose your faith?"

I laughed. "I prefer to think I *found* it—in a comparative religions class. It seems humans need to believe in something outside themselves . . . but . . . look at all the creation stories in different religions . . . they are similar. So why should I accept that a bunch of tribal writings from Israel are any more valid than the great-turtle-in-the-sky theory." I took a sip of my chocolate but it was still too hot. Not enough to burn my mouth, but not a comfortable temperature either. "Do you know how many people have died in battles of *my god is better than your god?*"

"Too many, I'll grant you that."

We sat as the breeze wrestled through the trees. It would be dark soon. Normally I stayed open until dark, but I had no regrets in closing early. It's not every day that one finds a long lost nephew.

"Do you celebrate anything?"

"Do not think I'm a witch, because I'm not, but I like to make days around the solstices special. These are natural, not man-made." I winked at him. "And no mass marketing maypoles or sun masks on sale at Carrefour or Casino."

"But Christmas trees and presents are around the time of the winter solstice," he said. "Christmas is a co-opted pagan holiday as is Easter. Then we buy chocolate rabbits and new clothes."

"*Touché.*"

The breeze became a wind and we were shivering.

"I suppose we should go before we both catch cold." He put a ten Euro note under the clip on the tray that the waiter had left with the bill when he served our drinks.

Then he revealed his secret. "I suppose I should tell you," he said, "that I'm a Catholic priest."

I did not feel that should change anything I felt about him. Nor was I embarrassed about what I had told him. "And I hope your religion brings you peace."

"In reality, it doesn't," he said.

Yves came back often. He was interested in the construction of the building, not like the many treasure hunters who wanted the leftover wealth from the priest. I knew they were on a wild goose chase, because my grandmother said the priest's whore had burned the money, old money no longer in circulation and money she could turn in without explaining where she got it from. I still found the word *whore* shocking in my grandmother's mouth. I swear, but only for emphasis, although rude words don't bother me, but she never did except for that time.

Whenever he came, he walked the slopes down the mountain. Sometimes I went with him. We talked about religion, we talked about history, but we also talked politics, literature and food.

Sometimes I cooked a meal for him at the end of the day. When one lives alone, cooking for someone who appreciates something as simple as vegetables and pasta in a cream sauce is a pleasure. And although I like to read with my meals, it was also lovely to continue the conversation of whatever topic came up.

Then one day he brought with him a young woman. At first, because of her accent, I thought she was Swiss, but she turned out to be American. Like the priest, she knew her history backwards and forwards, and like the priest she was fascinated with the daily life of other times.

Chapter 22
Argelès-sur-mer

Roger faced the congregation. Therefore, he was unable to see the gold-plated angels, saints and Biblical figures in bas-relief stumbling over each other behind the altar where Père Yves's coffin rested. What he could see was that every inch of the church was filled with villagers wanting to say good-bye to the priest. All the chairs were taken and the side aisles were packed with people standing.

Roger had not wanted to come. The last funeral Mass he'd attended had been his wife's and he hadn't wanted to go to that one either. However, it had been necessary to rise above his own grief to deal with his daughter's then and now. Gaëlle had adored the priest for his involvement with her youth group. She was sitting to Roger's right and he kept glancing her way to see how she was holding up.

At best he had never been religious, going to Mass first to please his mother, then his wife. It hadn't won him any favors with God, who'd somehow still seen fit to leave that wife in the path of a bullet.

His mobile phone rang. It was Gendarme Gault reporting that, outside, people who could not push themselves in flowed down the stairs onto the street. Roger knew that the shops had just closed out of respect for the priest. The owners and clerks had waited too long to make their way into the church.

"Je ne sais pas pourquoi je suis ici, Patron," Gault said.

"You're there to observe," Roger said. No one around could

hear him talking over the low drone of the organ. He had to block his free ear to hear his officer talking.

"Pour?"

"Anything that seems out of place, anyone that . . . just observe. You'll know." He couldn't have been more specific, because he didn't have the answer. It had to be an instinct that someone wasn't acting right. Gault was a good man with good instincts, although young and untested. He trusted him to pick up on anything strange, even if he was the youngest *flic* on the force. He had accomplished more in his six months than Boulet had done in his whole career. He set his phone to vibrate rather than have its ring disturb the service.

Unfortunately the call hadn't broken the heaviness he felt beyond his sadness at losing a friend. When he was young, he hadn't understood why his father refused to go into a hospital after his wife had died in one. Now he knew. All hospitals were that hospital. All funerals were his wife's funeral.

Five years afterwards there was a cover over the hole in him that her death had left. But the cover wasn't locked. Certain things still opened that damned hole. Not all were as dramatic as a funeral: the scent of Shalimar, the perfume she'd always worn; the taste of spaghetti Bolognese, their family celebration meal; the song "Alexandra, Alexandrie" playing on the radio. The first time he'd met her she was doing a Claude François imitation to the song. She had all the singer's movements down as she'd sung.

He wasn't there to be maudlin. He was there to say good-bye to his friend. He was there to see if he could spot anything that might lead to the killer. He knew he couldn't bring people back to life by attending their funerals, but he could bring their killers to justice.

The man that shot his wife was now in prison. Once Roger had thought that knowing the culprit was in prison, the pain would disappear forever. Now he knew better. Later he wondered if France had still had the death penalty, would it have helped, but had decided no. Another person's death still wouldn't bring his wife back to him and their daughter. An eye for an eye didn't work.

He believed the bad, the evil, had to be contained, separated from the good people who wanted to lead ordinary lives. But killing them put him on the same level as the murderers.

He had killed once in the line of duty and had felt sick for weeks after. There was something about stopping someone else's life that made him feel that a part of his own soul was destroyed. No matter that he had killed in self-defense, although that had helped him keep things in perspective: if he had another choice, he would have taken it. He wondered if the people who loved the boy he'd killed wished his killer dead.

He shuddered. Whenever he became maudlin like this, he would remember the light go out of the eyes of the seventeen-year-old he had shot. The kid still had the gun in his hand with the smell of gunpowder hovering in the air. His own emotions had been mixed between realizing that he could have been on the ground with his blood melting into the sidewalk, and the shock that he was responsible for the death of a kid. Television always made death look so easy. All those *flics* pulling guns, killing here and there and calmly going for coffee—it wasn't like that at all.

At the moment he wondered if he should even continue as a policeman. He wasn't solving any crimes, neither the priest's murder nor the petty robberies that happened from time to time in the village. His job in Argelès was much simpler than it had been in Paris. Stop some family violence, protect the tourists and residents, pull a drunk off the street, deal with petty robberies, usually done by kids or gypsies. He had lost his edge being in this small town.

What else would he do? Could he do? If he were free he could follow Annie wherever she wanted to go, but that would pull Gaëlle out of school. No, he was tied to Argelès at least until his daughter finished her *bac* and went off to university. Then they would see.

What if Annie wanted her own child? At one time he wouldn't have minded another, boy or girl, not important. But starting over? Diapers, teething, homework, he was too old to go through all that again.

He had just gotten Annie back, or rather almost back because he knew she could easily slip away from him again, not just to an assignment but to her lifestyle, and here he was worrying about if they should have children or not. Looking at the congregation, he sought her out.

She sat with her parents in the front row where Paul Bressands had reserved a place for them. Annie had told Roger that they had spent much time with Père Yves's brother, often taking their meals at the same table in the hotel where Bressands and Annie's parents were staying. Roger had been there as the Parisian had brushed aside the Youngs' reservations about being seated with family, even if it were only one person. "He loved Annie. And besides, I need support," Paul told them.

Although he couldn't specify why, Roger didn't like Bressands all that much. He'd known too many Parisians like him. Or maybe it was businessmen, self-impressed, treating others as if they were there merely to serve them. They were the ones who were impatient with waiters and thought *flics* should conduct any investigations around their business appointments. To be fair, Bressands hadn't manifested any of these characteristics, but his clothes and bearing matched those who did. If Roger were to be fair, he would admit that the man's attentiveness to Annie was responsible for his own attitude.

Nor had he ruled out Bressands as being a possible suspect,

not of actually pushing the priest, but perhaps of hiring someone. The family had been from money originally. His Parisian contacts reported that Bressands's business had suffered a reversal. But unless the priest's death added money to Paul's bank account, there would be no motive. A trust fund from the parents perhaps, that Père Yves hadn't turned over to the church. The chances of Bressands's guilt were remote, but not impossible.

Annie looked haggard, Roger thought, as Bressands slipped into the chair next to hers. He knelt, crossing himself. When he sat again, he murmured something in Annie's ear. She nodded and squeezed his arm.

Overall Roger didn't like to think of himself as jealous. Annie had lots of male friends, colleagues, buddies, brother wannabes. She picked up people as some women picked flowers. Her friends were her bouquets. Now that was a poetic thought, not like him, but the emotion of the funeral as well as his recent reunion with Annie had stirred feelings that he had too long suppressed. And he had to admit also, she was the one who had opened him up again. Until her the only people he had allowed himself to love were his wife and Gaëlle. He wouldn't have risked it. As he watched her with Bressands, he thought marriage might be a good idea. Not that he worried that Annie would cheat on him, but he was doubly sure if they were married, she wouldn't consider it. It would be his guarantee she would always come back.

Another row of seats had been reserved for the mayor and village council. They wore dark suits. Many of the townspeople were dressed in shirts and slacks. The man who owned the garden shop on the outskirts of the village wore his blue working smock. Père Yves wouldn't have minded.

The Boulet family had come early enough to get a good view. Madeleine held her new husband's hand tightly. Roger wondered if it were because she was moved and needed his comfort. More likely she was afraid he'd leave her, having been forced to spend their honeymoon together. Roger didn't know whom she'd married; just some poor *mec* from Banyuls where he had a small domain and a cave that offered wine tastings to tourists unless Madeleine scared them off with her whining. That wasn't a kind thought, he chided himself. However, all the Boulets were a royal pain in the ass—small villagers with an idea that they were more than they were. At least Bressands acted like what he was: a Parisian businessman who was used to money. Class was the difference.

Not that Roger was from anything more than a bourgeois family. His mother had been upset when he decided to go into police work after he graduated with a political science degree. She saw him as a diplomat. Went around telling everyone how he was studying at Aix-en-Provence. He'd liked his studies well enough, and planned to make a difference in the world as a policeman, but at his age now he was convinced that the chance to do it had passed him by.

Boulet was also on duty outside. All the police, town and national, were on duty today either surveying the village in case someone took the residents' preoccupation with the funeral as a carte blanche to help themselves to someone else's property or looking for the murderer.

His top men were in strategic places throughout the church. They had their instructions: look at the attendees.

For what, they'd asked, just like Gault had. He couldn't have told them. Not that he expected a dramatic confession. No one was apt to get up and throw themselves on the altar crying, "I can't live with the guilt. Arrest me. I killed Père Yves." That might happen on television, but television and reality were two very different things.

Still he hoped for something, Lord knows what, for he had

no other idea as to what to look for next, and he hated that not only did it make him feel like a failure but an impotent failure.

CHAPTER 23
ARGELÈS-SUR-MER

Hand-in-hand, Annie and Paul Bressands pushed their way through the crowd standing outside the church. Her hand ached under the force of his grip. Her eyes were red-rimmed. She had never managed to cry prettily like they do in the movies. Instead her skin blotched, and her nose resembled a wino's and one with liver disease at that. She had managed to get through the eulogy without crying, although more than once she had stopped to breathe deeply or she would have lost it. However, as soon as she returned to her seat, the tears would not stop and even the comforting arms of her father did nothing to help.

Realizing that the priest's brother was trying to leave the church, the crowd parted in waves, not unlike the Red Sea did for Moses. At the bottom of the stairs, the hearse waited with its rear door open. Annie's parents, Dave and Susan Young, caught up to their daughter.

The pallbearers carried the coffin through the new path then shifted it into the hearse. Other mourners carried the flowers and put them in behind the body. As more and more flowers came out it was obvious that the hearse would never be able to hold them all. Different people offered to carry them to the cemetery. Annie thought that some should be given to the hospital in Perpignan. She was sure that would have been Père Yves's preference, but she remained silent. This wasn't her call.

Paul reached out to arrange a vase that had been balanced precariously before the funeral director shut the door.

The hearse started down the wrong way on the one-way street, being the only vehicle allowed to do so. In many local funerals, especially those of older people, the men walked directly behind the hearse. Then the women followed. However, for the young, there was no such segregation, and Paul had said, after talking with Annie, that he was sure his brother would prefer no separation of the sexes.

In front of the hearse, a trumpet and a bagpipe played "Amazing Grace." Annie had told Paul that Père Yves had said that he'd first heard Joan Baez sing the hymn in a concert in Toulouse. She couldn't remember if it were 1987 or 88. She hadn't known about the two musicians, until she heard the first notes. By swallowing several times she was able to stop the tears from starting again and was able to listen to the Argelès Gospel singers who picked up the song and even if the pronunciation was strange, the emotion was perfect. That there was a local gospel group no longer amazed her. Globalization of culture transcended the business world.

Over a thousand people walked behind the hearse. Their footsteps made a background noise to the music and both drowned out the soft purr of the engine. The cemetery was behind the train station, a seven-minute walk at a good clip, but the cortege took double the time to arrive at the gates.

The first part of the cemetery was made up of small houses with anywhere from six to a dozen drawers holding individual bodies. Names were engraved outside. The hearse drove by them until it came to the section where vaults were at ground level covered not by grass but marble slabs. Names were engraved on the flat part. Resting on about ninety percent were ceramic books with messages in gold or black lettering saying: "From your loving wife," "Our cousin, we'll miss you." In some cases, a picture of the deceased was inserted in a frame of the book. In others there were carved images of what was important to the deceased: a tractor, a dog, a football.

Annie had always found local attitudes toward death fascinating. Widowers, who ignored their wives during their lifetime, preferring to drink Pastis in cafés than being at home, would lovingly attend their graves daily, showering them with flowers. The same widowers had probably never bought a bloom for their spouses while they were breathing. Widows, who screamed curses at their husbands while alive, likewise would regularly visit their deceased husbands. Practically the whole town turned out with chrysanthemums on All Saints Day, November 1. That wasn't even counting the carefully beaded flowers that were left in vases, or the pine boughs and candles at Christmas. She wondered who would take care of Père Yves's grave. She would, she decided.

The priest from Collioure was reciting the ritual. The crowd was silent as the coffin was lowered into the vault. The people who worked for the cemetery department shoved the marble slab over it and the flowers were put on top until none of the stone could be seen. One by one, the mourners spoke to Bressands and drifted back to their normal daily activities.

Annie's back ached. Her feet ached from the high heels worn for the first time in months.

Everyone drifted away, touching Bressands, mumbling different condolences. When he, the Youngs and Roger were the only ones left, Bressands bent to put a stone on the grave. He turned to leave then walked back and started to sob until his entire body throbbed. Annie gathered him in her arms, letting him cry himself out.

Dave Young put his hand on Bressands's back as he fought for control. "Let it come out now."

Bressands sighed and searched for a handkerchief. Dave handed him his. The grieving man blew his nose several times. "I'm sorry," he said.

"Don't be. It's normal," Susan said. "Come back to Annie's flat for lunch."

"Mom, I don't have anything to eat," Annie said.

"Yes you do. I cooked a big pot of spaghetti last night."

"Mother." Annie turned it into a five-syllable word.

"What? You come into our house in Geneva when we're not there and make yourself at home and you gave me a key," Susan said. "Did you think I would wear it as a necklace or use it when I needed to, like today?"

Strange to hold such a normal conversation in a cemetery after she had just said good-bye to a good friend, Annie thought. She wasn't used to losing people to death. Granted, friends had drifted out of her life because they moved or their interests changed, but that wasn't final like death. There was no Facebook, Myspace or blogs to track down where Père Yves had gone.

She was lucky at her age to still have both her parents. A couple of her school acquaintances' parents had been killed in a car crash and a teacher had died of cancer, but these had not been people that she'd been close to. Not like Père Yves, with whom she'd talked almost daily either in person or by e-mail for the past few years. Had he been old, it might have been easier, but she suspected not much.

Much of her life wouldn't change that much. She would still get excited about her research. She would run low on money. She would go back to work until she could get more time off. There would be regular conversations with her parents and visits back and forth. Roger and Gaëlle would be there. Life went on.

When her cat died during a time that she lived in an apartment building in Geneva, she'd told her concierge, who'd said, "C'est la vie." That's life. "Non, c'est la mort," that's death, she had replied. She hadn't liked it when she'd lost pets. She supposed, as she grew older, she would lose more and more people, but she doubted that she would ever get used to it.

Enough about herself; she needed to think more of Paul for Père Yves. "Do come back with us."

Bressands walked out with them. "Wait. Please, just one more moment." He turned and walked back to his brother's final resting place, scooched down and put his hand on the corner of the coffin. When he rejoined them there were fresh tears in his eyes that the others pretended not to notice.

Susan Young had opened Annie's table to full size and had set five places, in case Roger wanted to join them, she explained. She whipped out a salad from the refrigerator and put the pasta sauce on the stove to boil.

"What can I do?" Annie asked as if she were a guest in her own nest.

"Dress the salad. Dave, can you open the wine? Paul, sit down and stay out of the way." Susan, the ultimate hostess, was in charge. Her orders were followed without questions.

"My brother said you had made this flat a magic spot," Paul said, looking around. "He said one feels content just being here."

Annie swallowed several times before she could answer, "Did he now?"

"Annnnniiiieeee."

She went to the window and looked down. "Have you time to eat with us?" she called to Roger.

"*Oui.*"

She threw the keys down to him. When he came in, he kissed her on the mouth, shook Paul's hand and kissed both of Annie's parents on each cheek.

"I'm glad you guys are back together," Dave said.

Annie and Susan said "Dad" and "Dave" at the same time.

"What? I *am* glad," Dave said.

Both women shook their heads.

"I am, too. She's a handful, but I want her to be my handful. Did she tell you about . . . ?"

The phone rang before Annie could stop Roger from telling her parents about what was going on, thank goodness.

Roger said, "I'll answer it."

Susan looked from one to the other. Annie saw that her mother had picked up the fact that something was going on. She'd never been able to hide much from her mother. The woman was almost psychic, almost able to diagnose illness by the way Annie walked across the room. Because of it, Annie had never lied to her mother as her friends had lied to theirs, not so much out of honesty, but more because it would be a total waste of time. Also Susan had reacted well to all sorts of things that would have sent many mothers into spasms if their daughters had admitted the same thing. Thus Susan knew when Annie had lost her virginity, tried weed and had gotten drunk for the first time.

Annie also knew part of her mother's openness was because her mother had done the same things and didn't consider anything life threatening as long as condoms were used and cars not driven while under the influence. Her mother also made it very clear that certain things were age-acceptable or unacceptable, which is why Annie may have waited until she was eighteen to experiment with the things that many of her friends had tried in their early teens. Susan had a way of making her daughter feel that she wasn't a late-bloomer, but a wise young woman who would make healthy decisions.

Still, there were times that Susan's intuitiveness was a pain in the ass. Like now, when she didn't want her parents to know that she was being threatened. Why worry them needlessly?

Roger handed the phone to Annie.

"Annie, this is Christianne Holtzmann in Zurich. *Grützi.*"

Annie didn't need a last name. She knew the voice as she had worked for the agency on several projects over the last four years. Christianne had been a good agent, showing Annie what her cut was. A lot of agencies were staffed by cowboys taking up to fifty percent of the payments the client made to them while claiming they were making nothing. Christianne had had several tech writers at the same site as Annie on the last contract a year ago, and she had stepped in once to solve a dispute between client and contractor on the contractor side. Most agents never defended their contractors. Even the client had been satisfied.

"I've got an assignment for you. I heard you were free."

Annie, who had given up any hope of the holiday she'd planned for herself, listened.

"A software company in Paris needs a manual translated from French into Dutch, English, German and Italian. Normally, we'd have to hire a person for each language, but then *Schatzie,* I thought of you. They will love it when I tell them you've gone to school in Holland and Germany and your mother tongue, luckily enough, is English. *Voilà.*" Like all good sales people, Christianne stopped talking to let Annie think.

More than once the fact she'd studied in different languages that were almost like her mother tongue had gotten Annie work. Although many people were multilingual, it didn't mean they could write well in any language other than their own. Maybe they could produce a good letter or two but usually not professional writing nor tech writing, which needed to be clean, clear and crisp to be effective. Annie was more comfortable writing in either German or Dutch than in English or French, but she knew she could do a credible job, better than a nonprofessional native speaker. It wasn't conceit, but confidence in her skills.

Better not to appear too anxious. "I was taking a holiday," she said. Roger's eyes met hers, but they didn't have the same anti-new-work look that she would have seen before their break-and make-up. There was another expression she couldn't quite make out, and she wished she had the same intuition as her mother did.

"You can do most of the work *chez vous,*" Christianne said. Like Annie she was multilingual and they often went from English to French to German in the same conversation. Her voice was confident, business-like as always. As Annie remembered, the woman had an elegance, a scarf tied a certain way that no one else would think of over a sweater. She was one of those European women who could wear a sweater and jeans and make someone think she'd spent thousands.

"Chez moi?" It would give her a chance to accept an assignment near Roger until they could work out some of the bugs in their relationship. Hmm. She hadn't thought that way before about anyone. Maybe being thirty-three was giving her nesting instincts. Heaven forbid. Or maybe not.

"I suppose I could meet them," Annie said. "Any idea of payment?"

"Too early to negotiate, but I can probably get it up higher since they'll only be paying one person."

"I don't do Italian," Annie said.

"Macht nichts. They'll still save. You'll be totally familiar with the material. Get it to them sooner."

"And you'll show me the invoices *comme la dernière fois?*"

"Annie, you know me. I'm aboveboard. I've an idea of the rate, but if I can come up with one or two people instead of several, the client will love me. I'll be, how do you say, golden, *n'est pas, ma Chérie?*"

"And before you ask, no other agency has called yet." Annie knew how competitive the computer consulting agencies were. "When do they want to see me?"

"I'll call you back. I was afraid to send your CV before you gave me your okay. *Ciao.*"

"Possible job. Here," Annie said after she hung up.

"I almost wish it were away," Roger said.

Susan frowned, but Dave never minded charging in. "I thought you guys broke up because Annie was away too much. Now you want to get rid of her?"

"It will keep her out of danger."

"Danger?" Susan, David and Paul said the word together, their voices rising in inflection.

Annie held up her hands to stop the conversation, but Pandora's box was open and the demons jumped out and were pushing her parents' worry buttons.

As Roger told about the threatening calls, Dave put his arm around his daughter's shoulder. "That settles it," he said. "I'm not going home until everything is resolved."

Annie groaned. Sometimes being loved was a pain in the ass.

"I have to get ready for my *vernissage*," Susan said, referring to the exhibition of her paintings slated for the end of the month at their village town hall. She put her hand on her daughter's knee. "But your father can stay here. You'll stay at Roger's?"

"Good idea," Roger said.

"I can accompany her on the train," Paul said. "I need to get back to Paris, but I want to finish clearing out my brother's things. I'll make sure I'm ready to go home by the time she has to go for the interview, but not before."

"Do I get any say in this?" Annie asked.

"No," she was told by everyone in the room.

CHAPTER 24
ARGELÈS-SUR-MER

"I'll get the train tickets. You finish up," Annie said to Paul Bressands. They were in the entry of the rectory. Paper-filled boxes surrounded them. Three giant trash bags were filled with Père Yves's clothes, ready to be carried to the *Armée du Salut*'s charity box.

"Why not Catholic charities?" Paul had asked.

"Because your brother was particularly fond of the Captain who leads their church in Perpignan and the work they're doing with the poor. He said it was one of the best programs around."

Paul shrugged. "You know best what he would have wanted."

Annie didn't want to say that it wasn't her fault that Paul hadn't had time to visit, despite the number of invitations Père Yves had issued to his brother. The priest had gone a few times to Paris, but when he came back, he said that he and his brother had had little time together: Paul's business had interfered. Annie wondered had she had a sister or brother would they have been close. Hard to tell, but she suspected they would have been. In her family alienation wasn't allowed.

For the past two days, they'd been packing, then cleaning up as they finished each area in the rectory. The new priest would move in next week.

"I promised your papa I'd not let you out of my sight," he said.

"Jesus. I'm not helpless," she said. "It's not like there's no one around." She pushed her hair out of her eyes and replaced the comb that had not been doing a good job holding the strands back. For a moment she envied the women with straight hair that could be simply forced into a ponytail, but she knew they envied her the curls. They had a choice of styles, however, she could only wash it and wear it at many different lengths. She sighed deeply, not about her hair, but for everything that had happened since she arrived back in Argelès.

Paul took her by the shoulders and came a bit closer, almost as if he were going to kiss her. "I never said you were. It's just . . ."

Annie felt suddenly ill at ease, but the moment passed. "Just nothing. I can walk to the station alone, past all the shops that are open with customers going in and out."

Paul let go of her and stepped back. "I usually travel first class. Is that a problem for you?"

"I usually travel second, but no, it's not. It will be nice for a change."

"If money's a problem, I can pay for your ticket." He reached for his wallet and pulled out the cash.

"*Merci, mais j'ai l'argent.*" She had the money. However, she realized that she had sounded harsh. "*Mais, excusez-moi.*"

"*Tu,*" he reminded her. His smile was warm as he gave her enough Euros for his ticket.

As she was turning the corner, she saw Roger walking toward her. He kissed her, not on both cheeks but on her mouth. "Now everyone watching knows for sure, we're an item again," he said.

"Marking your territory?" Annie asked.

"If I were a dog, I'd have piddled or mounted you," he said. "Where are you off to?"

"Train station."

He fell in beside her. "I've got a full report on Bressands that differs a bit from earlier ones. He's almost bankrupt, which we knew, and he hasn't had much luck in raising capital, which we didn't. And I was able to find out that both he and his brother were co-beneficiaries on a trust fund. Draconian set-up."

"Draconian? I love it when you speak English and use words that only a native would use."

He frowned. "Do you want to hear or not?" When she nodded, he continued. "Neither brother could get at the capital, but they were paid the interest. Solid investments. Père Yves's went to charities, mostly peace stuff, left wing."

"Not surprising," she said.

"But, if either one died, the capital would go to the remaining brother. They could choose if they would take the capital as payment or use it as . . ."

"*Bonjour, Chef Perrin.*" Ex-mayor Boulet stepped out in front of them. Standing with him was his daughter, Madeleine.

Annie knew her tolerance level was low that day, but she forced a smile and said her *bonjours* as was expected. Being a foreigner meant following local mores strictly. It made acceptance much easier.

"How is the murder investigation going?" Boulet asked. "My son said you aren't even close to solving the crime."

If you knew why did you ask, Annie thought, but she said nothing. Boulet's mouth could do a great deal of damage and antagonizing him was the same as setting off a bomb, a verbal bomb.

"We've some ideas, but nothing solid."

"How do you know the murderer won't strike again?" Boulet asked.

"I thought you suspected one of the Paris urchins?" Roger said. Annie knew by the way that Roger said it that he was as annoyed at Boulet as she was. However, Boulet didn't know Roger as she did. Introspection wasn't his strong point, although he did have an animal cunning when it came to local politics. Annie had rejoiced when the cunning failed him, and he'd lost the last election. However, except for Père Yves she didn't discuss politics with her neighbors. She listened.

"He could come back. Really Perrin, what local would have attacked the priest?"

"I think it's a disgrace," Madeleine said. "I don't feel safe in my bed at night if my husband is late getting home."

"Your bridegroom is working late already?" Annie asked. She couldn't resist it. Well, maybe she could have if she tried.

"Will you two be getting married soon?" Madeleine asked.

"I'm not sure I believe in marriage," Annie said.

Madeleine looked confused. "Well, I love being a Madame rather than a Mademoiselle."

"After a certain age you're called Madame anyway," Annie said.

"But don't you want someone to take care of you?" Madeleine asked.

"I have more faith in myself taking care of myself." She eyed Roger. His lips were twitching.

"Still, with a murderer loose, you should be careful," Boulet told her. "The priest was much bigger and stronger than you are, and the Chief here can't watch you all the time."

They excused themselves.

As she watched them walk away, Annie shuddered. "There's something about that man that makes me want to take a shower. And as for her . . ."

"I know what you mean," Roger said. He put his arm through hers and walked in the direction of the train station. "Have time for a cup of tea?"

Annie stopped at the steps in front of Martinez's. "I'd love to, but I need to get train tickets and get back to helping Paul."

Roger frowned.

She knew that frown. "What?"

"I don't like the idea of you going to Paris with him."

She gave him a give-me-a-break look, but said, "Because he has business problems doesn't mean he's a killer. If everyone who had made bad investments turned into a murderer, we wouldn't have a population problem."

"Did you ever think he might be the one calling you? Putting on a fake Catalan accent?"

"Honestly, Roger." She started to walk away from him, but he grabbed her arm.

She pulled away. "I can't believe Paul killed his brother. I don't believe he'll hurt me." She debated telling Roger that Paul had invited her to go to his place so she could shower before her interviews, and she'd accepted. It would give her a chance to poke around his flat and disprove Roger. If there was anything Annie loved, it was being right, although she prided herself on being able to admit she was wrong and to be able to say she was sorry. This just wasn't one of those cases.

She passed all the shops until she came to *Brasserie à la Gare*. One of the town winos was slumped onto a table. This wasn't one of those cafés for the gentility. It catered to heavy drinkers, those who would gradually become more and more nasty.

The station, across the street from the *brasserie*, was a modern stucco building with a terraced entrance full of plants that she couldn't name except for general categories like cactus and pink flowers. To the right was a *boules* court where the men of the town arrived with their kits and discussed each game in detail, comparing it to other games. Annie loved watching them, holding the ball, estimating exactly how they had to throw it to get close to the target, the groans and ahs when someone did it right or wrong.

Inside Annie was third in line. Buying the tickets only took a few minutes. She knew the man behind the counter. He lived two streets over from her. Although he was always polite, she knew he was a strong Le Pen supporter, which probably meant she was too foreign for his liking. She was probably too feminist, too American, too everything that he didn't appreciate. However, this was just her instinct, for he never did or said anything out of line.

The man behind the counter had several more people to wait on, each with a complicated question. No one could seem to make up their mind about the time they wanted to leave and how many changes they were willing to make. A young couple that couldn't stop giggling wanted to go to Barcelona.

When the last person left the man took out his portable and dialed a number he knew by heart. "She just came in and bought two tickets to Paris. Only one was a return." And he gave the times and dates. Smiling, he knew he would have a hunk of cash, enough to buy a good bottle of wine.

CHAPTER 25
PARIS

Annie had not slept well. First-class couchettes had four beds, not six. But where the second-class compartments were usually filled, the first-class ones were more often empty. No one had boarded in Perpignan, Carcasonne or Toulouse, where most passengers joined the trip. She should have dropped off and not awakened until the train arrived at Gare d'Austerlitz in Paris as she usually did.

Some people could only sleep well in their own bed. Annie wasn't one of them. Normally, she could sleep anywhere, anytime. For example, she could put her head down on her desk and drift off in minutes. She had learned it was not wise to sleep with your head next to a telephone, because a sudden ring created a wake-up call that nullified any beneficial effect the nap might have had. Thus, on most overnight train trips, the swaying of the car acted as a cradle. Had Roger not planted some doubts about Paul Bressands, she would have slept well.

They had left the shade up so there was some light thrown into the compartment by whatever lamps they passed. She and Paul were in the lower two bunks. For most of the night she watched him sleep. His face appeared younger when he was relaxed. In fact, he looked almost like a little boy with his feet drawn up so that his knees hung over the edge of the cot. Roger had to be wrong, but he wasn't one who blamed people without reasons. And even if Paul were a murderer, he would surely be too clever to attack her when everyone knew they were together.

As a child Annie's imagination often kept her awake. After watching *Poltergeist* she was sure the apartment house where they lived was built on a graveyard. Even as an adult, the DVD of the movie *E.T.* had led to her spending hours awake in her bed. She wasn't afraid of aliens, but of what government officials might do. Her parents had reassured her that it was only a movie, and the government would *not* cordon off their house with billowy sheets like in the movie.

Nights were also the time that she thought about her bills, her next job, and the lists of things she needed to do. As long as she couldn't sleep, she thought about the interview ahead. However, interviews held no fear for her. She didn't need a job for a few more months. If it worked, it worked. If it didn't, it didn't. That was a good position to be in.

That taken care of, she next wondered how she would be able to check Paul out. She decided to leave it to opportunity.

As the train chugged into the station, she caught sight of the circular clock: eight-thirty. Because they had not undressed, it was simply a matter of throwing on jackets as protection against the cool September Paris morning air. The city was definitely in a different climate than the south of France, but then she had no reason to be surprised. It was further north than Boston was from Washington, D.C.

The train spat out its passengers into Gare d'Austerlitz where they moved herd-like down the platform. Annie Young never went in or out of any Paris train station without feeling as if she were a part of an Impressionist painting, even though the trains were now long and sleek and didn't billow clouds of smoke. This morning was no exception. A soft mist was falling, which added to the grayness and the artistic flavor.

Paul hefted Annie's brown backpack over his shoulder and pulled his own wheeled suitcase with his free hand. She had to run to keep up with him.

With the masses, they moved into the Metro. Paul handed her a narrow violet ticket for the machine to get them to their destination, the station La Motte-Piquet Grenelle in the 15th arrondissement where Paul had his flat.

"I hope you don't mind if I shower and leave you," he said as they stood in the swaying car with other commuters. Annie could have fainted and still have been held in position by the bodies jammed together.

"I don't mind at all. Do you mind if I stay until my appointment?"

"Not at all, but what time is that?" he asked.

"The agent said she wanted to meet me for lunch before we go to the client's." She smiled and felt like Judas. There would be time to shower, wash her hair, change into her one business suit that she only wore for interviews and search Paul's flat. That she felt badly about, but it should put to rest any doubts she had about him. Or rather that Roger had about him. Okay, she admitted it. It was a violation of the consideration he had shown.

Annie dried her hair. There was nothing she could do about the frizz. Between the dryer and the dampness outdoors, tame hair was just not one of her options.

Paul had shown her where she could find an iron stuffed in a closet that included his washer, dryer and cleaning products— all arranged magazine-perfect.

The flat was two stories, starting on the sixth floor of a building that went back to the early nineteen hundreds with a metal cage for an elevator. In a way she felt as if she were walking around a spread in an interior-decorating magazine that featured antiques. Paul and Père Yves had grown up here. After their parents died, Paul had moved in with his wife and children. He was now living alone in a space that would have been spacious for a family of six.

Before he'd left for work, his hair still wet from his shower, he'd given her a quick tour, pointing out which pieces of furniture had been in his family for years and which he had bought despite his wife's preference for the modern. "Her new place is totally modern, nothing older than five years," he told Annie, his lip barely hiding a sneer at the idea. She had thought that his wife had died. She was wrong but was it important? Maybe she was just dead to him.

Pictures of her with their children decorated a baby grand piano in the ample salon that looked over a small park and the aboveground Metro Station Cambronne in the background.

By contrast the kitchen was ultra modern. Annie made herself a pot of tea and cut a slice from the bread they had bought at the *boulangerie* they'd passed on the way to the flat. The woman behind the counter had welcomed Paul back. Annie spread jam thickly. As she waited for the kettle to heat, she searched through her bag for her new phone.

Roger picked up on the first ring. "Thank goodness, I was worried about you."

"I'm having breakfast in Paul's flat."

Roger sucked in air. "I don't like that and it has nothing—I repeat, nothing—to do with jealousy."

"I can do some investigating for you."

"Jesus, Mary and Joseph, that's dangerous."

"You make me feel like I'm in Bluebeard's lair, when in reality I'm having jam, bread and tea. Paul's not here."

"I hope he's not there if you're talking that way," he said. "I suppose as long as you are there, and he isn't, you might as well look around."

"The police chief in you is coming through," she said. She described the flat, adding, "It's old money and class. Certainly

189

higher than *bourgeoisie,* but we knew he went to a *Grand École.*"

"Elite," Roger said. "Nothing new."

Annie sighed. "He has an office. If there's a written contract to kill his brother, it'll be there."

"You don't have to be sarcastic," Roger said.

Annie cradled the phone under her chin as she poured hot water into her teacup. It was a Limoges, so delicate that when she held it to the light, she could see her fingers between the roses decorating the porcelain. There was no rule that a man with a lovely, inherited flat, furnished with excellent taste by his parents and himself, was a murderer who committed fratricide. Or wasn't. There was no correlation.

After hanging up, Annie walked around the flat. Although she didn't own an antique, she'd worked for a small auction house in Geneva for a year. Even working in their computer department, she had learned from the different dealers with whom she'd lunched what made a piece valuable. Although she would never have claimed herself an expert, she suspected that any of the pieces in the living room, from the Orientals on the floor to the heavy oak armoires, would bring in enough money to solve some of Paul's cash-flow problems. Certainly more than enough to fulfill whatever the terms of his divorce and child support settlements were.

On the top floor were six bedrooms, two of which had been the place for the nursery and governess. Another, so tiny she could touch each wall, must have been the maid's quarters. The spacious master bedroom was neat.

Paul was no slob—that was for certain. He had told her that a cleaning woman came in once a week and someone else came in to do the laundry and ironing. Neither was due today. She opened his armoire. He had three suits—black, gray and navy blue—all custom-made, hanging in perfect order. Next to those were casual slacks. A small number of sweaters and shirts were stacked with military precision on shelves. Shoes had shoetrees stuffed in them. There was one *smoking*. Annie loved that French word for tuxedo.

His clothes weren't as plentiful as an American's might have been, but that held no surprise for her. Most Europeans chose their clothes carefully. The majority of her women friends had maybe five to ten outfits maximum, usually of high quality and with great accessories. She wondered if it were childhood training, culture or personality that made both Paul and Père Yves neat.

A book about the former minister of culture, Jack Lange, was next to Paul's bedside. A metal bookmark stuck out in the middle. Do murderers refuse to turn over page corners? The drawer of the nightstand held tissues and a packet of sleeping pills with two of the ten gone. The prescription date was eight months old.

So far all she had learned was that he was extremely neat like his brother and read political books unlike his brother, which she knew from his library downstairs. The library also told her that he had bought books to read, not just display. Again nothing new, for she had seen him a couple of times with a book open in the hotel or sitting in a café. So what if he was a reader: it was hardly the stuff to help in a police investigation.

His bathroom cabinet revealed only aspirin, shaving cream, a razor, an extra pair of glasses, contact lens cleaner and two empty shelves. Under the sink were towels and face cloths, also folded in perfect stacks.

Annie went downstairs to Paul's office. She was a great hacker, but she seldom used this part of her skill set. She turned on his computer, wondering if she could come close to guessing his password. People often chose the name of a loved one, their animals, birth dates. She didn't know enough about Paul to crack those codes, but there was no need.

He had not set up his system to require a password. That made sense since he lived alone. What would he be protecting? Maybe he would have used one if he thought either the cleaning lady or the laundress would go into his files, but she was sure he was enough of a snob to consider hired help not interested in computers. If she were out to sabotage a company, she would have her spies be cleaning people for the top brass of the company. Servants were invisible unless they messed up their work. So were janitors, street cleaners, etc.

Excel was the first software she checked. There were spreadsheets for household expenses and personal tax records but nothing from his business. Word showed letters, a few to his brother, more to his children and one to a woman who lived in Chartres that he had taken to dinner a few times when he was there on business. It seemed like she wanted more than he did, which Annie gleaned from an e-mail where he discouraged her from coming to Paris for a weekend.

Before she could open more of his e-mails she looked up to see Paul standing there. He didn't need to ask what she was doing.

CHAPTER 26
A TRAIN

"Café, coca, biscuits?" The young man, who couldn't have been much more than twenty, pushed the metal cart down the train aisle of the Paris-Toulouse TGV. Outside, wet countryside sped by in a blur. Some brown-spotted cows huddled together in a field. The train cut through the late afternoon gray.

Annie's mood was as gray as the weather. She felt awful. Not that the day had been a total loss. She'd been able to muster herself together and eat with her agent. They had talked until almost five. She'd been given enough work to keep her busy at least until December. A good thing, for she had no energy to do her own historical work.

"Café, coca, biscuits?" The young man stopped in front of Annie, who had made eye contact. She shook her head. Maybe later she'd go to the dining car. It still amazed her that any country as food fanatic as France could have such horrible food on their national trains: dried baguettes with hardened cheese, salads with tired lettuce and tomatoes that probably had never seen the natural light of day but were locked away in some strange building with artificial light.

At least she was fairly sure that they weren't genetically modified artificially, just naturally bad. The French, terrified by the different food scandals in other countries, were determined to keep out mad cow disease, GM foods and any meat with hormones. Trade issues, Britain and the U.S. claimed. Quality, the French responded.

The agent, who had come in from Zurich, had taken her to a great restaurant in the Latin Quarter, but Annie had been in a haze, not noticing the name and only picked at her grilled salmon. Any other time she would have delighted in the atmosphere, with waiters standing at the doors of the different restaurants to entice customers inside. Not that it was necessary. The windows with vegetables and meats arranged as paintings would have been enough. She should have been hungry, but she was still too upset from her confrontation with Paul Bressands.

He had looked at her and asked, "What are you doing?" His tone had been soft and he had annunciated each letter. She could have been frozen in place by his stare.

She swallowed. "I was trying to find out if you had any secrets that might have caused you to have your brother killed." Had he been the real murderer, she knew she would never have said that, but she didn't believe he was guilty. For a second she thought of Angela Lansbury in the series *Arabesque* to the French or *Murder She Wrote* to Americans. At one point in a large number of episodes, Jessica Fletcher, Lansbury's character, would look at the camera very seriously and say, "I think I know who did it." Then she confronted the murderer, who would start to attack her just as the police burst in. There would be no police today. Nor did Annie know who did it, but her instinct told her it wasn't Paul.

He had nodded. "And what do you think?"

"I think I made a huge mistake."

"You did. And now would you please leave."

She didn't move for a moment. "Paul, I'm so sorry, I . . ."

"I don't want you here," he said so softly that she barely heard. Or maybe it was her heart that didn't want to hear. "And if Roger wants to know anything else, have him contact my attorney. He has her number." He turned to stare out the window as she departed. He didn't say good-bye, nor did she.

Annie had grabbed her suitcase and left with as much dignity as a sneak could muster.

The train chugged into Limoges. Several people got off; a few more got on, but overall the train was almost empty.

Annie picked up the French manual, which she was supposed to translate into English, German and Dutch. Her case also contained all the software that she could check if she didn't understand something. She was glad, for the French was written in an even more complicated style than she was used to. Figuring out the software would be a challenge and would keep her mind off the guilt she was feeling.

Of course, she *could* worry about the man that was stalking her by phone, but that didn't really bother her at all. Roger and her dad were taking care of worrying about that. She did have the problem of getting her father out of her nest long enough to begin work. More than once work had been her salvation when her life wasn't going all that well. It would help her get used to the village *sans* Père Yves.

At least her relationship with Roger had seemed to sort itself out. In a way she was glad she would be around for a while. When she had to leave again, that would be the real test.

A man walked by and stared at her. Probably he was in his early forties, a few gray hairs at his temple, jeans, turtleneck, all black. All he needed was a *Gitane* hanging from his lips and a beret to be the stereotypical Frenchman.

"Vous êtes seule?" He put his blue bag into the overhead compartment and sat down. His ticket and reservation stuck out of his pocket. Of course, she was alone. The other three seats were empty of people, coats, magazines or any other paraphernalia. The overhead rack only had one suitcase.

Not an original pick-up line. Annie could see from eyeing his reservation stub that this was not the seat he'd been assigned. The TGV always required reservations. If it were full, it could leave her stuck with a horrible traveling companion. More often than not she enjoyed whoever was her seatmate. Not this time. *"Oui, et je voudrais rester comme ça."* She could brush anyone off in four languages.

He ignored her statement that she wanted to stay alone and tried a few compliments, first on her beauty, then asked her about the materials. *"Je suis un programmer, aussi. Je peux vous aider."*

Annie didn't want to count the number of times men had tried to pick her up on a train. For women who wanted to hunt for men, she should tell them to forget the bars. Ride the TGV, she would say. Many times, she'd met some nice guy on a trip. One she'd dated for several months, until he became too possessive. Having a good man was nice, but being alone was better than having the wrong one around. *"Je n'ai pas besoin de l'aide. Laissez-moi."*

He shrugged, got up and gathered his things and went into the next car. She was alone until she reached Toulouse.

Since she had a two-hour wait for the train to Argelès, she left *Gare Mirabeau* and entered an Italian restaurant she'd eaten at often when she'd had an assignment for Airbus and lived not far from the station. The restaurant had high stools made of almost white wood. It only seated about sixteen people. As she entered, she saw the waitress was new. The one that had been there when she'd been a regular must have quit. What did she expect? Things change. The two women used to talk, but not enough for Annie to make any effort to keep in touch with her. There were a lot of people like that in her life. People came into her life and went out of it. The more she moved around, the more she realized that most of the people she dealt with were temporary. Temporary wasn't bad in itself. However, she wanted some roots. Père Yves had been a root. Her parents were two roots. Roger was growing into a root. Maybe she was a root for Gaëlle.

She ordered tortellini with pesto and a glass of wine. Both tasted identical to the last time she'd eaten there. The chef was probably the same, or had left his recipes. While she waited for *l'addition* to pay, she dialed Roger.

"Where are you?" he asked.

"Toulouse. My train gets in at 23:55."

"I'll meet you."

I don't want you walking through the streets late at night, she imagined him saying.

"I don't want you walking alone this late," he said. "Did you find out anything?"

"I'll tell you about it when I get in." She wasn't ready to talk about how embarrassed she'd been when Paul walked in and she'd been on his computer.

"Your Papa's with me. We had dinner at my place. We'll both meet you."

"Good because I want to go back to my place so I can get an early start on this project in the morning."

"Does that mean I don't get any loving tonight?"

The last thing Annie felt like was sharing a bed. She wanted to be in her own place. Alone.

"I'll give you a rain check. Or checks." Just because she wasn't in the mood today didn't mean that she wouldn't fancy Roger's body tomorrow and the day after and the day after that.

"I really don't want you alone, Annie, and your Papa agrees. I promise to take you back to your place as early as you want, or you can pick up some stuff tonight to take back to my place."

"And I agree." Dave must have grabbed the cell from Roger.

"I give up," she said, too tired to argue.

Walking back to the train station, she wondered what would

have happened had she said to Paul that she just wanted to check her e-mails. Stupid. He had seen she was in Excel.

She thought of all the things that she might have said to him had he let her.

She imagined seeing a trolley rumble over the aboveground tracks outside his window, stopping and discharging passengers.

She imagined seeing him with his head buried in his hands mumbling, "And I'd give my business, this flat and everything else to have my brother back."

"Paul, I am sorry," she would have said.

Maybe he would have forgiven her. More likely he wouldn't have, and anyway it didn't do one damn bit of good imagining other alternatives. What had happened, happened. She couldn't change it or delete it.

From Toulouse to Argelès she cursed herself for playing snoop. Even making up excuses for herself, such as she wanted to double-check for the sake of Père Yves, wouldn't wash. She had the habit of being too honest with herself.

Roger had told there were two kinds of *flics*, those that dealt only with facts and those who relied on feelings and facts. He fell into the later category.

The train pulled into Argelès. As soon as she swung down the three stairs, twenty-seven hours from when she left, she saw her father and Roger standing there. They walked up to her. Her father let Roger kiss her. It was a tender kiss that brushed her lips followed by a long look.

"Glad you're back, *Chérie.*"

Only then did Dave Young come forward and hug his daughter. "Me too." Had there been some unspoken passing of territory, father to daughter, written in the DNA of the male animal?

On the walk back to Annie's flat, she told them what had happened and how badly she felt. The streets of Argelès were deserted. Only one café was still open and its white plastic chairs were in piles and chained to the tree next to its terrace. The tables were behind the glass doors, and the waitress was wiping down the countertop.

The clock at the top of the church bonged twelve times.

"If I'm staying with you, Roger, I need to get some things from my flat," Annie said. Together they walked down the deserted streets.

Dave went to unlock the front door with his key. "I thought I locked it," Dave said.

They walked up the three flights. When Dave went to unlock the next door, it was already open. "I *know* I didn't leave it like that," he said. "I had forgotten to leave the new Keegan book with you. I loved it, your Mom did, too. It was in my backpack when Roger picked me up."

"I waited at the end of the street when he went up," Roger said.

Annie almost gagged. "God! It stinks!"

"Smelled okay when I left," Dave said.

Annie put on the lights and bounded up the steps. On the tile floor she stepped into a huge pile of cow shit or maybe horse shit. She wasn't an expert. Written in the same material on her wall were the words "Git out of town Hore."

"Someone needs a spelling lesson." She fought not to cry at the desecration.

Chapter 27
Argelès-sur-mer

"Shit! Shit! Shit!" Annie stood in the center of the flat and turned trying to take it all in. Finally, she focused on her curtains. The rusty fabric with the gray elephants that she had lovingly sewed onto a quilted backing to keep out the summer heat was smeared with excrement. Her walls that she had just lovingly painted would have to be redone for the same reason. Her refrigerator had handprints of shit. All she could see was devastation. How fast had whoever did this have to work to create so much mess in so little time? A voice cut into her consciousness.

Roger barked into his phone, "I don't care what time it is, get your butt out of bed and over here." He clicked off the phone and shoved it back into its case on his belt.

His voice penetrated through her emotional fog. "I've got to get this cleaned up." She must make everything normal: she didn't care how long it took. This was her nest, the place where she had chosen each thing in it. Some bastard had the nerve to desecrate it. She'd heard how people when robbed felt that they had been violated. She felt violated. She felt furious. Had they stolen anything?

She looked to the most valuable item in her flat. Her computer. She glanced at her desk, and it was there, but the laptop too had shit smeared all over the keys and screen. Damn! She'd have to buy another. This one was only six months old. She hadn't even had time to rub the letters off the keys, which was the fate of all her keyboards. She wore them out faster than new technology made them obsolete. Better that the sons-of-bitches had stolen it. That way at least someone might get some use out of it. And how would she ever get the information out of it? She bent down and looked at the USB port. That was clean. The backup drive was still in her lower right desk drawer, and she'd backed up everything just before she left for the train to go to Paris. Her back-up laptop was in the closet under her shoes, half of which were in the middle of the floor. A tiny, tiny comfort that she still had a working laptop.

Roger put his arms around her. "Annie, you can't clean up until we dust for prints."

Throwing his arm away from her, she started laughing and wanted to sit down, but she wasn't sure of which spot might be clean enough. She couldn't stop. Her laughter continued as she watched her lover and father stare at her.

"She's hysterical," Roger said to Dave.

Annie shook her head and forced herself to inhale deeply until the laughter was replaced by giggles, which she could no more stop than she could make her nest clean by wiggling her nose. Still between rolls, she was able to choke out, "I'm not . . . hysterical . . . think about what you said."

The two men looked at each other.

"Fingerprints," she gulped.

Both men stared at her.

"Fingerprints," she said again, this time without the laughter. They still stared at her.

"Do you really believe whoever did this used his bare hands to handle all this shit?"

"She has a point," Dave said.

As Annie paced the room, hiccups slowly replacing the giggles, Roger followed her. He grabbed her and tried to comfort her, but she pushed him away. "Water."

Dave found a glass that the vandal missed and ran a glass of water after putting on a rubber glove, handed to him by Roger. Annie put a finger in each ear and let her father feed her the water. "It's the Young family cure for hiccups," he said, and before she finished the glass, the spasms had stopped. "You okay?" Dave asked. His face had the same look that it did when she had fallen on a ski slope during a family outing and no one had realized it until she didn't show up. A search party had brought her down, and he had run out to meet her litter.

Dave Young was a father hen, no doubt about it, and most of the time, she was glad to be cloaked in his love, but this time, she had little patience for what she regarded as a really, really stupid question. "Just fine. My nest has become a toilet. I've got to buy a new computer. I've a project I should be working on tomorrow, one of my best friends is dead, I've insulted his brother, but other than that, it's just an average, lovely day."

Before they could answer her, they heard footsteps thumping up the stairs. The door opened. Officer Boulet's head came up the stairs followed by the rest of him. He wasn't in uniform, but wore a pair of black slacks and an off-white cotton knit sweater.

He pulled his handkerchief out of his back pocket and held it over his nose. *"Mon Dieu!"*

"Did you bring the camera?" Roger asked.

"You said nothing about a camera." He stuck his lower lip out.

Pouting in a child was bad enough in a child, Annie thought, but for a man in his thirties, it was even more disagreeable.

"I've my digital camera," she said. She wished she had some paper towels, but her sense of environment kept her from buying paper products, cling film or aluminum foil. It was just as easy to use bowls with plates over them and cheaper too.

She went into the bathroom. The towels hadn't been touched, and she grabbed one to use to open the drawer where her camera was kept. Thank God: it was still there. "Whoever it was didn't believe in robbery," she said.

"Unless you came back too quickly," Boulet said.

"If they heard us coming, there was no place they could go," Dave said. All eyes turned to the skylight that was at the top of the point of the wooden cathedral ceiling.

"If someone used the skylight, how did they get up there? It's at least twelve feet." Annie's comment was greeted by nodding heads.

"Well, maybe someone knew that you two were out eating at *Les Arbres* and Annie was away," Boulet said.

Annie took her camera and started photographing each section of the room. "Too bad we can't photograph the smell. I doubt there's enough *Monsieur Propre* in the world to clean this."

"One thing is for sure, you and your father can't stay here tonight," Roger said.

Boulet took the towel from Annie and used it to move a chair. He put it up against the bathroom door and opened the door in the closet that was built into the wall and pulled down a suitcase. Then he gave the towel to Dave who used it to open a drawer where he'd stashed his things.

"Annie, you want some extra clothes or do you have stuff at Roger's?" Dave asked.

"I want to stay here and clean," Annie said.

"Even if you wanted to, do you have enough of what you need to do it?" Roger asked.

"You use that tone with Gaëlle when you think she's being unreasonable," Annie snapped.

"Precisely," Roger said.

They drove to Roger's in silence. Annie let exhaustion wash over her. Let was the wrong word. She couldn't have stopped it no matter what she did. When they arrived she stomped into the house, ignoring the dog, and stripped as soon as she entered the bathroom where she took a long, long shower. It seemed the smell wouldn't wash away no matter how hard she scrubbed.

While she was washing, Roger had opened the clic-clac, as the sofa bed was affectionately known, for Dave and had given him a sheet and a duvet. Both men waited for their turn in the shower.

Dave knocked on the door, "You'll turn into a prune, Kitten."

Annie turned off the faucet and wrapped herself in a forest green bath sheet. One of Roger's good traits that Annie had always appreciated was that he had the rare ability not often found in men to make a home. He cared that things looked nice, and if he didn't like to do the cleaning himself, he did pick up after himself. And he made sure that there were those little touches, like bath sheets that you could get lost in. She knew his wife hadn't bought them, because he'd said that he and Gaëlle, when they started over down here, had decided to get as much new as they possibly could afford. And besides, they matched the tile. Annie had dated too many men since she left university who would sleep on mattresses rather than go to the trouble of making up a bed. These men had never met an iron.

When she opened the door to her father, he battled his way in through the fog left by the steam from her shower. "I hope there's some hot water left."

"It heats constantly," Annie said. "Towels are warming on the rack behind the screen."

She then went into the next room, which was the toilet. Like most French homes it was separate from the bathroom. Bidets were another civilized thing. She had to hold on to civilized ideas. Her nest, her poor nest, was too small to have a bidet, but some things had to be sacrificed for economic freedom. Right now she'd substitute economic freedom for peace of mind. Or maybe not.

In the bedroom, Roger had stripped to his underwear, waiting his turn in the shower. He had turned down the duvet. "I'd have put a chocolate on the pillow if I thought it would have helped."

Although Annie had not lost any of the outrage she had felt earlier, in these surroundings there was a greater feeling of security. She kissed Roger on the shoulder as she passed him.

Dave knocked on the door. "Bathroom's free, or relatively inexpensive."

Annie groaned. This had been a family joke for as long as she could remember.

"*Merci,*" Roger said. He patted the bed. "Get in, and let me tuck you in."

Under most circumstances, Annie would have bristled at being treated like a little girl. It was almost as if his next offer would be a bedtime story, but after this awful day, it felt good to be babied a little. No, it wasn't this awful day, it was that awful yesterday. The clock said it was 02:37.

Her eyes felt heavy. Although she wanted them to stay open until Roger came to bed, she couldn't.

The next thing she heard was Gaëlle's alarm going off. It wasn't a buzz, but a CD of Patrick Fiori. For a second she wasn't sure where she was or if Paris, Paul, the job and the trashing of her nest had all been a nightmare. Sometimes, when she dreamed, she put together vivid and strange details.

Looking around, she recognized the French windows with light fighting to break through the shutter slats. She heard Gaëlle stirring in the next room.

Roger moved in his sleep, throwing his arm around her, nestling his head into her shoulder.

Her mind began replaying the scene in her nest. "Shit," she

said and shook Roger who opened his eyes without really seeing her. "Boulet did it," she said.

"Huh?" Roger rubbed his eyes then looked up at her. "Did what?"

"My flat. It was him that trashed it."

Roger sat up. "Annie, you're nuts. Boulet is a total screw-up, but why would he do that?"

"He knew that I was away and that you and Dad were eating out and where." Annie knew the room smelled of sleep and mustiness. Roger's breath was also thick, but that was another thing she appreciated about him. Both accepted body odors as being part of life. However, none of his good traits negated the flash of anger she felt when he disregarded what she said.

Roger rubbed his chin stubble. "Half the village knew you were going to Paris. You told one of the *mamies*. Or at least you told me earlier that you told one of them."

She nodded. "I told them."

"And *Les Arbres* is in the middle of the village. There is a picture window. Your father and I were sitting there. We'd debated eating on the terrace, but we knew it would get dark before we finished. Anyone could have seen us." He threw off the duvet and swung his legs over the edge of the bed. "Besides, how could he have gotten a key? The locks weren't jimmied."

She pictured herself in a boxing ring, but instead of gloves, she was throwing out ideas.

Roger stopped halfway to the door. "Were there keys in your bag? The stolen one?"

"No. Mamie Couges has a set." She wasn't going to admit to him the time she'd arrived only to realize that her keys were in Zurich and Père Yves, who'd kept a spare set in case something needed being done in her nest, was away. Shit again. When she'd cleaned out the rectory, her keys hadn't been found. She hadn't even thought to look.

"I'll check with Mamie Couges today to see if she still has them." He left and Annie heard him asking Gaëlle how long she would be in the bathroom. Then she heard him suggest she dry her hair in the bedroom.

"Okay, maybe it wasn't Boulet. After all, why would he do that?" She lay down. She jumped up again and ran into the bathroom. "How did he know where my suitcase was?"

Roger stuck his head out of the shower. "Logic."

"Boulet?" Logic wasn't a word she could associate with the ex-mayor's aggressively stupid son.

"Even a clock set incorrectly is right twice a day." Roger shut the bathroom door.

Annie wasn't convinced, but it wasn't worth fighting about, not because she didn't care, but because she couldn't think of any more arguments to support her theory.

Chapter 28
Argelès-sur-mer

The smell of coffee perking on the gas stove filled Mamie Couges's kitchen. Floor space was almost nonexistent. The room was filled with a stove, refrigerator, sink, table, four kitchen chairs and two stuffed chairs flanking the large window looking out on the street. A fireplace, which for many centuries had been the sole cooking/heating method for the house, dominated one wall. Although logs had been laid with kindling and old copies of *Roussillon Sud*, the local paper, it was still too early in the year for a fire.

A half-dressed doll was propped against the shovel next to the fireplace. Children's trucks were scattered on the stairs leading to the next floor. The kitchen occupied the entire ground floor. Like many of the homes along the street, there was one room per story.

"*J'ai toujours dormi tôt,*" Mamie Couges said. "These old bones need their rest, you know."

She bustled around getting a demitasse with a blue flower that existed only in the artist's mind for Annie. Mamie Couges poured the black liquid into the cup, sloshing some on the faded oilcloth covering the table. "*Non,* I didn't see anything unusual. It isn't like the summer when people are on the street until all hours."

She launched into tales of her grandchildren doing homework, and how some of her friends' grandchildren should follow their example. As she talked, she threw out the dregs of her last cup of coffee and poured fresh. *"Pourquoi tu m'as demandé?"*

Annie debated telling her why she'd asked. Telling her was the same as telling the complete street. Well maybe that was a good thing. People would be watching their neighbors' places more carefully—at least until the novelty wore off. When she finished her story, she took the smallest sip possible of the coffee. Mamie Couges's coffee could be used to remove rust.

"C'est horrible," Mamie Couges said about the story, not the coffee. "The world is changing. Not for the better, I might add." She released a long sigh. "Sometimes, I think I've lived too long."

Annie reached out and patted her veined and age-spotted hand. "I can't imagine Argelès without you. And this street just wouldn't be the same."

Had Mamie Couges's skin been lighter, there would have been a blush. It was no secret that she still took great care with her appearance, making sure that she oiled herself before going to bed. More than once she had offered her own homemade cosmetics to Annie. Of the three *mamies,* her skin was still as wrinkle free as a woman forty years younger. "How'd they get in?"

"By key. Would you mind checking to see if you still have mine?"

"Mon Dieu!" She stood up so fast that she hit the table, knocking over a vase of wildflowers that should have been thrown out a few days before. A two-door cabinet was over the sink and held mismatched dishes and glasses. There were many hooks on the inside of the door, each with a set of keys. Mamie Couges was the key guardian for many of the foreigners on the street and also for a substantial number of locals.

She plucked two keys off a peg revealing a piece of cloth tape with the word *Annie* in Mamie Couges's spindly writing. "These are yours. To my knowledge, they haven't been out of my sight.

No one broke in last night." She frowned, which was unusual. Mamie Couges was the most smiling person Annie had ever met. "I suppose someone could have snuck in when I wasn't looking, I don't always lock my house when I run to the store, but it's hard to think who would do such a thing."

Annie calculated the amount of time it would take for someone to slip in and grab the keys, then go upstairs and trash her place and replace them. It was workable, but not probable. Although the break-in was done at night while her father and Roger were dining at *Les Arbres,* that was when Mamie Couges was home. "Do you lock up when you go to bed?"

"Not always. I can't imagine anyone breaking in to either rape or rob me." Her eyes twinkled. "Although if he were young and handsome, I might show him a trick or two."

The vision of Mamie Couges chasing a rapist around the room frolicked through Annie's mind, and only with willpower was she able to control her smile. "Okay, so no one could have gotten this key." There was the remote possibility that someone could have made a wax print, but that was too remote. The key maker in town only matched blanks to existing keys. They were barely low tech. She looked carefully at the key. No wax in any crevice. The key was as shiny and new as the day she had it made and had given it to the old woman. More likely the key came from the church, for she had given one to Père Yves as well.

"Did you see Gendarme Boulet by any chance last night?"

The old lady made a *pftt,* that dismissive sound with her mouth that the French are so good at. *"Con,"* she said. "I don't see how your sweetheart puts up with him." She thought about it. "I saw him, but I usually see him at least once a day. Poorer I am for it, too."

A knock at the door made both women look up.

Dave Young stuck his head in the door. "I'm looking for my

daughter, and I've found her." He and the old women exchanged cheek kisses, although Dave had to bend down.

Without giving him a choice, Mamie Couges poured another cup of coffee and set it front of Annie's father. "Terrible thing that happened to your daughter's apartment. I hope you'll stay around and protect this girl."

Annie, who only wanted things to be back to normal, said, "Well he does have to get back sooner or later."

Mamie Couges cocked her head, "Later is better, but of course, the handsome Chief can protect you."

"I'd like to think I can protect myself," she said.

"*Pftt,*" Mamie Couges said. "Independence can be carried too far."

Annie and her father loaded up on *Monsieur Propre,* sponges and rubber gloves as they walked around *A Dix Balles,* the store that had a bit of anything and everything for sale. Although they claimed it all cost under ten Euros, there were a few items that cost more. Dave once said the store was the French equivalent of a Vermont General Store, only without the food.

He picked up a pail.

"I've a pail," she said.

"With the amount of work we have ahead of us, we both need a pail."

It pissed Annie off that in her tiny studio she would now have two pails. That she was spending her day doing what she was about to be doing caused the rage that she'd been shoving aside to surface again.

As they entered her desecrated nest, the smell hit her and she held her breath trying not to gag.

"I've just the thing," Dave said. He handed her a mask like a surgeon might wear that covered her nose and mouth. "I got it from the medical center." He took out a bottle and poured a drop of green liquid into it.

Annie slipped it over her nose and opened her eyes wide. Her eyes watered.

"Wintergreen oil. I read somewhere that pathologists use it when they've got a really smelly corpse, although they say they need to smell things like alcohol or almonds. Helps them figure out what the person died of, but they don't have to suffer through the entire autopsy." He then took a second mask, added the oil and slipped it over his nose and mouth. "Whoa! Strong!"

"Better than the other smell," she said.

They'd been working for a good hour when there was a call from outside. Annie stuck her head out the window.

It was the locksmith. "The Chief sent me over to change the locks," he called.

Half of Annie was annoyed that Roger had taken this on himself, and half of her appreciated it being taken off her shoulders. At least he could have discussed it with her. She tossed the keys out the window to the street below. Having locked the door last night and again behind them today gave a wry truth to the saying about rustled horses and barn doors.

When the man, who was about the same age as Annie, entered he started talking through his nose. "What the hell happened? Smells like a damned barn."

She told him. At this point there was no point in hiding anything. "What is my best choice for a new lock, so I don't have to go through this again?"

He listed her choices.

Dave said, "I remember a police lock, when your mom and I were first married. We lived in Roxbury and there were a lot of break-ins."

"What is that?" the locksmith said. "Never heard of it."

Dave took a piece of paper and drew one. "There was a bar that was sealed into the floor and the middle of the inside of the door. It took a key from the outside to release the bar enough to open the door. Someone has to literally break the door down to get in."

The man stared at the sketch. "I could make that for you, Annie. Only problem is that the way your door opens onto stairs." He paused and ran down the steps. "Come here. I think that would make it even stronger. See. We could have the point on the second step." He rapped on the door. "This whole door is flimsy. If I were you, I'd replace it entirely."

"Definitely," Dave said.

Annie sighed. "I don't see why I have to worry about anything. Everyone else can do it for me," she said in English to her father.

"I can get the door for you. In fact, we can go to the store right now if you want. I'll put on a solid lock until I can make that." The locksmith pointed at the sketch.

"You go ahead," Dave said. "I'll keep cleaning."

As they jumped into the locksmith's truck, he said, "Chief Perrin said to change the locks on the front door too. And also to change the grill so no one can put their hands through the window."

"And what about the other owners when they come down and want to let themselves in?"

"You could mail them their keys."

Annie thought of the grouch who spent vacations on the first floor. He'd been in charge of building insurance. When she hadn't paid her share after one week he had sent her second bill with the price of two stamps added to it. He'd hate her changing the locks. She'd only met him a few times, but each time his face had been contorted in annoyance over something. "Good idea," she said. "Go ahead."

By the end of the day, the overpowering smell was lemon

cleaner. The walls, however, were streaked and dingy.

"Needs repainting," Dave said. He was stretched out on a wooden chair. Annie was sitting opposite. They had borrowed a neighbor's car and taken the clic-clac to the dump. It had been a struggle to get the sofa bed down the narrow stairs while holding their breath against the stink. "We could do that tomorrow before you buy a new clic-clac."

Annie knew her father was well aware of how much she wanted her life back to normal. "I had thought of changing the color. Slightly more ice blue. I'm so bored with white." That was about the only thing Annie was bored with. Boredom would be nice right about now.

"I'm going to call Paul. Ask him about the keys that I gave to Père Yves." She didn't care that he had basically told her never to darken his door again. She'd darken his phone.

"Allo," Paul's voice renewed Annie's sense of shame that she'd been snooping, or maybe her shame that she'd been caught snooping, if she were totally honest with herself.

"Don't hang up please, it's important."

There was a long sigh. "It better be."

Annie told him what happened and then asked about the keys.

"The only keys I found were church keys," Paul said. "And Annie, although I'm sorry about your studio, perhaps you can understand what I felt the other day when I . . ."

"Paul, I understood then. I can only apologize from the bottom of my h—"

He hung up on her.

CHAPTER 29
ARGELÈS-SUR-MER

Sylvie Fontaine had moved her office from her home to the old police station that had been renovated after the police moved to their new building just outside the village center. Annie had not yet visited her in the new place and Sylvie's phone call asking her to stop by was a good reason to do so. When she and Hannibal arrived, her raincoat and his fur were soaked.

Sylvie came out of her office, looking especially chic with her black hair cut in a 1920s bob. She always wore long flowing skirts with matching tops and accessorized them with shawl-size scarves and earrings that looked so heavy that Annie expected the *notaire*'s head to fall to her ample chest. Today's were red butterflies and when Annie followed Sylvie into her office, she saw a big butterfly embroidered on her shawl.

"I hate business suits," Sylvie had once said over coffee at *Les Arbres*. "I have my own style, and what I wear has no bearing on my professional ability."

At that moment Annie decided the *notaire* would be worth cultivating as a friend. The only problem was that they were both so often tied up with work that they didn't have the time to get together as much as either of them would have liked.

A Yorkie, about the size of Hannibal's head, ran out from under Sylvie's desk and yapped at the big dog. *"Sois sage,"* Annie said as she imagined the big dog might be considering the little one as a snack. Hannibal looked at her as if to say that he was always good.

"*Tais-toi,* you're a good dog," Sylvie said to her animal. The dog stopped barking. "Once I tell her it is okay, she thinks she has notified me and now that I'm in charge, she is off the hook. I read it in a dog psychology book."

A sniff here and there were followed by dog licks and both animals settled at their respective companions' feet.

"How was Australia?" Annie asked, looking around at the new place. Unlike Sylvie's clothing, her desk, computer and file cabinets were stark. Her diplomas were on the wall. A shelf held law books. Besides the desk with a chair on each side was a small round table in a corner with two directors' chairs. The only feminine touch was a vase of mixed flowers.

"Wonderful. Do you think I now talk like an Aussie? G'day, Mate. Shrimp on the barbie for lunch?" Sylvie spoke in English.

Annie broke into a laugh. "Not unless the Australians are now speaking with sexy French accents. You've got the vocabulary down though."

"The Australian men seemed to like it. *Oh là là.* I've stories to tell."

Annie smiled. Men were always a good topic for the two women. Sylvie had never married, saying she preferred having lovers. They demanded less. Sylvie's mother had been equally vocal about wanting her daughter to marry and settle down. When these discussions came up when the three women were together, Sylvie would look at her mother and ask, "Now what is settled down?"

"Married for security," her mother would say. Then Sylvie would remind her mother that she owned her own home and had a thriving practice.

"But I want grandchildren."

"You've a grand-dog," Sylvie would counter.

Each time Annie was grateful for her own mother's hands-off-the-marriage-and-grandchildren subject. She did not bother to ask if any of the men Sylvie had met had any possibilities of a longer commitment. Even being almost a day's travel away, Sylvie did attract men to the point that had an Aussie showed up in town looking for her, Annie would not have been surprised. "When did you get back?"

Sylvie leaned back in her chair. "Two days ago. I was so shocked about Père Yves."

"Everyone was."

"Is Roger close to an arrest?" Sylvie leaned forward in her chair before Annie could answer. "I hear you two are back together."

"He hasn't a clue," Annie said, feeling a bit disloyal in saying so, but it was the truth. Then she added, "The gossip flows freely and fast."

Sylvie nodded.

"We're working on it. As long as I've got stuff to do here, I think we'll be fine, but when I've another assignment away . . ." She shrugged. "On the phone you said something about a letter."

Sylvie reached into a drawer and brought out a red folder with the corners held by attached elastics. "When I got back this was amongst my mail. It was from Père Yves." She handed it to Annie. "I've left his note to me inside."

Annie undid the elastics and folded back the sides. "There's also a USB key. Have you looked at it?"

"Tempted, but I figured it was private."

The note was scrawled on a Post-it note, unlike his normal handwriting that made Annie claim his true calling should have been a scribe in a medieval monastery. "Maybe I was," he'd answered. The memory and the handwriting made her eyes tear. She wiped them.

"You look like a ghost. Do you want to be alone?" Sylvie asked.

Annie shook her head. "I'm okay. More or less."

"I've read about messages like this in books and seen stuff in the movies, but it's never happened to me before," Sylvie said. "Most of my practice involves house-closings and wills. But here's the note that went with it."

Her eyes bored into Annie. Their intensity made Annie determined not to cry. Then Sylvie excused herself and went into the other room while Annie searched for her glasses.

Dear Sylvie . . .

If anything happens to me (doesn't that sound dramatic?) would you make sure that Annie gets this letter and USB key.

As always,
Père Yves

In the next letter Père Yves's handwriting was normal. Seeing each flourish made it hard to believe that she couldn't just run up to the rectory and talk to him.

Dearest Annie,

Old friend, fellow historian, do I feel silly doing this. I know by this time tomorrow that you'll be home. We'll have talked, and I will have told you all about this, and then I'll really feel stupid. But I have this feeling of foreboding, which you know is nothing like me.

Some strange things have been happening. First, when I went to Rennes-le-Château two weeks ago, I was convinced I was followed, at least until the turn-off up the mountain. Anyone following there would be noticed of course. When I got back I was convinced someone had gone through my papers. Again it was a feeling, I suppose I could have left some of my things out of place, but I doubt it. And there have been too many hang-ups when I answer the phone. I know it could be a parishioner who has decided at the last minute not to confide in me, but again, based solely on feeling, I think someone does not wish me well.

When I began, I was looking for proof that Mary Magdalene had been married to Christ and that she and her children ended up somewhere in southern France. We both know this isn't a new theory. But the more I've traced black Madonnas, the more reading I've done on early texts, the more convinced I've become that it is more than a possibility. All of this would not put me in the Church's good graces. And how many times have you and I tried to tie the black Madonnas to the goddess Isis. And, and, and looking for Roman temples built as they trooped through here, although most places have only been way stations.

We might have done better had we been more focused instead of hopping from one idea to other, but at the same time that made it fun. And in proving theories, you can't discard new evidence, can you?

However, so many people think I'm chasing the treasure along with so many other treasure hunters that my true goals are hidden under all this religious stuff. This isn't deliberate on my part, as you well know, although I've always thought it is better to let people believe what they want about others.

If there's still treasure anywhere, be it the Cathar's, the Knight Templar's or Dagobert's, it really isn't as important as the knowledge of finding out the truth about earlier times, and for me, it is also a question of wanting to be able to believe that what my Church has told me is true.

Ah, there I go, questioning my faith. I did find in reading Pope Benedict XII's papers that he didn't believe in the Virgin birth. He made a very good case as well. I mentioned it to the Bishop, and he told me that I had better be careful what I went around saying.

And faith. How can I, as a Catholic priest, doubt the Bible and the divinity of Christ? I've been so close to leaving the priesthood, but I believe so deeply in the teachings of Christ no matter if he were man or God, and think I can still do good in this world, that I've stayed. I just don't know for how much longer I can stay. Doing good? Maybe I would be better working outside the Church for some charity or . . . ?????

However, I believe we have a major find in Rennes-le-Château. The rest is on the USB key. I know you'll be able to think of the password. It's related to our first trip together.

If you are reading this something has happened to me. Don't grieve for me, for I really did lead a blessed life. Continue with our/your research if not for your own development then to share with the world. I still think you're misplaced and should be a history prof, but that discussion we'll have at another time if there is to be another time. I hope so. Forgive my ramblings. I love you.

Je t'embrasse très fort, je t'aime,
Yves

The "I love you," jolted Annie for a moment, but then she put it into the friendship type of love, the same she felt for him because his collar stopped any other kind. She did not need to be a Catholic to respect the boundaries of the Church.

Not for the first time, Annie wondered if the Church were responsible for the murder because of his discoveries, but she threw out the thought. Too much like a thriller. The Catholic Church didn't go around murdering heretics, much less doubters, in the twenty-first century.

Sylvie had slipped back into the room without Annie hearing. Although Annie didn't ask, the *notaire* handed Annie a tissue from a box hidden in her drawer. Annie blew her nose. Hannibal got up and put his head in her lap. "It's all right, boy," she said, stroking his head. But she knew it wasn't.

"Do you want to use my computer?" Sylvie asked.

Annie inserted the USB key. The request for the password appeared on the screen. Damn it. What could it be? Their first discovery? The first day when she had been walking the area with Père Yves, they'd followed the old Roman road, merely a path now. But everyone knew that was there. Still she put in the words: road, roman, roman road and romanroad. Nothing.

What else had they done? They'd discovered the fireplace in the ruin with the millstone that had come a while later, that even Roger had noticed when she had shown him the village. They'd been drinking a cold beer in a restaurant when Père Yves had said, "Fireplaces are dangerous in mills." Both of them had cried, "Click."

She tried a series of words: well, mill, Christ, Mary. On the fiftieth failure she looked at Sylvie, "I can't keep you longer. I'll do this at home."

"Tell you what," Sylvie said, "Let me treat you to lunch at *Les Arbres*. I haven't been there since I've been back."

Chapter 30
Argelès-sur-Mer

To enter *Les Arbres* it was necessary to take one step down into the wood-paneled dining room. A huge fire was lit in the fireplace. It sizzled as rain dropped down the chimney, adding a second melody to the crackle of the wood.

Only two other patrons were there, ex-mayor Boulet and the Crédit Agricole bank manager, Etienne Pujoc. Two bowls of lightly fermented cider sat in front of them. Boulet's was untouched, but the bank manager's was almost gone. The ex-mayor was hunched toward the bank manager, who sat back in his seat with one arm over the chair back. He appeared to be only half listening.

When Marie-France, the owner, saw Annie and Sylvie standing there with the dogs, she ran up to them with a smile that erased the gloominess of the day. She kissed both women on both cheeks then hugged Sylvie. "When did you get back?" The restaurant owner patted both animals, although the Yorkie tried to insert herself between a caress and Hannibal, just to give Marie-France every chance to make more out of her than the German shepherd.

As Sylvie told her, she ushered them to a table near the fireplace. "Did you take lots of photos?" When Sylvie nodded, Marie-France said, "You'll have to come over and show us on the night we're closed. You too Annie, and bring Roger. Now the season is over, we've a chance to breathe again." She pulled out two chairs and Annie and Sylvie plunked themselves down.

The heat from the fireplace was as welcoming as the owner had been. The dogs, who had trotted in next to them unobtrusively, settled under the table in such a way that each woman had to angle their chairs not to step on them.

Marie-France brought the menus, but Sylvie said, "I've wanted one of your *Norvégiennes* crepes for a while. And cider."

"Make it two."

When Marie-France had left, Annie said, "I've a book for you. The latest Amelie Northrup."

"Is it as good as the one about the Japanese company?"

"Better. Wait here, I'll run and get it. Can I borrow your umbrella?"

Hannibal raised his head as she put on her coat, but when she told him to stay he returned to his spot. It was less than a five-minute walk to Annie's. When she came back, she handed Sylvie the book. "I put it in an envelope so it wouldn't get ruined. Pass it on to your mother when you're through. She'll like it too."

"Thanks, I'll start it tonight. I haven't had a chance to stock up on new books since I've been back. In fact, I'm still jet-lagged."

The door opened creating a breeze and the current Mayor Galy and a man that Annie didn't know walked in.

As the two men walked past Boulet and the banker, the banker almost stood and had his hand half out to greet Galy, but Boulet said, "If it isn't Monsieur Socialist himself. Going to put anyone else in danger next summer by inviting those ruffians back?"

The bank manager set down, a ruddy glow moving across his face.

Galy smiled at the banker, but did not make eye contact with Boulet.

"Not smart to ignore a voter, Galy." Boulet's voice could be described as a snarl.

"I really don't think you would ever vote for me, Boulet," the current mayor said.

Boulet turned his back on Galy and went back to his conversation with the banker.

"And to think our taxes actually paid Boulet's salary for years," Sylvie said.

"If I could vote here, I wouldn't have voted for him," Annie said.

"It's too bad you're not a European citizen, then you could vote in local elections," Sylvie said. "Have you thought of getting a French passport?"

"As long as I don't have to give up my American one, yes, but I always put it off. I could get a Swiss passport too."

"But that's not EU and you couldn't vote here."

"But I could vote in Switzerland. Even though I've sublet my old flat, it's my legal address."

"But if you marry Roger . . ." Sylvie said. "Now tell me all about him, how you got back together, and I'll tell you all about the sexy Australian men I met."

CHAPTER 31
ARGELÈS-SUR-MER

Père Yves had been too devious in his choice of password for the USB key. Annie tried cathar, poulet, champagne, church, blanche, blanchefort, ladyblanchefort, stone, snake, Benedict, inquisition, mountain, triangle, rexmundi, mundirex, salamander, museum, musée, baptism, Isis, Ptah, abbey, Bethany, hautpoul, plague, 5000bc, magdala, tourmagdala, towermagdala, magdalatower, marie, Bérenger, Saunière, Bérenger-Saunière, entrecote, fitouwine, fitou, wine, mousse, chocolate, chocolatemousse, frites, ketchup, stream, poissonrouge.

But it wasn't the woman who was the descendent of those that had allegedly brought Christ's descendent to Rennes-le-Château. And it wasn't the ugly statue of Rex Mundi in the church, and it wasn't anything to do with their lunch, or the salamander on top of Rex Mundi where the Virgin rested her foot in the Rennes-le-Château church.

By the time she had tried every bloody word she could think of associated with their visits to the mountaintop village—almost one hundred by her estimate—Annie was so frustrated that she threw her pen across the room. It bounced and hit the sleeping Hannibal on the head. He woke with a start.

She got up to rub his head. "I'm sorry, *mon chien*. Too bad you can't talk. Maybe you could help me with that damned password." On the top of her fridge was an open box of dog biscuits that she'd bought at the corner grocery on her way back from *Les Arbres*. The dog accepted one as an apology, returned to the couch, scoffed it down, put his head on his paws and closed his eyes.

Annie couldn't decide whether to go back to work or to try more passwords, except she couldn't think of any more. She'd racked her brain to remember every minute that she'd spent with Père Yves those first days, trying bits of conversations, things they saw, things they discussed, things they ate. Every time she picked up her document to translate, another idea came and she'd switch windows from her hard drive to the USB key. If Père Yves were alive now, she'd kill him for putting her through this.

It was getting dark. She snapped on several lights and made herself a cup of tea. As she drank it, she paced around the room. "I'm bouncing around too much. I need to think of one thing and try and eliminate it," she said to the dog who opened one eye.

January241917, January24, 012417, 01241917, 19170124. As many combinations of the Rennes-le-Château's priest Bérenger Saunière's death date that she tried, none worked. At least there wasn't a limit on the number of times she could try before she'd be locked out. It wasn't like an ATM card in that respect. However, she didn't feel grateful for that small favor.

Her phone rang.

"Hi, love of my life," Roger said.

"I love you too," she said. The words slipped out. Funny how once she'd made such a big thing of saying them. "When are you finishing up?"

"I'll be off about seven. You and Hannibal want to meet me at the *gendarmerie?*"

Annie had glanced out the window. The rain had stopped. Over the roofs she could see the moon beginning its nightly climb. "Sure. I'll stop at the grocery and pick up something for supper. Any preferences? Speak now or forever hold your peace."

"Piece of what? Bacon, you?"

"Consider I've stuck my tongue out at you. Okay, you'll get what I feel like cooking, and I won't know that until I see it."

She finished her tea. January 17, 1781, was the next date she tried in all combinations. That was the day the Marchioness of Hautpoul died. She allegedly had given documents to Père Antoine Bigou of Rennes-le-Château and those were what Père Bérenger Saunière allegedly had found that led him to the alleged treasure. Alleged, alleged, alleged. Nothing was certain except that January 17 was the date of several important happenings in the village. They'd talked about it for a long time the first day and thereafter, but that still wasn't the lost password.

What had she been thinking? She was using English. She tried all the dates with *janvier*. Nothing. She rummaged through her photos and found one that she'd taken of Père Yves on their first visit to Rennes-le-Château standing in front of the mill. "If you were alive, I'd curse you," she said to the priest's face. He'd been squinting into the sun. Squint wasn't the password either. "I always thought we were on the exact same track, that we could read each other's thoughts about this stuff. I was wrong."

She took out the photos of the Stations of the Cross that they had taken that day. Père Yves had pointed out they ran in the opposite direction to normal. Not being a Catholic, she hadn't noticed. She retried every password backwards.

In a *pique* she pulled the USB key from her laptop. She'd try again later on Gaëlle's computer.

"*On y va*," she said to the dog, who grabbed the leash in his mouth.

Annie stopped at the grocery store on the corner. It was tiny and dark inside with a refrigerated counter for fresh cheeses and a small selection of sausages, but outside on the sidewalk were fresh vegetables, almost all from the region—a perfect night for vegetable soup. She bought onions, carrots, celery, parsnips and a turnip and the last of the fresh figs for the season and the first of the kaki fruits. Inside she grabbed a can of beans and tomato juice to use as a base for the soup. She knew there was macaroni in Roger's cupboard.

At Martinez's she picked up a baguette. "Last of the last batch of the day," Gabriel Martinez said to her as he wrapped a piece of paper around the bread. This late they were no longer warm from the oven.

As they headed toward the *gendarmerie,* they had to pass Sylvie's office in the old police station. Hannibal stopped, whined. No matter how she pulled, he refused to budge.

"You just want to see your tiny girlfriend, who is much too small for you?" Annie asked. "Not now." She pulled on his lead, but he pulled her toward the door. This was strange behavior for the dog. Annie decided it would be faster to let him see what he wanted. However, he walked past the old police station and going around the building he sniffed under the bush that backed up to the wall of the building.

Annie looked. Trembling, as far back as possible beneath the shrubbery, was Sylvie's Yorkie. First, Annie patted Hannibal then she called the small dog that just looked at her and shook more, if that were possible. "Shit," Annie said. She put her groceries and briefcase on the ground. Scooching down so she was resting on her heels, she made her way under the bush. Water dripped from the leaves, making little icy attacks on the bare skin of her neck. A branch scratched her face.

The little dog continued to cower out of reach. There was no choice but to get down on her hands and knees and crawl to the dog. The knees of her jeans were soaked through in seconds. The dog didn't fight her, just snuggled against Annie's jacket, turning it muddy. The trembles went through the material.

As Annie walked toward Sylvie's, the dog in one arm, Hannibal by her side, she tried to balance her shopping and briefcase as best as possible. By now she was under a street lamp and could see her hands that were filthy from her crawl and what had come from the poor dog. The color was red not brown, blood not dirt.

"What is it, sweetheart? You weren't hit by a car, were you?" There was a waist-high stone wall around the house they were passing, and Annie put the dog on the wall to take a better look at her. Her muzzle was bloody. She ran her hands over the dog's tiny body. She didn't whimper or wince. Nothing seemed broken. "We'll get you back to Sylvie and let her take care of you, okay?"

Sylvie's front door was slightly ajar. The receptionist only worked mornings. Sylvie kept her practice as streamlined as possible. The Yorkie whimpered as they walked up the steps. Annie pushed the door open and called out.

There was no answer. An unlocked door wasn't that unusual out of tourist season. Especially for a business that had clients coming in and out. Nor would it be unusual for Sylvie to dash out for a package of cigarettes or the newspaper and forget to lock the door. In her work, the woman was orderly. In her private life, scattered. Schizophrenic, but in a good sense, Sylvie had described herself.

Annie took a seat in the waiting room, still holding the little dog and making soothing sounds, yet the pooch kept whimpering. Hannibal, ignoring the command to sit, pushed the door to Sylvie's office open with his nose. From her position Annie could see her friend's feet and legs splayed on the rug in front of the desk. She dropped the Yorkie onto the chair and rushed in.

Blood was spattered everywhere: on the papers, the desk, wallpaper, carpet. Nothing in the office was in place. Either the place had been ransacked or Sylvie had put up a great battle. Or both.

Annie knew that Sylvie was dead: she was face-down on the carpet. Hoping for a miracle, she put her two fingers under her neck to where there should have been a pulse.

"Hannibal, no." She ordered the dog to stop sniffing the body. "Let's get out of here."

Outside she dialed the police station.

Chapter 32
Rennes-le-Château

I didn't go to Yves's funeral. I never go to funerals, but I try to be there for the mourners after others have gone back to their daily lives. When she was alive, my grandmother chided me, "Miriam," she'd say with that frown that said she was unhappy with a child, "you have to do what people expect."

Well I didn't then, and I don't now. That doesn't mean I don't care about those that are in pain for losing someone they loved. I am the one who helps mourners pack up the clothes of their deceased family members and invites the survivors to dinner when others no longer want to be bothered, especially with widows.

Wives feel threatened by the widow as if she were ready to pounce on their husbands. It is my experience that it is usually the husbands who go after the widows or divorcées. When Michel and I broke up, I had many offers from husbands of friends. Needless to say, I never took them up on it.

Because there were so few tourists, I did not bother to open the shop the day of the funeral. I found myself hiking down to where Yves thought there might be the remains of a Roman temple.

He wasn't totally crazy. In the name of all the gods and goddesses, people have been living here for over fifty thousand years. When I was little, a strange grave had been opened, and archeologists from the University of Toulouse came out and told us how old the bones were and they went back well before the Romans. Later when I was at the University I had coffee with the professor who came, although he didn't remember me. And every now and then someone turns up a Roman coin or an artifact belonging to some unidentified era.

Which brings me back on how to deal with Sebastian and his bloody documentary: he just wants to deal with Saunière and the effect he had on the town, but there is so much more here. If I were being totally selfish, I would encourage him to go deeper, turn the town into a dig, which would bring lots of business but ruin the soul of the village. I am not that selfish.

When I stand on the spot that Yves thinks is the source of the temple, I don't feel anything at all, not a vibe, not a shiver. It is down on Perez's land. His family was originally from Catalonia a couple of centuries back, thus some of the villagers still think of them as newcomers. His land was rich, and he farmed it well. He is now in a nursing home. His son works in Paris and at one point hired guards to keep people off the land. Who can blame him really, when they came with shovels and pick axes and dug just to dig in the hopes of finding a long-lost treasure.

How stupid!

Land that was farmed has been turned over hundreds and hundreds of times over the centuries and would have given up treasure long ago, but the older I get, the more I realize that people are not all that intelligent. Even the supposedly smart ones.

Then there was the painting of the tomb that resembled a tomb on the land that was supposed to be painted by one of the masters in the secret society of Sion, or something like that. With everyone stomping around taking pictures, young Perez had the tomb opened. There was nothing in it, so he had a workman take a drill to it and scatter the stones. Thus fewer tourists went down there, but if I had a Euro for each one who asked me where it went, I could close up business and retire.

From where I am standing I can look up on the rock-strewn hill with the village perched on top. I can see the houses of my neighbors. My house is across the street from the second yellow one, but invisible. The first yellow house is blocking the view of mine.

The wind is less strong down here in the valley. I pick my way up. I've been doing a lot of climbing up and down hills and mountains for an old lady these past couple of years, which brings my thoughts back to Yves.

I feel sorry that he was never able to express his love for Annie to her. Oh yes, he loved her all right. How do I know? Besides it was obvious to anyone who looked closely and didn't think of him as a priest? And he told me he was, merely confirming what I already knew.

Annie wasn't with him when he showed up that July. I think she was in Zurich or Geneva, but I'm not sure. During the summer, he seldom came to research this or that. Too many people. Tourist season was in full swing, but he had visited me for the sake of visiting me.

I had closed the shop about eight. Because it was early July, not more than three weeks after the summer solstice, there was light until almost ten. He had arrived at the shop, gone upstairs to my kitchen and prepared a big salad filled with all kinds of summer vegetables for me. We took it to the tiny courtyard behind my house. I had bricked it over and along the sides were flowers that didn't mind the shade that made it cool even on the hottest summer days.

There were four metal chairs with cushions and a small filigreed circle table where Yves had put the salad bowl, a multigrain baguette and cheeses he had brought from Argelès and a bottle of rosé. Between the food, wine and dishes only a small patch of the ironwork of the table was visible.

He planned to stay over. My clic-clac opens into a double

bed. Yves was the ideal guest, although he was more family than guest. Each morning he returned the clic-clac to couch status. He even brought a sleeping bag so I would not have to wash sheets. What more could an aunt want?

We sat in the courtyard. Yves reached for the knife to cut us more bread. His knife stopped in mid-air. "I love her."

I didn't have to ask who. "I know."

"You know?" He sat back in his chair, the knife in one hand, the baguette in the other.

"Of course. It shows on your face when you look at her."

"Do you think she knows?"

"Annie may be a smart woman, but I don't think she has a clue how you feel other than friendship. That collar of yours, even when it isn't on, like tonight, is as much of a barrier for her as if you were gay."

He cocked his head.

"Women mark certain men off-limits and that opens the way for friendship in the same way they have women friends."

"*Merde.*"

"Were you planning to tell her?"

"*Jamais*, never."

I wanted to ask him if he left the church would he pursue her, but when he stood up and walked over to the rear wall and stood there for a long time, still holding the knife and baguette, I let him be with his thoughts. When he came back, he finished cutting the bread and said, "Do you want more brie or the *chèvre* with *feneguk*?" as if the earlier words were never spoken.

In my heart of hearts I would love to have had them become a couple. I'm a romantic, I know, and even if I'm cynical about couples in general, I would like to believe that someone, somewhere could live happily ever after. But in this case Yves isn't living at all, and although I haven't gone to the funeral, I still mourn him.

Annie never knew how he felt.

There was one more time it came up. When was it? About a year ago. He had come up by himself. Annie, I think was working in Amsterdam at the time. It was close to the winter solstice. I had brought in my Christmas tree. I see it as a way of keeping the sun alive, a symbol of hope that after the shortest day, the sun will see fit to slowly increase its blessings on the earth so we may once again grow food. I never bought an artificial tree. Can you imagine a pagan discovering plastic trees?

I always decorated it with nuts, strings of berries, popcorn and cookies. Pagans of olden times I doubt baked cookies or popped corn because corn came from the new world, but I suspect if they could have, they would have. Besides, each civilization adds its own stamp to the past.

I had roasted chestnuts for myself to eat for lunch and had some leftover *cassoulet* that I planned to reheat when Yves knocked at my door. He stamped the snow off his boots before entering.

I mulled some wine and invited him to eat with me and it popped out of my mouth, "So what are you going to do about your love for Annie?"

He had been about to take a sip of the wine and he held the mug in both hands. "Why are you bringing that up now?"

"Because I know you want to talk about it, and I'm the only one you can talk with."

"You deny it, but you *are* a witch, albeit a white one," he said.

I let the silence hang. No, that's not true. It was not totally silent. I had a fire going in the fireplace and there was a crackle and a thud as one of the logs shifted when the one under it had burned to a point that it could no longer support the weight of the log above.

Yves was a bit like that. He could no longer support the

secret of his love and we spent the afternoon discussing his feelings. We both knew when he went to leave to drive back to Argelès that we would pretend the conversation had never happened. He would never tell Annie how he felt, nor would I. After he had wound the scarf around his neck, buttoned his coat, put on his hat and gloves, Yves leaned over and kissed me on both cheeks, but he hesitated then whispered, although there was no one around to hear, "I feel better that someone knows, that I can talk to someone about it."

He was right. Sharing means a person is no longer alone. Sharing with a trusted friend is also safe, and his secret would stay safe with me, but now that he is dead, I wonder if Annie should be told. Maybe not, it might make the loss of her good friend harder, and Yves wouldn't want that. I need to think about it, because words spoken can never be taken back.

Chapter 33
Argelès-sur-mer

The windows of the cruiser were steamed up. Although the rain had stopped, Annie's, Hannibal's and the Yorkie's breath fogged up the windows so that all the passing headlights, street lights and lamps in windows were surreal. The little dog had fallen asleep, curled into a ball in Annie's lap.

Annie rolled down the window and looked toward Sylvie's office. She couldn't make out who the three policemen standing in front of the door were, but she knew they were Roger, Boulet and Gault. They were all about the same size and weight and had their backs to her as they kept shifting their weight from one foot to another, blowing on their hands. The light over the door had been broken and the streetlight was too far away to illuminate their faces as they turned around. She could hear them talking though.

"Come on, Patron," Boulet said, not for the first time.

"No one goes in until the medical examiner arrives," Roger said.

"*Oui*, but he's coming from Montpellier. That will take at least another hour. More, maybe, with the rain and traffic."

"Not my fault the guy in Perpignan wasn't available. We wait," Roger said. He walked over to the cruiser and got in, turned on the engine and let the defroster clear the windows. "And frankly, I'm glad he was busy. The local guy is incompetent." Boulet and Gault got into the back seat, pushing the dogs aside.

"Montepellier is better?" Annie asked.

"He could write the definitive book on investigating murder scenes. Only because of his wife's family is he down here. They want him in Paris." He scratched Hannibal's ears. The dog had rested his head in the middle between Annie and Roger. "How's the little one doing?"

"I still wish you'd let me take her to the vet. She might be hurt."

"She's evidence. The blood on her could be hers, Sylvie's or the murderer's. Call Gaëlle and tell her we'll be late."

"I already did." As if fate were on her on side she glanced at the rearview mirror to see the new vet, Dr. Joseph Bournet, walking toward the car. She pointed him out to Roger. "Let me ask the vet to look at her here."

Roger followed her finger. "As long as he doesn't try and get rid of any of the blood."

"And fingerprints?" Annie asked.

"You don't need to be sarcastic," he said.

"I'm sorry," she said. She really hadn't meant to be nasty, but she couldn't stop trembling. She wanted to do something to help her friend, but it was too late. The only thing left was to help the dog.

The vet carried a bottle of wine and a bouquet of flowers with the petals pointing to the ground. Annie had always noticed that Americans carry flowers up, but the French carried them blossoms down. Stupid thing to think of at the moment, but carrying flowers was so nice and normal. Murdered friends were neither nice nor normal. As the vet slowed as he got closer to the cruiser, she said, "Dr. Bournet, over here."

At first he looked around trying to identify where the voice was coming from. At the moment no one was on the street. Roger opened the car door so the overhead light would go on. When the vet spotted it, he came over or rather he loped over. If the word *lanky* hadn't existed it would have been invented for the young veterinarian. *"Qu'est ce que c'est?"* His head tilted toward the policemen.

"Sylvie Fontaine was murdered a short while ago; we're waiting for the medical examiner," Roger said.

"Mon Dieu!" the vet said.

Annie explained about finding the Yorkie. "I want to make sure she isn't hurt."

"Chou-Chou," he said, reaching for the dog.

The dog stood in Annie's lap and wagged her tail as he patted her.

"We're old friends." The vet walked around the cruiser. When Roger vacated the driver's side, he got in. He handed his wine and flowers to the two *flics* in the back. "Hello, Hannibal." The shepherd, wedged between Boulet and Gault, wagged his tail and nuzzled the vet against his ear.

Annie began to believe the rumors she'd heard about him. A regular Dr. Doolittle was the word on the street. Stories abounded about his care and saving of all kinds of animals, a parrot with a cold, a dog hit by a car, another with a heart condition that was approaching Methuselah in dog years kept alive by the vet's potions and will power. And although he was far from good-looking, Annie knew that more than one Argelès woman plotted how to end his single status. All this in the six months he'd been practicing in town.

"Viens, Chou-Chou." The small dog came. The vet opened the door enough so that the overhead light would stay on. He ran his hands up and down the small animal's body. When he came to her ribs, she moaned slightly. "Could be a bruised or cracked rib. I'd need an X-ray, but she doesn't seem in that much pain. And we all know you're a real actress when you want to make us think you're suffering, don't we, Chou-Chou?" He pried open her mouth and stuck his finger toward the back of her throat. The small dog struggled and gagged. The vet

smelled his fingers then wiped them on a handkerchief. "No internal bleeding. Can you bring her in tomorrow? No charge, since she's not yours."

"Guess you're an orphan," Annie said to the dog as she took her back from the vet. "I'll keep her until I talk to Sylvie's mother. She may want her."

The medical examiner arrived. Annie watched fascinated as the man dressed in what looked like a space alien suit went into the office. The policemen waited outside. Annie so wanted to be inside watching, not her poor dead friend, but to see the procedures. For her friend she wished she could be taken away and properly laid to rest. Tears welled up in her eyes. Why hadn't she cried before? Too shocked probably. Just as she was blowing her nose, Roger came over.

"I need the dog for the examiner, but I'll bring her home tonight. Meanwhile, I'm going to have Gault run you to my place. I don't want Gaëlle alone any longer."

Annie agreed. She'd had enough.

Enough death.

Enough cruelty.

Enough mysteries.

In fact, she had had too much. All she wanted was a hot shower and to slip into bed. Although she knew she couldn't sleep the evil in the world away, she wanted to try if only for a few hours.

Chapter 34
Argelès-sur-mer

Gaëlle's head was cradled on her arms. All that Annie could see was hair making a blue fan. The kitchen table shook from her sobs. Annie started to stroke her, but her hand hovered just above the teenager's head.

Annie wondered what had brought on such a reaction. Gaëlle had barely known Sylvie. The three of them had never gone anywhere together, and in fact, the only contact Annie remembered was when they'd been in Martinez's for hot chocolate and she'd introduced them. Gaëlle had said how pretty and chic Sylvie was. Nothing more.

How Annie wished she'd waited until Roger could have told the girl, but Gaëlle had wanted to know why her father was late. Honesty was the only way Annie had ever dealt with her, and although the alternative might have been more peaceful short term, long term, it wasn't the way she wanted their relationship to work. And besides, who could have predicted this devastation over an almost stranger.

Comfort was needed, but Annie wasn't sure how to give it. Even if she had been the girl's natural mother, she was sure she would be confused. Mothers of enough teenagers had confided in her that they didn't have any idea what was going on in their children's heads.

Annie tried to think back to when she was that age. How could she compare? No one had been murdered in her life until she was an adult. Lord knows, she was having enough difficulty dealing with two violent deaths, and this was Gaëlle's third, the first being her mother. That was it. Sylvie's death had triggered feelings left over from her mother's murder. All Annie could do was to pull up a chair, throw her arm over the weeping girl and wait it out.

Several minutes went by before the sobs slowed. They were replaced by hiccups and sniffles. Annie got a glass of water and held it as Gaëlle blocked both ears. As Annie fed her the water, Gaëlle drank deeply. When Annie lowered the glass, the hiccups were gone.

Gaëlle's face was red and tear-streaked. The mascara she was forbidden to wear outside the house had streaked, transforming her pretty face into something that would have looked good if she had been part of the rock group Kiss.

As always Annie was tissue-less, but she pulled a paper towel from the rack and gently patted the girl's cheeks. Gaëlle's skin had to hurt; her eyes had to hurt.

"There's been too many. Just too many. I don't understand why." Gaëlle's voice was hoarse. She followed the words by a sigh that even hurt Annie.

Annie nodded. Although she hadn't known the girl's mother, Roger had said often enough that she'd been a great mom. And then Gaëlle had a good relationship with the priest. As far as Annie knew, the teenager had never cried for Père Yves.

She knew the girl had been one of the kids he'd taken on nature hikes. Gaëlle had frequented the hall behind the altar that the priest had turned into a room where they could come on Saturdays and Sundays to hang out. He was quick to show a kid how to hit a good tennis shot, ride a horse or anything else that the kid might be interested in. He'd even set up a computer center and gave basic lessons in how to use it. He convinced the one programmer in the village to give programming lessons to those kids who were interested. Gaëlle was one of them. The girl even had the priest intercede once with her father when she'd thought him too strict. Roger had listened, and modified his edict only slightly, but Gaëlle had been content.

Hannibal came over and stood between them, then dropped his head on Gaëlle's lap. He looked from one human to another as if they could explain what was going on and then he would know how to act. Gaëlle patted him without appearing to be aware she was doing so.

Annie drew in a deep breath. She needed to find the words to help. Normal adolescent angst she could handle. Pimples, a boy ignoring her, or worse, talking to another girl—all that she could deal with, no sweat. All those things she'd suffered. Even the alleged unfairness of a strict father, and she would be able to find the right words or to plot a strategy to solve the problem. But three murders before the age of fourteen, no, that she couldn't do much about. She didn't even have the words to come to grips with Père Yves's death for herself. Sylvie, she'd have to wait, for Annie knew that she was on overload. Too much had happened in the two and a half months she'd been back. She wondered what Gaëlle would do if she broke down and cried until she ran out of tears and pain as she wanted to. No, she was the adult. She'd put her pain on hold.

If she told Gaëlle that of course she knew how she felt, she would insult the girl. And in fact, she didn't know how Gaëlle felt. Annie's mother was still alive and healthy, ready for a chat whenever Annie picked up the phone or connected to the computer. No telephone lines were strung to where Gaëlle's mother was.

Gaëlle folded her hands in her lap. Annie took them in hers. Their eyes met.

"I don't want to hear life isn't fair. I want it to be fair."

"I wasn't going to say that." Annie looked at the girl. "Okay, I was going to say that. But it would have been the wrong thing to say, even if it is true." She reached over to brush the hair away from where it was plastered by the tears Annie had failed to wipe away. The short points on top, contrasting with the long strands, were wilder than ever. "Look Gaëlle, I'm not very good at this. I do know I love you, and what you've experienced makes me mad."

Gaëlle cocked her head. "Why mad?"

"Because it isn't right." She deliberately chose a word different from fair. "Someone as nice and sweet and brave as you shouldn't have had to experience your *maman*'s death in any form, much less how it happened. Your papa told me she was really a good mother, and I don't believe he was idolizing her after losing her."

The teenager nodded several times. "She was the type who played with me a lot. We did lots of things together even though she worked."

"Part time, though."

Gaëlle smiled. "Part time. She said she'd rather have less money and not be stressed out like lots of her friends were when they worked full time and tried to run a house and take care of the kids. Papa was away a lot at work."

The story was the same as Roger had told her. Annie knew that with all his heart he was trying to fill the hole that his wife had left in both their lives, but more than once he admitted he didn't have the knack to see the world through Gaëlle's eyes. More than once Annie had to explain how his daughter was thinking. At the end of the conversations they would all agree that it was not his fault because he'd never been a teenage girl. Annie and Gaëlle had the advantage of having a similar hormonal structure that saw the world the same way.

"You still miss her." Maybe not the best thing to say.

Gaëlle's eyes filled, but she brushed the tears away with the back of her hand. "That doesn't mean I don't love you."

"Of course it doesn't. When I was little I used to think you only had so much love to give, but now, I know the more you give, the more you have." Not bad, Annie thought. She could tell it worked because no more tears came. This girl could have been her daughter, had she been a teenage mother. Boy would she have been unprepared. And at thirty-three she felt no more ready than she would have been at nineteen. Ready wasn't important. Gaëlle needed her now. "Besides, I'm not a mother replacement. We have a different relationship where sometimes I act as a mother, but mostly I act as an older friend. Everyone needs one of those, even if their mother is still alive."

"Really? Did you have one?"

"Yup, a neighbor that was also my mother's good friend. That was after we moved to Geneva. I could often tell her things I couldn't tell my own mother."

"Wouldn't she have understood?"

"I think the problem was that Mom would have understood all too well, and I was at the stage I didn't want understanding from her. I wanted to blame her. My Dad too."

"I don't think I would have ever felt that way about my mother," Gaëlle said.

"As much as I don't want to tell you how you would or wouldn't have felt, I've never known a teenager who hasn't wanted to rebel against their parents at some point. It's part of growing up."

"I suppose then I'm mad that I didn't get the chance to be angry at my mother. Or afraid by being angry, I was somehow responsible for her murder. In some strange way I willed fate to kill her."

"I don't understand."

There was a long silence. The girl stood up and went to the refrigerator and poured a glass of water. She held the bottle up offering it to Annie, who shook her head. The girl sat back down, the glass between her hands. She didn't drink any.

Annie said nothing, letting the silence talk.

"I've never told anyone this." Her eyes did not meet Annie's.

Annie turned Gaëlle's chin so they were eye to eye. "You know anything you tell me, I'll keep as a secret."

Gaëlle nodded. "The day before she was shot, we had a big fight. She wanted me to clean my room. She called it a pigsty."

"Mothers often call kids' rooms pigsties. They're experts on them," Annie said. I shouldn't have said anything, she thought. Now she'll shut up and won't tell me the rest of the story. She needs a prompt. "And . . ."

"I was being a real brat. I slammed the door to my room and told her I wished she were dead." She looked away from Annie. "And the next day . . . she . . . was . . ." The sobs burst through again.

Annie gathered the child into her arms, rocking her back and forth. Finally, they stopped.

"Did you ever tell your father that?"

Gaëlle shook her head violently on that. "He wouldn't have understood."

"Congratulations. You are now an official teenager with a parent that doesn't understand."

Gaëlle laughed. Then she got very serious. "I couldn't help feeling like I killed her."

"That's normal again. A lot of kids take responsibility for things about which they are innocent. Unfortunately, they also refuse to take responsibility for some of the things they should, like a clean room and good grades."

Gaëlle looked at Annie.

What next, she thought. "You didn't kill your *maman*. The man with the gun did. I hate to burst your bubble, but you aren't that powerful."

That brought another smile. "I suppose I know it in my head, but . . ."

"But in your heart you've your doubts."

Again the teenager nodded. "You know what scares me?"

"No, tell me."

"That Papa or you'll get murdered next. I don't think I could handle any more." Instead of saying anything, Annie gathered the girl into her arms and rocked her back and forth as if she were a baby.

CHAPTER 35
RENNES-LE-CHÂTEAU

Sebastian called on my cell. My ex must have given him the number, because I give it out to very few people and Sebastian definitely wasn't one of them. "What do you think?" he asked me. "Do we have a deal?"

I let the silence hang.

"Can't you just picture this little girl staring around a bush, watching the bitch burn money? We would pay you for the information, even let you work with the writers to make sure your grandmother is properly represented." This phrase had almost become his mantra, but each time he said it as if it were the first. How stupid did he think I was????

Yet each time he called he sweetened the offer. He had gone from saccharine, to sugar, to honey and was working his way up to chocolate. I wasn't playing hard to get, I had been in a state of shock since Annie had called me back to tell me Yves had been murdered. The first time she had just said he was dead. Murdered? My first thought had been that it was suicide or an accident, only because he seemed to be in such good health. The suicide thought only lasted a few seconds. I knew he wouldn't kill himself. I have a sixth sense for people who are suicidal. I've been right at least four times, starting with my roommate when I was at university.

I knew my nephew was upset about losing his faith, which he had talked to me about time after time, when he was looking for something that might prove there was a Roman temple buried below the town. He was tracking down old documents at various museums, and right before he died, he had called me to tell me about the aerial photo that showed what might be the outline of a building. He was going to come back with Annie as soon as she got back from her assignment in Switzerland.

Annie and I had a good cry.

When I hung up I sat in the chair for a long, long time.

A stout, older man came to the store. He spoke with a heavy Catalan accent, but that wasn't so surprising. Many of the treasure hunters are Catalan. There are some people whom I take to immediately, like the priest, like Annie, and even my ex. Most of the time my first impressions are right.

Much has been written about auras, that a witch or a sensitive can see colors around people and get an idea of their character. However, I can never remember what color is supposed to represent what. Although I thought it was a load of you know what, when a client asks me I always direct them to one of the books I sell on the subject. "How can I cover all that is in this book in such a short time?" I say, holding it out. Then there is a bit of information on the back cover that jogs my memory, and I say, "But I can tell you . . ." If they are really interested, they will buy it. I usually start to put it back on the shelf, so they won't feel pressured. Most often they will take the book and thumb through it. About half will buy it.

Some will ask if I can read auras, and of course I say no. I'm not in business to cheat people, but I do imagine from time to time making up stories.

However, this man did have an aura. It was as if there was a dark cloud hanging over him. At first I thought it was just because he was standing in the one spot in the store where the track lighting didn't shine, but as he moved toward the counter where I was sitting, there still seemed to be darkness surrounding him.

Ptah had entered the store as he often does. I don't like him in here because he likes to sit in the window and he often knocks over some of the books and incense burners to make himself comfortable. Still, people come in to see him; however, I've never been able to find a correlation between those who come in to ask about the cat and those that turn into actual customers.

Ptah looked at the man and his fur stood up, although not as much as when a dog comes into the store. It would be too melodramatic to say he hissed, and Ptah is able to get out a very reliable hiss if it suits him. I felt his tension in the same way I could feel when he was hungry or happy. I read cat body language. I don't know if there is any such thing as a cat whisperer, but I'm probably close.

"May I help you?" I asked and he said that he was merely browsing, perhaps trying to find something for his daughter. It was then I could hear the thick Catalan accent. Ordinarily I might have asked him where he was from, but I just didn't like him enough to do so.

"Have you been here long?" he asked.

"About twelve years."

"I imagine there are a lot of treasure hunters."

"Or history buffs," I answered. It would be self-defeating to say I thought the treasure hunters were reaching for stars that would never descend to earth.

Before he could ask anything else, the door opened and three American women came in. They immediately headed toward my books in English about the different mysteries in the region. I long ago learned to have English, German and even a few in Japanese. Any Japanese that came in always bought a book. The Dutch never do. I finally trashed my Dutch editions.

One of the women lived in Toulouse and the other two were her friends from Boston. As I was chatting with them in my broken English, I saw from the corner of my eye the man ooze out the door.

So many of my customers I forget as soon as they leave, but the man left me uncomfortable.

That night I had taken a warm shower, was dressed in sweats against the fall chill and was sitting and reading when Michel knocked on the door and came in without waiting for me to tell him too. I have to admit he looked handsome with his gray hair curling over his navy blue turtleneck. He was still slim and adorable.

"Sebastian called me," he said.

"I'm sure he did." I wondered why he was so interested in this. He had his cat swallowing not just the canary but the entire aviary smile. "Why are you so happy?"

He came over to the chair and pulled me up and danced around the room. "I've a showing in a gallery in Paris . . . and . . ."

Not only was he the cat who swallowed an aviary, he was playing with the last remaining bird by stringing out his story.

"They are going to use my paintings as a backdrop for *Thé ou Café* and that will be tremendous publicity. They are doing it the day they are interviewing Lianne Foley."

"That's wonderful. I'll get the champagne." I meant it. He was a wonderful painter, but he still hadn't had his break and with each passing year it seemed less and less likely. Although he had a local following, the big galleries in Paris had rejected his work regularly.

I always had a bottle of Limoux *blanc des blancs,* which couldn't call itself champagne, but was just as good at a fraction of the price. I once had friends blind taste it against two much more expensive champagnes and they chose it over the pricey ones. Of course at the time we felt forced to finish all three bottles. It was New Year's Eve and we also had *foie gras,* smoked salmon, caviar and all the other end-of-year treats, but I am getting off the subject.

I got the crystal glasses from the cupboard, and Michel eased off the top. I have never seen him open a bottle badly, never seen him leave any foam on the table. "And what is the catch?"

"Why do you think there's a catch?"

I shrugged. When talking with Michel, it is easier to let silence work. After all these years he still hasn't caught on. It is not that he is stupid, he is just one of those persons who have never really developed people skills. We clicked glasses.

"Well, the catch, and it is not really a catch, is that you help them with the documentary."

I put down my glass and walked over to where Ptah was curled up in a ball on the afghan over the clic-clac. Did I really have anything against doing the documentary? There really was no one to protect, although if it came out that there was no mystery here, the tourists would go away. That would thrill some of the villagers that were tired of strangers peering in their windows and each of the store owners that lived by the tourists would find work elsewhere, including myself. Then again, it would only be shown on French TV and we would still get the international tourists.

I could imagine my grandmother being thrilled at being on television, although the television of today with its flat screens was so different from the tiny black-and-white set she used to sit in front of nights toward the end of her life.

And I thought back to her saying how she saw the bitch burning the money.

Michel looked frozen waiting for my answer.

I held out my hand. "Give me your cell phone."

I wasn't going to pay for the call. I wasn't surprised that he had Sebastian on speed dial.

CHAPTER 36
ARGELÈS-SUR-MER

The duvet was wrapped around Annie cocoon style. When she felt a weight on the bed, she thought it was Roger. In a state more asleep than awake she reached over to kiss him. Instead of a cuddle her face was given a huge lick. Hannibal lay next to her. She swore that if he could have talked, he would have asked, "Was it good for you too?" She snapped on the small lamp on the nightstand. A warm light pervaded the room. The dog's tail thumped several times.

At the same moment Roger opened the bedroom door and came in. Chou-Chou was in his arms. The dog's side had been shaved. Annie could see a purple bruise surrounded by the pink skin unused to exposure to air.

Hannibal wagged his tail, but showed no willingness to surrender his place on the bed to either the small dog or Roger.

"Do I have to be jealous of my pet?" he asked.

"What time is it?"

"Almost two. I'm beat." He held the dog out to her.

"I'm not surprised. What happened?" Annie reached for the small animal as Hannibal sniffed her. Both tails wagged.

"Off the bed. Both of you," Roger ordered. The animals obeyed. He pulled the police uniform sweater over his head and tossed it on the chair in the corner. He took a clean pair of pajamas from the dresser and changed as if on automatic pilot. "That man is brilliant."

"Who?"

"Medical examiner from Montpellier. He just finished. I've never seen anything like it. He even had a white body bag."

Annie looked confused.

"The old black ones don't show up hair or fibers. Things for which the guy from Perpignan probably wouldn't even think of doing or looking for. He went over every centimeter of the murder scene. I mean every centimeter has been photographed. He even went over Chou-Chou." He went to his side of the bed. "I'm sure she's hungry and thirsty, but I'm wiped out."

Annie unrolled herself out of the duvet. "I'll take care of it." She looked closer at the small dog. "If she's shaved you must have met up with the vet."

"I did."

"And what did he say about her?"

"She's only bruised. He took X-rays. No bones broken." Roger lay down and stretched out and gave a deep sigh. "Heaven." He adjusted one of the pillows. "She's evidence. The blood on her could be Sylvie's or the murderer's."

Annie looked at the purple mark more closely. "Poor thing."

"The examiner thinks she was kicked. The bruise is consistent with a kick from a size forty-four or forty-six shoe." He reached out to pat the dog. "Poor baby, you've had a worse day than I've had. You've lost your mistress. But don't worry; we'll keep you until Sylvie's mother gets back from holiday."

By the time Annie had finished watching the small dog inhale dinner with the speed of a vacuum cleaner and went back into the bedroom, Roger was asleep with the light shining in his face. She crawled under the duvet and snuggled up to him. He automatically turned, throwing his arm around her. Chou-Chou jumped up and nestled into Annie's stomach, three spoons nestling.

"I'm taking you to school, Gaëlle, and Annie, you can go to

your flat, but only if you keep the dogs with you," Roger said to Gaëlle and Annie the next morning at breakfast.

He hadn't shaved. For the first time Annie knew what he would look like as an old man. Exhaustion seemed to deepen the laugh lines by his eyes, which had deep circles. His curls were matted. Tousled had given way a long time before. Not surprising considering he would have been given a gold medal for the way he thrashed around in the bed during the night if medals were awarded for such things. "This morning I need to get my car from the mechanic. He found out what was making that funny noise, so Annie you drive that. Once you're in the village, you should be safe."

Although Annie had expected Gaëlle to complain, because the *college,* where she was in her seventh year, was within walking distance and she usually met her girlfriends for all the latest gossip en route. The girl said nothing.

"And I'll pick you up at school."

"I can do it," Annie said. "I'll have the dogs with me, and so often you get tied up."

Gaëlle just nodded.

He didn't need to explain why he hadn't had time to pick up the car the night before. No one had to say that this acquiescence was so abnormal, so out of character for Annie and Gaëlle that their fear hung silently in the air. Roger looked at each of them in turn. He opened his mouth to say something then shut it. Annie knew that he thought there was no need to waste good arguments when the battle was won.

Gaëlle hopped out of the cruiser, kissing both cheeks of Annie and Roger as she slid across the back seat, missing contact but not the emotion. She slammed the door before either Hannibal or Chou-Chou could escape. *"Coucou,"* she called to a group of girls walking ahead of where the car had parked. Her friends were all dressed as she was in jeans with large rectangle school bags on their backs. They turned and waited for her. She started to head toward them but then turned and knocked on the cruiser's window. "Be careful. Both of you," she said before melding into the crowd.

"She's such a good kid," Annie said as Roger did a U-turn and headed toward the garage.

Roger nodded as he put his hand over hers. "I think there's a connection between the murders. But because the methods are so different no one agrees with me."

Annie had been thinking the same thing. But that didn't take a genius to figure out. She and Père Yves were closely connected. She'd been with Sylvie the day before. "The killer had to make a connection between the three of us," she said.

"That's what scares me," Roger said. "I'm so afraid you'll be next. I know admitting fear sounds unmanly, but maybe it's more manly to admit it. I don't want to get good at losing people I love."

Annie touched his cheek. "Until yesterday, I really felt you were being overprotective, and I understood why. If you're macho about some things it's okay as long as it isn't everything."

They drove on in silence. Roger's garage was right before the beach, but he drove past it up to the Mediterranean. Argelès had one of the last white sand beach before black rock took over down the coast and into Spain. At this time of year the area was deserted: all the shops on the two paths running parallel with the sand were shuttered, except for the one hotel that stayed open all year round. Sometimes during the week it was empty, despite the popularity of its restaurant with the locals. However, people would come from Paris for a weekend, usually to select their next summer-time rentals. It allowed the owners to survive.

There was nothing honky-tonk about the area. The shops

resembled a small well-built southern French village except there was a wide paved street in between that was forbidden to cars. During July and August there were times of the day that it would be difficult to walk down the street because tourists swarmed the passage way on their way to restaurants and boutiques between bouts of sunning and swimming.

Annie preferred this time of year. The sea had always drawn her with its changing moods and power. When they lived in New England her parents would rent a cottage in Maine for two weeks in the summer and each day they would go to the beach. Sometimes they would take a boat ride and at night they would eat lobster, clams or fish either in a restaurant or on the porch of whatever cottage they had rented. Those weeks went faster than any other in the year.

In Holland they went to The Hague. The sea was different there, gray and colder, if possible, than the Atlantic.

Annie had missed the ocean during the Stuttgart and Geneva years. Neither Lake Constance nor Lake Geneva had the same force. And if the Alps were wonderful for hiking and skiing, they were not an ocean replacement. Maybe it was like she had told Gaëlle last night, there was enough love to go around: love for people, love for the sea, love for the mountains.

The Mediterranean was not as powerful as the Atlantic. There were no tides, but during a storm, it still became a worthy opponent for anyone out on a boat. Periodically, in anger, it flooded out the beach and the stores. A pine grove was between the last row of buildings and the sea. The grass under the trees had been replanted in the spring because one of the winter storms had washed away the lawn. Roger parked between the grove and the tiled area leading to the sand.

Annie looked out at the panorama. To the right low mountains led to Spain. Here, she had it all—both sea and mountains.

The sky was a brilliant blue, matching the water. Not a wave marred the surface. It was as if yesterday's storm had never happened. If only yesterday had never happened.

On this day only one man walked the beach. A Golden Lab, a piece of driftwood in his mouth, ran alongside him. Periodically, the man would take the wood and throw it for the Lab to retrieve. He reminded Annie of Paul. She wondered how he was doing, if he were coming to terms with his brother's death.

When Roger opened the cruiser, the two dogs jumped out. Hannibal ran to the closest tree to notify the world he was there and claim that part of the world as his own. Chou-Chou squatted.

"Í know I have to start my day, but I want some time with you. Just the two of us," Roger said.

"The two of us, the two dogs, that man and his Lab," Annie said.

"Same thing, smart ass," Roger said.

The air was mild enough that they took off their jackets and threw them over their shoulders almost in unison. They walked under three flags: the red, white and blue French flag; the orange and red striped Catalan flag; and the blue flag that the European Union gave beaches that had safe swimming water. All hung in folds, perfectly still. As they stepped onto the beach, the Lab ran to check out the two new dogs and soon the three animals were romping together, ignoring their respective humans.

"Marry me," Roger said. He wasn't looking at Annie. He continued to walk toward the high-rise apartment buildings of Port Argelès.

She stopped.

He continued looking straight ahead, his eyes fixed on Madeloc, the single tower left from a medieval fortress on top of the mountain that led into Spain. His concentration was such it was almost as if he were a Catalan soldier studying the mountainside for approaching enemy soldiers.

It took her a few seconds to not only catch up with him, but to run ahead of him. Walking backwards as he continued to advance, she asked, "What did you say?"

He stopped, put his hands on her shoulders and looked into her eyes. "I love you. Losing you, getting back together again and then having you in danger, has only shown me how much."

Annie's thoughts were a jumble. Never as a child had she played bride or house. Her games were anthropologist, archeologist, explorer. From the time she'd discovered her father's old Landmark children's history books in her grandmother's attic her goal had been to go to university and to research stuff. To not just read about what someone else thought, but to dig out the original documents or sites where possible.

Although she'd dated many people, some for a couple of years, any move on their part to make it permanent had always caused her to flee. Living with someone had seemed like too much of a sacrifice for how she wanted to live her life.

Roger had been different. Where many of her former lovers had seemed to be stealing time from her life, he added to it. Except for the big fight about the Zurich job, he had accepted her as herself more than anyone else she'd met. But marriage? That was for grown-ups and she wasn't sure that at thirty-three she was ready to fall into that category officially.

And of her *lycée* and university friends who had married, almost all were divorced for reasons that had sounded good at the time. As one friend had said when they had a girls' night out, "What's the matter, Annie? You're in your thirties and you haven't even been divorced yet."

"You don't want to, I can see it in your eyes," Roger said.

She reached out, putting her arms around his neck. His expression made her want to cry. "Don't put words in my mouth."

"Then you . . ."

His quick change from hopelessness to hope made her feel even sadder. There wasn't even a flicker of doubt that she loved him more than she'd ever loved any man, but the idea of being a wife and all the melding of her desires to his was beyond frightening.

"Tell me exactly what you're thinking." His voice was how she thought he'd sound if he were interrogating a suspect.

She did.

"Whoever said you'd have to? Give up everything, that is?" Roger asked.

"I keep thinking of my mother who would just find her footing with her art, making all the right contacts, only to have to pick up everything and follow my father to his next job."

Roger put his head back and laughed. "In our case, it would be you that moved us with your crazy assignments and desire to poke into the past."

Annie wanted to get angry, but she couldn't. He was so right. She was the wanderer.

"And not only that, your parents have a pretty good marriage. If we could do half as well we'd be doing okay."

"How traditional would you want us to be?" she asked.

"Sounds like you're negotiating," he said. "I'll take that as a good sign."

She stood on tiptoe to kiss him. "I do know I want to spend the rest of my life with you. I'm just not sure about marriage."

He kissed her back, his tongue exploring hers. "I'll take that as a yes."

"Almost yes," she said.

Instead of driving to the garage they walked hand in hand, their faces thoughtful neither smiling nor frowning. They said nothing. The car was ready and Annie got behind the wheel to drive him back to where they'd left the cruiser.

When they got back to the beach parking lot to pick up the

cruiser, he got out and walked over to the driver's side. The window was down. "Gaëlle gets out at 17:00 today, don't forget. And keep me posted on where you are." He bent over to kiss her.

"Will do." She unsnapped her seat belt so she could push her head through the window to accept another kiss.

CHAPTER 37
ARGELÈS-SUR-MER

Before Annie started to work on her translations for the Paris firm, she decided to wash Chou-Chou. Despite the veterinarian's attentions, the poor creature was still stained with blood in places and her fur was knotted and matted. Nothing like the sleek, silky dog that had challenged Hannibal the day before when the two animals had settled down under a table in *Les Arbres.*

A long time ago Annie had mastered project avoidance. Not that she used it often, but there were times when she couldn't focus on work that the talent came in handy. This was one of them.

Who could blame her? Within the last twenty-four hours she'd had a message from the grave, a second friend murdered and a marriage proposal. How she wished for the calm of her last project where the only problem was an idiot boss who micro-managed. He would interrupt the team so they would have to start over and over in an office that hadn't been air-conditioned. The atmosphere had been suffocating as the Zurich temperatures climbed to record highs. During those times she could shut everything out. Those were outside problems that never touched her being because they were all part of collecting a salary. The good old days, only she hadn't known they were the good old days at the time.

Because Annie only had a shower stall, which would not work well as a dog bath, she removed the dishes from the drain on the side of the sink and filled the basin with warm water.

No way was she able to justify her action as the love of giving dogs baths, but cleaning the pup was something she could start and finish. There were no big decisions, just the obvious wash, rinse and dry, a simple act. Every ion in her being wanted a simpler life. She wanted everyone back alive. If someone had to die, she wished it were something normal like a heart attack. Something quick, not lingering like cancer, and something definitely natural. Knowing two people murdered within three months was not normal, nor did she wish it to become normal.

As soon as she took off Chou-Chou's collar, the small dog began to tremble. The shaking increased the closer they got to the sink and continued until Annie shut off the hair dryer. Then, as if she knew how lovely she looked in Yorkie terms, she pranced around the room, trying to get Hannibal to play. Hannibal, who was only bathed by a hose in his yard, felt he was in no danger of a bath and went into play position.

"Down," Annie hollered. Her nest was much too small for one dog to bounce around much less two, especially when the larger animal was a German shepherd.

The USB key that Sylvie had given her was on her desk. She reinserted it into her laptop. If only she could open the bloody thing, she could copy it, but the password protection that Père Yves had given made that impossible. Any of the passwords she thought of, she'd already tried. She cursed her lack of imagination or memory.

She sat at the computer staring at the little box on the screen and tapping a pencil as if the beat would trigger the right word. When the telephone rang, she jumped.

"Annie, we were wondering where you stand with the project?" The woman on the phone was the secretary of her client. She spoke in heavily accented English, one of the many who loved to practice their English when the chance arose. At one time Annie would have responded in French, but now she was content to let others choose the language.

"The English is done on the document you wanted first. The German I was starting today, and I probably can get to the Dutch by early next week."

"Could you send the English to us?"

"I'll e-mail it this afternoon."

There was a sigh at the other end of the phone. "We're under siege here. We don't know if it's a virus or what, but everything is down. Our IT guys are going, how do you say, nuts. Would it be possible to snail mail hard copy and a USB key with what you've done so far?"

"Of course," Annie said. "This afternoon?"

"Wonderful," the secretary said. "We've been down two days and no one can predict how long. They can use their laptops." The tone of the word *they* was laden with what Annie assumed could only have been brought on by the frustration of everyone venting on her.

"I'll do it this afternoon."

"*Merci.* This is about the only thing that's gone right in the last couple of days."

"I understand," Annie said. She almost said a broken computer system seemed rather unimportant compared to murder, but she resisted. She wanted to print out a hard copy to give it a last onceover. Whenever she looked at a hard copy she found errors she had missed on screen.

Her printer had been dying for a long time. The ink cartridge was new, but seemed no more willing to release ink than the old. Annie tried everything. Not that she could complain. The machine was over eight years old and had pushed out enough reams of paper to dwarf the Eiffel Tower several times. It owed her nothing.

Unlike many computer people, Annie didn't always feel the

need to have the latest equipment. Nor did she feel the need to shop at all. Shopping was something to do when there was absolutely no other choice. Today was one of those days. If she were to get a copy that she was sure was error-free to her client, she would need to buy a new printer.

"Come on guys," she said to the dogs. They jumped up.

La Porte d'Espagne was probably the best shopping mall to buy a new printer and unlike in the village, stores stayed open over lunch. In fact, she could grab lunch at Flunch, choose the printer, get back to her nest and . . . and then what? Not think of her dead friends? Keep failing on password guessing? Not feel trapped by Roger?

A deep sigh escaped. One way she had developed over the years to work through any of her problems was to concentrate on something else. First it was her studies and later it was either work or whatever history project had captured her attention at the time. However, she had already broken the back of the project of the Paris documentation. The rest was hours of writing down the details.

As she walked down her street, Mamie Couges rushed out of the house. A dishtowel was in one hand and a plate in the other. "What do you know about Sylvie?" No cheek kisses. No *bonjour.*

This was not a subject that Annie wanted to get into, but she gave Mamie Couges the essentials: stabbing, sudden, no idea of whom.

"*Alors,* and her poor pup. Will you keep her?"

"Until I talk to Sylvie's mother. She hasn't answered her cell phone. Maybe it's off because she's away."

"You've a good heart. I know her mother is visiting her sister, somewhere near Lyon, but I don't have the number, and I can't remember the sister's married name." The old woman bent closer. "They only started getting along recently. If I find out,

I'll tell that beautiful man of yours. She needs to know about her daughter."

"Do you know where and when she'll be back?" Annie asked.

The old woman shook her head.

She left the old woman standing with her dishtowel and plate. Although she wanted to double-check to see if Mamie Couges was knocking on the other *mamies'* doors, she resisted. Village life was village life and without the gossip, something would have been missing.

The mall's parking lot was not overly full, but then it was a weekday. Planters held semi-tropical plants. Annie grouped them under cactus and palms because she wasn't able to tell one plant from another any more than she could identify birds. Overall, she had to admit she was more a city girl than a country girl.

Since she didn't drive often, and hated parking more, she pulled in where there were less cars, farther away from the entrance, because then she didn't have to angle the car carefully. If she scratched the car, she had no doubt that Roger would understand. He had put enough nicks into it himself. Still it would be an annoyance that she didn't need.

The dogs were in the back seat. Of course, she could take them in with her, although getting a tray at the Flunch cafeteria might be a little hard to handle with two dog leashes. There was a pizza place that had waitress service, but Flunch would be quicker. Besides, she loved the cafeteria with all its choices. Had it been summer, she would not have been able to leave them in the car. Hot dogs should be served in buns. However, it was a lovely, need-a-light-jacket kind of day, and she wouldn't be gone that long. Still, she left all the windows open a small crack.

Although she'd promised Roger to keep Hannibal with her, he was, sort of, with her, if she wanted to stretch the truth a bit.

Cracking the windows slightly so the dogs would have air, she said. *"Soyez sage, les deux."* The dogs rested their heads on the rear window ledge so that they could see people walk by. They'd be good.

Annie selected the printer in less than five minutes. The clerk handed her a large box with a plastic handle. If she'd thought juggling two dog leashes and a tray would have been hard, two dog leashes, a tray and a printer would have been impossible.

At Flunch the line was almost nonexistent. Only an older woman with her grandson who wanted to eat just dessert, a big bowl of chocolate mousse, was in front of her. "But it has lots of vitamins," he said. His eyes sparkled and he cocked his head.

"If you eat the vitamins in your meat and vegetables first, the vitamins in the mousse work better," his grandmother said. To the man serving she said, *"S'il vous plaît,* more beans than *frites."*

Annie took her vegetarian couscous to a table where she could look out on the parking lot. Roger's car with the dogs was out of sight. She was sure they were okay, although she knew there would be a doggy smell when she got into the car.

She moved the couscous around her plate until she had a circle, then lined the carrots into a row of orange soldiers. The turnips and cabbage made clouds. She heard her grandmother saying, "Don't play with your food," two tables away. However, the older woman was talking to the boy who had built a house with his *frites,* not to her.

Annie forced down a few mouthfuls. Some people eat extra when upset. Annie was not one of those people. When she and Roger had broken up she'd lost fifteen pounds, putting her into a size six dress. Or a thirty-six European. European sizes sounded fatter. However, Annie never worried about her weight. She considered how she looked more a problem for those looking at her. Nor was she one of those women who constantly checked her appearance in the windows.

"You have to eat at least half, or you can't have any dessert." The grandmother spooned beans into the child's mouth. Annie felt that the woman might come over to her table at any minute and start feeding her the same way. However, Annie hadn't taken any dessert.

This is stupid, she thought. I'm grown up. I can eat what I want. I can leave food on my plate and have dessert. I can even have dessert before my meal if I want. She was tempted to tell the small boy there was hope in the future, but knew that wasn't the right thing. Still it was tempting, but part of being thirty-three was resisting some temptations, just not all.

She gathered the napkins and plates onto her tray and put them in the carousel that moved automatically to the kitchen.

In the car the dogs greeted her with huge licks and little licks, depending on the size of their respective tongues. Face washing was a form of doggy greeting along with sniffing in places humans wouldn't, both of which made Annie happy she was human. Annie thought of a program about chimpanzees in the wild that had been on BBC Prime right before she'd left Zurich. One chimp had hurt his leg, and his friend slept next to him hand in hand. Although chimps didn't always show such compassion, Annie wished for similar compassion among all creatures.

She turned the key in the ignition. There was only a growl. Several attempts flooded the engine. Shit, she thought, nothing to do but wait. When enough time had passed she tried the engine again, but there was no welcoming purr.

So often when a car went into the garage to be fixed, another problem would occur within a few days. This wasn't the first time it had happened, and Roger had said that he would change garages if it happened again. Sometimes being police chief wasn't an advantage. Roger had come to the conclusion that maybe the garage owner risked this with him, because no one would believe that anyone would try to fool the police chief. Maybe he hadn't counted on the Catalan attitude that a police chief from Paris was still a foreigner.

Annie fumbled in the bag for her mobile, but before she could turn it on there was a tap on the window.

"Avez-vous un problème?"

Ex-mayor Jean-Pierre Boulet definitely didn't match her image of a man in shining armor, but he might be able to reduce the time she needed to spend on dealing with the stupid car. She rolled down her window. "It won't start."

"I know. I heard the engine grinding as I was heading for my car." He had a bag from C&A in his left hand. It looked ratty to Annie. Probably he was returning something, not buying.

"Let me take a look," he said. Before Annie could say anything he had his hands on the hood. "Pop the button, will you?"

She did as she hopped out of the car, being careful to keep the two dogs inside. They both stared at the engine. He fiddled with a wire here and there, unscrewed the oil cap and tested the oil in the car.

"Do you know much about engines?" he asked.

"Not really. I'm going to call Roger." She reached into the bag for her phone.

At the same time he dropped the hood. It hit his hand and he did a little dance around the area, shaking it. Then he bumped into Annie, knocking the phone not just out of her hand but down a small embankment covered with thistles. "Oh, I'm so sorry. I don't see how we can get it back."

By swallowing several times Annie was able to control her annoyance. "If I had a long stick I could, but I don't. Do you?"

"No, I don't, but let me take you to the garage. We can borrow a broom and have then come look at the car at the same time."

Annie sighed. This was the last way possible she wanted to spend her afternoon. Still she had several hours before Gaëlle was due to get out of school. She did have her printer, and if the stuff was one day late so be it.

They got into a new sand-colored Volvo, a rather big model by Argelès standards. Some streets were narrower than the car. Typical for the ex-mayor, she thought, although the idea of status cars amused her. Her goal was to not have a car at all. Not only was it better for the environment, it was one less thing to take up her time. Like now. She glanced back at Roger's car. The dogs would be okay for a short time more.

"Fine," she said. What else was there to say?

He pulled out of the parking lot onto the main route. "You can see Canigou," he said.

The mountain was beautiful with its snow-covered peak. The mountains came down to the vineyards, stripped of their fruit but still with leaves. The vines were lower than those in Switzerland. According to what the local vintners had told her, it was a quality control thing. She liked wine, knew the difference between a pinot noir and a gamay, but had no idea which would be considered more prestigious. She often chose a bottle by the attractiveness of the label. Then if it married well with her meal, she was content to buy the same wine a second time.

They were heading toward Prades and had passed the third gas station when she jolted herself back to the present. "Where are you going?" she asked.

"I don't know where my mind is," he said. "I'll pull over." He swung the car off the main road onto a dirt path that was too narrow to turn at all. "I'll have to go a bit further to turn."

Annie shifted in her seat. She did not like this and wished she'd never come, but couldn't quite understand her apprehensiveness. Don't be silly, she told herself. You know this person. You may dislike him, but there's nothing to worry about.

About half a mile from the roadway a small copse of olive trees stood in the middle of a vineyard. A grassy area in front of the trees had been cut back. Boulet swung his car onto a dusty road and parked it between the trees. "Can you excuse me a moment? As long as we are here, I need to answer nature's call. That was one of my goals when I stopped to help a fair damsel in distress."

What could Annie say? No, don't go to the bathroom. I want to get out of here. They both got out of the car.

"I'll look in that direction." She turned toward Canigou. A few seconds later she heard footsteps. She swung around to see the man behind her, his arm raised and a stone in his hand, heading toward her skull.

CHAPTER 38
ARGELÈS-SUR-MER

Roger sat at his desk. His files were stacked in color-coded piles, blue for robbery, red for missing persons, yellow for annoyances like drunks, white for family violence, green for murder. The files reminded him of a wall built of Legos, only he didn't remember any green Legos. Gaëlle had played with the blocks as a child, but he remembered them as yellow, blue and red. His wife wanted their daughter to be exposed to more than girl toys, so she was given cars and trucks, which she ignored. The Legos were different. She'd spent hours building things, but seldom houses. Her Legos were used to make flowers, boats, horses, cats, dogs and a playmate she'd named Chloë. The arms, legs and head had been yellow, the hair red and the body blue. Maybe that was why she dyed her hair blue. At least that was growing out.

If she'd built flowers, there must have been green Legos, or maybe she'd painted them green. He separated the two green files from the pile. If there were no green Legos, maybe there should be no green files and therefore no murders. He liked that idea.

He remembered Père Yves's color-coded files and for a short moment felt a trace of jealousy when it came to Annie and the priest, even though he knew there was nothing sexual in it. Couples didn't have to have identical interests to be happy. God, he wanted to solve that murder. Both murders. Never had he run into such clueless crimes. He didn't believe in a perfect

273

crime. If he had to guess, he would say that the person that killed the priest hadn't meant to kill him, but wanted information about that stupid alleged treasure. Perhaps the same thing had happened with Sylvie. The lack of similarity between the murder methods could be explained by the fact that neither had been pre-planned.

However, Annie's situation was different. The threatening phone calls and the trashing of her apartment had to be pre-planned. Could that mean another person was involved, one who was totally unrelated to the murders? Yet if someone were after the treasure, his love's connection to the priest made her a likely target. He wondered if Sylvie had any strange things happen to her before she was murdered. Probably not, for she'd been in Australia for the past month. He must check her telephone records against Annie's. If they were to solve either crime it would mean a lot of detail work, most of which would prove useless.

A deep sigh escaped him. He was tired, not physically, but mentally. Man's cruelty was wearing on him. Sometimes it was hard to remember that he had joined the police force to help people. The idealism of youth had soon given way to the reality of the job: drugs, robbery, violence. People who didn't want to be helped. Victims whose lives were shattered.

In a huge city like Paris, what should he have expected? People from all nationalities crowded together, many without a way to earn a good living. Granted, it had been that way since the people had stormed the Bastille, fighting for a better way of life. What he didn't understand was crime among those who had so much and just wanted more and more, although he had read the political and psychological books. But theory seemed to break down when he looked into the barrel of a gun held by a scared teenager in need of a fix.

He knew part of the reason for the dissonance between his

idealism and reality was that he had come from what was known as a good home. His mother was the read-a-bedtime-story type of mother and his father, although strict, always had time to kick a football after work. And if they didn't have much money, there was enough to go camping every summer in different parts of the country. Nor did he have any question about what the punishment would be for infractions.

Maybe his biggest shock was to discover others didn't have the same rules. Some had no rules at all or believed that the rules were for others, not themselves.

He went to his gray metal file cabinet and opened the drawer with the P and pulled out his file labeled personal. In it was a framed montage of Gaëlle and his wife, the kind where photos were slipped into circles, squares, rectangles and ovals. There was only one studio portrait with Gaëlle and Stephanie looking in different directions. It was the largest and in the middle of the frame. Gaëlle had been eight. Stephanie had just found her first wrinkle and had been worrying that she would be starting menopause as their daughter went through puberty. They had joked about how Roger would not be able to cope with all those raging female hormones.

The other photos were of his women unwrapping Christmas presents, on horseback during a summer holiday, mugging for the camera with both dressed in pajamas. His favorite was the two of them carrying Hannibal as a puppy into their house. When he remembered the dog's milky breath that day, he shoved the frame back into the cabinet as fast as he could.

How stupid he'd been to think Argelès was different. All the same problems existed, only lower in total number. Per capita they were probably the same. People might be a little slower to act because they knew their neighbors, or rather knew their neighbors were looking, but they still had all the same abilities to do harm to each other.

So much for philosophy. Time to get to work. He needed a new way of looking at things. Before he and Annie had fought about Zurich, he had watched her help Gaëlle organize her thoughts for an essay. It was far different from the Cartesian logic taught in the French schools. Annie had called it mind mapping and had Gaëlle write all the ideas as fast as she could on a piece of paper, drawing lines between connected thoughts.

He took a bunch of file cards from his right drawer and picked up a pen. Across the room was a corkboard that had a number of notices about holidays, work schedules and two missing girls, one eighteen, the other twelve. He got up and removed the pins one by one and put the notices in a pile on the file cabinet.

He wrote Père Yves on one card and pinned it in the middle of the board. He wrote the word treasure and put it on another card above Père Yves. Then he wrote Sylvie. Fifteen minutes later the board was almost solid white. Standing back he waited for a revelation. No clouds parted, no voice spoke.

Roger had spent almost that entire day interviewing people who might have seen or heard something related to Sylvie's murder. Because her office was right next to the parking lot where the village's only supermarket was, and across the street from the school, many people had been around, but no one had heard a scream or seen anything unusual. The murder, the medical examiner had guessed, took place at approximately four o'clock, too early for parents to pick up schoolchildren.

The grocery store had opened after their lunch break a half-hour before so no lines would have been waiting. At this time of year, lines were uncommon. The flower shop next to the grocery store was closed for two weeks for the annual vacation of the owners. The beauty shop owner hadn't heard anything, but pointed out that her store was full of chattering women and running hair blowers. The owner always had a radio playing music in the background. All right, there was a good chance Sylvie might not have screamed if she had been caught unawares. The theory that she put up a fight had been ruled out by the blood spatters. The mess was ransacking, the examiner said.

Too bad none of the other offices in the building had been rented. Other tenants would have been a big help. No matter where he looked, there was just no breakthrough.

A knock on the door broke his concentration. Gendarme Boulet pushed his head in. *"Téléphone, Chef. Votre fille."* All the gendarmes knew to always interrupt Roger if Gaëlle called.

Roger leaned back in his chair and picked up the phone. *"Allo, Chérie,"* he said.

"Salut Papa. Annie isn't here. Should I walk home?"

Roger stood up. "What do you mean?" He glanced at his watch. School had ended a half-hour before. That wasn't like Annie. She was always on time. Or she would have called.

"Annie didn't show up. Should I walk home?" Gaëlle repeated.

"Is there anyone around?"

"A couple of teachers are still here."

"Go inside and wait for me."

When Roger pulled up to the school, he saw his daughter talking to a young woman. He got out of the cruiser and went up to them. Gaëlle introduced her literature teacher. They shook hands while Gaëlle explained the teacher had stayed with her rather than leave her alone outside the deserted building. Word of Sylvie's murder must have gotten around. Murders in small towns made everyone jittery, while in big cities, it was just another bit of news. The college was far enough back from the road and hidden by a grove of cork trees so that Gaëlle would have been totally isolated.

Roger thanked the teacher and held the passenger door for his daughter. "Nothing from Annie? Nothing on her mobile?"

"Maybe she forgot. Or got really involved in her work," Gaëlle said.

"Let's go to her flat," Roger said.

They drove back into the village and parked by the river. Because of the rain yesterday there was a small amount of water, but not enough to totally cover the grass that grew lush and thick up to the banks. The river was so often empty that two roads leading into the village crossed the river by actually going through the bed. River was probably too grandiose a word. Even creek would have been giving it more than it merited. Roger assumed that it was called a river based on water flow from a bygone era.

They parked next to the washing shed, a long low building filled with sinks, where some of the *mamies* still did their weekly wash. At one time all the women of the village washed their clothes in these sinks, but progress proved washing machines easier. Still, women without dryers would bring sheets here to dry on the lines provided by the village rather than hang them out their windows over the street. Sheets blocked the windows of their neighbors below, but it was normal to see socks, pants, pajamas and face cloths hanging from all windows. When Roger was first in the village he dropped in to the washing shed, figuring it was a good way to introduce himself to the older citizens. By carrying baskets of dripping laundry to the lines outside, he had endeared himself to more than one old lady, which was precisely what he had intended to happen.

Today there was only one woman taking down her dry sheets. She waved to the chief as he got out of his car. He waved back, but didn't want to take the time to talk.

Gaëlle had to run to catch up with her father. His imagination pictured Annie in a pool of blood in front of her desk.

The new lock on the front door and her entrance were both fully in place. Still, he held his breath, afraid of finding her body. No dogs barked as he took the stairs two at a time. Annie's apartment was empty. An almost empty teacup stood on the counter separating the kitchen and living areas. The teabag was in the sink. He knew it was from today. Annie wasn't the type to leave dirty dishes when she left her flat for the day. A wet towel smelling of dog was draped over the open washing machine door. More than once he'd waited as she checked to make sure everything was neat when she returned. "She was coming back," he said to Gaëlle who had caught up with her father.

Gaëlle looked around. "Nothing out of order, except . . ." She went over to the printer, which was open with the cartridge next to it on the desk.

Roger looked at her phone. There were no messages. Too bad. It might have given him an idea of where she'd gone. "Can you find her cell phone?" he asked.

"She usually keeps it in her pocket, and her pocketbook is gone also," Gaëlle said after opening and closing all the closet doors and drawers.

He sat at the table and dialed his own telephone number. There was only his recording. "Annie, if you're there, pick up please. Please be there."

Out on the street he locked the front door.

"What next, Papa?"

He thought for a moment and knocked on Mamie Couges door. The old woman answered. She had a spoon in her hand. He could smell something with lots of garlic cooking. *"Bonjour, Chef Perrin."*

"I wondered if you'd seen Mademoiselle Young today?" he asked.

"As a matter of fact I did. She seemed in a hurry. I wished

she could have told me more about the latest murder."

"Any idea where she was going?" Roger wanted to stay on the topic and not get quizzed on Sylvie's death.

"I know she had the dogs with her and keys in her hand. Both hers and another set. Maybe car keys? No, she doesn't have a car, but I remember the chain they were on, it was a big football."

"My car keys, of course." His car hadn't been at the river. He walked over to the parking lot by the library and the *salle des fêtes*. He and Gaëlle checked all four rows, but his car wasn't there. Nor was it at the parking lot by the supermarket.

"Where could she have gone?"

"Shopping?" Gaëlle said.

"Annie?" They both knew Annie's attitude toward shopping.

"Wait a minute, she mentioned something about having printer problems. Her printer was open," Gaëlle said.

Roger hugged her. "Do you know her favorite computer store?"

Gaëlle shrugged.

Roger picked up his phone. "Boulet, I want you and Gault to take two different cruisers and go to each shopping center in the region."

"Why?" Boulet said. "It's almost the end of our shift."

"I don't care. My car is missing. You're looking for my car." His tone was such that Boulet made no more complaints. "I'll do Auchon's and those going toward Prades." He wished he knew what shopping malls had the best computer stores, but he wasn't into computers. Only a few years before the police had electric typewriters, and although they were computerized now, it was minimal. Annie worked in a world he didn't understand, nor did he want to understand. He knew enough to do his job, e-mail and an Internet search or two. That's all.

"Do you talk about computers with Annie?" he asked his daughter.

She shook her head. "We talk about school, clothes, Patrick Fiori, television, makeup, books sometimes, Hannibal, but not computers. Except when we play computer games."

"She never mentioned where she buys her computer stuff?"

Again Gaëlle shook her head. "I do know she doesn't know much about shopping around here. *Porte d'Espagne,* maybe, because that's where she got stuff for her apartment. I went with her once to pick up some curtain rods. That is when she doesn't go to Weldom's because she can walk there."

"Weldom's doesn't have computer stuff." By now they had reached the cruiser. With the late afternoon traffic, he needed to put on the siren if he didn't want to sit in traffic.

They passed the turn-off to the farm nestled at the foot of the mountain where a bearded farmer made goat cheese to sell at the Saturday *marché.* The man looked as if he were from another time, except that he ran a video of the process. Several times she and Roger had gone there to buy cheese mid-week. He wondered if maybe she'd stopped there and had a flat. No, the farmer would have been able to change the tire, and she would have called.

Something had happened to her. He had no doubt of it. She was too responsible to not pick up his daughter without calling him. That the dogs were missing with her gave him some comfort.

"Don't worry, Papa. Hannibal is with her and we all know what a good watchdog he is," Gaëlle said as if she were reading his thoughts.

If Hannibal got a chance to protect her, Roger thought.

"When we find her, don't be mad at her," Gaëlle said.

Mad? He would be ecstatic, if only she was all right. He tried not to show how worried he was, so to not upset his daughter.

There were mainly vineyards between that turn-off and the shopping center. He shut off the siren. By now it was later in the day and the parking lot was beginning to fill up with people who were stopping on their way home from work in Perpignan to whatever nearby village they lived in.

"You look right, I'll look left," Roger said as he cruised up one lane and down another.

"Over there," Gaëlle said.

He saw it as soon as she did. He parked the cruiser in front of the car. Hannibal and Chou-Chou barked their welcomes.

"Got a key, Papa?"

He tried the driver's door. It opened. Then he saw the keys in the ignition, and he knew that whatever had happened to Annie, it wasn't of her own choice. He had to be calm. Calm for Gaëlle. Calm for himself. He needed to be at his best to find her before anything happened to her, if it weren't too late.

"Maybe she went for help," Gaëlle said.

"She'd phone."

"Try her portable again."

On the off chance she would answer, he did. He heard it ring in his ear, and he heard it ring down the embankment behind the rear fender of the car. He and Gaëlle looked at each other.

"*Merde*," Gaëlle said and her father did not correct her.

Roger tried to start the car but it did not turn over. He got out to look under the hood. "Some of the wires are disconnected." He dialed the *gendarmerie*. "My car is at *Porte d'Espagne*."

"We'll call off the search," the dispatcher said.

"No. I need you to check the gas stations around the shopping center to see if Annie went to one of them for help." He knew she hadn't, but he needed to make sure, needed to hope. He looked at his daughter who stared at him. Her expression was almost the same as when she had learned about Stephanie's murder.

"You think something's happened to her too?" The girl's voice was a whisper.

He scooped her into his arms. "I don't know," he said. But he knew.

CHAPTER 39
THE ROAD TO
RENNES-LE-CHÂTEAU

Annie fought to open her eyes. She felt pulled and tugged. Nothing was solid. She felt folded over. Her hands were grabbed. A cloth floated over her. Or maybe it was a dream. More likely it was a nightmare. Nothing was scary, though, just uncertain. Why could she only feel half her body? Something stung her arm, but when she went to brush it away her hands wouldn't move. Her world started moving or, more aptly, bumping. A fog descended, hiding everything. Then nothing.

God, her head hurt. She'd never had headaches, or almost never. She'd only remembered one bad hangover in her life, not because she didn't drink, but because she was the type of drinker that got sick on more than three glasses of anything. Her system rejected alcohol long before it changed her behavior, speech or movements. So she limited herself to two drinks at the most. Hangovers needed alcohol. She couldn't remember having had a drink. Memory was not something she could call up at all. She drifted into more sleep.

She tried to force her eyes open. Where was she? What was that smell? A new car smell. She must be in a car's backseat. It was moving. She was stretched out on her side. She fought off a wave of nausea. Her arms and hands prickled. When she tried to move them, she realized that they were tied behind her back. No wonder they prickled.

She couldn't see the driver in the front seat. It was so dark. Night must have fallen. Wherever she was didn't have street-lights. Or maybe there was something over her face. Then she fell back into unconsciousness.

The next time she opened her eyes it was easier. She was no longer in a car but on something flat and softer. In the grayness she could make out ropes around her hands. Her eyes followed them to bedposts. She was spread-eagled on a bed. Her eyes tried to make out more, but there wasn't enough light. Where the hell was she? Something had happened, but the memory was just out of her grasp. Her head hurt. She wanted to throw up.

Her bladder felt as if it were going to burst. Drifting into her consciousness was a memory of a conversation with Gaëlle, who had been complaining about having to get up to put Hannibal out.

"You have a choice," Annie had said.

"If I don't he'll mess in the house," Gaëlle had said.

"*Voilà,* that's your choice. Get up or clean up."

Annie knew she had a choice now. She could wet herself. Or she could call for help. If help came, she was sure it would most likely be from her captor. Try as she might, she still couldn't remember coming here. If she were here alone, she would just have to wet herself. If she could clear her thoughts, she would be able to figure out which was worse.

A loud snore came from the other side of the wall where the bedpost rested. Okay, she wasn't alone. Would her captor be angry to be awakened? What the hell did she care? He had no right to do this to her.

Sylvie and Père Yves. My God . . . it was the murderer who had taken her prisoner . . . Think. Focus. . . . Try and remember.

Boulet. Shit. He wouldn't hesitate to kill again. Kill her. Why else would he have kidnapped her? If she only knew why the ex-mayor had killed Père Yves and Sylvie, maybe she could convince him to keep her alive.

Her head throbbed. Her bladder throbbed. If she were to live, it would take all her brains to save herself. Although she would like to think she was smarter than the ex-mayor, she was at a disadvantage. If her head didn't hurt so much, she would be able to think more clearly.

"I have to go to the toilet." She called three times, each time a little louder.

The snoring stopped. There was shuffling. The door opened. A switch clicked and Annie found herself almost blinded by the overhead light. Still she could make out the ex-mayor standing there, wisps of hair standing on end around his balding head. It reminded her of a halo, but the man was no holy figure.

"I have to go to the toilet."

"I'll bring you a bedpan," he mumbled.

When she saw him last he had been fully clothed. Now he was in blue and green striped pajamas. Murderers don't change into pajamas before killing people, surely. What a stupid thought. There's no correct way to dress to kill someone.

Could she be in his house? What time was it? The sun was just beginning to come up. "That's too embarrassing."

"Do you want a bedpan or not?" his voice was heavy, a morning voice, the voice of someone who had been asleep for a while.

Annie shuddered. She hated bedpans and the idea of him pulling down her pants was more than she could imagine. "Please untie me. Let me go to a real toilet. I promise I won't run away."

He scratched his stomach and then rubbed his cheeks, which were overdue for a shave.

Maybe his desire to pull her pants down was minimal too, because he left the room. What if he didn't come back? Maybe he had gone to get a bedpan.

She didn't have long to wait.

A moment later he was back with a pistol. Annie didn't know one gun from another, but it looked old. Nothing like weapons she'd seen in modern crime movies, nothing like Roger's gun. Someone might talk about a Glock or a Winchester, but that meant nothing to her. A gun was a gun was a gun, and he had a gun that could kill her if he so decided. She decided not to use the words *kill* or *gun* or say anything. Moreover, she'd pretend things were normal. Compared to the gun, she wished she had the bedpan and had not opened her big mouth.

He approached the bed.

My God, what was he going to do? She shut her eyes. Her breath came in short gasps. Was this how she would die? Then she felt him tugging on the rope of her left hand. It hurt. Then the hand was free. She opened her eyes. He stood there with the gun in one hand and the piece of rope in another.

"You undo your right hand, and don't try anything. I would have no problems shooting you. In fact, I might quite enjoy it."

Annie wondered why he hadn't already, but she wasn't going to ask. She worked at the knots as best she could. The rope had left both wrists raw. A few drops of blood were on her right hand. As she sat up the room began to spin. "I'm dizzy."

"Maybe you've a concussion. I also gave you a sedative, some of my wife's old medicine. Used to cut her pain."

Annie knew that his wife had died of cancer some time ago. She didn't know the shelf life of sedatives, but it didn't matter. She felt awful, and what difference did it make if she had a concussion or a drug reaction? She swung her legs over the bed and let them dangle the way she'd been told to do when she was recovering from having her appendix removed. The pressure on her bladder felt worse. She minced her way to the door, hoping she wouldn't pass out.

"Why am I here?"

"You know."

"I really don't."

"You and the priest. You found a treasure. I need it."

He needed it. Not that he wanted it. What she would do with the difference, she had no idea, but if she were to get out of this she had to use everything she could muster.

As she passed the window, she couldn't make out any buildings. The ex-mayor's house was surrounded on three sides by houses. The front faced the principal road in Argelès. Obviously, they weren't in the village. There were no streetlights. Had she heard he had a villa up in the mountains? Hadn't there been some gossip about his using village employees to help him build it, and supplies meant for the *salle des fêtes* that were missing? Nothing seemed certain.

If only her head would stop hurting. If only she could keep from throwing up. Or if she did, maybe she could cover him with vomit.

That wouldn't do any good. He'd probably shoot her for doing it. But if he hadn't shot her already, maybe there was a reason.

Outside the room where she'd been, she saw a corridor. As she inched through the door she noticed that that the floors were well-waxed parquet. A nice rug, probably Moroccan considering the color and pattern, ran down the middle. A huge chest, elaborately carved in the Catalan style, was on her left. The wallpaper was flecked with gold. Wherever she was, it had been furnished with money, but everything looked dusty and unused.

"First door on your right. And I'm right behind you."

Annie started to shut the door, but his hand stopped her. "Leave it open."

Looking around, she didn't see any escape. It was a small

room, no windows with only a toilet—so typically French with the bath, bidet and sink in a different room from the toilet. "Where would I go? What could I do? There's not even a medicine chest in here. No towel."

"You can push the door to, but don't click it shut."

Annie sat, sure the ex-mayor could hear everything as clearly as she could. In a way it was embarrassing, but embarrassment wasn't her biggest problem. She needed a plan.

"What's keeping you? I can't hear you anymore."

"Sometimes nature can't be rushed."

"I never thought you Americans could be so delicate," Boulet said.

Annie could hear him walking about. His steps were never far enough away for her to make a break, and even so, what good would it do? Even if she had the strength, which she didn't, she didn't know how to get out of this house. And if she did, she didn't know where she was nor how she could find help.

Play it calm, she kept telling herself. Calm, calm, calm. With that, she turned and vomited.

CHAPTER 40
ARGELÈS-SUR-MER

Roger ran his hand through his hair. The Argelès police forces, national and village, were sitting in front of him, nine men and one woman. A very small base force kept the peace for the village all year round. In summer they had temporaries, usually from the army, to swell their ranks. That might change now that serving time in the Army was no longer obligatory for all young men.

However, this wasn't summer. Right now he wished he could order in all kinds of reinforcements. He had called headquarters in Paris to request help, but the person who needed to authorize it hadn't been available. Roger had sworn at the bureaucracy and slammed down the phone.

A copy of the morning's *Roussillon South* with Annie's photo dominated the front page. The editor had changed their lead for him.

He was in the middle of a nightmare, a bloody, unfair nightmare from which he could not wake. For the second time in his life the woman he loved had disappeared.

His men were all seated in folding chairs arranged haphazardly around the meeting room. Roger was sitting on a scarred wooden table in front of them. Behind him was a blackboard that had been washed clean.

"You don't know the killer got her," said Gendarme Boulet, the mayor's idiot son.

Con, asshole, Roger wanted to say but didn't. "And where

else would she be?"

"Well women like to shop," Boulet said. "She could have gone to another shopping center."

"And how did she get there? Walk down a major road leaving my car and the dogs? I don't think so." The image of his hands tightening around Boulet's neck flashed through Roger's mind, a pleasant thought. In training, one of his teachers had said something about bad ideas leading to good. Obviously the man had never met this asshole. Boulet's bad ideas stayed bad and only triggered anger.

"It's six in the morning. The stores closed how many hours ago, Boulet?" He stared at the man who looked away and refused to meet Roger's eyes. "Any more bright ideas?"

"Maybe she met a friend," Boulet said. "Got gabbing."

"Annie was supposed to meet Gaëlle at school at 17:00 yesterday," Roger said.

"*Oui*, Boulet. The Patron's woman would never have forgotten Gaëlle. Annie may be different, she may be American, but she's responsible," Gault said.

"But . . ."

"Boulet, shut the fuck up," Roger spat the words out.

Boulet examined his fingernails. The other *flics* said nothing. Normally, their Patron was calm under all circumstances.

Roger knew they were seeing a different side of him. For once he didn't care. At this moment, he was Annie's lover first and their boss second. He needed them, as he had never needed them before. "Around lunch time we know she was in the village then . . ." The phone rang. He grabbed it.

"Help me! My husband's drunk. He's going to beat me." There was a crash in the background that sounded like breaking glass followed by a scream.

Roger knew the voice. He covered the mouthpiece and said, "Boulet—no, wait a minute—Gerard get over to 23 Mirabeau."

Just because he wanted to get rid of the asshole before he put his fist through his face didn't give him the right to jeopardize someone else. Gerard was good at family violence situations. Boulet was a disaster.

"The Lemoines?" Gerard asked.

"Who else? And try and get back as fast as possible," Roger said.

"If I have to bring him in?" Gerard tilted his head to the cell area behind the conference room where they were sitting. Gaëlle had gone to sleep in one, covered by a blanket with the dogs curled up under the bunk. Roger wasn't about to let her out of his sight or at least out of the building where he was until he found Annie alive or . . .

"I can take your kid to my house. My wife won't mind," Gault said.

Roger wondered how much protection a woman in her early twenties and six months pregnant could offer his daughter. Yet, he knew Gault was trying to be helpful. "See what happens first. Get going, Gerard."

"Let's go over this again," Roger said.

Each *flic* reviewed where he'd looked. When it had become obvious that Roger's car had been tampered with, they'd checked the nearby gas stations. No woman of any description had come in to ask for help. The Automobile Association hadn't been called.

"Why would your woman mess with your car, is what I don't get," Boulet said.

"She probably didn't. Whoever kidnapped her did," Gault said. He spoke through clenched teeth.

"It has to be someone she knows. Annie wouldn't have gone with a stranger. Especially not now," Roger said.

"So what do we do? Knock on every door in town and ask if she's there?" Boulet asked.

"No identification yet on the prints on the hood of the car?" Roger asked.

"*Patron*, we won't get that report back for several days," Gault said. His voice was gentle.

Roger shook his head. He had made the same mistake that Boulet had made in misjudging time. He was so tired, but he couldn't let himself sleep until Annie was found.

"You have to consider that the prints on the hood may be Annie's," Gault said. "She probably opened the hood to see what was wrong."

"Is there anyone we haven't notified? Think," Roger said.

"I called every police station between here and Toulouse, the Spanish and the Andorra borders. And I called the customs people as well. I faxed the photo of her you gave me," Perez said from the back of the room. Of all the *flics*, he was the quietest, but his work was always done on time. Roger had never heard him make an excuse. If he were wrong, he admitted it.

"And going north?"

"All the way to Avignon. They'll be looking out for her," Perez said.

"*Flics* look out for *flics*." Gault put his hand on his boss's shoulder. "We'll find her."

Alive, promise me you'll find her alive, Roger wanted to say. But he couldn't articulate the words because then he would have to admit out loud that he wasn't sure she was alive and that he would have to go through losing a woman he loved again. Although he knew it was possible to love more than one woman in a lifetime, he believed the number of soul mates assigned to any one man was a finite quantity. He had gone through his quota, and even if he hadn't, he knew that he would never allow himself to be this vulnerable with another person.

"Patron, go home, there's nothing more you can do now," Gault said.

There was a scuffling sound outside the door. Gerard shoved a handcuffed man who staggered and swore as he passed the door to the cells. The smell of alcohol and urine overwhelmed the room.

Roger raced from the room to the holding cells.

The drunk stopped in front of the cell where Gaëlle was sleeping and mumbled, "Young for a hooker. Whatda the dogs do?" Gerard was not the least gentle in shoving the man into the next cell. "Shut your face."

Hannibal growled as Gaëlle sat up and rubbed her eyes.

"Wake up, *Chérie*," Roger said, shaking her. "We're going home."

She squinted at the light. She looked at the drunk then at her father. "Did you find Annie?"

Roger shook his head. "Nothing more I can do right now. I'll start over when I've had some sleep." Only he knew that there was no way he *would* sleep until he found her. The most he could hope for was a little rest so he would be better able to deal with everything later.

CHAPTER 41

Annie thought of the hostages she'd read about, people who had been kept prisoner in Iran, Guantanamo or Iraq for many years and wondered how they had stayed sane. When she'd scanned their biographies, she never envisioned herself in the same situation.

As she lay spread eagled in the bed, her hands and feet again tied to the bedposts, she tried to remember the stories. One told of a man who had been given a Bible that he read and reread. After he was released he did a television documentary about places mentioned. Another prisoner tried to remember certain days of his life in exact detail. There was an English journalist and his girlfriend who had worked to free him despite a non-negotiating stance from Thatcher's government. They wrote a book that alternated points of view during their several-year struggle to secure his release.

What had given them their inner courage to go on day after endless day? She'd been a prisoner less than twenty-four hours and already she was feeling, was feeling . . . she wasn't sure what she was feeling.

Her mouth tasted foul, like she'd eaten too much garlic. For a woman who jumped out of bed and brushed her teeth and showered each morning, she felt just plain grimy. None of the prisoner stories had touched on basic hygiene at all.

Her arms prickled from the crucifix position they were in. Now that it was daylight she could see the room was well furnished with solid English furniture, a thick rug over beige tiles, matching floral spread and curtains. The green in the leaves matched the paint on the wall. Someone had taken great care in its decoration. She couldn't picture the ex-mayor with swatches of cloth and paint. Nor could she imagine that Madeleine had such good taste. She thought that she'd heard he had bought a second vacation home somewhere in the mountains. Maybe this was it. Maybe he'd bought it furnished from someone who went back to the U.K. Maybe she hadn't heard anything about a second home, and her imagination was working overtime. However, if she had heard something and if she could remember where the alleged second home was she might be in a better position.

Better position?

Her body was in a terrible position physically in an unknown place. There was no better position under these circumstances.

Rays of sun flattened themselves across her bed, warming her. In one place there was a rainbow. She had to twist around to see a prism hanging in the window. If she were the type to believe in omens, she would take it as a good one. Where was a leprechaun when you needed one? Off chasing a pot of gold? Like ex-mayor Boulet.

Well, one thing was clear. Boulet wouldn't kill her as long he thought she could help him find the treasure. The only problem—there was no treasure. Although she knew better than to underestimate an opponent, she was smarter then he was. Cunning. That was the quality he had that she lacked. As long as she could make him believe that she could lead him to the treasure, she might have a chance.

Her head still hurt, but less than earlier. She needed to think clearly if she were to survive.

From the other end of the corridor she could hear water running and Boulet singing. His voice was cracked and off key.

Neither the melody nor the words meant anything to her. It could be the drone of a Catalan folk song or maybe he just couldn't carry a tune.

An hour or so later, she wasn't sure of the time, he entered the room with a tray. "I've coffee and bread for you." He put it on the nightstand and fed her as if she were a baby, a mouthful of bread and a sip of coffee.

"Not too much coffee," she said.

"You don't like my coffee?" He wore a freshly ironed shirt open at the neck. His trousers were creased. A drop of blood glued a piece of toilet paper to his chin. His repulsiveness was in his character, never in his clothing. By local standards he was a bit of a dandy. At least four times, she had witnessed one of his favorite tricks. When talking to a peasant he would roll up his sleeves. It reminded her of the adults who scooch down to be on the same level as a child. She had to do the same, now. Try to remove the barriers between them.

"I'm tied up. Coffee makes me want to go to the bathroom."

He set the cup down on the tray. He had not bothered with a saucer. "We need to discuss the treasure."

His weight on the mattress made her half roll toward him. The last thing she wanted was to touch him. "I don't have it."

"Did you give it to Sylvie?"

Why would he think that?

"I saw you give her a package." When she frowned, he said, "At *Les Arbres*. When you had lunch with her."

For a moment she couldn't think what he was talking about. Sylvie had given her the diskette. Then she remembered. "That was a novel. I had it wrapped up so it wouldn't get wet."

"I don't remember a novel in her office."

Had he realized that he almost had admitted to the *notaire*'s murder? She summoned all her strength to ignore the admission. Of course his search hadn't produced anything but Sylvie's death, there was nothing to find. Everything was in his imagination. She looked into his eyes. It hit her that it wasn't just avarice that she had observed, but insanity.

He reached out to stroke her cheek. She shrank back as if his hand carried some contagious germ. "You don't like me," he said.

She refused to answer. He wouldn't believe she liked the man that killed two of her friends. And if he didn't know that he was fat and ugly, she didn't want to aggravate him by pointing it out.

"That's all right. I don't like you either. Argelès has too many foreigners. It was better in the old days when I was a child. A few summer people at the beach." He chuckled. "At least I took a lot of their money." When she looked confused he added, "From building those summer places. Better than a church collection. Opened my purse, and they filled it."

Annie knew not to mention his losses. She had heard rumors that the buyers had later brought a lawsuit, which was hushed up, but Roger had confirmed it. The French weren't lawsuit happy, but the workmanship had been so poor that when the toilets wouldn't flush, paint peeled within weeks of moving in, water heaters didn't heat, the elevator stopped working, and the wiring had started a fire, they made an exception. All this she had forgotten until now.

"Ungrateful bastards. What do you expect when you buy low? A mansion?"

Annie swallowed what her expectations would be: hot water, paint adhering to walls, things like that.

"The banks are hounding me. I need money. I want the treasure you found. You do want to help me, don't you?" He stroked her cheek.

Annie forced herself not to pull back as she debated what to do. Saying the treasure was nonexistent would be the most stupid thing she could do. "I can show you where the treasure is."

"Tell me." His voice shook.

"I can't. It's too complicated."

"No, no, no. That's the wrong answer. It's not complicated. You just say, go here or there."

"It's near Rennes-le-Château, but you have to walk over rocks, down the Roman road and I need to see the land to show you where exactly." Don't let him ask why they left the treasure there, she prayed. Dear God, help me. Take control, she thought. "Do you have a toothbrush? My mouth tastes horrible. Then we can get on the road."

His head snapped back in disbelief.

"Well, why wouldn't I cooperate with you? The treasure means nothing to me."

"What is it?"

"Gold, silver, old coins, jewelry. Part of the Knights Templar's money that Philippe the Fair wanted to get his hands on, but failed." She hoped he didn't know much of the history of Rennes-le-Château. "You've heard how people have been looking for it for years."

"Of course, but why didn't you take it with you when you found it?"

"Père Yves was a priest. He would have turned it over to the Church. We argued about it. I wanted to give it to the Louvre. So we decided to leave it where it was. A compromise." Where in hell had that idea come from? Imagination is a wonderful thing, she decided.

"That's just like you crazy leftists. You don't know what to do with money and power. You squander it on others."

Surreal! Sitting here, chatting about politics, being fed by a murderer. She looked closely at him for the first time.

"You are well dressed. I'm grubby. It'll look funny to people who might be there. I need a toothbrush and a shower. Then we can get going."

He stood up. "Now that pleases me. I thought you'd give me a lot of fight. You seemed more aggressive." He chuckled, but it was the type of chuckle that Jack Nicholson might have given in a Stephen King film.

Annie shrugged as best she could.

"Madeleine has some clean clothes in the dresser. You can borrow them after you take a shower." The ex-mayor untied her and let her rummage through his daughter's dresser.

Although she wasn't thrilled at wearing another woman's underwear, it was better than putting her own stuff back on. The undies were lacy, embarrassing to take out in front of Boulet, although she was not worried about rape here.

"She has some dresses in the armoire."

"We'll be walking over rough terrain in places. I'd prefer jeans and my boots."

Madeleine had no jeans, but she did have slacks that fit and socks to wear, although they were the kind with ruffles at the edge, perfect for a five-year-old or a First Communion, not good for hiking boots. Annie wasn't worried that she'd be going on a real hike. Once she got to a place where other people were, she would look for an opportunity to escape. "Wear good walking shoes, the rocks are slippery. Hiking boots would be better." She was grateful that she wore her boots so much of the time and just happened to have had them on yesterday.

He seemed to believe her concern. "I don't have any hiking boots."

"Sneakers with a good sole?"

"Good idea. *Merci.*"

It was as if they were planning a day out and they were chatting as a couple about what was the best thing to wear.

She resisted rubbing her wrists until she locked Boulet out of the bathroom. Like the toilet, the bathroom had no window. No escape—nor could she stay in there forever. He would just break the door down. The murder scene in *Psycho* dominated her thoughts. Her usual morning shower took ten minutes or until the water ran out. This shower was more a wash–rinse–dry race.

When she opened the door, he was sitting in a chair waiting. "You sure aren't like my daughter. She takes hours."

"We have things to do."

He shook his head. "So American. Time is money, right?"

She smiled. "That's right. And you're going to need a shovel."

He chuckled. "You can dig up the treasure. How deep is it buried?"

Annie forced her face to stay open and friendly. She could be digging her own grave, literally. "Well, we buried the pieces in different places."

"Why?"

"We thought that it would be better protected that way. If it were together and someone found it, it would be all gone."

"You're smart. Smart enough not to fight me, too."

CHAPTER 42

Boulet's car pulled out of the driveway onto a tree-lined dirt road, which twisted and turned. For the first twenty minutes they didn't see any other houses, then they passed through a hamlet with three houses and a *crêperie* all made of stone. The trees were pine, olive and cork. The cork bark had been stripped recently leaving the underskin exposed and light. Annie realized that even had she been able to escape, she could easily have become lost. These mountains still had wild boar and big cats. A few years back and with great controversy, bears, once plentiful then nonexistent, had been reintroduced.

He turned on the radio to the station *Nostalgie,* a station that played pop music from the fifties through the nineties. Not what she would expect him to listen to, but she wasn't going to complain. Claude François sang *"d'Habitude,"* Johnny Hallyday sang *"Souvenirs, Souvenirs."* Then there was an English song, "Staying Alive." Amen, Annie thought.

Chapter 43
Argelès-sur-mer

"You look like hell, Patron," Gault said when Roger walked into the gendarmerie at eight the next morning. His daughter said the same thing as he drove her to school. They were right. His hair needed a shampoo, and he had circles under his eyes. A shave would have been in order. His uniform was rumpled because he'd slept in it.

He ignored the comment to go into his office, leaving Gault and Boulet shrugging.

He pulled off his uniform sweater with the gray stripe across the chest, arms and back and undid his shirt collar. He shut the blinds to keep the sun out and felt the radiator to make sure it was off. Granted, shirt-sleeve weather during the days wasn't that abnormal for October, but this was more like June temperatures. In June what would life be like? With every atom of his being, he hoped he'd be in the midst of wedding plans, not in mourning.

One by one he telephoned all the other chiefs in the surrounding communities. Nothing. They all offered encouragement, but their reminders of how difficult it was to find a person with nothing other than a description made him want to yell at them.

He had always been a doer. The world needed passive people who would stand back and let the doers do. Being forced into a passive role was his idea of a living hell, especially when there was so much at stake. All night long he had tried to think of actions to take.

By now everyone in town knew Annie was missing. Signs were on all the shop windows by midnight last night. Gabriel Martinez had promised to talk to each client that came in for bread. Short of organizing a house-by-house search, there was nothing more he could do. The village had over eight thousand houses and flats with about half closed for the winter. She could be in any one of them.

He didn't really believe she was in Argelès. She'd been kidnapped from a shopping center on the main road to Perpignan. Only a fool would have brought her back into the village. The killer had been smart enough to kill two people and trash Annie's flat without leaving any visible clues. He wasn't dealing with a stupid adversary. Unlike many of the crimes he solved, which he considered an intellectual challenge, this was a personal battle, too personal.

To make matters worse, Gaëlle had refused to go stay with a friend of theirs in Paris. He wanted her out of harm's way. Although he doubted his daughter was a target, he didn't want to risk it.

"Annie will be back in time to take me to the Patrick Fiori concert. I know it," she insisted as she had tossed her book bag onto the backseat of the cruiser. He was not sure at all. He regretted blowing up at her and calling her a selfish brat. Putting the concert before Annie's welfare. And her own. He didn't give in, but they compromised. She would stay with a girlfriend whose parents promised that Gaëlle would never be left alone. Still, Gaëlle had sulked all the way to school. As she had gotten out of the car she'd said to him, "I'm scared for her too, Papa."

He had driven off without offering his daughter any comfort. He had none to give. His own fears had taken possession of him like a demon waiting to take over his immortal soul.

A photo of Annie, Hannibal and Gaëlle taken on a ski trip

two years before was on his desk. Even when they were broken up, he had never put the photo away. He took out a handkerchief and dusted it. He could almost smell the cold air. It had only been a day trip to Grindelwald. Annie had been working in Zurich and during Gaëlle's school holiday the two of them had gone to see her.

Although Gaëlle had taken lessons, on her second run she'd torn ligaments in her ankle. The photo had been snapped an hour before the accident, when they'd been laughing at Hannibal who upon seeing his first snow had rolled and rolled in it and used his snout as a shovel to throw it in the air. They'd spent the rest of the vacation in their rented chalet doing jigsaw puzzles.

He then realized the irony of the situation. He and Annie had fought about her working away from Argelès. Had she been away on assignment, she would have been safe in Geneva, Zurich, Paris, Amsterdam, anywhere but where she was. He had thought of Argelès being safer than other cities where she'd worked. How wrong he had been.

He blew his nose several times. It was better than bawling, which was what he wanted to do, to cry out like a little boy who has lost his favorite toy. Big boys don't cry. Big police chiefs don't either.

There must be something he could do, besides sitting at his desk.

Roger wasn't sure there was a God. If there were, he wanted to rail at him, but didn't dare. Had the God been vengeful enough to take Annie, then Roger didn't want to do anything to antagonize him further. If there weren't a God, then even blasphemy was useless.

Gault pushed his head through the door. "*Patron,* medical examiner. The Montpellier one, not Perpignan."

He grabbed the telephone. "*Bonjour,*" Roger said.

The examiner had a perpetually hoarse voice like American movie stars playing Italian gangsters.

"*Bonjour.* I've finished the autopsy."

"What did you find?" He wished the examiner could name the killer, but forensic science had a long way to go before they could do that.

"No real surprises. She was stabbed in the back seven times. Probably the second or third cut punctured her lungs. Another went through to her heart. Her ribs were damaged, as was the knife. Part of the knife was broken off in the body. Ordinary kitchen knife."

"Could have been bought anywhere then," Roger said. Had it been an unusual knife, he might have checked with the hunting and fishing supply store to see who might have purchased it. The owner of that store had an incredible memory.

"Because he attacked from the back, she didn't have a chance to fight him. Nothing under the nails. We did find a gray hair in the blood that could have fallen from the killer's head. Or she could have picked it up from the back of a chair. The sweater she was wearing is the type of knit that fur and hairs stick to."

His first clue. One gray hair. Not much to put out on a description. Search for a gray-haired man with one hair missing, especially in a village with many retirees. Talk about proverbial needles in proverbial haystacks. This was more like trying to find a certain straw in a haystack. The image he'd had of the killer was a person in their thirties. Some young men are gray haired.

"It was about one inch and straight."

"That narrows it down to several hundred thousand people."

"How are you doing on fingerprints?" the examiner asked.

"Hundreds." They could have been from any of Sylvie's clients, friends who had stopped by, the cleaner, the postman, anyone. Assuming the killer had gone in without gloves.

"We're having her receptionist try and find out if anything is missing, but she wasn't aware of everything that Sylvie had been working on. Not to mention that she was just back from holiday. If he could only get into the killer's mind, he might discover what the killer was looking for.

"I didn't examine the priest, but I talked to my colleague in Perpignan. Nothing similar in the two, so I couldn't say if there were a connection or not. My guess, solely based on different methods, is there's no connection."

Roger thanked him and hung up. He sat back in his chair. The force of his weight caused it to skid back about three inches. Rather than fall, he jumped up. He paced the room.

He picked up the phone again and called a Parisian number. *"Amélie d'Arvoir, s'il vous plaît."*

There was a long wait: no music, just dead air. As he waited he tapped his desk with a pencil. Then the phone disconnected. He pushed the redial button and the receptionist apologized. Again he waited.

"D'Arvoir."

"Amélie, ça va?"

"Ça va bien. C'est qui?"

"Roger. Roger Perrin."

"What a surprise. Are you in Paris?"

"Non." He caught her up on all that had been going on.

"I'm so sorry."

Her voice reminded him of all the cases they had worked on. Until he had met her, he had been skeptical of profiling, but she was almost clairvoyant. Together they'd solved a number of cases. Several of their friends had tried to turn them into a couple, but he hadn't been ready, and she knew it. At one point she suggested they pretend to be involved to get people off their backs. She was the one who showed him the opening in Argelès, pushing him to apply.

"I want your opinion." He told her everything that he could think of.

She interrupted with questions: How long between the murders? Any warnings issued? Had the priest's house been searched? She continued to probe in details.

"I forgot to tell you about Annie's flat being trashed."

Again she asked question after question. "It would help if I could come down and walk over the scenes. I'll catch the night train and be there in the morning."

Roger wondered if that would be too late. "Do you see any pattern?"

"I wish I did. But you have a priest pushed off a tower, which could have been an accident."

"But the body was moved."

"If someone wanted to search his place, it could have been someone taking advantage of the situation. Or not. Still innocent people don't move bodies. I get a feeling of desperation, especially in the savageness of the second attack. Oooo, my leg," she said.

He imagined her leaning back in her chair, one leg folded under, the way she always sat until her leg was asleep.

He could hear her footsteps as she moved around and he was sure she was cradling the telephone receiver between her cheek and shoulder.

"You're afraid I'm going to be too late, I can tell," she said. "But I'm off for the next two days. I'll come down. In fact, let me take the rest of the day off. I'll be in at some point tonight."

Chapter 44
Rennes-le-Château

Annie watched the countryside pass through the car window. Vineyard after vineyard flashed by. About every twenty minutes ex-mayor Boulet would propel the Volvo through another small town, announced by a white sign with black letters, a few houses, shops and a speed bump. The French called them sleeping policemen. She wanted a real policeman, an awake one.

Then there would be another name sign with a red line through it. She recognized them all, including some houses along the way: it was the same route she'd traveled with Roger not that long ago and Père Yves too many times to count.

What she also knew was that none of the villages had even a traffic light. When they walked to the car back at the ex-mayor's place, Annie had hoped that she would be able to jump out if he stopped, but the first thing the ex-mayor had done was to handcuff her right hand to the armrest. A few tugs and twists when Boulet had walked around the car to the driver's side proved to her that there would be no way she could slip out of the cuffs. There was no hope that anyone would notice. To make sure, he had covered her lap with a red plaid wool blanket.

As the temperature rose within the car, the armpits of her sweatshirt developed wet circles. Her forehead glistened with sweat. Boulet, too, was sweating. She could smell him. He was of the generation that didn't believe in deodorant. Both of them grew riper by the moment.

Not a word had passed between them for the last half-hour.

Annie wasn't sure if she would be better off engaging him in conversation or staying quiet. Anyone looking in would merely think they were just two people out on a drive. It was like being trapped in a Dali painting with melting watches. Nothing was right. Nothing was like it seemed.

To try to control her rising panic, she stared at a field that was filled with sheep. More than once on the way back to Argelès she and Père Yves had bought some cheese from the herd owner at his crude wooden roadside stand. Her breathing returned to normal as she tried to concentrate. She must develop a plan.

If he admitted to her that he had killed her friends, then he would begin thinking of killing her if he weren't already.

Who was she kidding?

Although he had never come out and said, "I am the murderer," and then tell all like they did on television shows, she was sure he knew she knew. She would be dead too, if he didn't believe that she was showing him what his other victims refused to give him. Her safety was limited until the moment that he realized she was no help to him.

Her earlier revelation that the man was not totally sane could give her both advantages and disadvantages. He might believe the most cockamamie things that would buy her time. On the other hand, if she said the wrong thing, or what he considered the wrong thing, her own words would put her in greater danger.

Her hope was that there would be enough people around when they reached Rennes-le-Château that she would be able to get away. "I'm hot," she said. "The blanket."

"If a truck passes, they'll see the handcuffs."

He hunched over the wheel.

"These aren't the kind of roads where a lot of trucks overtake cars. They use the Autoroute," she said.

"Shut up. I don't understand how your boyfriend puts up

with you. Women should be seen and not heard." He put on the air-conditioning.

Not the time to give him a lecture on women's rights.

"How much? How many?" he asked.

"What?"

He sighed as if he were dealing with a child, a stupid child at that. "The treasure? Value, number of pieces?"

"There are lots of pieces, I told you." She hadn't remembered exactly what she said. Her head still had a dull ache, milder than earlier, but she was still aware of it. "You're asking the wrong person. We never had anything evaluated."

"I need half a million Euros. Do you think we can get that much?"

If there were treasure, Annie was sure that the French government would want it as national treasure, that it would need to be authenticated, and there would be no way to dispose of it easily. Anyone who would pay real money for it would want it authenticated and ownership verified. The ex-mayor didn't need to hear this. More importantly, she didn't need to tell him. "We've about thirty kilometers to go. There's a parking place at the end of the village."

Let someone see her handcuffs when he tried to get her out of the car.

Let someone think it strange they were walking through the village with a shovel.

Let someone ask if they had a permit to dig. Let someone—anyone—get help. Let this be one time when people were about.

"What do the pieces look like?" he asked.

"There was one cup, gold. Père Yves said he knew it was gold, and it was encrusted with rubies and emeralds. They alternated the two stones around the edge. I remember thinking how hard it would be to drink out of it, the stones were so close to the rim." Maybe with enough details he would believe her.

He frowned. "Maybe the stones would have fallen out when you reburied it."

"It was in a case . . . a box, wooden. We used the same case to rebury it." Stupid choice. Wood might have rotted if it been buried in the seven hundreds or eight hundreds.

He didn't pick up on it. He hit the steering wheel several times. "This is wonderful. All my problems are going to be over."

The Volvo pulled up next to the Tour Magdala, the house and library built by the mysterious priest of Rennes-le-Château at the beginning of the last century. The round tower jutted out over a cliff leading to a valley flanked by two mountains. She had seen a six-star figure drawn with the mountain peaks making three equal distance points and three churches in the valley making the other three.

The exact distances always made her wonder how anyone could have measured it so carefully over seven hundred years before. Also, how could a medieval person without access to an airplane know that the three mountaintops were an equal distance apart? What kind of mathematical mind would have been able to figure out exactly where to build those churches? But then, when she had first read that the Gothic Cathedrals of Notre Dame at Paris, Chartres, etc., were at the points of the constellation of Virgo, she doubted it. Someday she wanted to work it out on a map, but it had always slipped to the bottom of her to-do list because she was working on other things. And if it were true, was it deliberate or accidental and why?

Both she and Père Yves had spent hours and hours playing with the geometrical theories that surrounded this place. Coincidence? Maybe. As Père Yves often said, the victors write the history. Much was lost over the years, deliberately or by accident. It didn't matter. When bits and pieces surfaced, they often contradicted what conventional history told—a bit like a jigsaw with major pieces missing. Today, she hoped she could just stay alive to continue her research.

Two other cars were parked in the graveled parking area, but the other places were empty. Since the cars had local plates they could have belonged to anyone who lived in the village itself.

Late October was not high tourist season, although people drifted through all year round. After the book *Holy Blood, Holy Grail* had been published, more and more people came, especially from Britain. That was the book that had originally drawn Annie's attention to the area. She'd been reading it at Martinez's when Père Yves had come in and said that he'd just come back from Rennes-le-Château. He had taken her with him the next week.

Both she and the priest had deplored how a small local industry had grown up in Rennes with its museum and bookstores. Today, she was grateful, because it would increase the chances of her escape. The only problem was that she and Boulet had arrived at lunch when everything would be closed. Her hopes of seeing someone who could have helped dropped. Since they had entered Rennes-le-Château, not one person had been visible.

Ex-mayor Boulet got out of the car and opened the trunk. Annie could hear him rummaging around, and when he appeared next to her he carried not one but two shovels, which he rested against the hood over the right front tire. He started to open the passenger door, then realized as she leaned forward that she was attached.

The door was slammed shut so sharply that pain radiated through Annie's hand, arm and shoulder. Boulet went around to the driver's side, sat down and leaned over her. For a second she wished she had something to hit him with, but her free hand was not even close to any semi-lethal weapon. To free her, he reached under the blanket.

"No one will see your handcuffs," he said.

"No one is around." A bottle of water had been rolling around at her feet. She drained half. It was fizzy water, something she found less quenching, but she had sweated so much liquid that anything would have helped.

"All the better. Let's go." He took her by the elbow.

She rubbed her wrist and arm. "Can I stop and go to the toilet? It's right over there." She pointed to a small building at the end of the parking area.

A frown passed over the ex-mayor's face.

Her only escape route would be to flush herself down the drain. "Walk around it, there's no way out. I can't escape. And even if I slipped out the back, you'd see me. I really, really have to go."

He threw his hands up. "All right, all right. God, I've never see a woman have to piss so often." She started to walk toward the toilet when he said, "Halt."

"What?"

"Empty your pockets."

Annie put her hand in her pockets. "What do you think I have?"

"A pencil. A pen. You could write a message on the mirror."

How Annie wished she were the type of woman that wore lipstick. She could have palmed it, but she had asked to go to the toilet because she really had to go.

Inside the room was the old-fashioned French ceramic square with two ceramic feet and a hole. She had used this type of toilet so often that she no longer even thought about it. She had mastered balancing with one of her feet on each ceramic foot and angling her rear over the opening. The greatest danger was when she pulled the chain to flush that water would flood her shoes, but she had learned to stand far enough away from the square.

The tap spit out cold water. Although there was a hot water faucet, no pipe connected it. Annie splashed the water on her face. A knock at the door interrupted her.

"What are you doing?" Boulet said through the door.

"Do you really want the details?" she asked.

"Hurry."

"There's no place I can pee once we get to where the treasure is. Give me time." Time was what she wanted, but unless she ran into someone and begged for help, there wasn't much hope. She opened the door. She thought of Miriam's shop, but she was afraid she would put her friend in danger. If there was some way to signal her as they walked by the charm shop, she would do it, but the location of the shop was at the other entrance of the village. She needed to keep somehow in sight of people or not travel in circles. "Ready."

"I didn't tell you before, but I brought the gun with me," he said. He took her hand and pressed it against a lump in his pocket. With anyone else it would have been a very sexual act.

Most of the first floors of the houses they passed were shuttered. Dishes clattering and chatter could be heard through the wood. She could scream for help, but if Boulet shot her, she would be dead. He might be caught, but that wouldn't do her any good. He might not be caught. That would do her even less good. Death had no appeal. Death for nothing had even less, if possible.

She tripped.

"Your boot is untied," he said.

She bent down and double tied it. The dust on the street transferred to the right knee of her slacks. She switched knees to tie the other boot. Now both her knees were dusty, but this wasn't a fashion show. She wanted to get out of this alive, not win cleanliness awards. Funny, she thought, that she had chosen the work boots that she always wore to go tramping around Rennes-le-Château when she last dressed in her nest, little thinking she would end up actually going there. The soles kept her from slipping on the rocks and the height was protection against vipers.

She looked at the mayor's feet and thought how the French called them baskets. Americans called them sneakers, the English trainers. It would give him some traction on the path she planned to take, but she would choose the most difficult descent.

As they walked through the village she thought that if her father had never taken a job in Holland then kept the family moving, she just might have been a history professor in some American college. A nice, dull, boring job where she would wend her way through the political landmines of academic life. Until today, she'd liked her life. Not everyone could balance vocation and avocation so successfully, even if she did sacrifice some of the material comforts for which her friends had opted. No one can have it all.

All she wanted was a tomorrow, a day after and a week after, etc. She was too young to die.

Chapter 45
Rennes-le-Château

"You can't be serious," ex-mayor Boulet said to Annie.

They stood with the walled village of Rennes-le-Château at their backs. A rocky path led to a valley, although the path was probably giving the route more credit than it merited. It was a combination of boulders and steep slopes. There was a much easier path down into the valley, but it could not be seen from this perspective.

Houses rose above the village walls. Shit, Annie thought. Although the houses had windows, almost all were shuttered. Damn the French and their shutters. Probably the residents didn't want the bright sunshine to fade their furniture and rugs. Why couldn't some housewife look out, get curious and watch them. Where was the nosy woman that would report that they were digging illegally and send the local *flics* to stop them? Were their local *flics?* She had never seen one. Maybe they were garrisoned down the mountain and served this small village, which couldn't have more than three hundred residents.

Annie pointed. "Over there is where the Poussin painting *Arcadia* was. There was a tomb that was a clue relating to the original treasure. Everyone thought that it was a fictional painting." She doubted that Boulet had ever heard of the painter. The part about the painting was true, but the significance was only theorized about.

"I don't see any tomb." The ex-mayor sounded sulky.

"The man who owns the land destroyed it. He got tired of

317

people tramping over his land." What a stupid thing to say. The ex-mayor wouldn't want to be caught as a trespasser. "He owns that house there." She pointed to a small villa, the only one in the valley. The rest of the land was grass. "He's almost never there. Don't think he is today."

"The house is shuttered. No car."

She didn't say there never was a car. A car, even a four-wheel vehicle, couldn't get into the valley. The owner parked in the village and walked down the easier path.

Boulet turned around and looked at the village. "Anyone can see us."

"I can't help that. We buried the treasure down there." God, don't let him ask about why we weren't seen, or if it were possible that someone else had found it. Hopefully by telling him that they had buried it in several places, he'd think some of it was safe. And if she had him dig and found nothing, she could say someone had, indeed, found it, but they should go onto the next place.

Don't let him want to wait till dark. Despite all her hopes of being spotted, she knew that the villagers didn't usually pay any attention to people poking around. There'd been so much written about the area that if they paid attention to everyone who came for a look-see, they'd never have any lives of their own. "We could go to the museum first so maybe you'll have a better idea."

He snorted. "All I want to see is the treasure. Let's get going. You first."

No matter how many times Annie had descended into the valley, she had never liked climbing up and down this route. It was hard going. Père Yves had convinced her that humans had placed some of the huge rocks in ritualized patterns. One was not even a stone geologically true to the area. Although they had speculated on the equipment it would take to drag it here, the greater problem was that they could not figure out the reason anyone would want to. There was no relation to anything they knew from any of the cultures they had investigated.

Père Yves had pointed out that dinosaurs had inhabited the area from prehistoric times. Remains of cave men also had dotted the region.

Although they usually had gone by the easy road, there were times they used this path, especially when they wanted to photograph certain things from a different perspective.

Annie hated the route because she was afraid of snakes. More than once she and Père Yves had seen vipers. Some years were worse than others, but this past summer had been a good year from a human point a view. If there were a viper point of view, she didn't care. Père Yves had bought a snake bite kit, partially to humor her, and partially because many of the pharmacy windows in the region had displays, showing snakes and the kits. Both of them had always worn pants and boots. If a snake wanted to bite, they weren't going to make it easy for him.

Annie had always thought of snakes as male, which had nothing to do with the fact that in French the word for snake was masculine, *le serpent*. Père Yves had said it had to do with the Garden of Eden. A female snake would not have been as tempting to Eve as a male snake. He also mentioned the Disney movie *The Jungle Book*.

If she hated snakes, then Père Yves hated heights. He always kept as far from the edge as possible. Today Annie walked where Père Yves would have. Boulet didn't seem to have any such fear. He walked, inched, climbed and maneuvered himself much closer to the edge then Père Yves ever would have.

Boulet pulled a handkerchief from his pocket and wiped his brow. He unbuttoned his shirt. His clothes had lost their freshly ironed look. "I'm not used to all this exercise," he said.

She was hot, but she, unlike Boulet, was in excellent physical shape. Even without a mirror she knew her hair was frizzed to the point that anyone looking at her would have said she was like a cartoon character that had put her finger in an electric socket. She wished she had something to tie it back because it kept falling over her eyes.

"How far down do we go?"

Standing back from the edge she pointed down to the valley and to the right. "See that tree?"

He nodded.

"That's where we buried the cup. On the path to the left, at eleven o'clock . . ."

"What are you talking about?" The ex-mayor almost growled.

"Think of the valley as a clock. We're at six o'clock. Straight ahead is twelve, three is over there. It makes describing positions easier. Like going into a rotary. You enter at six and take the three, the first right."

He sighed. "What's buried at eleven o'clock?"

"A necklace. And at ten there's plates." She didn't want to tell him that if this were treasure from the seven hundreds, plates weren't used. People used trenchers of stale bread, putting the food on top, then eating the bread last when it had absorbed the juices. The Knights Templar might have had plates, such was the extent of their wealth, even if the peasants at the time didn't. "My God, I never thought of it before." She slapped her forehead. "The cup. The Holy Grail. No, it isn't possible. But it was old enough. It was not of the period. It seemed more Roman to me. I wonder why we didn't think of it before. What if Père Yves found the cup the Lord himself drank from when he created Holy Communion."

He put his hand over his mouth. "Maybe that was what he wanted to share with you."

So he did know that Père Yves wanted to share something with me, Annie thought. She forced herself not to react and went on. "I wonder if there would be DNA on it from him." This might be going too far, but she could see in Boulet's eyes that he believed in the possibility. There was no way she was going to say the bread and wine ceremony had been part of the Essene culture. Christ was an Essene. "No fingerprints of Christ would still be on the cup. It was too long ago. But maybe his DNA might be. In any case imagine holding a cup that Christ held." As she thought all this, she almost believed her own story.

Annie saw that Boulet's face had taken on an expression that might be described as ecstasy. Unlike many men in the village she saw him coming out of Mass regularly. He even went sometimes midweek. She couldn't imagine how he could justify murder with his religion. "With or without it being the Holy Grail, it will bring a lot of money. The stones alone would be worth millions. But why do you need so much?"

He was facing away from her toward the valley. She couldn't hear what he said.

"I'm sorry, but I can't hear you." She had to keep him talking.

He turned around to face her. He put his shovel against a large rock and wiped his brow again. "I'm overextended. The banks with their new-fangled ideas won't loan me any more money, even now the lawsuit is gone. Not like when my brother was alive. All I had to do then was walk in the door. Didn't even have to do that. Just picked up the phone and my brother saw I had what I needed."

Annie had heard about all the trouble the bank was in from loans made by his brother to his cronies. The brother had moved to Burkina Faso to escape prosecution, or so it was rumored.

The ex-mayor frowned. "But if it is the Holy Grail, I'd have to give it to the Church."

Shit, that was the wrong track for him to be on. "You'd still make a fortune. Imagine being the man who found the Holy

Grail. You'd have interviews all over the world. You'd be made a saint." Saint Murderer, she thought. Her head ached. "And imagine drinking from the grail. Your lips where Christ's lips had been."

"We'd better get going." He reached for the shovel. The handle was next to a small ledge with an overhang. The ex-mayor let out a scream. Annie jumped. The ex-mayor jumped and shook his hand. A viper whipped through the air. He swung his hand and the snake's diamonds danced in the sun before it dropped off and slithered across the path. Boulet pulled out his gun and started shooting.

Annie stood frozen, afraid one of the bullets would ricochet and hit her. Before she could do or say anything, Boulet took several steps back but ran out of ledge and tumbled over the edge. Annie went as close to the edge as she dared and watched as he tumbled down the path. Rocks went with him, starting a small landslide. She peeked over the edge. The ex-mayor had come to rest more than six hundred feet below and lay half buried in rubble.

She turned and ran up the hill to the village.

Chapter 46
Perpignan

As Gaëlle and Annie walked up to the ticket booth at the *Palais des Rois Majorque*, Annie felt a hand on her shoulder. She screamed.

"My God, I didn't realize you were so nervous." The spoken voice would have made a good baritone had the speaker chosen to sing.

Annie turned to see the director of the Palais. "Charlie." She fought the urge to sit on the floor. She willed her legs to hold her. Roger had been right: she was stupid to take Gaëlle to the concert just hours after escaping ex-Mayor Boulet. Her head hurt. Her muscles ached. It took work to keep her hands from shaking.

Charlie kissed her on both cheeks. "I tried to call you today, but there was no answer. So I staked out the entrance."

"I was busy," Annie said. Busy being the prisoner of a murderer. She introduced Gaëlle.

"Let me show you lovely ladies to your seats."

They walked behind him, through the ticket booth and into the theater. The crowd was so thick someone could have walked on their shoulders. Charlie led them to a side door, backstage and then to the front row. Annie glanced behind her to see Gaëlle's eyes open wider and wider.

"Wait here when it's over. I'll get you backstage."

Gaëlle opened her mouth and closed it without saying a word. When Patrick Fiori walked on stage, the teenager jumped up and down cheering and screaming. As he sang, she grabbed Annie's arm so hard that the older woman was sure that she would be bruised. Without taking her eyes off the singer for a second, Gaëlle whispered into Annie's ear, "Isn't he wonderful?" For most of the songs she mouthed the words along with the singer, who strutted up and down the stage. At one point he walked to the edge of the stage and appeared to be staring directly at them.

Annie had to admit he did have a great voice and was equally good-looking. Mostly, she was thrilled that Gaëlle was so happy. Watching her made her forget how much she was longing for a bed and a long sleep.

As the crowd filed out, Annie and Gaëlle waited in their seats. The drummer disassembled his drums. Technicians unscrewed wires and moved the speakers, each large enough to house two or three derelicts for a good night's sleep.

"Don't jump this time. I'm behind you," Charlie said softer then Annie ever remembered him speaking. "Gaëlle, I'm taking you to meet Fiori. *D'accord?*"

"*D'accord!*"

Annie suspected Gaëlle would have considered selling her soul for this chance. Charlie led the way holding Annie's hand, and Annie held Gaëlle's. Because the concert was in a château from the twelfth century, the backstage wasn't like a theater's. Temporary walls carved out rooms. Annie knew from when she'd been there before that they were used as offices and storage. During performances, which were often held at the palace, they doubled as dressing rooms.

Charlie stopped at the third on the left and knocked three hard raps against the wood. The door had a rounded arch and the hinges were made by some ironmonger of the fifteenth century. They were pitted from repeated rust removals over the century.

"*Qui est là?* Who is it?"

"Charlie."

"*Entrez.*"

Charlie pushed down on the handle. The star pulled a T-shirt over a muscled and hairy chest. He stood in front of a desk. A computer had been pushed aside to make way for a mirror. "I'm sorry to interrupt you Monsieur Fiori, this is the fan I was telling you about this afternoon."

Fiori smiled and went over and kissed Gaëlle on both cheeks. He pointed to a chair. "I'm hiding here for the next hour. By then most of the people will be tired of waiting for me."

"*Mon Dieu,* I don't know what to say," Gaëlle said.

"Then I'll talk." Fiori asked her questions about school, which of his songs she liked the best, had she been to any other concerts. He autographed a photo. He looked at Annie, "Do you want my autograph, too?"

"*Non merci,* but would you like mine?"

Fiori stared at her for moment then burst out laughing. "That's a good one," he said. Then he looked at his watch. "I guess the coast is clear enough."

After Fiori left, Charlie said, "And now anytime I need a translator you owe me big time."

"I was beginning to get worried when you two didn't come out," Roger said after he had met them and was driving them home. The weather had changed, and once again it was appropriately cold for November.

Annie had already undressed and was under the covers, grateful for the mattress that supported her and the knowledge she didn't have to move if she didn't want, but could if she did want to. Never again would she be in a bed and take being free to leave for granted. She rubbed her wrists. The cold sheets had begun to warm.

Roger pulled on his pajama bottom. "But then I didn't see any ambulances for stubborn Americans who insisted on going to a concert when they should have been in bed."

Annie thought of Gaëlle tucking Patrick Fiori's photograph under her pillow and thanking Annie over and over. "This was so exciting for your daughter. And I'm okay. Did you get news on Boulet?" She hadn't really wanted to ask while Gaëlle could hear. Although she had been so busy babbling about Patrick Fiori, probably she wouldn't have paid any attention.

He slipped under the covers. "I talked to the hospital. They say he's still on the critical list. They won't let anyone talk to him. There's a policeman from the area outside at all times who will take a statement if he can make it." He put his arm around her, "You want to talk about it?"

Annie thought of how she looked down at Boulet laying at the bottom of the incline and how tempted she had been to just keep running and not tell anyone, but once back in Rennes-le-Château she ran to Miriam Fournier's. Her friend was napping after lunch, but had quickly run two doors down to the house with the plate saying Dr. Azèma, *Medicine Générale*. He had answered the door to her rapid pounding. When he had asked her to describe the snake, she wanted to say medium height, balding, brown eyes. Within a few minutes the doctor and several other men were on the way to rescue Boulet. Annie had called Roger who had come to get her as fast as he could. When he entered the doctor's office and found her sitting in the waiting room, he had cried. The memory caused her to shiver.

"It's okay, you're safe. But you really should take it easy for the next few days." Both of them knew he would have loved to lecture her more on insisting on going to the concert, but both also knew that Gaëlle's pleasure had been worth her discomfort.

Annie closed her eyes. Her headache was less from the blow than exhaustion, but every muscle in her body ached. Tension, the doctor, who had checked her over, had decreed she should relax for the next few days. She had no intention of going easy. Her plans included work and getting her life back to normal.

No sooner had they fallen asleep when the phone rang. Roger fumbled until he found the receiver. *"Perrin ici."*

Through the fog of sleep Annie could hear him say, "Really, tomorrow, no it's fine you woke me up, I'll be there early, no thank you."

"What?" she asked after he hung up.

"Boulet. The doctor says I can talk to him in the morning. He's stable. The snake didn't kill him. However, he will be a quadriplegic the rest of his life."

Annie felt no guilt at his suffering.

When Annie woke the next morning, Roger had left. She hadn't heard him at all. She padded into the kitchen. A teapot with leaves already measured inside was on the table and the kettle was filled with water. A note was propped up: *I'll call you. I left too early to get bread, but there's some eggs.* She made tea and decided to lie down for a few minutes before scrambling some eggs and taking her shower. She woke at two in the afternoon.

The phone rang. "Hi *Chérie*," Roger said. "What are you doing?"

"I'm in bed." She started crying.

"I'll come home."

"There's every reason in the world for you to feel terrible," Roger said. He sat on the edge of the bed. Annie's face was blotched and she snuffled. The bed looked like snow was melting in patches from the tissues that she had cried into.

"I feel like such a weakling." She tore a tissue into miniscule bits. At no time did her eyes meet his.

"Weaklings fall apart during the crisis, not after. You did what you had to do, now you're dealing with it." He took her chin in his hand and forced her to look at him. "I love you."

"I love you, too."

"On the drive out and back to Rennes-le-Château all I could think of was how lucky I was that I still have you, and I'm so proud of you."

She manipulated her head so she could kiss his hand.

"I got a full confession for both murders. He thought the treasure would give him the money he needed to bail him out of his financial problems."

"The port development?" she asked.

"That, and once he wasn't mayor, he couldn't extort as much money."

Annie nodded. "What will happen?"

"The doctors say he'll be on a respirator for the rest of his life. He says he doesn't want to face a trial. We can transfer him to a prison hospital."

"He's imprisoned in his own body."

In a way she felt better as she lay back against the pillows. When she shut her eyes, she didn't have any bad pictures on the inside of her eyelids. Nor did she hear Roger tiptoe out of the room.

CHAPTER 47
ARGELÈS-SUR-MER

Annie opened the door to her nest. The metal of the police lock squeaked. She took the bar and carried it upstairs. It was easy to hide it behind her clothes in the closet. It would be a good idea to keep the police lock on the front door, especially when she wasn't there, but for the first time since she had arrived in Argelès after her Zurich job, she felt free.

Not totally free. She still had an assignment to finish. She called her client to explain why she hadn't mailed the materials as promised.

"We know," they said. "You made the news on TF1, F2 and F3, but you can e-mail it now."

They asked her more questions. Her reaction varied from not wanting to talk about it to wanting to talk about it. Each time she talked about it made it seem a little further away.

No one had called Roger's home, but his phone number had been red listed. No policeman in his right mind would have his private phone number available to the public at large. When Annie listened to her messages, there were several from reporters. She erased each one. By tonight there would be another story and they'd lose interest in her.

One call she didn't erase. Paul Bressands. Him, she called back.

"Are you all right?" he asked.

"I'm getting there."

There was silence on the line. Annie blurted out, "I'm so

sorry about what happened in Paris."

"I think my brother would have understood. I do now. And you risked your life to catch his murderer."

Annie sighed. "Not out of choice."

"It doesn't matter."

They promised to keep in touch, but Annie was sure they wouldn't.

She walked around her nest touching everything. Then she spied the USB key Sylvie had given her. God, she'd miss their friendship. Friendship? That was it.

She powered up the computer and put the USB key in. When it asked for her password she typed in *amitié*, friendship. They had discussed friendship the first day they'd gone to Rennes-le-Château. The A drive showed a file called Annie. A quick click and it appeared.

Chére Annie . . .

If you're reading this, it means something has happened to me. I'm convinced that Boulet, the father, not the son, is following me. I've seen him sneaking around. When I went to R-l-C the other day his car was behind mine. He teases me about the treasure, but he is not the type of man to joke. I know he has great financial problems.

And speaking of treasure—I think I've found a group of archeologists that will be willing to excavate the building below the well and mill. By the size, I'm convinced it's a temple, but only they can determine if it is to Isis or Mary or maybe to neither. When we think how little is left from the time of Dagobert, the size implies a skill set that has to be Roman or earlier. Another mystery. The archeologist is André Limoux and he's at the University of Toulouse. Please follow up.

Now is the harder part. I want you to know how much our friendship has meant to me. It's beyond the sharing of our love of history. You know that with all the research we've done, I've lost my belief in the tenants of the Church without losing a belief that there is something far greater than mankind. It's just that man had to explain the world with legends.

There were times that I thought I was in love with you, but I knew I'd never act on it. I watched you with Roger and thought that the two of you would be so good for each other. He is a good man, and a man good enough for you. Granted you have different interests, but with training he'll respect yours. It won't hurt you to learn to give a little as well. He doesn't want to cut your freedom, but I understand why he wants you close to him. Time with you is delightful.

Think about it. This advice is not from a priest, but a friend.

Much love,

Yves

Annie read the letter at least ten times. Despite the awareness he was gone, it made her feel as if she could run around the corner to talk with him. Should she show it to Roger? In a way it was evidence, but there would be no trial. Even if the ex-mayor recanted his confession, whatever powers there were in the universe, the powers that Père Yves was trying to find had made sure Boulet would pay for his crimes.

Had he been alive, Père Yves would have told her to marry Roger, she knew that. No matter what his doubts were about the Church, he believed in families. If she married Roger she'd have a ready-made family.

Strange to think of herself as a stepmother. Being a stepmother to Gaëlle sounded pretty good. Being a step-owner to Hannibal was also good. It was the wife part that bothered her. If she wanted to marry, Roger would certainly be her choice, but did she want to marry at all?

Even as a little girl, she had never dreamed of walking down the aisle in a white gown. She could hear Roger saying, "So wear blue, or red or yellow. Just don't wear black to our wedding."

Maybe he'd be happy with a long engagement to give her time to get used to the idea of being a wife.

FRENCH WORDS AND PHRASES USED IN *MURDER IN ARGELÈS*

A bientôt— See you soon

Alors— Now or then, often used at the beginning of sentences

Aoili— mayonaise with garlic used in fish soup, on potatoes, etc.

Apéro— Before-dinner drink most often served with nuts or potato chips

Armée du Salut— Salvation Army

Aussi— Also

Au four— Oven

Bac— The diploma a student gets after sitting a test upon finishing the lycée (high school). It is a source of great worry.

Bien sûr— Of course

Bienvenue— Welcome

Bon (ne)— Good

Bonne chance— Good luck

Boulangerie— Bakery

Ça va— How are you as a question, fine as an answer

C'est difficile— That's hard

C'est la vie— That's life

C'est moi— It's me

C'est vrai?— Is it true?

Charcuterie— Butcher who also may serve ready-to-heat dishes

Chien— dog

Clic-clac— A sofa bed that folds in half and makes a click and clack sound as it is being opened and closed.

Collège— In France it is equivalent to junior high school

Comme la dernière fois— Like the last time

Con, Connard— Ass or asshole

Copine, copain— Male or female friend with the connotation of buddy

Couchette— French train sleeping car

Coucou— Used to call hello and get someone's attention

Coup de foudre— Literally bolt of thunder, but used as love at first sight

D'accord— All right, okay

Diabolo frais— Fizzy water mixed with a strawberry syrup

Dormir— To sleep

Écouter— To listen

Entrecôte— Steak

Excusez-moi— Excuse me

Et puis— And then, often used in telling stories . . . *Et puis* this and *et puis* that.

Flic— Slang for policeman, cop

Fou, folle— Nuts, crazy

Frigo— Refrigerator

Gendarme— National policeman

Grenier— Attic, it comes from when seeds and grain were stored in the attic

Grippe— Flu

J'écoute— I'm listening . . . some people answer the phone this way

Je t'embrasse très fort— A common sign-off on letters and e-mails to friends, I embrace you strongly

Kir royale— Champagne mixed with kir, which can be peach, apricot, etc.

Macht nichts— German for it really doesn't matter, it's not important

Mamie— Grandmother

Maquis— French resistance fighter in World War II

Marché— Open-air market held in almost every village once or twice a week

Mec— Slang for male, guy

Menthe— Mint

Merde— Shit

Mon Dieu— My God

Natel— cell phone

Nid— Nest

Notaire— Notary public lawyer

On y va— Let's go

Papi— Grandfather, affectionate

Pique— Being annoyed

Poubelle— Trash

Pourquoi— Why

Prochains arrêts après— Next stop after

"Sais-tu ce-que cet idiot a fait?"— Do you know what that idiot has done?

Putain— Whore

Qu'est ce que c'est?— What is it?

Regarder— To look

Réglisse— Licorice

Sais pas— Don't know

Salade verte— Green salad

Sans— Without

Schatzie— German for dear

S'il te plâit— Informal for s'il vous plaît, please

Soyez sage— Be good

Tais-toi— Be quiet

Tartine— A baguette cut in half and served with butter and jam, usually for breakfast

Tisane— Herb tea

Toujours— Always

Tôt— Early

Tramantane— A wind that strikes the area with regularity

Tutoyer— When a person goes from using the formal *vous*, to the informal *tu* for you

Vendre— To sell

Vernissage— The first night of an exhibition, usually with wine/champagne and finger foods

Look for the next Five Star Publishing
Third-Culture Kid Mystery:
Murder in Geneva,
due out in late 2012

Geneva, Switzerland
October 27, 1553

The smell of burning wood and wool floated through the air. Then the odor of human flesh cooking wafted into the mixture. It reminded Elizabeth of feast days and meat turning on a spit. She shuddered. Knowing a man was about to die in agony, the sixteen-year-old couldn't stop herself from wanting to see. She stood on tiptoe to peer over the heads of the crowd.

The wood crackled and the flames rose higher and higher as the huge stack of wood caught and shot yellow spikes against the gray sky. Everything but the fire was gray—the clothing of the witnesses, the frosted ground, the sky, gravel and stones as well as the leafless trees.

The babble of the crowd stopped the second the faggots were lit. Elizabeth had expected to hear cries, but the victim, Michel Servetus, was as silent as the crowd.

She should not be here. If her uncle caught her she would be punished, but she risked his temper to see the man who had dared to challenge Calvin on the trinity.

When the subject of Servetus came up at the dinner table,

Elizabeth had to hold her tongue. She had too many heretical ideas herself. Much of religion did not make sense to her, but she would never say it. Expressing doubts was far too dangerous. Too often what God wanted seemed to match what the people in power wanted, another thought best kept to herself.

What made someone feel so strongly that they would sacrifice their life for it? There was nothing she believed in so much that she would be willing to die. What was he feeling? How much could flames hurt before he would pass out, pass away?

Because she was shorter than the people standing in the six rows in front of her, she couldn't see. She pushed, twisted and moved through the crowd heading up the knoll without looking at any of the faces she passed. She was disgusted that they wanted to see the gore and mad at herself for being like them.

"Elizabeth, what are you doing here?" It was Jean-Michel, the young man who lived next door to her aunt and uncle's house. Elizabeth had been forced to move in with them after her mother and brother died this past January; her father had disappeared last year. Her aunt and uncle raged on that it was improper for a young woman to live on her own.

Jean-Michel's hands were discolored by the inks that he used as he learned the printing trade, the trade that would eventually give them a good life together if he had his way.

She pulled the hood of her cape closer over her face—half to protect herself from the chilly October air and half to not be recognized. She really didn't want Aunt Mathilde and Uncle Jacques to discover she had been here. They disapproved of everything she did from the spelling of her name with a z instead of s given by her English mother and the half-English blood running in her veins, to her posture during prayers. She never was as good or as obedient as their children—her cousins. From seven births and seven miscarriages that followed too closely one after another, three boys and two girls had survived. Her aunt seemed to never know a non-pregnant year.

"Wild child," they called her, even though at sixteen she was more woman than child. They employed other terms: Satan's offspring, clumsy, hopeless, disobedient were those most often dropping from their lips.

"Don't tell my aunt and uncle you saw me," she said.

"It's our secret." Jean-Michel followed her further up the hill where they had a better view of the burning. He bent over and kissed her on the cheek.

"Don't," she said. "If anyone sees us . . ."

He nodded. "If you would let me talk to your uncle about marrying . . ."

"Not yet." Her eyes were riveted on the scene below. The flames were so thick, it was impossible to see what or whom they were burning. She did not know how to tell him that she did not want to marry, which made her completely out of step with every other young woman living in Geneva. She knew her childhood had made her different from others. No matter how hard she tried, she could not think the way her aunt, uncle and neighbors did. Although she was able to hide her ideas and mimic their behaviors, too often she was caught out and earned a lashing either with her aunt's tongue or a broomstick.

She felt nothing but love for Jean-Michel.

ABOUT THE AUTHOR

D-L Nelson is a Swiss-American writer and the author of five other Five Star novels: *Murder in Caleb's Landing, Running from the Puppet Master, Family Value, The Card* and *Chickpea Lover: not a cookbook.* She lives in Geneva, Switzerland, and Argelès-sur-mer, France. Like Annie, she knows what it is like to be torn between cultures. She only wishes she had as many languages as Annie does. Visit her blog at http://theexpatwriter.blogspot.com